Candy Cane *Wishes* and *Saltwater* Dreams

A Christmas Novella Collection

Amy R. Anguish
Hope Toler Dougherty
Linda Fulkerson
Regina Rudd Merrick
Shannon Taylor Vannatter

Scrivenings
PRESS
Quench your thirst for story.
www.ScriveningsPress.com

Mistletoe Make-believe ©2021 by Amy R. Anguish
A Hatteras Surprise ©2021 by Hope Toler Dougherty
A Pennie for Your Thoughts ©2021 by Linda Fulkerson
Mr. Sandman ©2021 by Regina Rudd Merrick
Coastal Christmas Charade ©2021 by Shannon Taylor Vannatter

Published by Scrivenings Press LLC
15 Lucky Lane
Morrilton, Arkansas 72110
https://scriveningspress.com

Printed in the United States of America

Paperback ISBN 978-1-64917-149-8
eBook 978-1-64917-150-4

Library of Congress Control Number: 2021944491

Editors: K. Banks, Linda Fulkerson, Elena Hill, Erin R. Howard, and Shannon Taylor Vannatter

Cover by Linda Fulkerson at bookmarketinggraphics.com

Some scriptures are taken from the KING JAMES VERSION (KJV): King James Version, public domain.

THE HOLY BIBLE, NEW INTERNATIONAL VERSION®, NIV® Copyright © 1973, 1978, 1984, 2011 by Biblica, Inc.™ Used by permission. All rights reserved worldwide.

CONTENTS

Mistletoe
Make-believe

A Novella by

Amy R. Anguish

For Heather Greer and Erin Howard, my two crazy writing sisters. You keep me sane, are great at bouncing ideas around, and make me laugh more than just about anyone. Thanks so much for being my tribe-let. I love you both!

L ying in the church building.

Such audacity. And yet the desperation Charlie Hill's family was fueling drove him on. He'd been raised to know better, but the very same people who'd equipped him with moral values had driven him to this brink.

He didn't even know her. Wasn't sure she'd be here long enough for this plan to work. But he had to try.

Charlie maneuvered his way down the aisle, past the confused glances of his relatives, and leaned over next to the pretty blonde—the only girl in the building who wasn't sitting beside someone. "This seat taken?"

Wide chocolate eyes met his. She blinked and gave a short nod before gathering her purse and scooting toward the middle of the pew. When she didn't stop until the center, he swallowed a grimace, hiked up his courage a bit more, and followed her in.

Before she could move again, he dropped the bulletin on her lap.

"Oh, I already have—"

His finger tapped the hastily scribbled request on the bottom. No need to look at the words. He'd rewritten them a dozen times before giving up and hoping they conveyed enough of his misery that she'd take pity on him and agree.

To participate in his lie.

What was he doing? Dragging someone else into the deceit. On the Sunday before Christmas. It was not only sinful but probably sacrilegious.

Before he could reach over and snatch the paper back, the service began. She set her things aside and grabbed a songbook. Nothing in her expression indicated whether she'd even read his scribbles, if she agreed, if she might jump up and escape at any second.

Well, no worries there. An older couple occupied the far end, and another man had filled in her original spot. Without climbing over people and making a scene, she was trapped. And she hadn't moved any farther away. That was a good sign, right?

The song leader announced the first hymn. "Let's sing."

She held her hymnal between them so he could share.

He glanced her way. She raised an eyebrow, gave a tilt of the head, and then cut her gaze back to the front. Okay, then. Maybe he had a chance. He slid his arm across the pew behind her and forced his focus on the worship service. Time enough to figure out details later.

At least, he hoped so.

SAMANTHA ARWINE HAD NEVER BELIEVED in the muses before. Not really. And when Marcus suggested she take a vacation to get hers to work once more, she'd been skeptical. Yet here she sat in a church building on St. Simons Island,

Georgia. And an idea for a romance novel literally dropped in her lap.

I'm desperate. My family won't quit bugging me about dating someone, and I'm not ready. Is there any possible way you could pretend to be my girlfriend this week while we're on the island for Christmas?

The fact that the man wasn't hard to look at, with his wavy brown hair and hazel eyes, sweetened the proposal—if that's what it could be called. What kind of family would drive a man to pick up a girl during a church service? If she agreed to this, what was she getting herself into?

'Your deadline is looming, Sam, and you haven't turned in a thing. Do you even have any plot ideas right now?' Marcus's words from the week before bounced around in her mind.

And she could honestly say she didn't have a single concept for a new novel. Not that there weren't stories to be found, but nothing that begged to be written. A block formed in her brain the moment her romance fell apart after Christmas last year.

If she hadn't had two practically complete manuscripts in January, she would've been in a world of trouble. As it was, she had to drag the few pieces out of her very soul to finish those the way the editor wanted. And now Marcus demanded more. How was a girl supposed to write about romance when she couldn't even maintain one of her own?

"Jesus is the reason for this season, yes." The preacher grew louder as he wrapped up the message she'd barely even heard. "But He's also the reason for all the other seasons too. We need to keep Him in our hearts all year long. If that means keeping your Christmas tree up ... or your nativity out, do it."

Laughter tittered around the small auditorium. Sam shifted, and her Bible slipped from her lap. He caught it before it could *thunk* to the wooden floor but didn't give it back right away. Instead, his fingers traced her name, embossed in gold.

He plucked the bulletin back out and grabbed a stubby pencil from the back of the pew in front of them. "Charlie Hill."

Oh. He was exchanging names. With the service wrapping up, she needed to finalize her decision in a hurry. Could she do this—pretend to be his girlfriend for a week? She had no other story ideas, and it was only for seven days. How could she turn him down?

"Okay. I'll do it." She scrawled.

He relaxed as if a boulder-sized weight slipped from his shoulders. When she glanced into his eyes, they crinkled at the edges, sending a fissure through her middle. Okay. With a smile like that, it should be no trouble at all convincing his family she was in love with him. She was halfway convinced herself.

The congregation stood, and she quickly hopped up, smoothing her creamy skirt. The last few songs flew by, and during the final prayer, his fingers twined through hers and held tight. Was he nervous too?

After the *amen*, most people headed for the doors, chatting and laughing, talking about plans for Christmas week. But one group moved against the flow, heading their way. Sam sat and gathered her things, willing her hands not to tremble.

"Sorry we won't have time to work out a plan right now. Looks like my family wants to meet sooner rather than later." Charlie whispered, leaning over to replace the pencil. "I'm staying at the resort. Are you?"

"Renting a small home near the beach." She stuck a pen in her purse's pocket.

"Here for the whole week?"

"I leave the twenty-sixth."

He gave a nod right as an older woman placed a hand on his shoulder.

"Charlie, are you going to explain?" There were a few

similarities in her face and his—same nose shape, same cowlick to the right side of their foreheads.

"Mama, this is Samantha, my girlfriend." Charlie straightened to his full height, and Sam realized how tall he was —at least ten inches more than her five foot four.

Sam stuck out her hand. "Please call me Sam."

The woman hesitated for only a second before grasping Sam's fingers. "Sam. Amazing we haven't heard about you before this."

"It's a fairly recent development." Charlie hedged the truth nicely.

"And where did you meet?" Another woman asked.

"We met at church, Aunt Meg."

"You'll join us for lunch, won't you ... Sam?" Charlie's mom asked. "We'd love to get to know you better."

"Sounds great." Sam nodded, even though inside she braced herself for an inquisition like she'd never experienced before.

"We'll grab Hailey from children's worship and meet you at the restaurant." Charlie pointed toward the west side of the building.

Hailey? Who was Hailey?

Sam followed Charlie toward a large classroom where several parents gathered their offspring. Charlie waved at a girl sitting sullenly near the door. She jumped up and smiled. Sam guessed her age to be around seven or eight as the girl wrapped herself around Charlie's middle.

What had she agreed to? She was playing girlfriend to a guy with a daughter?

"Hailey, I want you to meet someone. This is Sam. She and I are dating, and we decided it would be fun for her to join some of our family events this week." Charlie made it sound like no big deal, but the girl's smile evaporated quicker than a drop of rain in an Atlanta August.

"What?" Hailey spun around and shot Sam a glare so sharp she could feel it in her forehead. "Dating? When did that happen, Daddy?"

"It hasn't been long. This was all pretty ... sudden."

"And you didn't tell me before now?"

"I just found out that she could spend time with us this week." Charlie walked his daughter toward the door. "Let's go meet everyone at the restaurant."

"Sure." Sam fell in beside him and noticed Hailey kept Charlie between them.

Charlie glanced at Sam and worried his lower lip. "There are going to be a lot of questions at lunch."

"I've no doubt." Sam tucked her Bible under her arm. "I can probably come up with a few of my own."

"Like?"

"Much planned this week? I'm actually supposed to be working while I'm here."

"I'm so sorry. I should've asked—"

She held up a hand. "I agreed, didn't I? Don't worry about it."

"We'll probably do a few things every day, but the point of going away for Christmas is to relax, so I doubt we'll stay too busy. Anything you need to miss, just let me know."

"Okay. I can handle that."

The church building was only a few blocks from the island's main shopping area, so it didn't take long to arrive at a seafood place. Charlie opened the door for Sam, and southern coastal smells surrounded her. She took a deep breath. If nothing else came from this meal, at least she'd be well fed.

Her eyes widened as she counted the heads of the group

waiting. One, two, three ... twelve, thirteen. With her, fourteen total.

"That's Grandma Hill. She's the matriarch of the family, and my dad's mom. His sister is the one standing there, Aunt Meg. She's married to Uncle Jacob." Charlie's finger indicated each person as he whispered the names in Samantha's ear. "Meg and Jacob have four kids, but only the two unmarried ones are here this week. Aunt Linda isn't here today, but those three are her children. Her husband Paul is standing by Dad. I'm the oldest grandchild and Hailey is the oldest great-grand."

His family gathering was bigger than she expected. The waitress pushed three tables together to accommodate them, and they spanned the full length of the restaurant. She, Charlie, and Hailey were right in the middle. A spot that felt more like a hot seat.

Right after they ordered, Charlie's grandma leaned forward and yelled down the table. "Did you say your name is Sam? Like a boy?"

"Short for Samantha." Sam took a quick sip of her water. "Samantha Arwine."

"Sounds familiar, but I don't recognize you."

"Maybe you've read one of my books."

Was it her imagination or did the table freeze for three seconds? Charlie didn't meet her eyes. Had she said something wrong?

"Books?" Grandma Hill cocked an eyebrow.

"I write romance novels."

Several shifted in their seats but seemed to be waiting for something now.

"Smut." Grandma Hill made a spitting sound.

"I don't write that kind." Sam straightened her back. "I write Christian romance."

Aunt Meg scoffed. "Get your ideas for all that romance from past boyfriends?"

Sam pursed her lips. "No. I haven't dated much. My one real past relationship turned out to be one-sided."

"Sam doesn't have to tell you all her history." Charlie cut off his aunt's inquisition. "What matters is, she's with me now."

Evidently, his family disapproved. She was grateful when the waitress placed her crab cakes in front of her. Now the family could focus more on eating than questioning.

Would she change herself just to make this week easier? No. Lying about a relationship was more than enough deceit. Even if it gave her fodder for another story. She had to draw the line somewhere.

2

"No way, Daddy." Hailey's arms crossed over her chest. "You can't make me do this baby tea party with *her*."

"Your grandmother thought it'd be fun for you and Sam. Plus, Santa will be there."

"Daddy." Hailey looked and sounded more like a thirteen-year-old instead of an eight-year-old. "You're kidding, right?"

Charlie counted to ten and released a slow breath. "Look, if Mimi, the aunts, and Grandma weren't headed to the spa today, I'd leave you with them. But they made these plans before I realized they conflicted with mine. I already agreed to a round of golf with Grandpa and our uncles. And no. You can't hang out with Meg's or Linda's kids. I think they're going to Sea Island today."

When his mom suggested this solution, he'd agreed to make his and Sam's relationship look real. But last night, after Hailey was in bed, he'd done a little digging. One of the good things about accidentally picking a published author as a fake girlfriend was the fact she had interviews and bios online so he could learn more about her. And he believed leaving his daughter with her a few hours wouldn't hurt anything.

He widened his stance. "What am I supposed to do with you if you don't go to the Teddy Bear Tea Party with Sam?"

"I guess just leave me in the hotel room."

"No way. But we better work this out fast—Sam should be here any minute."

"What's up with her anyway? Where did she come from?" Hailey narrowed her eyes.

"Atlanta, just like us." He spat the words.

"Right. Since when are you dating again? And someone who isn't your type?" Hailey moved her arms from her chest and propped her fists on her hips. The body language reminded him quite forcibly of Hailey's mom, Jennifer.

"My type? And what's that?"

"Someone who *isn't* artsy. Usually with long, brown hair."

Everything that wasn't Jennifer. So, he had a type. Not necessarily something he was proud of. But was it wrong? Especially since he wasn't actually dating Samantha?

This was a means to an end. He wasn't looking for anything serious. What was the phrase? Once bitten, twice less-likely-to-go-there-again? Or something like that. After Jennifer, he had no desire to go down a path that led to more heartache.

How had this become so complicated? Probably when Jennifer told him she was pregnant from the one night they'd gone too far. Hailey was the best thing to come from that relationship. But some days ...

Before he could explain why he was dating a woman who was 'not his type,' someone knocked. Good or bad, that's the way it was. He shot his daughter a warning glare and opened the door.

Sam had her fist raised to knock again. Her chunky blue

sweater and light corduroys looked comfy but cute. She pushed her sunglasses back on her head. "Are we ready?"

Charlie ran a hand over the back of his neck and grimaced. "I'm not sure—"

"I'm not going!" Hailey interrupted behind him.

Sam pinched her lips together, and a look of uncertainty crossed her face.

"Come on in."

"What's up?" Sam focused on his daughter.

"I'm too old for that stupid tea. I don't even have a teddy bear anymore."

"That's a lie. You have one in the next room." Charlie swatted Hailey's arm.

"Fine, but that doesn't mean I play with him anymore. I'm used to having him in bed at night, is all." She pouted. "And it's just going to be a bunch of babies and their mommies. And we're neither of those things."

Charlie cringed. She had him there. Sam wasn't a mom—that he knew. He really needed some time for the two of them to talk through things. Though, on second thought, did their story have to be elaborate if it wouldn't last more than a week?

"But what about Santa? Don't you want to tell him what you want for Christmas?" Sam set her purse on a table near the door.

"You don't really think eight-year-olds believe in Santa anymore, do you?"

"You know people who don't believe in Santa only get socks and underwear in their stockings, right?" Sam raised an eyebrow and tilted her head.

Charlie turned his head to stifle a snicker. Hailey looked a bit ruffled. Score one for the 'girlfriend.'

"You get socks and underwear in your stocking?" Hailey scoffed.

"I believe in Santa. I only get those things when I ask for them." Sam winked. "Okay. So, no tea party. What's the backup plan?"

"I'm supposed to be golfing with the guys ..." Charlie glanced at his watch. He was already late, not that he was gung-ho for the plan. But he had promised.

"And Mimi, Aunt Meg, Aunt Linda, and Grandma Hill are all at the spa. But I figure that's not something you'd want to join." Hailey rolled her eyes.

Charlie opened his mouth to protest. He could picture Sam getting pampered despite her neatly trimmed, paintless nails and pixie hairstyle. But Hailey had obviously decided Sam wouldn't be good enough for anything this week.

"I mean, I'm always up for a pedicure, but what's the point right now? It's too cold to wear sandals." A laugh burst from Sam that didn't sound authentic.

❧❧❧❧ 🍬 ❦❦❦❦

WHAT WAS she supposed to do now? Charlie was no help. Why would he expect her to concoct an idea to entertain his daughter? She didn't have much experience with eight-year-olds, but this one seemed very ... teenager-ish. Was that normal?

"Ice cream?" Sam suggested the first thing that popped in her head.

"At ten in the morning?" Charlie's eyebrows rose.

"It's Christmas week. Why not?" Sam grabbed her purse and eyed Hailey's T-shirt. "Grab a jacket, kiddo. We'll find something sweet and then walk along the beach to my rental house until your dad's done with golf."

"Why do I need a jacket?"

"Because it's only sixty degrees outside and the wind

coming off the ocean is cold." Charlie's answer saved Sam from having to enforce authority she wasn't sure she had.

Hailey huffed but spun on her heel and stomped to a room off the main area of their suite.

"Sorry about all this." Charlie pitched his voice low enough it wouldn't carry. "I know I didn't mention her when I wrote that note yesterday. And hadn't planned on shoving her off on you either."

"If we were a real couple, I'd be spending time with her too. And one morning won't kill me. You'll be done around when? Lunch?" Sam glanced Hailey's direction, but couldn't see anything past the bed's corner.

"That's the plan. Thanks for this. I'll text you where we can meet for lunch as soon as I know, okay?" He reached up and brushed the strand of hair off her forehead that seemed to perpetually want to be out of place.

Her breath caught at the tender touch—just like something she'd have a hero do in the romances she wrote. She inhaled deeply to clear her head. "Sure. That sounds good."

"Okay, I have a jacket." Hailey came back out with a denim coat, unbuttoned, and some sort of ball cap pulled low on her head.

"Great! Let's go." Sam forced more enthusiasm in her voice than was really there.

Charlie squeezed her hand before she corralled his daughter out the door, and her heart fluttered. What was going on? This was pretend. There weren't supposed to be breathing hitches or heart skips.

She focused on the task at hand. Entertaining a surly preteen for a couple of hours instead of polishing the scene she'd pounded out the night before. She aimed them toward the shopping area and into the confectionary.

Several flavors of fudge, pralines, brittle, truffles, and

various other desserts filled glass counters, with candy of just about every variety along the opposite wall. Did Hailey make a sound like "Mmmm?" Sam swallowed a smirk.

"Ice cream's in the back."

"What if I want something up here?" Hailey planted her feet.

"Up to you. But I'm only buying one thing, so make it good."

Hailey hesitated and then peered at every single item as they worked their way back toward Sam's goal. The ice cream tubs came into view, and Sam kept one eye on Hailey while reading the tags marking flavors. Once she saw peach, though, her decision was made.

Sam ordered herself a double cone of the peach ice cream and faced Hailey. "Okay, did you decide?"

Hailey nibbled her bottom lip, then ordered some hot-chocolate-flavored ice cream for herself. Sam swallowed her smart remark and paid for their treats. They stepped back into the windy day, grateful the sunshine softened the bitterness.

"Which way now?" Hailey looked around.

"This way. I found a little cottage not too far away. It's older but in good shape. Just big enough for my purposes this week."

"Purposes?" Hailey licked a drip from the side of her cone.

"I'm hoping to get my muses back in working order. They've been silent almost all year." Sam savored a bite of her own dessert.

"What's a muse?"

"Well ..." Sam tried to figure out how to make her explanation simple enough. "A long time ago, in the land of Greece, they believed in a lot of gods, and not just one God like we do."

"Right. We learned about that in social studies."

"Okay." Sam blew out a breath of relief. "Well, the muses were like minor gods. They were supposed to give people creative ideas. And authors refer to their inspiration as their muse—where we get our ideas."

"Would my mom call them muses too?" Hailey paused and Sam stopped to look back at her.

"What?"

"My mom's a painter. Does she have muses too?"

Sam's heart skipped for a whole different reason than earlier. "I don't know."

Charlie had been with an artist before. Was that why his family was so up in arms about her being an author? Because it was an art too? Did they expect her to be like Hailey's mom? Not that Sam had a clue what happened there.

"Probably." Hailey walked again, and Sam steered them down the little side street that led to her cottage.

Sam unlocked the door and switched on the lights in the small living room. "Make yourself at home."

"Cute place." Hailey looked around.

"I think so too." Sam's phone rang, interrupting her. Marcus. "I've got to take this. You gonna be okay if I step out on the porch?"

"Sure." Hailey flopped down on the sofa.

"Hello." Sam answered as she walked back out the door.

"How's my favorite romance author?" Marcus's smooth voice came through the line, and she could picture him chewing on the end of a pen as he leaned back in his leather chair.

"Okay, cuz. I admit it. Vacation on a beach was a great idea." Sam perched on her steps.

"So, you're writing?"

"I'm writing. Let's just say an idea literally fell in my lap yesterday."

"I don't care how you got it, but I'm glad to hear you have one again." Marcus barked a laugh. "I was beginning to think you'd run your course."

"Thanks a lot." Sam watched several seagulls swoop down over the beach and then back up again.

"You know what I mean." Marcus tutted. "So, will you make that deadline after all?"

"I'll do my best."

"That's my girl." Marcus snapped into the phone. "Don't play too much down there on the beach. I need those words of yours."

"I know, I know. I'm working too. Four thousand words last night."

"Good. Keep it up. I'll check in again later."

She knew he would.

While she didn't mind being Marcus's only client most of the time, the pressure her cousin put on her to do well could sometimes be overwhelming. A normal agent wouldn't bother her about deadlines or wordcounts. But Marcus hoped if he helped Samantha succeed, he'd be more likely to lure in future clients and build up his business.

Three years earlier, his suggestion seemed like a great deal. Now, though, Sam doubted her sanity in hiring a family member. He was a good agent, but he was also more businessman than friend. He wanted what she'd been contracted to give. She couldn't take it personally.

Easier to tell herself than believe.

She headed back into the house, but Hailey wasn't on the couch. "Hailey?"

Hailey appeared in the kitchen doorway, and if Sam wasn't wrong, a bit shamefaced. "I'm here."

"Ready for a walk on the beach?" Sam peeked around the doorframe, but the kitchen looked as it had before. Her laptop sat on the counter, coffee cup next to the sink, drying. Nothing appeared disturbed.

"Sure." Hailey headed out ahead of her.

Sam cast one more glance around the space, a foreboding feeling trickling down her spine. What was she missing? If only she were a mystery author. Then maybe she'd be able to pick up on invisible clues.

No such luck. Her romance genes didn't help a lick. Except in giving her way too many emotions when it came to a certain pretend boyfriend she barely knew. And would see again in an hour or so. Then, what?

3

"Hailey, not so close to the edge, please."

Thanks to Hailey and his aunts begging, some of the family were on a dolphin tour. They'd traveled to Jekyll Island because the St. Simons tour was closed until February. Not that it took long to drive over the causeway.

Charlie cut a glance at Sam who sat next to him on the bench. She strained her neck from side to side, probably looking for the dolphins like everyone else. His daughter was the only one on her knees, leaning over much too far.

"Hailey. If you can't sit safely by the edge of the boat, I'll make you move over to this side of me." Charlie tugged at his daughter's jacket.

"Dad, I'm fine." Hailey shot a grin over her shoulder that held more excitement and joy than he'd seen in a while.

"I'll grab her if she slips." Sam murmured the words where only he could hear.

And even though they'd known each other only a day, he trusted her.

"There!" Someone behind them shouted, and the captain slowed the boat.

"Ah, ah, ah. Look over here to the starboard side. Looks like a small pod of about three—no, four dolphins playing." The captain's voice came over the speaker, giving more details about the mammals darting in and out of the water.

"Wow." Sam rose and leaned beside Hailey.

If they were both going to hang their necks out, Charlie should probably at least stand so he'd have a better chance of grabbing them if they slipped on the wet deck. He stepped behind Sam and reached for the rail but his hand landed on top of hers instead. Though he should pull away, the feel of her fingers between his was so right, he couldn't. And she didn't move either.

"Looks like we've got a few more joining the fun." The captain commented as more people moved to their side of the boat.

Would they end up flipping over with all the weight on one side? But the vessel remained stable. Hailey bounced on her knees as if she wanted to launch herself into the water. And as much fun as that might be in the summer, this was December, with temperatures dipping into the low forties at night. That marsh would be frigid.

"Daddy, can I go stand with Aunt Meg and Mimi and Grandpa and Uncle Jacob?" Hailey pointed.

"Only if you promise to listen to them and quit leaning over the edge." Charlie tweaked her nose.

And she was off with a call over her shoulder. "Promise!"

"Finally. What I always assumed an eight-year-old acted like." Sam laughed as she watched his daughter weave her way through the crowd.

"Yeah. The preteen drama snuck in fast lately, and I miss my little girl." Charlie noticed Sam still hadn't shifted away despite having more room now, and her nearness warmed him more than his jacket.

"I can't imagine how hard it must be to raise her on your own. You're doing a great job, by the way."

"Thanks. Some days I wonder why I took on such a task, but I couldn't give her up for anything. She's the best thing to come out of that relationship. The only thing, if I'm honest. Everything else ..." He shook his head.

"Rough divorce?" Sam turned a sympathetic face his way.

"Never married. We'd only dated a few times and ended up making a big mistake one night. No. I can't call it a mistake because it gave me Hailey. But you get the idea. I knew better. Jennifer knew better too, despite not being a Christian. When she wound up pregnant, she freaked. I had to talk her out of an abortion.

"I couldn't stand the thought of trying to fix one mistake with another. And for a while I thought she wouldn't listen. But she decided if I paid the bills, she'd go through with the pregnancy. And she made me promise to take care of the child by myself because she wanted nothing to do with motherhood. She was just getting established as an artist and couldn't have anything come between her and her dreams."

"How sad that she put her dreams before the life of her child." Sam turned her hand over and gave his a squeeze.

Her words made him blink. Sam, as an author, was an artist too. If she were to have a baby, it would take away from her writing time. Wouldn't she be upset?

His heart skipped a beat, and he swallowed a few times before he could answer. "Needless to say, we're doing okay, but my family thinks Hailey needs a steadier female influence. Hence my original problem that prompted my note on Sunday."

"I can see where they're coming from, but I also don't think it's a good idea to base a marriage on finding your daughter a mom." Sam lifted a shoulder. "Though I know people have done it and it worked out okay. You're not exactly on a wagon train."

He chuckled. "No. This is definitely not a wagon train."

❧❧❧❧ ❄ ❦❦❦❦

OF ALL THE inane comments she could've made! A wagon train? Where had that come from? Sam berated herself, though he didn't seem upset.

"And you? You mentioned a one-sided romance?" Charlie broke through her mental beating.

"Oh. Yeah. It's an age-old tale really. I expected him to propose. He informed me he was moving on. That was last January." Sam focused her attention back on the dolphins, now a bit farther away.

"That's a rough way to start a year."

"Tell me about it." A mirthless laugh escaped her lips. "I was so broken up I couldn't think of a single thing to write about. That's why I'm here. My agent suggested getting away for a week—thought a place more romantic might stir up the old muses. So, I came where my parents honeymooned thirty-five years ago."

"An island for Christmas."

"Why not, right? My parents are spending the holidays up north with my brother's family this year. But I have a January deadline, and I had to do something."

"So, your lousy boyfriend ruined not only your year but also your Christmas, because now you're away from your family." Charlie's voice sounded slightly guilty.

"I'm not even sure I can use the word *boyfriend*. I've done a lot of soul-searching and thinking this year. And I wonder if I projected things that weren't really there onto our relationship. Hazard of the occupation, I guess. When you write romance for a living, you can find it anywhere."

"Hey." Charlie nudged her until she looked at him. "Don't be so hard on yourself. Do you love your job?"

"I adore my job." Easy to say because it was true. "Having people tell me my books touched them in some way ... it's one of the best feelings in the world. It's why I keep up my editing gig on the side—so I can afford to keep writing."

"Then don't worry about the hazards. Every job has a downside. Although I doubt you actually did read more into the relationship than was there. You seem pretty levelheaded."

"I don't know about that. Going in expecting a happily ever after and finding out he'd just needed a girlfriend through the holidays? Wow. Ironic, isn't it? This is the second year in a row I'm basically being someone's pretend girlfriend." She pulled her hand away and stuffed it in her jacket pocket, immediately missing the feel of his fingers through hers. Strange, considering what she'd just said.

"I'm so sorry, Sam. I had no idea this was such a bad plan."

She sank back onto the bench as the captain announced they were about to move again. He lowered himself beside her, and she glanced over with a quick, half-hearted grin.

"At least this time I know it isn't real."

"If you want out—"

"No. Believe it or not, I think this is helping my muses. And I know it's giving you at least a little peace about needing someone in your life." She glanced a couple rows back where his family members sat, casting glances somewhere between skepticism and disapproval their way.

"I don't know about that. I don't think they'll be happy no matter who I bring to the dinner table."

"Well, don't look now, but they're watching us." Sam

giggled, a feeling of being a teenager on a group date creeping over her.

"Guess we better give them something to watch, then, huh?" He raised an eyebrow and then slid an arm around her shoulders. "You want to skip dinner tonight so you can have the stamina to join us tomorrow?"

Sam cringed. "Is that an option? I hate to leave you hanging after agreeing to this."

"Don't worry about it. I'll let them know you're working and will join us for beach time tomorrow morning."

"Please tell me we're not getting in the water. It took everything I had to keep Hailey dry this morning." Sam shivered.

"Nope. Just looking for shells, walking around, picnicking. We might check out the lighthouse."

"Sounds like fun."

The boat bumped gently against the dock, and everyone rose and made their way back to land. As they walked up the pier, Hailey pointed to a notice board. Sam and Charlie moved closer.

"Look. Ice skating. And miniature golf all done up like a winter wonderland!" Hailey turned eyes the epitome of puppy-dog style on her daddy. "Can't we go, Daddy?"

"Not today. But maybe later this week."

"Tomorrow?" Hailey tugged his arm.

"You'd rather drive back over here to Jekyll than go to the beach?"

"Oh." Hailey slumped a moment, then perked again. "Wednesday?"

"We'll see."

"Sam wants to go, I bet. Don't you want to go ice skating?"

Sam's eyes widened. When did Hailey decide she wanted

to spend time together? "Um. It's been a while since I've skated, but I'm game for trying if you are."

"See, Daddy? That's two against one."

So, Hailey was using her to get her way? Or was there another reason?

"Let's talk about it tomorrow, okay? Sam needs to get back and work some this evening."

"Right. Work. Okay." Hailey shot her a look Sam couldn't begin to decipher, but the discussion dropped, so she'd let it slide for now. If nothing else, this week was much more interesting than she'd expected. And now she could anticipate ice skating.

4

The next morning, Charlie and Sam meandered down the beach. "I don't think I've ever had a white Christmas," he said, kicking a piece of driftwood out of the way.

"Never?" Sam carried her shoes in one hand despite the sixty-degree weather. He'd probably suggest she don them when her toes turned blue.

"Me, being an only child—and Hailey too—we always go where the family has gathered. And Grandma Hill always wants to spend the holidays at the beach. A different one each year."

"I bet it's fun to see all the different coastal areas, though." Sam gazed out at the horizon. With the dark gray skies, the clouds and ocean blended, making it hard to discern where one ended and the other began.

"I don't know. After a while, they sort of look the same." Charlie ruffled his hair and followed Hailey, who dashed ahead, searching for shells and other interesting finds. "It might be nice to spend at least one year where it's colder than the forties at night and with a chance of snow."

"My brother and sister-in-law live in Michigan. I think they'd tell you snow isn't all it's cracked up to be." Sam motioned around them. "And how can you say this beach is like all the others? I haven't done much exploring of this island, but the parts I've seen ... man! I can see why my parents wanted to honeymoon here."

"Why?" He stopped walking and waited for her answer, wondering what he'd missed.

"The trees stretching out giant arms, dripping with Spanish moss—it's like wandering into an enchanted wood. And waves pounding the sandy beaches with a rhythm that makes my heart beat faster. The cute, little touristy areas. And the history that stretches back ages ... religious history, as well as other kinds."

Sam spun in a circle. "If I weren't so settled in my condo near Atlanta and if I had the money, I wouldn't mind having a place here to escape and write. Or just escape."

"I imagine an author could work from anywhere. What holds you to the Atlanta area?"

"Mostly? The fact I haven't lived anywhere else." Sam laughed and the sound did something to his heart he wasn't quite sure he wanted to analyze right now. "Although there are more opportunities for book signings there."

"I can believe that. Is there even a bookstore on this island?"

"Yes. Oh! I forgot to tell you." Sam bumped her forehead with her palm in a way he found utterly adorable. "I contacted the shop before coming, and they agreed to do a signing Thursday. Christmas Eve. Can you believe it? I hope you didn't have other plans for us that morning. It completely slipped my mind."

"Oh, wow." Why was he upset about her working

Thursday morning instead of hanging out with him? "That's amazing for you."

"I know. I mean, who knows how many will actually show up, but if I can get my books in the hands of a few more people. Well, it's always good to find new readers." Sam shivered and wrapped her arms around herself as a breeze blustered past them.

"You'd probably be warmer if you'd wear your shoes."

Sam let out a sigh so deep he was surprised she had any air left. "I know. But I haven't been to a beach in ages. It just seems wrong to not feel the sand between my toes."

"The wind doesn't help either. Maybe we should move on to something warmer." Before he knew what he was doing, he wrapped an arm around her shoulder and snugged her to his side, sharing some warmth. The last woman he'd held this close was Jennifer. Yet, he couldn't deny the sense of rightness having Sam in such close proximity.

She stiffened for a second and then relaxed again. "I don't want to ruin Hailey's fun. Does she have a collection?"

"She gathers seashells from every beach we Christmas at and stores them in these plastic globe ornaments I found online with the name of the beach and the year painted on the side. Not that we're actually home Christmas day to enjoy our own tree, but we get to see them when we put it up shortly after Thanksgiving."

"That's a very cool tradition. You're such a good dad to help her make memories like that." Sam leaned a little further into him, and he found he couldn't complain. "Does she have ... well, maternal grandparents?"

Charlie let out a breath. Their situation was different than most, and he knew it. But how to explain it all?

"Only a grandfather. And he's moved farther away since there's no family left down in Georgia. I send him pictures and updates, and he contributes a little to a college fund for her each year."

"I guess it's better than nothing, but how sad to not have that family around to love on."

"The fact he has anything to do with her, considering his daughter wanted nothing—"

"You're right. I'm sorry." Sam straightened and slipped from his hold, a cool breeze replacing the warmth she'd shared the moment before. "Mind if I stop and put my shoes back on?"

"Sure. I'll go chase Hailey down, and we'll meet you back here in a minute."

She lowered herself to the ground with a nod. He hesitated, wondering how to bring back the closeness that had formed earlier. But nothing sprang to mind. And it wasn't like this was a permanent thing anyway. Sam had only agreed to this week. He needed to remember that.

⋙⋙⋙ 🍭 ⋘⋘⋘

What was she doing? Cuddling up to a man she'd known only a few days as they walked along the beach was fine and dandy for one of her characters, but for herself? Sam needed to remember she wasn't actually living a romance novel right now. Best to just use this as fodder for her work in progress and then forget about it. Mutually beneficial situation and nothing more.

If only her heart didn't twinge in regret at moving away from Charlie's strong, warm arm. Or at the fact she more than likely would not be spending next Christmas on a beach. Or that she'd lined up the book signing Thursday morning, taking her away from one of her few days left living this fantasy.

"Hey, Sam!" Hailey waved from farther down the beach and pointed toward something just out of sight.

"Hang on. I'm coming." Sam hopped up, dusting sand from her bottom.

She worked her way toward the people she liked more every moment she spent with them, though the ground was harder to walk on while wearing shoes. Hailey was animated about something, but Sam still couldn't see what. Charlie was shaking his head and motioning as if trying to remove an idea from the eight-year-old's head.

"Sam, tell him it's a good idea." Hailey crossed her arms and glared at her father.

"Until I know what it is, I can't say." Sam refused to be drawn into taking sides.

"Look." Hailey pointed to a large piece of driftwood now visible. Its branches dripped with brightly colored balls and bits of shiny tinsel and garland.

Sam couldn't help but smile. "Someone decorated the driftwood."

"Now don't you start too." Charlie's voice held a note of exasperation.

"I'm only admiring it." Sam walked a bit closer. "I still don't know what Hailey wants to do."

"Decorate one of our own, of course."

"Oh." Sam didn't see the problem, but maybe she lacked some information.

"And when are you thinking we'll do that?" Charlie asked. "And with what decorations?"

"Daddy." Hailey tugged his sleeve, her voice wheedling. "We can do it tomorrow. We'll just pick up a few things at a store."

"Tomorrow you said you wanted to do putt-putt and ice skating."

"Right. How about Thursday? Perfect. Christmas Eve."

"Maybe after my signing?" Sam asked before she could stop

herself.

"Not helping." Charlie muttered near her ear, his breath tickling the hairs on her neck and sending a jolt through her tummy.

A giggle burst from her lips. "Well, I'll stay out of it and just let Hailey keep working on you. But I thought we were going to go climb that lighthouse."

"Right." Charlie nodded. "Let's go."

"Will your family mind that we left them on the beach?"

"No. My mom and grandmother love to spend at least one day simply sitting in the sand and reading. They have no desire to *climb all those stairs*." His voice at the end mimicked an old-lady voice that sounded nothing like his relatives.

"Okay then." Sam didn't dare ask what his mother and grandmother were reading. Certainly not 'smut.' "And the others?"

"The other men said something about a fort. And my aunts mentioned shopping with their girls."

They meandered up the wooden steps from the sand to the sidewalk and made their way past more of those giant oak trees that fascinated Sam. The lighthouse rose ahead of them, a white giant standing guard on the tip of the island. Charlie pointed to a place where they could play miniature golf without leaving the island.

"But no ice skating. And it's not decorated for Christmas." Hailey pouted.

"Right." Charlie led them into the lighthouse museum. "Can't blame a guy for trying."

Hailey quickly lost interest in the history behind the landmark, so they gave up skimming the facts in the house and headed to the tower itself. Sam stared up the spiral staircase, counting steps as they ascended.

"You gonna make it?" Charlie asked from behind her.

"Hailey, slow down a bit. I want to be able to at least see your feet, please."

"I'll make it. A hundred twenty-nine steps is nothing, right?" Sam pushed onward. "Though it's a bit crazy to think we're inside a structure that's been standing since 1871."

"I believe the sign said 1872." Charlie's voice held a hint of teasing.

"Are you sure?" Sam turned back to face him and realized her position on the steps placed her at the perfect height to stare into his hazel eyes. They were greener today, matching his fleece pullover. And only inches from hers. She blinked, mind blank on what they'd been discussing.

"Pretty sure, but we can check again when we go back down." His voice was breathy—just from climbing halfway up?

"Right." Her own reply was barely above a whisper.

"Daddy? I can't go any slower. Did you stop or something?" Hailey's voice drifted down from above them.

Sam swallowed and spun back around to climb again. What was wrong with her? This was only a pretend relationship. No need to get all flustered just because a guy was closer than she expected. Or had color-changing eyes that happened to be her favorite shade of spring grass.

"Man." Sam muttered to herself.

"What?" Charlie asked.

"Nothing." She stepped out onto the platform at the top, and the rest of the air whooshed from her lungs as the ocean and island stretched out around them. "Wow."

"Wow, indeed." Charlie stepped right behind her, his hand on her shoulder.

She chided her heart once more. Because it didn't leap at the view nearly as much as at the slight touch of the man next to her. And that wasn't what she'd agreed to. What would happen in four days when the pretense ended?

5

"I can't believe I paid good money to utterly humiliate myself." Charlie willed his right foot to straighten instead of tipping precariously toward his other foot. The man-made frozen rink underneath his cheap skates didn't help matters.

"You're doing fine." Sam gave his arm a little tug. "And look how happy this makes Hailey."

His daughter breezed by him, having no trouble finding her balance on the slippery surface.

"Sure. Well, she's shorter, so the gravity's not as strong."

Sam's laugh rang out and his heart tripped over itself for a few moments. Maybe the situation wasn't as bad as it could be. After all, he had a great excuse to hold her hand as they inched along the rink. Who cared that everyone else moved much faster, including several of his cousins? Speeding was overrated. He just wanted to enjoy the moment, savor it, relish ice skating in almost seventy-degree weather with a beautiful woman by his side.

They eased into a turn, and his left foot took off faster than his right. He tried to pull it back in line, but it was too late. Up went his legs, and down went everything else. "Oof!"

And, unfortunately for Sam, she came tumbling after. The downside—literally—of holding the hand of someone who can't skate.

Charlie stared at the blue sky sprinkled with clouds. Maybe he'd just stay here a minute. Nothing wrong with admiring God's handiwork from another direction, right?

"You okay?" Sam eased into a sitting position next to him and leaned over.

"Just pretending I meant to do that. Makes it a tad less humiliating."

"And how's that working out for you?" Sam's brown eyes danced with merriment.

"About as well as you'd expect." He pushed up with his elbows until he was sitting.

"Daddy!" Hailey skidded into him, her arms windmilling as she stopped too fast.

"Careful, Hailey. This seat's a bit cold. I don't recommend it."

"You stayed down a really long time. I thought maybe you were hurt." Hailey placed a hand on his head as if she were the parent and he the child.

"I'm fine. Just maneuvering back to a standing position. It's harder for me, you know. Taller."

"I don't think that's the way it works, Dad." Hailey propped her fists on her hips.

"I'll remind you of that when you're my age." Charlie looked around, trying to decide the best way to get up. "You about ready to go play some mini golf?"

"Not yet! We haven't even been here half an hour."

"Are you sure?" Charlie glanced at his watch. "It feels much longer."

Sam patted his arm. When did she get back to her feet?

"C'mon old man. Let's get you to that bench, where you can watch your daughter from a better angle."

"Old man." He sputtered. "The girlfriend isn't supposed to take sides with the daughter, you know. Pretty sure it's supposed to be the other way around."

"Terribly sorry." She tugged his hand until he wobbled his way back up. "I'm new at all this."

"Mm."

"So? Bench?"

Much as he hated to admit defeat, every muscle in his backside ached too much to contemplate going around again, even to save face. He nodded, and they moseyed toward the seat. At least it wasn't near the one where his parents and aunt perched. Grandma Hill had claimed her arthritis was too severe to leave the resort today, and several of the others kept her company playing card games.

"It hurts to be bested by an eight-year-old, huh?"

"I think it hurts more to be bested by frozen water." He rubbed the back of his head and grimaced.

"Want me to go fetch your shoes?"

"Just sit a few minutes. I'll be okay."

"All right. Still going to be able to play putt-putt after that fall? Hailey is counting on it."

"I'm not dead yet, am I?" He smirked. "I think I can beat a couple of women."

"Oh, a challenge. Okay then." Sam rubbed her hands together and settled in beside him, a perfect fit under the arm he rested on the back of the bench.

If Sam hadn't agreed to his plan, this week would've been much different. But she livened things up, added some laughter and color, and even awakened a few stirrings he hadn't felt in a long time. Could there be more to this than they'd originally planned? What if he suggested not ending the charade after this week? Was he really contemplating a serious relationship again with an artistic woman?

"Daddy, Mimi said we won't have time for putt-putt and lunch before her massage appointment this afternoon if we don't go now." Hailey flew into them at full speed and it took all their arms to keep anyone from getting hurt.

"I guess we better go then." Charlie eased to his feet and caught his mom staring with a contemplative expression.

Was time really the problem, or had she simply not liked seeing him cozied up with Sam?

✤✤✤ ❀ ✦✦✦

"A HOLE IN ONE!" Hailey jumped up and down as Sam's ball clunked into the hole at the other end of the green. "Sam, you did it."

"Wow." Sam leaned on her putter. She'd never finished with less than two strokes before. There must be something magical about this place ... or the people she was with.

"Great putt." Charlie pointed toward her ball. "Go stand over there, and I'll take your picture."

"Oh." Sam laughed. "I don't need documentation. I won't forget today."

Charlie studied her a moment. "Still. Just for fun."

"Okay, sure." She knelt next to the hole, her smile wide.

"Let's take a picture by the polar bear, Daddy." Hailey pointed to the next green.

"Are we taking photos, or are we playing golf?" Aunt Meg nudged Charlie out of her way and lined up her lime green ball on the starting spot.

"We're having fun, Aunt Meg." Hailey tugged her dad's hand until he stood with her in front of the bear. Charlie

39

stretched his hand out and snapped a selfie of the two of them.

Sam gave them a thumb's up as they glanced her way.

"Now you too, Sam." Hailey motioned her over.

"Oh, no. You don't want a picture with me."

"Please." Hailey folded her hands and put on her begging face.

"Why not?" Charlie raised a brow.

And she knew why not. Because she was getting much too wrapped up in these two people. It would hurt to leave them in a few days if she wasn't careful. And yet, who could resist when people seemed to want you around?

She stepped next to Charlie, Hailey in front of her. Charlie's hand slid around her waist, nestling her into his side. She held herself stiff, trying to ignore the flutters in her tummy.

"Relax." Charlie's whisper tickled her ear and sent shivers down her back.

She glanced his way, and he winked before motioning her focus back to the phone. Snap. Hailey grinned from ear to ear in the shot, but Sam was caught off guard by the expression on Charlie's face. Because he hadn't looked at the camera like he'd urged her to. Instead, he'd kept his gaze on her, and she could almost believe he really liked her.

"Are you done playing photographer yet, or should we go around?" Mimi bustled past them.

"Play away. We don't mind being passed." Charlie motioned for her to start. "Show us how it's done, Mom."

"It's done by not stopping to document every hole. The way you kids abuse the cameras on those phones, it's a wonder more people haven't gotten in trouble for taking a photo of something they shouldn't have." Aunt Meg shot a look Sam's way although Sam couldn't fathom what picture Meg seemed to think she'd taken.

"Oh, come on, Mom." One of Meg's children laughed as she putted through. "If I quit posting pictures on social media, you'd think I'd died or something and start worrying. Leave the love birds to their fun."

After the older women moved on, Hailey rolled her eyes. She set her ball down to take her turn.

"I'm sorry we had to have them along today." Charlie squeezed Sam's shoulder.

"It's probably best. Keeps me grounded and helps me remember what happens after Christmas." She pitched her voice low so Hailey wouldn't hear.

"About that—"

"Your turn, Daddy." Hailey pointed to the hole. "I got three!"

"Good job, Hailey." He scribbled her score on the card and then took his shot.

What had he been about to say? Was he wanting to end their arrangement earlier? The more time they spent together, the tighter the web of lies became. How hard would it be to untangle things after this week? Especially with Hailey growing more attached now.

The rest of the course offered no chance for that conversation to pick up again. When they returned to the clubhouse, Mimi and Meg and a few others were waiting for them. Now that discussion would be postponed even longer. Charlie helped hang all the clubs and then escorted them back to the SUV.

"Lunch?"

"Sure." Sam swallowed a sigh. "But then I probably need to work this afternoon."

"Understood. See you at the mid-week worship service this evening?"

She hesitated. Why? Normally nothing would keep her

from going. But this week, everything was different. "I'll be there."

"Great." Charlie's smile sent a warmth through her middle that had nothing to do with the un-Christmas-like weather.

Sam sent up a prayer that God would forgive them for their deceit. Surely God would understand why they did it, right? Maybe it wasn't as important as when Rahab lied about the spies on her roof, but ... well ... Sam sighed. She'd just have to pray for more forgiveness when the week was up.

6

Bells jangled as Charlie and Hailey pushed through the bookstore door Thursday morning. It was his daughter's idea to swing by Sam's book signing. Although they hadn't told his relatives their real purpose in coming here.

His eyes immediately sought out the blonde head seated in a windowed area to the right of the entrance. Sam signed a book with a flourish and grinned when she presented it to a lady. As they chatted, the love of her work shone in Sam's expression and her animated hand motions.

While Jennifer was caught up in her own world when she painted, she hadn't been as ... vibrant about the end results as Sam. It had been personal to her. As if she didn't want to include anyone else in her life. Sam seemed the opposite— drawing him to her with every expression and emotion that flitted across her heart-shaped face.

"Humph. Guess they'll let anyone do a book signing here." Aunt Meg muttered as she pushed past him and headed toward the suspense section.

"I'm going over to say *hi* to Sam." Hailey started off that direction, but he caught her.

"Wait until she's finished talking to the customer."

"Right. Okay."

Charlie glanced around. The bookstore was cute and well stocked, considering its small size. He didn't have time to browse, though, because Hailey dragged him toward Sam as soon as the other lady moved away. Sam flashed them a smile.

"What are you two doing here?"

"We came to see you!" Hailey bounced on the balls of her feet. "I hoped maybe if Mimi and Aunt Meg could see you with your books, they wouldn't be so against you being a writer."

Sam's mouth formed a perfect *O*, and she glanced at Charlie as if for guidance on how to respond.

"You said you wanted to find another book to read on the way home in a few days." Charlie nudged his daughter toward the chapter books. "Why don't you go see what catches your eye?"

"I hope you sell lots of books today, Sam." Hailey winked and then scurried away.

"She's something else." Charlie shot Sam an apologetic smile.

"In a good way." Sam straightened a stack of novels on the edge of the table.

"These are all yours?" He counted five different titles.

"All mine. I have another, but they didn't have any copies with such short notice."

"Wow."

"Thanks." She ducked her head.

"I wondered why Hailey was so adamant about going to the bookstore when she knows I always get her books for Christmas. Hello, Samantha." His mom stepped up beside him and peered at the novels, her lips twitching. Was she trying not to smile? "So, this is your ... not smut, huh?"

Sam's mouth quivered as if fighting a grin of her own before she nodded. "Yes. These are my romances."

"Hmm." Mom picked one up between two fingers and flipped it over to see the back.

Charlie rolled his eyes. "If you want to get one today, Mom, it'll be my treat."

"No, I don't think so." She returned the book and meandered away.

Heat crept up Charlie's neck. "I'm so sorry, Sam. She's not usually this bad. You'd think as much as she harps on me to find a girlfriend that she'd be happy. Not like this."

"She's trying to take care of you." Sam reached forward and straightened the paperback. "I get it. After seeing you burned by Hailey's mom, I imagine it's hard to see you even pretend to have interest in someone else with artistic leanings."

"That doesn't make it right."

"Maybe not. But it's still okay."

Another customer stepped up.

"I'll catch you later? Hailey still has her heart set on decorating the driftwood. And the trolley ride tonight."

"Sounds great. I'll text when I'm done here." Sam nodded and then turned her smile on the reader waiting to ask questions.

"I'm ready, Daddy." Hailey walked up with a stack of four or five books.

"Think you have enough?" He cocked an eyebrow.

"It should hold me for a few days." She shrugged.

He shook his head but motioned her to the checkout counter. At least she wanted to spend money on books and decorations instead of makeup and jewelry and even worse things.

"Dɪᴅ you have enough writing time today? We monopolized a good chunk of your afternoon decorating that crazy driftwood." Charlie's voice pulled Sam away from her thoughts as they waited for the next trolley to arrive for the island Christmas lights tour.

A paper cup of warm cocoa gave her hands something to do. "It's Christmas Eve. A girl shouldn't have to work the whole day." She flashed him a grin. "And the driftwood project wouldn't have taken so long if we'd found a piece 'worthy' enough for Hailey's tinsel sooner."

"True." His laugh sent pleasure through her.

Sam couldn't complain about the hours spent shopping and decorating the driftwood this afternoon. Not when it meant more time getting to know Charlie and Hailey. Besides, writer's block had hit late last night. Twenty thousand words in, she had a ways to go yet, but now she had more ideas for her characters.

"Finally." Grandma Hill huffed as the trolley pulled up, Christmas lights strung around its windows and carols playing from the speakers.

"Festive." Charlie's uncle's voice held a note of sarcasm.

Sam quickly swallowed a snort of laughter. Charlie's face said he fought the same problem.

"If they don't want to do this, why are we here?" Sam stood on tiptoes to whisper in Charlie's ear.

"Hailey, for one." His stubble scratched against her cheek as he answered her. "Family compromise for another. Majority rules."

Emotions swirled through her insides at their close proximity, and Sam almost missed his answer. A throat cleared loudly behind them. Sam sprang away from Charlie, tearing her gaze from where his focus had been—on her and only her. What were they doing? This was fake.

"They're loading now." Charlie's mom looked between her and him, an eyebrow raised. "If you two are finished telling secrets."

"Sweet nothings, Mom. Not secrets."

Charlie's flippant reply had her torn between wanting to laugh and wishing they weren't getting on a bus full of other people. What would it be like to spend time just the two of them?

Would the pretense vanish? Or would they remember it better that way? Was Charlie that good of an actor, or was she projecting the emotions from her novel into real life?

Charlie steered her up the narrow steps and toward the middle, where Hailey claimed a window seat. There wasn't enough room for all three, though, so he motioned her across the aisle. Sam swallowed her disappointment at the idea of him being several feet away. But then he nudged her over and slid in beside her instead of his daughter.

Sam's gaze wandered to where Charlie's grandmother frowned in the doorway still. Directly under a sprig of mistletoe. Sam glanced around, but no one else seemed to notice the traditional decoration. Did she want Charlie to see it?

No.

Pretending, Sam. Remember?

Right. Maybe if she reminded herself about five million more times tonight, she'd believe it. Or at least be able to fight the growing attraction to the man next to her. After all, she'd come down here to write a romance—not live one.

As the trolley started its route past the best decorations on the island, Charlie slid his arm around her shoulders. Sam tried to relax, but knowing his family was behind them, probably paying more attention to what might be happening in their seat than out the windows, made it hard. Maybe if she focused more on the lights, they would do the same.

Cottages and plantation houses and other structures glowed with Christmas spirit. Some even decorated the giant oak trees, and the Spanish moss appeared a bit unearthly in the multihued glow of the strands. Santas and snowmen and other traditional décor were everywhere. She sipped her chocolate and hummed along with the songs, enjoying the sound of Hailey exclaiming over each new sight.

How long would the magic of Christmas remain in Hailey? Would she grow bitter like her Mimi and great-aunt and Grandma Hill? Would finding out her dad and Sam had deceived her break her eight-year-old heart? She'd already been abandoned by her mom.

"Penny for your thoughts." Charlie nudged her. "You got awful quiet there."

"I—" How did Sam explain they might have made a mistake? Would she have agreed to this plan if she'd known about his daughter? She still would've had the story idea but wouldn't have to worry about ruining anyone else's Christmas.

"Hey." Charlie frowned. "What's wrong?"

Sam glanced over at his daughter and back again. "Just worried about how she'll take all this ... when ..."

He leaned back and huffed out a breath. "Yeah. But I have an idea. I'm hoping we can have some time to talk tomorrow. Maybe after presents are opened but before the meal."

"I don't know, Charlie. I mean—"

"You shouldn't spend Christmas alone, no matter what." He didn't let her say anything else. "Come as a friend if nothing else."

She sighed but nodded. How could she resist one more day with them?

"I forgot to tell you earlier my grandma thinks we all need to wear Sunday attire for Christmas dinner. Don't stress, though. What you wore on Sunday was fine."

"I have another dress. No worries."

The trolley pulled back into the starting spot. How had an hour passed so quickly? People slowly filed off the vehicle, thanking their guide. As Charlie and Sam passed under the doorway, she didn't dare glance up. With the conflict roiling through her all evening, adding mistletoe would only make matters worse.

7

Despite the griping his grandma had done that morning about him inviting 'that girl,' Charlie's heart skipped when Sam arrived for Christmas. Besides, his grandma never liked anyone's date the first few times she met them.

After Sam voiced her doubts the night before, he wondered if he'd lost his chance for good. As much as he'd wanted to take advantage of the mistletoe hanging above the door of the trolley, until they could talk things through, that tradition would have to wait.

"Hi." Sam's voice was a little breathless, as if she'd run the last mile to the resort.

"Merry Christmas. Come on in." How he kept his own words from coming out breathy, he had no idea. Not when she tugged her jacket off, revealing a simply cut, deep-red dress and pearls. Wow.

"Sam!" Hailey threw herself at Sam, wrapping her arms around her waist. Was this the same girl who'd pitched a huge tantrum earlier this week over him dating someone 'not his type'?

"Hi, Hailey. Merry Christmas." Sam embraced his daughter, a joyous expression on her face. An affectionate look for his child. And that stirred the feelings up in his own heart even more. They needed to have that talk—and soon.

"Are we ready to get started now?" Grandma Hill's voice rang out above everyone's talking. "I'm not getting any younger, you know."

"Come on in. Do you want anything to drink? Aunt Meg has some cider in a crockpot." Charlie linked Sam's arm through his and led her farther into the suite.

The hotel decorated with a tree in the window, and his grandmother sat to the right, her frown at odds with the merry surroundings. When was the last time he'd seen Grandma Hill happy? And for someone who'd been egging him on to date, shouldn't she be pleased?

"What'd ya get me this year, Mimi?" Hailey plopped down by the tree, her skirt billowing up in a bubble.

"You'll see soon enough." From her chair on the other side of the tree, his mom smoothed Hailey's brown hair. "Want to help pass out presents?"

"Sure." Hailey bounced back up and skipped a gift to Aunt Meg.

One by one the packages under the tree diminished, piling up next to their recipients until time for opening. Hailey grinned as she presented two different boxes to Sam. Sam's eyebrows raised, but she set the gifts in her lap. Charlie knew about the green box—the one from Hailey and him—but curiosity tugged as he spotted his mom's name on the other.

"Okay, that's it." Hailey looked around the room. "Now can we start opening?"

"Yes, dear girl." Grandma Hill nodded. "You're still the youngest, so you go first."

"We open by age order." Charlie whispered to Sam so she'd understand. "It helps keep things a bit less chaotic."

Sam gave a nod and then smiled as Hailey tugged an outfit free from tissue paper. The eight-year-old didn't look thrilled with getting clothes, but she'd appreciate them when it came time to wear them. Several of Charlie's cousins opened their gifts. Then there was a pause as all eyes turned their way.

"Oh. I'm sorry. It's rude of us to ask how old you are." Charlie's cheeks heated. "Why don't you go next?"

"Um. Okay." Sam pulled the paper back from the box Hailey helped him wrap the night before. "Oh."

The picture frame had raised oak trees on the edges, like the ones on the island. He'd had the photo of them at the putt-putt course printed and put it among the branches. If Sam's misty eyes were any indicator, he'd chosen well.

"Okay, Charlie, now you." Grandma Hill's command didn't let the moment linger.

He also got clothes, and then it was his mom's turn.

"Open mine first, Mimi." Hailey bounced in front of her grandmother.

"All right."

Hailey got his mom something? Charlie frowned and tried to see around his daughter. He didn't remember this gift.

"A book." His mom displayed one of Sam's novels, her eyebrows raised his direction.

Sam tensed next to him, and he covered her hand with his, afraid she might bolt. What had his daughter been thinking?

"I picked it out at the bookstore yesterday." Hailey pointed to the cover. "See? It's set on a beach. And I couldn't get Sam to sign it because I wanted it to be a surprise. But I bet she would now."

"Maybe later." His mother flashed a half-hearted smile at

her granddaughter and then looked at Meg to indicate it was her turn.

His dad leaned over and told Hailey, "Good choice."

Had Charlie heard that right?

Soon enough, they got through everyone else, and once more it was Sam's turn. Charlie braced himself as Sam glanced his way before tugging a corner free of the wrapping paper. He didn't know what to expect. His mom was smirking now.

Sam lifted the lid and gasped.

"What is it?" Hailey stuck her head between Sam and the gift, impeding Charlie's view.

"Hailey Marie! Step back." Charlie moved his daughter and then glanced at the culprit of his mother and aunt's laughter. Mistletoe. What?

"Don't you like it, Samantha?" His mom asked between chuckles. "We didn't catch you two kissing all week, so we figured—as a romance writer—you might appreciate a little help in that department."

Sam's face wasn't quite the same shade as her dress, but it was close. Charlie shot a glare at his mother. What was she thinking? All week long she hovered and scowled, and now she wanted them to kiss in front of the whole family?

"Mom, really?" He positioned himself at the edge of the chair though there was no way to shield Sam from everyone looking.

"Oh, go on. We've given you enough grief this week." His mom waved her hands at him. "Let's just call this a truce, huh? It is Christmas, after all."

A truce. Charlie's heart hammered against his ribs. Of all the situations he'd imagined this week, this one never crossed his mind. What should he do now? He'd decided earlier they shouldn't kiss until after they'd talked, but his mom didn't know any of that.

Sam's fingers tugged his shirt sleeve, and he slowly twisted to face her. She lifted the sprig of mistletoe inch by inch until it dangled above her head. One of her perfectly shaped brows lifted as her eyes scanned his face. If only he could read the emotions in those brown depths better.

"Go on, Daddy. Kiss her!" Hailey bounced up and down across the room.

Everything stilled, and he leaned Sam's way. His pulse pounded in his ears. Her breath fanned his face. And then her eyes closed, and he was lost. He crossed the tiny distance left between them and pressed his lips to hers.

SOFT AND FIRM all at once, Charlie's mouth molded to hers, pausing a moment as if enjoying its spot. Then his lips moved in a bit deeper, one of his hands spreading over her back while the other cupped her cheek. The mistletoe fell from her grip as her fingers moved to clasp the shoulder of his sweater.

Murmurs around them slowly filtered through the fog in her head, penetrating the senses so completely wrapped up in Charlie Hill. Her eyes fluttered open as he pulled away, leisurely enough to indicate he hadn't wanted the kiss to end any more than she had. Whoa.

One corner of his lips tilted up, and she ducked her head as a smile enveloped her own mouth. If she learned nothing else this week, she'd learned this—all the kissing scenes she'd written before now were wrong. Dull and lifeless and completely empty compared to the caress of Charlie Hill.

"See? That wasn't so hard, now was it?" Charlie's mom teased them from across the room. Was this new attitude a Christmas miracle? It wasn't like anything Sam had seen so far this week.

"I take it that was part of my Christmas present too?" Charlie turned and smirked at his mother.

"If you want to consider it yours too, go ahead. Won't bother me a bit."

"So, do I get to open another package now or not?" Charlie's voice was much more unaffected than Sam figured her own would be.

She was still recovering from the most perfect kiss she'd ever had.

The rest of the gift opening went on around her as if a life-changing event hadn't happened only moments before. Hailey squealed when she opened the earrings Sam gave her—tiny sand dollars from a gift shop downtown. Maybe she'd figured out how to get along with an eight-year-old better than she thought.

Sam's phone trilled as everyone collected wrapping paper. She shot an apologetic glance at Charlie and motioned that she needed to answer. He waved his understanding, and stashed the mistletoe in his back pocket before gathering the trash around it.

"Hello?" Sam placed the phone to her ear and stepped into the alcove that led to the bedrooms.

"Samantha, darling. Merry Christmas!"

"Marcus." Sam kept her voice low so she wouldn't interrupt the festivities. "Merry Christmas to you too."

"Marcus?" Grandma Hill's hearing must be better than most women her age. "Who's Marcus?"

"I just wanted to tell you I was going through these pages you sent me, and I think this is going well, Sam. A bit different than what you usually write though. Are you sure you need the little girl in the story?"

Sam glanced over her shoulder and discovered most of the activity stilled and herself the center of attention. "Listen,

Marcus. It's a holiday. Let's talk about this tomorrow when I get home, okay? Or better yet, maybe Monday?"

"Am I interrupting something? I saw that picture of you on social media with the guy and girl." Marcus's laughter grated on her nerves.

"Are you cheating on my son?" Charlie's mom stepped over to Sam, her look the fiercest Sam had seen yet.

"No." Sam shook her head. "You've got it all wrong."

"Oh, have I?" Marcus evidently thought Sam was still talking to him instead of the people in the room because he just kept going.

Charlie's mom snatched the phone from Sam's hand, her finger bumping the button for speaker as she jerked the device away.

"Please tell me you're not using those people as inspiration for your story, darling." Marcus's voice filled the silent room. "Because I never would've believed you had it in you. But I know you didn't have any significant other before you headed down there."

Sam sought out Charlie across the room, where he stood frozen. The gig was up. They'd been found out.

"Sam?" Marcus asked. "Hello?"

"I'll call you back." Sam said loudly and then accepted the phone back from Charlie's mom.

"Just what's going on here?" Grandma Hill rose to her feet.

"Daddy?" Hailey looked back and forth between Charlie and Sam.

Sam swallowed a lump creeping up the back of her throat. The one thing she hadn't wanted to happen was now reality. She'd hurt Hailey. Her own heart didn't feel great right now either, but to disappoint an eight-year-old?

"Sam and I never met before last Sunday. I saw her alone in the church building and thought maybe if I asked her to pretend to be my girlfriend it would give me some peace this week. You all have been harping on me for years now to date and marry and get a mom for Hailey. I couldn't stand the thought of having to hear it through another family holiday." Charlie's words rushed into the heavy quiet.

Voices erupted all around them, questioning, protesting, scolding ... The attention was off of Sam now and all on Charlie. Much as she wished she could help, something told her staying here would only make matters worse. She snatched her coat from beside the door and slipped into the hallway.

For a few moments there, she'd forgotten everything was imaginary. That she and Charlie hadn't been together longer than five days. That this would end after today.

But the finish line arrived before either of them were ready. It was rather like a polar bear plunge, going from that kiss to Marcus announcing her hoax to the whole family. Marcus. Why on earth was he working on Christmas anyway? What a perfectly horrid finish to a delightful week.

And now she had nothing to look forward to except writing scenes for her characters to live out their romances. Back to living vicariously through her books. No more amazing kisses for her. Not even the prospect of a Christmas dinner. She had no food at the cottage except a few toaster pastries and a frozen pot pie. Worst Christmas ever.

With the best gift.

Oh! She'd forgotten her picture frame. She spun around to go back for it and then changed her mind. Maybe it was better to leave the memories behind. Why hold on to something that was never real to begin with?

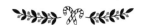

"HAILEY!" Charlie had waited long enough. Even if the eight-year-old didn't want something to eat this evening, he did. And she was going with him.

He pushed open her door and froze. The bed was made, nothing was strewn over the floor, and her backpack was missing. No trace of her.

Sure, they'd dealt with tears and anger earlier, but he thought she'd come to grips with it. Understood Sam could still be her friend even if she wasn't really dating Charlie. Not that Charlie didn't yearn to change that, but he wasn't about to let his daughter in on that plan. Not yet.

How had Hailey snuck out without him noticing? Where could she have gone?

8

B anging on her door later that afternoon startled Sam from the scene she was writing. She hadn't achieved success recreating that kiss from earlier, anyway. But who could be here now?

Charlie?

Her heart sped up, hoping and fearing at the same time. She inched the door open and sucked in a breath. Hailey stood there, hair plastered to the tear streaks on her cheeks, her arms wrapped around the frame Sam left behind when she fled.

"Hailey." Sam pulled her to her. "Did you come here by yourself?"

Hailey's head bobbed against Sam's chest.

"What were you thinking? Your dad must be beside himself." Sam pushed her back and held her by the shoulders.

"Please don't tell him. Not yet. I needed to talk to you, and I knew after this morning he wouldn't want me to come." A hiccup erupted after the plea.

"Come on. Let's find some hot chocolate. But I will need to at least let him know you're safe."

"Okay." Hailey mumbled.

⁘ ⸎ ⸎

CHARLIE'S PHONE buzzed across the room, and he dove for it. Maybe a family member was letting him know his daughter was with them.

The text was from Sam. His heart pounded as he opened the message.

Hailey just showed up on my doorstep.

Thank you, God.

His fingers shook so that it was almost impossible for him to reply.

Can you keep her there? I'll come get her.

Give us a bit? I think she needs to talk.

Charlie slumped into the closest chair. Leave Hailey with the woman who wasn't supposed to be in their lives anymore after today? The one who turned their whole family upside down this week. The one who'd thawed his heart ... and kissed him with a passion mixed with purity and affection he had never experienced before.

It took all his willpower not to rush out the door and head that way now, but maybe Sam could explain things better than he could.

Okay.

Had she been using them all week too? Like the guy—

Marcus—said on the phone earlier. How did things get more complicated than he'd imagined?

Sam situated Hailey at a stool by the counter, and heated some water

"What did you need to talk to me about?"

"Your story."

Sam stilled. So, she hadn't been completely crazy thinking someone had messed with her laptop earlier in the week. Apparently, Hailey had snuck a peek.

"What about my story?" Sam stirred in the chocolate powder and added a swirl of whipped cream.

"It's about us, right?" Hailey ran a finger through the fluffy white floating on top of her mug and licked it off.

Sam eased onto a stool and debated what to say. "Yes and no."

A furrow ran down Hailey's forehead. "Why can't grownups just give a straight answer?"

A laugh burst from Sam before she could stop it. "Okay, here's the deal. Yes. I'm using this week as inspiration for my story. Did it sound familiar?"

Hailey nodded and took a long drink.

"Well, that's because I based my characters on you and your daddy. But they're not exactly the same. And the story will have its own ending instead of the craziness that happened today. I didn't mean to hurt anyone. Your dad and I thought the arrangement would work well for both of us. We didn't think things through as much as we should have."

"Mimi was pretty mad." Hailey swung her legs back and forth as she ducked her head.

"I'm sorry I messed up Christmas, Hailey. I never meant to

make anyone mad or upset or hurt." Sam reached over and squeezed her hand.

"So, it was all pretend?" A hint of tears laced Hailey's voice. "Like in your book?"

Sam had to swallow her own rising tears. "Not all of it. I really did have fun with you guys this week. I never would've ridden the trolley or decorated a piece of driftwood or ice skated if I hadn't met you guys."

"But now you're going to quit hanging out with us."

Sam released a long breath. Much as she wanted to reassure this sweet girl otherwise, it was best to stick to the original plan.

"We're both going home tomorrow anyway, so we wouldn't have much more time together no matter what. I just wish we'd ended on a better note."

Hailey shook her head. "But why do we have to quit spending time together? Don't we live in the same place?"

"Atlanta's pretty big. Not like St. Simons. We might not live as close as you think."

"You're not any better than my mom. You only want to be around when it's convenient for you." Hailey hopped off the stool and dashed in the living room.

Sam's heart shattered, but what could she do? She refused to make promises she couldn't keep. That wouldn't be any better than Jennifer, either.

CHARLIE CRADLED his head in his hands, elbows on his knees. *God, I really messed up. I need your help to fix this. The problem is, Lord, I'm not sorry I asked her to pretend with me. Doesn't your Bible say that good can come from all situations? Please, bring some good from this disaster I created.*

A knock interrupted his prayer. He had no desire to see anyone right now, but when another knock quickly followed the first, he eased himself up and opened the door, lest the intruder continue to pound. His mother. He swallowed back the urge to slam the door in her face.

"Charlie." He stepped back, and she walked in, looking around. "Where's Hailey?"

"She ran away."

She spun on her heel, her arms akimbo. "What?"

"Don't worry. Sam just texted me Hailey went there." He held his phone up. "I'll go get her in a bit."

His mother's stance eased a bit, and she nodded. Did that mean she'd grown to trust Sam this week too? Despite what happened earlier.

"What brings you to our suite?"

"First, I felt I should apologize."

Charlie's knees wobbled. He needed that chair again and pointed to the seating arrangement. Thankfully, she headed that way without questioning it.

"When you explained you felt the need for a fake girlfriend this week because of our ... urging you to marry so Hailey would have a mom, at first I denied we'd been that bad." She twisted her wedding rings around her fingers, looking at the gems instead of him.

"And then?" He prompted.

"And then I wondered if you didn't have a point. If we really had driven you to take such a drastic measure. To ask a complete stranger to spend time with you—to hang out with your daughter!"

"Sam wasn't so bad, was she?" Charlie leaned back, arms folded across his chest. "I mean, we did meet in a church service."

She huffed, still not meeting his eyes. "I admit she was

growing on me. But we didn't really get to know her that well—"

"Maybe because all week long you looked down on her and treated her like dirt." Charlie cocked an eyebrow.

"Not like dirt."

"Mom."

"Okay, we didn't treat her like we should have. Especially since we didn't know you hadn't even met her before Sunday morning." She shook her head. "I still can't believe you did that. In a church service, no less. I raised you better."

He tapped his fingers against his biceps.

"Anyway, we're sorry we've made such a nuisance of ourselves, trying to make your life better."

His mother couldn't help herself. Trying to twist the words to make them sound like what she and her sister-in-law and mother-in-law had done wasn't really that bad. But he appreciated her effort anyway.

"I didn't mean for things to be so ... tense. I thought if I proved to you that I was at least trying to consider what you wanted, maybe you'd let me relax this week instead of constantly harping—"

She made a squeak of protest.

"Harping," he reiterated, "on me to find a mom for Hailey. Don't you think I want what's best for my daughter too?"

His mom finally looked up and pursed her lips. "Yes."

"I know she needs more female influence in her life. That it's not enough for her to have only me. But she has you and Grandma and Aunt Meg and several others. It's not like she doesn't have some strong women in her life already.

"And I didn't want to date *only* to find her a mom. A marriage needs to be based on more than that or it won't work. It's why it was good that I didn't convince Jennifer to marry me.

It would've been for the wrong reason, and we both would've been miserable."

"When did you get so smart?" His mom sighed.

"Like you said a few minutes ago—you raised me that way."

One side of her lips turned up.

They sat in mutual silence for a few minutes.

"But, Charlie, are you sure about her career?"

He jerked his head her way. "What?"

His mom barked out a rough laugh. "I can see the way you've looked at Sam through the week. As if you want to keep her around for a while. But she's got a career that demands a lot of her time and energy and emotion. Writing isn't the same as painting, but it's not always going to be easy."

"She's not Jennifer, Mom. She's ... she sees other people and puts their needs above her own. Just look how she handled this week. She was supposed to be writing a novel, and how many times did we interrupt that to keep her with us?" He spread his hands out on the armrests. "She never complained or tried to get out of anything, despite knowing she might get glared at the whole time."

His mom had the good sense to look sheepish.

"And look how Hailey's taken to her. You know that girl doesn't latch on to just anyone."

"I know." His mom pushed up from the sofa. "Just be careful, okay? It's not only your heart on the line here. It's Sam's and Hailey's too."

"I know that better than anyone." Charlie pointed to the door. "My child ran away over all this."

"I love you both." His mom pressed a kiss to his forehead. "And if you choose Sam, I'll learn to love her too."

Charlie sat, too stunned to walk his mom to the door. Had that just happened? And now what? Was it too little too late?

FOR THE SECOND time that day, a knock at the kitchen door drew Sam's attention from her laptop. After Hailey drifted off in front of the television, she'd been working some of her frustration and hurt out through her characters—the poor dears. They were having all sorts of problems this evening.

She pulled open the door and caught her breath. Charlie stood there, a basket in hand. His grey sweater had his eyes looking like the sky and ocean when the rain had moved in, and his hair was tousled from the wind.

"May I come in?"

"Yes." She stepped back quickly. "Sorry."

"It's okay. Hailey?" He glanced around as if his daughter were hiding.

"She fell asleep on the couch a little while ago. I know it's not late, but she had quite a day." Sam moved to head that way, but he caught her.

"Let her sleep awhile. You're right. She's had quite a day. But so have you. Have you eaten?" He held up the basket.

"Not much. A frozen pot pie earlier. And then I forgot to eat anything this evening."

"That's no Christmas fare." He made a tutting noise and pulled out food. "Try some of this. I had the resort pack it up for me."

Sam accepted the ham sandwich he offered, made with thick slabs of meat, probably leftover from the main meal earlier in the day. Her tummy rumbled with approval as she took a big bite. He smirked and opened a container of fruit and another of potato wedges.

"I take it from what your agent said—" Charlie perched on a stool and motioned toward her computer "—that's who you were talking to, right—that the craziness this week has inspired you?"

Sam ducked her head and worked to swallow her food. "Yes, Marcus is my cousin and agent. Although the agent part might change after this week. Yes, I got some writing done. And some of it was inspired from this week."

"So ..." Charlie paused, as if unsure how to phrase what he wanted to ask. "When Marcus said you were using us—"

"No." Sam flattened her hands on the countertop. "I wasn't using you. Yes, the idea for my novel came from your original note and everything that spurred from it. But you and Hailey ... you've made my week so much better than it could've been."

"I'm glad some good has come from it."

She nodded and wiped her lips with a napkin. "I'm just sorry it wreaked so much havoc with Hailey. Not to mention ruining your Christmas this morning."

"I had a very good Christmas, thank you." Charlie grinned at her, and her cheeks heated. Was he thinking of the same thing she was? That kiss?

Setting her sandwich down, she picked at the crust. "I'm glad I didn't ruin your Christmas."

"Nope. Did I ruin yours? After all, this was all my idea."

She shook her head. "No. I think if I had to go back and make the decision all over again, I'd still say *yes.*'"

"Good to know." Charlie fiddled with a spoon she'd stirred her coffee with earlier. "My mom came and talked with me this afternoon."

"Oh? Did she ream you out about lying all week? Or congratulate you on getting rid of such a horrible person who would write trashy romance novels?" Sam forced a smile, though it felt fake even to her.

"Neither, believe it or not." Charlie glanced at her, something in his eyes she couldn't quite decipher.

"Oh?"

"She actually gave her blessing."

Sam shifted on her stool, unsure if she'd heard right. The woman who'd glared at her all week now approved their relationship? Knowing it was all fake? What did that even mean?

"Before everything happened this morning, I wanted to get you alone and talk. About maybe continuing this ... whatever it is that's been building between us. Seeing if we could make things work in the real world of Atlanta instead of here on a romantic isle."

She struggled to draw a full breath. Had she fallen asleep too? Was she really in the living room recliner, next to Hailey, snoozing away, her brain conjuring up all the right things? She pinched her arm and winced. Nope. Not asleep.

"You okay?" Charlie reached toward her, obviously having seen her grimace.

"I'm not sure."

"Not sure if you're okay or not sure about my suggestion?"

"Not sure about any of it." Sam stood and paced to the fridge for a bottle of water. "I mean, when I came to this island where my parents honeymooned, I was looking for a romantic idea, and then it happened. Like Christmas magic. But I don't think I can believe any of it."

"What do you mean?"

She twisted off the lid of her drink as she talked, trying to find the right words to say exactly what she meant. "Charlie, I've made this mistake in the past."

"Mistake?" He leaned forward. "You've pretended to be someone else's girlfriend?"

She shook her head. "No. But remember what I said about my last relationship? I was projecting. I saw things that weren't there, things that were more romantic in my mind than in real life. I let my imagination run away with me because that's what I do."

"Sam, you can't be serious. Are you saying there wasn't anything real between us this week? That it was all in your head?"

"I make up romance for a living!" Sam threw her hands up, forgetting she'd just loosened the lid on her bottle. Water splashed on her head, dousing more reality on her than already weighed down her heart.

Charlie jumped up and grabbed a towel, bringing it over to help mop the mess. He ran it over her hair, then stilled and clasped her shoulder. Her heart and mind warred within her, one minute urging her to shove him away and the next, to throw herself into his arms.

"Sam, if it's only you making things up, then how could I feel it too? Maybe this time, it's not all in your head."

The words were a balm to her soul that had berated her for being so heartbroken over the last relationship. And yet, the little girl who'd spent over an hour crying in the room next door this afternoon made the decision even harder. How could she risk hurting Hailey even more than she already had? More was at stake this time than her muse and her self-esteem.

"I just can't, Charlie." She took a step back. "I can't do this to Hailey."

His jaw clenched and relaxed again. "I guess I better go wake her up and take her back to the resort. We're leaving fairly early tomorrow."

A sob demanded release. Sam swallowed it back. "If you want to leave her and fetch her first thing tomorrow, she's fine to sleep on my couch. I don't want to steal her rest."

He hesitated, but then nodded. "It'll be early when I come."

"Just text on your way over, and I'll wake her."

"Do me a favor?" Charlie reached out but stopped short of actually touching her.

"What's that?"

"Pray about what I said earlier. Don't simply rely on what's happened in the past."

It was a hard request. Because as much as she wanted to believe something could grow between her and Charlie, a bigger part was terrified God would say *no*. And this time would hurt much worse than the last.

9

The tide rolled out as Charlie made his way along the beach to pick up Hailey the next morning. Truth be told, he wasn't ready for the week to be over. Sure, he had Sam's phone number—assuming she didn't change it when she got home—but Atlanta was huge. How could he find her again once they were back to reality?

He'd texted her he was on his way, but she hadn't replied. Maybe she thought having less contact with him would make it easier. Whatever the reason, he already missed her.

Her cottage still looked dark as he climbed the back steps. Had she not received his message? He rapped on the back door, his heart beating faster than any other time he'd picked up Hailey from a friend's.

Right as he was about to knock again, the door inched open a crack. Sam blinked at him, several of her hairs waving in a direction he was pretty sure they didn't usually go. He pinched his lips together to keep from grinning.

"I'm so sorry." Her voice was a bit hoarse. "I forgot to plug my phone in last night, and it must have died."

"It's okay. Is Hailey up?"

"Oh. Um, I don't think so. Come on in." She backed away from the entrance so he could step through.

He glanced her way and then averted his eyes. Better not enjoy the view of those bare legs underneath her pajama shorts if she wasn't interested in continuing their relationship after this morning. Besides, a pair of beautiful legs got him Hailey all those years ago. And he'd learned that lesson well. No more of that until he had a wedding ring to go with it.

"Hailey." Sam touched his daughter's back. Hailey sprawled across the sofa, an afghan over her, one arm dangling off the edge. And the pat did nothing to raise his sleep-like-the-dead child.

"Here." Charlie gently nudged Sam. "She's hard to get up in the mornings."

Sam stepped aside, hugging her middle.

"Hailey." He tugged the blanket off her and tickled her ribs. "Hailey-girl. C'mon, baby."

His daughter groaned and threw an arm over her eyes. "It's too early."

"Agreed. But we've got to get on the road soon. Time to go home."

Hailey shifted just enough to squint at him and then glare. "I don't want to."

"I'm sorry about that, Hailey, but it's time."

Another groan and then she rolled into a sitting position. "Can I go to the bathroom first?"

"Go on." He stood and noticed Sam had disappeared.

The smell of coffee wafted from the kitchen, and he followed the alluring aroma. Sam tapped her fingers against the countertop, her focus on the liquid dripping into the pot.

"Thanks for letting her stay the night." He stepped up behind her and clasped her shoulder.

"Oh." Sam turned and leaned against the cabinet. "No problem. I don't think she moved at all. Or if she did, I didn't hear anything. Want some coffee?" She nibbled her lower lip as if regretting asking.

"The sun was just coming up as I walked over. I bet we could find all sorts of treasures on the beach if you want to take it out there for a few minutes." He held his breath. Had he pushed too far?

Finally, she nodded. "Let me grab some pants and a jacket."

Hailey stumbled in as Sam poured them both a mug of coffee. He wrapped his daughter up against his side, treasuring the sweet moment.

"Thought we might go look for sand dollars for a few minutes before we head back to the resort."

"Really?" Hailey perked up.

"For as long as it takes to drink our coffee."

"Drink slow." Hailey slipped her shoes on and headed out the backdoor before they could reply.

"Guess we better follow." Charlie allowed Sam to go ahead and fell into step beside her.

The sun's rays cast a golden glow on everything in sight. The trees Sam described earlier in the week as being from a fairyland looked even more magical now. Hailey dashed from one object on the beach to another, excitement written in every motion.

"Look!" His daughter galloped over, her hands full of sand dollars.

"I've never seen so many." Sam ran a finger along the edge of one.

"There's usually more right after the tide goes out in the morning before anyone else has been on the beach." Charlie motioned around them. "It's why I always try to come out early at least one morning on our Christmas trips."

"Thanks for sharing it with me." Sam studied the depths of her cup as if all the answers needed would be there.

"I'd like to share more than this with you." Charlie risked the statement as his daughter rushed off again. "Did you consider it more last night?"

"Charlie—" Sam sighed. "It's too much right now. We've been looking at everything through the spirit of Christmas and vacation and island life. You can't base a relationship on that. There's no substance."

"I don't know if I believe that." He swallowed the last few drops of coffee. "But I won't push today. I'll just remind you that you have my number if you change your mind. And I hope you do."

"I—"

With a kiss to her cheek, he cut off another protest. "I think there's something real growing between us this week. Think about it. Pray about it. And I'll do the same." He turned and focused on his daughter once more. "Hailey!"

The eight-year-old groaned when he handed his mug to Sam. "Already?"

He nodded.

She bustled over and thrust an armful of treasures in his hands before throwing her arms around Sam. "I'm sorry for what I said last night. I'll miss you, Sam."

"I'll miss you too, kiddo." Sam stroked his daughter's hair before stepping out of the embrace. "You be good for your daddy, okay?"

Sam rushed back to her cottage, gone from their lives as quickly as she'd arrived. Charlie inhaled deeply, trying to ease the ache in his chest. Nothing more he could do today. Hopefully time and prayer would change her mind.

Hailey tugged on his arm, and he turned his gaze to her. "Daddy, I think I have a plan."

"A plan for what?" He steered her toward the resort—no need to linger here any longer.

"A plan for you to win Sam."

SAM DID one more round through the cottage, making sure she hadn't forgotten any socks or earrings. No sign of anything that wasn't here to begin with. She meandered into the kitchen to pack her laptop.

As she passed a mirror, she made a face at herself. No telling what she'd looked like this morning when she'd answered the door for Charlie. But he'd kissed her cheek anyway. She caressed the spot on her face, wondering for the thousandth time if he might be right. She sighed.

When she ran her finger over the touchpad on her computer, something caught her eye. That's not where she'd left off last night. She frowned as she scanned the page. Had someone messed with her computer when she wasn't looking? The words all appeared the same. What was going on? More of Hailey's shenanigans?

"Strange."

She saved her work and shut things down. She could figure it out better at her condo. Time to head back to reality.

The drive across the island didn't take nearly long enough as she meandered past the oaks and beautiful homes. Would she get to come back in the summertime when everything was green instead of yellow and brown? Maybe explore the fort and old church buildings and other history?

Maybe Marcus would suggest another working vacation and she could justify it. Marcus. She groaned. That was a problem better handled right away. What was wrong with him lately? Since when did he check in so frequently on her progress?

"Call Marcus." She told her phone.

"Sam, darling! To what do I owe this pleasure? Don't tell me you're done already." Marcus's cheerful voice grated on her nerves.

"No. Not done. Not with the manuscript anyway. What I have is rough, as you saw. And I need at least another week to finish the first draft." She touched the roof of her car as she drove across the bridge to Brunswick, a silent promise to cross again someday.

"That's fine. We have a few more weeks before it's due to the editor."

"I know." Sam followed the signs to head out of Brunswick and back north toward Savannah and then on to Atlanta.

"O-kaay." Marcus dragged the word out. "So, what's up?"

"I'm trying to figure out why you felt the need to call me yesterday. On Christmas, no less." Her voice was full of anger, but she didn't care.

"I mean, I didn't realize you were actually going to be with the guy and his family." Marcus chuckled, though it sounded nervous. "How was I supposed to know I'd end up on speaker phone?"

"Marcus, there was no need for you to call at all. You knew I'd been working. You should've been off celebrating the holiday, not checking in on your author."

"I thought you'd be alone, Sam. I mean, you went down there alone."

"Not the point." Her grip tightened on the steering wheel.

"So, what is the point?" Marcus's voice sounded more business-like now, and less friendly.

"The point is, if you want to keep representing me, please back off a bit. You've been a great agent for me the last few years, but this week you crossed a line. We're family, and I agreed to be your first author because I trusted you. But I thought the deal was that you'd help get me better established and then build your agency from there."

"Right. That's what I'm doing."

"Marcus, most agents don't check in on their authors. They wait until the author sends them something. And even then, it's not full manuscripts." Sam sighed. "Family or not, we need to set some better boundaries."

"So, what exactly are my boundaries? I always thought the agents decided those—not the authors."

"Your job, as I understand it, is to help me find contracts, make sure my manuscripts are ready and that they find the best homes, and then help market."

"And where did I cease doing that?"

"When did you quit trusting me?"

He huffed. "Maybe when you let reality take away your ability to write."

"I'm writing again, aren't I?" She banged on the console. "I even sent you proof. But you called about five times over the course of the week."

"I just wanted to make sure we weren't going to lose that contract." His voice was raised.

"Well, we aren't." She wanted to make more demands, but knew she'd already pushed too far. "I promise. My eyes are back open, and I can do this. But you've got to quit relying on me to be your only source of income too. Go find some more authors to represent."

He didn't say anything for a long moment. "Check in with me when you're done, okay, Sam? And be careful driving back. I hope you didn't get yourself in too much trouble with that family. It's one thing to use people you don't know for inspiration. Something else entirely to play pretend just to get a story."

"Tell me about it." Sam swallowed a lump of sadness. "I'm fine. I'll talk to you next week."

She ended the call and breathed deeply. If she focused solely on how to end the story she'd been writing, it should occupy her thoughts enough that she wouldn't be able to think about what Charlie had said. Only one problem with that plan. Charlie was her inspiration for the story.

10

T*en months later*
    "Is this it, Daddy?" Hailey peered in the bookstore window, bouncing on her toes.

"This is it." He took a steadying breath. Was this plan going to work, or was it sure to fail? Only one way to find out.

"Do you think she's going to be excited to see us?" Hailey pulled the door open and stepped inside.

"I hope so." He kept the words under his breath, not wanting to put a damper on his daughter's excitement. If nothing else, he knew Sam would be kind to Hailey. But how would she welcome him?

"There she is!" Hailey pointed toward a corner on the other side of the cash register. "I see her."

"I see her too. Let's get in line."

Only three others waited to get their books signed, but he knew it could still take a while because Sam made sure each reader had all their questions answered. He caught glimpses of her blonde hair over the customers' shoulders in front of him. And each second they remained in line, the knots in his stomach tightened more than the five-o'clock traffic on the top end perimeter.

"Sam!" Hailey jumped up to the table as soon as it was their turn.

"Hailey." Sam rose to her feet and caught the girl as she threw her arms around her. "What are you doing here?"

The question might have been aimed at his daughter, but Sam's eyes met his.

"Hi." He rubbed the back of his neck. "I looked you up. Your signings are all listed on your website."

"Yeah. Marcus suggested making sure people know where to find me." One corner of her lips drew up.

"Daddy bought your book for me as soon as it came out. I couldn't wait any longer. I had to know how it ended." Hailey tugged on Sam's hand.

"How it ended?" Sam's mouth formed an O. "You're the reason my laptop wasn't exactly where I left it. Did you read more of my story that last night on the island?"

Hailey had the grace to look sheepish. "Ye-ah. I was curious."

"When she told me the premise of your story, I sort of wanted to see how it ended too." Charlie raised an eyebrow.

<hr/>

"You read my story?" Sam's cheeks heated. What did he think? While it began based on their St. Simons experience, she'd changed the ending to be more romantic than how they'd left things.

"I did." Charlie took a step closer.

"Oh, um." The back of her knees bumped into the chair she'd occupied moments before.

"I'm not sure about the ending, though."

Her heart skittered. He'd hated it. Thought her touched in the head. Or just figured her imagination was skewed. Warped.

"I don't know. The way he holds her car keys captive until she promises a date when they return to reality ... it was great and all. But I thought of something that might be more romantic."

She swallowed, wishing she could draw a full breath. "More romantic?"

"Yep." Charlie took another step, and Sam bumped into the bookshelf behind her. How had she worked herself all the way back here? "What if he found her at a book signing and asked her for a date in front of all her fans? Because he knew from the way she wrote the story she really did like him too. And he'd kept alive the hope of finding her again all those months—couldn't get her out of his head."

"Oh." He couldn't? Were they still talking about her story? "That would be romantic."

"And then, maybe they could work up to the epilogue."

"The epilogue?"

"Mm, hmm." His face was maybe an inch from hers now, and she could barely think straight. "You know. Where they promise to spend Christmas together for the rest of their lives."

Good thing she didn't have a response because he didn't let her speak, covering her lips with his in a kiss she'd experienced over and over again in her dreams since she left St. Simons.

But this kiss was better.

So much better.

When Hailey's arms wrapped around them, and the cheers erupted in the store, she couldn't help but bury her head in his shoulder and grin.

"You were my best Christmas ever. And I really think we should continue that trend. What do you think?" Charlie's whisper tickled her ear.

"I think I like that idea. I've missed you so much."

"Yay! My plan worked!" Hailey danced beside them, and they shared a smile.

"What about your family? Will they be upset about you dating someone in the arts?"

"My mom read your book and passed it around to the others." Charlie winked. "You're in."

She was *in*.

Going to St. Simons for Christmas had given her much more than a kick to her muse. She'd found love. She leaned in and pressed another quick kiss to Charlie's lips.

"So, which beach are we visiting next Christmas?"

ABOUT THE AUTHOR

Amy R Anguish grew up a preacher's kid, and in spite of having lived in seven different states that are all south of the Mason Dixon line, she is not a football fan. Currently, she resides in Tennessee with her husband, daughter, and son, and usually a bossy cat or two. Amy has an English degree from Freed-Hardeman University that she intends to use to glorify God, and she wants her stories to show that while Christians face real struggles, it can still work out for good.

A Hatteras Surprise

A Novella by

Hope Toler Dougherty

For all the people who help me tell my stories, especially Jeff Radford who helped me with fishing tournaments and boat details, Earl W. Worley, Jr., Chief Operating Officer of KS Bank who answered banking questions, and Walt Wolfram, PhD, William C. Friday Distinguished University Professor and Director of the Language & Life Project at NC State University who spent an engaging half hour discussing the Hoi Toide dialect with me. It takes a village, and I'm indebted to many gracious people. Thank you!

1

For a moment, Ben Daniels was fifteen again. The tackle shop matched exactly the one in his memory. The same weathered planks. The same signs for bait and ice. A side portion had been added, but the front cast him back to ice cream cones and Popsicles with his siblings on melting afternoons.

"This is it. Nice job, man." Talking out loud. To himself. Must be more tired than he thought.

He exited his car to stretch as scenes from that long ago summer vacation flooded his head—climbing the Hatteras Lighthouse, riding the waves, and a little girl with blond braids who tagged along or, rather, led them on other adventures.

What was her name? Would she, like the tackle shop, still be here?

He smiled and shut his door, a refreshing breeze blowing off the sound. The extended weather report promised more temperate days like this one on the Outer Banks for the remainder of October. Fantastic. He rolled his shoulders and headed inside.

A beach music favorite he recognized from college greeted him along with a woman sporting cropped gray hair. "Good afternoon. What can we help you with today?" She turned from a rod and reel display and moved to the cash register.

"Hey." He blinked, pulling himself to the present. "I'm looking for a beach cottage."

"For rentals, Island Realty is back up the road a bit." The woman jerked her head toward the way he'd just come.

"No, ma'am, I'm staying at the Teachy Bed and Breakfast. I'm looking for the cottage my family rented years ago. I don't have the address, but it's near this store."

"When we talkin', sonny?"

"2000 or so."

"Pretty good chance the cottage is gone by now. Storms, rebuilding, and such."

"Sure. I wanted to find it for old time's sake. It was a special place, a special time for my family."

A door behind the counter opened, and a woman with sandy blond hair stepped into the shop. He sucked in a breath.

"Hazel, do you have—" she froze in the doorway, a deer caught in a flood light. She dragged her wide eyes from his, muttered, "Excuse me," and vanished into the back room.

"That's too bad. Ahm." He glanced at the office door, squinting his eyes. A crazy idea lit in his mind. "I'm also looking for someone I met back then. Someone named Ginny?" The name popped out of his mouth before he could question it. "Do you know her?"

An eyebrow arced to Hazel's gray hair, and she stiffened like a momma bear growling in front of her den. "Maybe. Maybe not. Who wants to know?"

Ben glanced again at the door and offered his hand across the counter. "I'm Ben Daniels. I think you know her, and I think she's in that office."

She clasped his hand in a firm grip, warning of a strong will. "If that's true, why did she turn around when she laid eyes on you? Why doesn't she want to see you? Are you that fellow from N.C. State? The one who broke her heart?" She raked her almost-black eyes over him and back again.

"No, ma'am. When we vacationed here, she showed us around the island. I'd love to say hello. That's all." He smiled, hoping his eyes crinkled like his sister teased him about. Would charm work on this fierce gatekeeper? "She's in the office, right?"

"She must not recognize you since she closed the door." Hazel slid a small pumpkin closer to the cash register and flattened her palms on the counter, leaning toward him. "Or maybe she did recognize you. Just doesn't want to talk to you."

Buckling under her guilt-inducing gaze, he grabbed onto the first excuse. "It's been around twenty years. She probably forgot some tourists here for just one week." He raised his eyebrows. "Do you mind if I knock and say hello?"

Hazel studied him and consented on her terms. "I'll knock and see if she's busy."

❧❧❧ 🎄 ❧❧❧

GINNY CLICKED the door closed and leaned against it, blowing out a raggedy breath. Old humiliation blanketed her. Twenty-year-old humiliation with ample doses of worthlessness and betrayal pressed on her shoulders. Ben. After all these years.

If he isn't Ben, he's a dead ringer. He's taller, more filled out. His voice is deeper, but his sea green eyes are the same.

Hey, God. That stranger dredged up a memory that makes me feel less than. I know. I know. I'm not that little girl with the hand-me-down bike, the faded shorts, the funny speech. My self-

worth comes from You. I know You love me, but I just got blindsided. I need some peace.

The back window showed a tranquil scene of sea oats waving in the breeze, clouds floating over the Pamlico Sound. Three tiny boats sailed on the horizon. The normal island scenes calmed her heart and regulated her breath. Ben. After all these years. She shook her head. Her first crush. Her handsome boy from a far away, great big city—Charlotte. Ben. One of the ones who'd laughed at her behind her back, mocked her speech.

The memory, decades old now, still stung.

Just breathe. The guy would be gone in a few minutes.

Sunlight danced on the waves outside her window, casting her mind to the week for the first time in years. She'd nursed the crush, tainted with humiliation, for years until Matt Tomes asked her to the prom. That relationship lasted until she left for East Carolina University and met a boy from New Jersey who loved her island accent and never made fun of it. To her face at least.

Other guys piqued her interest in subsequent years, but Ben's memory and green eyes hovered in the back of her mind, always a silent yardstick.

Twenty-year-old pictures flickered in her mind from that golden week. Ben, helping her into her boat even though she didn't need it. Praising her island skills. Making her feel like she was sixteen instead of ten. Stirring boyfriend-girlfriend fantasies. Oh, what silly thoughts of a ten-year-old.

Breathe, Ginny. You can show the quarterly reports to Hazel in a few minutes.

As soon as the screen door slams.

A KNOCK JERKED her heart rate into high gear again. Hazel never knocked—even when the door was closed. Not a good sign.

"Yes."

Hazel slid in through a just-big-enough crack in the door and closed it behind her. "Why are you hiding in here?"

"I'm not—"

"You walked out front, saw that man, turned right around, and shut the door. Why? Is he the jerk who broke your heart in Raleigh?"

"No one—"

"You came back here with your tail between your legs and started keeping the office for your daddy."

"Wrong." Ginny fingered a fishing lure of her father's she kept on his desk. "Daddy passed. The store needed me, and my video project was finished."

"But you hadn't finished your doctorate. Plus, my version's better." Hazel shrugged. "Anyway, he's singing some song about vacationing here a long time ago. Wants to say hey."

Heat climbed up her neck.

So, Ben's back on the island. Remembered her after all these years. Asked for her.

Calm down, heart. Saying hello for a quick minute should be fine. No problem.

God, some help with a problem, please.

Filling her lungs with a good breath, she followed Hazel back into the shop. Her gaze flickered toward his face, fell to a button on his chest. She released the breath and forced her eyes up to meet his. Yep. Same green ones she remembered.

"Hello. Hazel said you wanted to see me."

"Yeah. Ginny, it's good to see you again. Ben Daniels. We met a long time ago when my family stayed in a cottage not too far from here."

"Oh." She smiled. "We get a lot of visitors on the island. I'm sure you can imagine."

Hesitating, Ben tilted his head. "Right, but you showed my family, my two brothers and sister, to some of your haunts. Took us crabbing and ate what we caught for supper with my parents. We climbed the lighthouse together too."

"Oh." Her eyes widened. "Of course, I remember you. Wow. A long time ago. I hope your family's doing well." Did she sound kind and welcoming but non-committal at the same time?

Ginny caught Hazel watching her pleat the hem of her blouse. She smoothed down the creased fabric and stuck her hand in the pocket of her jeans.

"You helped us look for shells too. My sister dreamed of finding a conch shell, but we never did."

"Right. Your sister." Ginny cocked her head. "What was her name?" Josie.

Behind the counter, Hazel coughed twice, then cleared her throat for an exclamation point.

His eyes narrowed. "Josie."

Focusing on him, she refused to look at Hazel. "Josie. Right. It's a shame she didn't get one. I'm usually pretty good at finding shells."

"We heard about her disappointment for months afterward." He grinned at her.

"Oh, no. Well, maybe you can find one for her before you go back to Charlotte." Her stomach dropped. Big mouth. Big mouth.

His head jerked. "You—"

"It's been nice to see you again." Backing toward her office, she felt for the doorknob. "I'm glad you stopped by. Enjoy your stay on the island." She slipped through the crack in the doorway and disappeared.

2

"Well, well, well. You do remember our visitor." Arms crossed in front of her, Hazel leaned against the door frame, daring Ginny to deny it. "Worrying the hem of your shirt gave you away. Uh-huh." She nodded. "It's a telltale sign you're lying, by the way." A smile stretched across her face.

"I don't lie." Ginny rolled her swivel chair back, planning her escape from the determined woman heading her way.

"You were evading the truth. Telling part of it anyway. Then you stuck your foot right in it when you said, 'Charlotte.'" Hazel slapped the desktop and hooted.

Ginny gritted her teeth. "How long until you retire?"

"Never. I'll be a sand burr on your heel for as long as I can figure math in my head."

"The cash register calculates for us." Ginny circled the desk and headed to the front of the store.

"Not when the power goes out."

"Don't bank on family ties to keep your job."

"Speaking of replacements, have you found yours yet? Shoulder season is here and just about gone. We need to train somebody before peak season starts next spring, and you need to get back to Raleigh."

Ginny grimaced. "I'll let you know. And did I overhear you offer my services to show him around the island? I have work to do here. Thank you very much." Ginny straightened a box of Snickers in the glass display case, reminded herself to buy candy for the Trick or Treaters who'd be knocking soon.

"Your daddy left the store to you and," Hazel made a face, "your brother, but you don't have to work here to own it. You're not the only one who can run it."

"Trying to get rid of me?"

"I'm trying to be serious. We haven't talked about Raleigh in a while."

Good reasons too. A bad breakup, a pass-over for lead on a new speech video, and her daddy's funeral ... not interesting topics. Licking her wounds for months at home helped, the island rhythms soothing her raw feelings.

"You're in this office too much. Get out and about. Have some fun. Plus, how're you going to finish your dissertation if you're hiding in here?"

As always, dissertation talk bristled her back. "My project's fine, and anyway he'll have his own vacation plans." She moved a box of promotional keychains to a more prominent place on the counter near the family photo. Mom, Dad, herself with her arm around her big brother's waist. Where are you? Are you okay? Come home and run the store like Daddy—

"Nope. Not here on vacation. He's taking Thumb Nelson's place at the bank. You didn't hear that part when you were eavesdropping?"

Her breath caught, and her eyes flew to Hazel. "He's moving here?" Too late, she couldn't tamper the curiosity in her voice.

Hazel shot her a gotcha smile. "Temporarily. While they

find a permanent manager." An idea animated her face. "Hey. Invite him to church, then go eat at Calmside for the Sunday Special."

"I don't think ..." She fiddled with the price tag on a sun visor. Why not help him discover Hatteras? Her social calendar certainly had time for fun excursions, but too much time with this blast from the past could fan the flame of her schoolgirl crush, lighting some serious heartache for her when he returned to Charlotte.

Too many site seeing trips with the handsome bank manager and Hazel would be buying a wedding magazine at the Red and White or saving wedding dress pins on her Pinterest page. Maybe not yet, but the thought would absolutely cross Hazel's mind. She'd already mentioned two different dating apps in the last month and tried to set Ginny up with a new UPS driver. The plan might have worked if not for his wife and twin daughters.

"That boy's new to the island. He needs a guide to show him around, give a little history. Think about it and go finish up. It's almost quittin' time." Hazel shooed Ginny toward the office.

"He's not a boy." He's a grown man with a lovely face and nicely shaped arms and—

"You noticed, did you?"

Ginny slammed the office door on the throaty chuckle coming from her irritating second cousin once-removed, behind the counter. She really needed to get back to Raleigh.

❧❧❧❧ 🍬 ❦❦❦❦

BEN'S LUGGAGE thumped on the floor of the Teachy Bed & Breakfast. The B & B offered an off-season, extended rate, which, of course, made his Charlotte boss happy since the assignment could last several weeks, maybe even months. The job listing would go live sometime in the coming week. How many résumés would flood the listing?

Working in a resort location must be a coveted placement for most people. As remote as Hatteras was, thirty miles into the ocean off the main coast, its beautiful shores enticed people year-round. Or so the pamphlet from the front desk claimed. He dropped the pamphlet and the to-go bag of popcorn shrimp on the bedside table and flopped onto the queen-sized bed like a starfish, releasing a long, road-weary sigh.

The scenic but lengthy drive zapped his physical and mental energy, especially the last sixty miles or so with the three long bridges connecting the mainland to the island. Seven hours in the car made for cramped legs and a crick in his neck. He rolled it to loosen the knots, wincing at the crackle and pops.

He reached for the bag marked with tracings of grease waiting on his bedside table and stabbed the wooden fork into the boat tray of fried shrimp. He speared two at once and crammed them into his mouth. Delicious. Crunchy. Still warm from the takeout grill.

Mental note: *Get a list of the best restaurants the locals frequent from Ginny.* Mental note number two: *Invite Ginny to dinner.* He smiled to himself. Nice mental note.

Stopping by the bait and tackle shop? Genius. Reconnecting with Ginny? An interesting surprise. Could it be more? A friend to re-introduce him to the island would be more than welcome.

He picked up the remote and turned on the TV to a music channel. More stress evaporated with the melody of soft rhythm and blues in the background. Swallowing some orange sports drink, he let his mind return to his family's vacation.

A hazy picture of a pigtailed little girl teased him, parking her bike beside the screened-in porch of the cottage, taking Josie for rides in her Jon boat. Her hair, darker today, swung over her shoulder in a single braid. Her blue eyes still flashed like way back then, but they held a guarded look now. Twenty years ago, she'd warmed up to his family in less than a day, sharing story after story about the island during their excursions. She didn't send the same open vibe today, however.

Listening to her back then fascinated him on two points, the island lore as well as her accent. Ben had heard about the Hoi Toide speech of the North Carolina coast on TV, but that summer he experienced it firsthand. If the locals spoke too fast, the language almost sounded like a foreign one.

She didn't really have a detectable accent today. Had she lived off the island? Was she trying to speak without any discernible accent?

Grabbing his phone, he punched his sister's number. She answered on the first ring.

"Hey. You left at eight o'clock. You should've been there by three. It's almost six. What gives?"

"Hello to you too. I rode around the island a bit. Trying to get the lay of the land. I'm in my room now." He slipped off his shoes and let them drop to the hardwood floor. "You'll never guess who I saw this afternoon." He stuffed three french fries into his mouth.

"Who?"

"Ginny from Hatteras Island." He arched his foot, enjoying the pull in his calf.

A quick silence filled the line, then a gasp. "Vacation Ginny? What a fierce and funny girl. Just the best. I was so jealous of what she knew how to do. All you boys thought she was fabulous too."

"Yeah, she had skills all right."

"I thought she liked us too. I never understood why she

didn't come to our cottage to tell us bye before we left. I had a friendship bracelet for her. Maybe she was too sad to see us go."

He took another swallow. "Maybe she was glad to be rid of us." She didn't seem too happy to see him today. Not really into revisiting memory lane. Very skittish. Cool, in fact.

"Maybe. How'd you find her?"

"I wanted to find the cottage we stayed in." He balled up his napkin and banked it off the back wall into the waste basket. "Remember the bait and tackle shop with the ice cream treats? There she was."

"I'm so happy you found her. Tell her hello if she remembers me. Anyway, when you coming home? You got about two, two and a half months, then Christmas!"

"I just got here, Josie."

"Right. Just wanted you to know you're missed. Plus, your promotion that includes the fancy office is waiting."

"If this assignment goes well, and that's a big if. Sally Grimes is targeting the promotion too." He yawned. "Keep Heath and Sam in line."

"A tough job for a little sister, but you know I will. Come home soon. I need help planning the wedding."

"Ha. You're goofy."

"Just missing my big brother. Hey, a Christmas present from the beach would be really special this year."

"Come home soon with Christmas presents and a promotion. Got it. I'll see what I can do."

3

Was this a good idea?
Ben shifted his car into park in front of Ginny's tackle shop and killed the engine. How much would this new venture set him back? Quick online searches had revealed hefty prices for fancy equipment, but he'd spend his dollars locally, especially if spending them at this local establishment fostered more conversations with Ginny. If the purchase included more chats with the crusty gatekeeper and her beautiful colleague then money well spent, for sure.

Thoughts of Ginny occupied his mind off and on all week. Her mention of Charlotte belied her faulty memory and dismayed her too. Why else would she scramble back to her office the moment the word fell out of her mouth? What did the Charlotte slip up mean? Puzzling. Intriguing even. Maybe learning to fish would lead to a distraction for the island stay and a mystery solved.

Time to feed the local economy.

He cracked open the door, and a bell jingled. The smell of coffee greeted him. Hazel, dressed in an untucked plaid shirt, looked up from, according to his online search, an expensive reel.

"Well, you're back. How was your week on the island? Got any money to lend out? I could use about a pound of twenties." She laughed at her own faded joke.

"I'll let you know if I have any extra. How's that?"

"Don't tease me, son!" She laid down the reel and leaned her hands on the counter. "What can I do for you today?"

"I thought I'd see how the fish were running this morning." He nodded to the reel. "I need a few supplies."

"Is that right?" She hooked her thumbs into the loops of her jeans. "You're a fisherman, are you?"

His eyes wandered to the closed office door. Are you in there, Ginny? "Ah, to tell the truth—"

"I expect you to."

"I guess I'm a learning fisherman." He grinned.

She nodded. "Gotcha. No shame in that. Everybody starts somewhere. You fished at all?"

"Of course."

"With anything other than a cane pole and a cork?"

"Ah." He glanced again at the door.

"Shush." She cut off his answer before he began. "We'll fix you up, buddy. Pier or boat? And what kind of fish you plannin' to catch?"

Raised eyebrows transformed a blank look. "Definitely pier. And big ones?"

Hazel hooted again. "Right. I like a man with confidence. And by the way. Ginny's not here yet."

"Ahh."

"No need to say a thing. Anyway, she's turning in now." Hazel's gaze skirted over his shoulder.

He followed her glance. A bright yellow Jeep crunched on the gravel and rolled past the building.

"She'll be right in." Hazel grinned.

An uptick in his heart rate surprised him. Yes, she's beautiful, but he was here on business, supporting her business, minding his own business. Then why did his heart beat like he'd been caught stealing a candy bar from a checkout line? Yeah, she had impressive skills at ten years old that wowed teen-aged boys, but they were both adults now. He had plenty of successes and skills too. They just didn't include fishing.

Not to mention, his promotion waited for him in Charlotte.

The back door creaked open, and a cinnamon aroma wafted in with Ginny. "Morning, Hazel. Apple Ugly in the house. I got the last one." She froze, a paper bag raised and swinging in her left hand. "Ben."

❧❧❧ ⚜ ❦❦❦

HER BREATH CAUGHT MID-SENTENCE. Ben. What was he doing here? On a Saturday morning? She placed the bag of gooey, apple-laden pastry near the pot of coffee on the back counter. Hazel prided herself with brewing delicious coffee, and Ginny learned quickly not to bring outside coffee with the morning breakfast treat. She breathed in a long breath of the strong aroma.

Thoughts of him interrupted her concentration all week, but she denied herself trips to the bank. Hazel's knowing eyes detected the ruse forcing her to make the cash deposits, but for once, kept her commentary to herself.

She sought Ben's gaze and nodded at him. "Good morning."

"Hey," he nodded back.

"This young man is here for fishing gear." Hazel moved to the wall displaying rods. "Wants to try his hand at an island pastime." She removed one to inspect it, but her attention bounced between them.

"Oh, right." She relaxed and leaned against the counter. "We can outfit you with whatever you need. What kind of fish do you want to catch?"

"Big ones!" Hazel chuckled and wiggled her eyebrows.

"Start at the top. Aim for the stars. Conceive, believe, achieve, right?" Ben laughed along with Hazel, encouraging a laugh from Ginny too.

"You're a positive person, young man. I like that." Hazel's eyes flashed as she handed a rod to Ben. "I just had a fantastic idea."

Ginny's heart fluttered. Hazel's ideas seldom worked in her favor.

❧❧❧❧ ❀ ❧❧❧❧

A FEW HOURS LATER, Ben let fly another cast off the Avon Pier, fatigue tugging at his forearms.

"Nice one. Did you see the arc? You're getting really good." Ginny's praise boosted his flagging enthusiasm.

He reeled in the line as his stomach growled. Hoping the wind swallowed up the sound, he angled away from her.

"I guess the Apple Ugly's gone, huh?" She grinned.

"Well, we've been out here most of the morning. That Death by Sugar blob you shared is history." He reeled in the lure, the tug in his biceps reminding him to upgrade his upper body workouts.

She cast her line into the rolling water several feet farther than his had reached. "Hazel must have a crush on you. She never relinquishes her portion of our Apply Ugly. In fact, she sometimes cuts the halves more toward the third, two-thirds portions. She loves those things."

"Another fan right here. Tell me again what time I have to get to the Apple Blossom Cafe to buy some."

"Orange Blossom. During shoulder or off season, at least by mid-morning. Depends on how many visitors are on the island really. During the summer, good luck getting one. Once the day's offering is gone, you're out of luck."

"Like the fish, apparently." He flicked his wrist mimicking Ginny's cast and plopped the sinker a decent distance from the pier.

"Nice. That's your longest cast right there." She turned back to him. "Fishing is all about patience. Some days the fish are biting. Some days, not so much. Today's a not-so-much day. Next time, you can start earlier. You won't have to buy all this sweet new equipment." She laughed. "You had some good casts, though, and you caught a fish. Don't forget your fish."

"Right. The tiny fish clearly didn't know better than to bump up against my hook."

"When Hazel asks, say you caught a fish. She doesn't have to have details. Less is more."

"Got it." He nodded. "To hear her tell it, you're an A-number-one fisherman, ah, fisherwoman?" He chuckled. "But you didn't really fish today, just casted and reeled in to show me the ropes. Didn't want to make me look bad, huh?"

Sand-colored tendrils of hair danced around her up-tilted face.

"You held your own very well, and you didn't hook yourself. Good job." She smoothed a wind-battered wisp behind her ear. "Take everything Hazel says with a grain of salt. Maybe a bag of salt sometimes."

His stomach growled again, disrupting his attention on her tresses.

Ginny captured his glance with sparkling eyes, and air caught in his lungs. She pressed her lips together.

"Go ahead. Laugh. I can take it."

"Why don't we call it a day, so you can quiet your rumbling stomach?" She leaned her pole against the railing.

After the requisite new employee lunch with his coworkers at the branch, he'd eaten every meal solo all week. Conversation with an interesting and lovely companion, however, enticed him more than a double cheeseburger with a side of fries.

"Sounds great. Where should we go?" He grabbed his rod and reel in one hand and his tacklebox with the other.

She slid the strap of the empty, brand new soft cooler onto her shoulder.

"My treat. For teaching me how to fish." Come on. Say, yes. Let's keep this day going a little longer.

"Well, I have—"

"To eat. Save me from another boring meal with this guy." He thumbed his chest. "Take me to a place only the locals know. Please?"

A tiny smile bloomed on her mouth. "Okay."

4

B en slid in the door of the Kennekeet Community Church as members of the praise team took their places in front of microphones and instruments. Turning his phone back on this morning had revealed multiple family texts he'd respond to this afternoon and one interesting text from Ginny listing the worship service time. Not exactly an invitation but helpful information, perhaps, in developing this fledgling friendship.

Too bad he missed the early meet and greet time, but rolling out of bed twenty minutes till the service begins diminished the window of arriving early into a doggy door.

He scanned the sanctuary for a familiar head of dark blond hair. A movement near the arrangement of sunflowers caught his attention. Hazel. Hazel sitting behind the drum set. Behind the drum set? Holding a drumstick, she rubbed underneath her nose with an exaggerated movement.

Catching his eye, she turned her head toward her left. He looked toward his right and found her. Ginny sitting halfway up at the end of the pew. Instead of a braid today, she'd twisted her hair into a low knot on the side of her neck. Nice. He glanced back at Hazel and nodded his thanks. She smiled.

As he tiptoed up the side aisle, the worship leader signaled for the congregation to stand, and the beginning measures of a popular song floated through the sanctuary. Ben stopped at Ginny's pew and tapped her shoulder. The fleeting look of happy surprise on her face pinged through his chest.

"Sorry I'm late. Just saw your text a few minutes ago. Thanks for the invitation." He whispered.

"Glad you're here." Ginny shifted her gaze to the front, joining along with the singing.

After the last song, Hazel zigged and zagged, winding up right behind them in the aisle. "Welcome. Glad you made it."

"Me too." Ben stepped closer to Ginny to make room for Hazel and caught a whiff of some floral scent. Very glad.

"How was fishing?"

"Great. She's a good teacher."

"He's a fast learner."

"Wonderful." Delight animated Hazel's face. "You know, our first Christmas fishing tournament is in December. A great place to show your skills. And don't forget the gala planned to celebrate the winners."

"He might not be here then."

Ben started at Ginny's high-speed comment. True. A permanent replacement could happen any time, and he'd be back home, but still ... He pushed the thought from his mind.

"Pshaw." Hazel's eyes lit up. "Hey, where're you two headed for lunch? Need a suggestion?"

"We ate lunch yesterday." Ginny lobbed a pointed glance to Hazel.

"You don't eat lunch every day?" She served one right back.

"Funny as ever, Hazel. I meant—"

Ben chimed in. "She means I hadn't asked her yet."

"Gotcha. So, where're you going?"

"She hasn't said yes either."

A faint pink tiptoed up Ginny's neck.

"Of course, she'll say yes, Virginia Rae. Why wouldn't she?" Exasperation punctuated Hazel's words.

"How about both of you joining me for lunch? My treat." Ben shifted his stance. "We went to Pete's yesterday, so—"

"You took him to Pete's?" Hazel's eyebrows doubled the space over her eyes. "Of all the places on the island." She shook her head.

"He wanted to go where the locals go." Ginny hugged her Bible in front of her.

"We had a great lunch."

"Yeah. Fish on wax paper. Standing at the bar."

"You can't beat delicious food, Hazel. It was delicious." Ben stepped an inch closer to Ginny.

"Wax paper and no ambiance. White walls all around except the Jesus wall. "

Ben chuckled. She had the decor down. The Jesus wall had a portrait of Jesus, Jesus Knocking on the Door, Jesus in Gethsemane, and several crosses for good measure.

"We ate at a picnic table. We could see the lighthouse, smell the ocean, hear the sea gulls. Plenty of ambiance."

"And the wax paper kept the fish tacos intact." He rubbed his hands together. "So, where're we going, ladies? I'm starving."

"Sorry. No can do. I got sweet potato biscuits and a bowl of fish chowder waiting for me." Hazel moved backward. "Thank you anyway. Take him to Calmside. They gotta view and fish on plates too."

"You up for it? Sounds good to me." Ben pushed his point, hoping to quell Ginny's hesitation.

"Sure. You can follow me. I'll wait at the first entrance."

She pointed at the driveway on the south side of the parking lot.

"No. Better leave one car here and drive together. Then you just need one parking place." Hazel focused her attention on Ben.

"She has a point."

Ginny sighed. "I know the way. I'll drive."

WHY DID Hazel play matchmaker to every male who crossed the shop's threshold? Poor Ben. He didn't know what he'd gotten into when he walked into the store last week. Ginny rotated the glass vase of yellow carnations and black-eyed Susans, considering ways to irritate Hazel. Not sharing an Apple Ugly this week. Having her start inventory early. Hmm. Not a bad idea.

Ben cleared his throat and made eye contact. "Hey, thanks for having lunch with me again. I'll thank Hazel too, for kinda elbowing you into it. I'm missing my weekly meal with my siblings, so ..."

Score a point for Hazel's insight. He'd been lonely all week and missed his sister and brothers. No wonder he'd visited the store twice in a row. A touch point from a long-ago memory, the store led him to two new friends on the island. His sudden appearance after two decades didn't mean anything and shouldn't stoke a schoolgirl crush.

Irritating Hazel might not be wise. She'd share the pastry, but the inventory idea ... "Happy to help." Enjoying some meals with him could work as long as she kept his temporary status in mind.

He leaned his forearms on the table. "So, Hazel's a

drummer, eh? She sounded good up there with the praise band."

"She earned a music degree from Meredith College. If you're lucky, maybe you'll hear her sing sometime. She's got a beautiful voice. Music talent runs in that side of our family."

"You're related?"

"My dad's cousin. She moved back after retiring from teaching music for decades in Chocowinity and helps out with the store now."

A waiter appeared and took their orders, leaving a basket of steaming hushpuppies.

Ben raised his eyebrows. "A Poke bowl? Is sushi an authentic Hatteras dish?" Grabbing a golden-brown nugget of fried cornmeal, he bit it in half.

She shook her head. "You can find it around the island now, but I discovered it in Raleigh when I lived there." She chose a small hushpuppy.

"College?"

"Grad school."

"Impressive. Business degree?"

"Linguistics." Her satisfaction enjoyed the surprise lighting his eyes.

"Didn't see that coming. What led you there?"

Her mind jumped back to the first day she'd seen them, three boys and a girl, eating ice cream in front of her dad's tackle shop. They jostled each other, teasing back and forth, oblivious to the little girl watching at the edge of the parking lot. Fascinated, she crept closer to eavesdrop. Hearing their desire to go crabbing, she jumped on a crazy plan before her courage disappeared like a sand bar at high tide.

"Wanna do us some crabbin'? Moy haise is right dain the road to the saind soid."

The four looked at her like she'd just spoken gibberish.

Every *Ow* sound, the long *I* sounds had set her apart from the spellbinding, big city siblings.

"What did she say?" The youngest boy, the one they called Sam, asked.

But the sister, Josie, approached her, smiling. "You want to take us crabbing?"

And so began her week with the Daniels family. She'd spent time every day with them, showing off her part of the island. It was also her first lesson in speech differences and how her Hoi Toide language told stories way beyond her ten years.

"Hey, Ginny. Where'd you go?" Ben popped a second hush puppy into his mouth.

She blinked. "Sorry. A memory highjacked me for a minute. I wanted to study the Hoi Toide speech of the Outer Banks."

"Right. You don't sound like you have much of an accent now."

Shrugging, she explained, "I lived off the island for a while."

"But the accent sounds so cool. Why would you want to change?"

The waiter set dishes in front of them, saving her from answering.

"Speaking of your dad ..." He unrolled his utensils.

"He passed away last fall. Would you like to try some of the sushi?"

"I like my seafood with an internal temperature of cooked, but thanks for offering. This clam chowder looks good." He studied his bowl.

"New England and Manhattan have their offerings, but this one, Hatteras clam chowder, is the best. No cream. No tomatoes. Just sweet clam broth in all its goodness." She dug into her Poke bowl, spearing a cube of salmon.

She still worked on her salad when Ben pushed his empty bowl to the side of the table, snagging one last hushpuppy. "I need some more practice fishing with a pro. You game?"

"I'm no pro—"

"You own a tackle shop. Don't sell yourself short. Help this landlubber get better."

"Dingbatter." She threw out the island word and waited for his reaction.

"What?"

"You're a dingbatter."

"Hey, now. I wasn't that bad. I caught a fish, remember?"

She chuckled and shook her head. "It means you're not from here. That's all." And here only for the interim, not forever. Remember that, Ginny. Still, pretending he lived here full-time—

"Hey, you know something else I'd love to try? Hang gliding." His eyes widened in excitement.

"You want to what?"

"Hang glide. It has to be crazy fun. Go with me. Give me pointers."

"I've never done it."

"You haven't? Then, for sure, we're going. I'm booking lessons. Maybe next weekend. The fish can wait."

5

B en swiveled on the bench and leaned his back against the picnic tabletop in the green space behind the bank. A breeze from the sound ruffled the remnants of his takeout lunch. He grabbed his phone and found Ginny's thread. They'd taken to texting every other day or so. Nothing earth shattering, but he'd come to look forward to her humorous take on current events and instances from his workday and hers.

Hey. Hang gliding is booked for this weekend and beyond. I'm on a wait list. How about another fishing lesson instead?

He tapped the family thread.

If I can get us lessons, who's up for hang gliding Thanksgiving weekend?

He researched Hidden Hatteras Gems while he waited for responses. He hadn't read past the third suggestion when the first sounds buzzed his phone.

In like Flynn

Sam, of course. Always ready for anything.

Absolutely

Heath responded in the affirmative.

Hello? Thanksgiving. Three people from church are coming.

Josie. Planning ahead.

I'll try for the Saturday. Sound good?

About Thanksgiving.

Josie. Still hopeful for his appearance for the holiday.

It's a no go, sis. I'm working Friday. You travel here Friday. Hang glide Saturday.

Another text buzzed through. Ginny. Nice.

Fishing works for Saturday. We need to start earlier.

When?

Sunup at the pier. I'll bring the bait.

Yes!

I'll bring the apple ugly and coffee.

Deal.

✺✺✺✺ ❀❀ ✺✺✺✺

"Good afternoon, Ms. ..." Ben glanced at the folder on his desk.

"Burris. Yancy Burris."

He rounded his desk and gestured for her to sit in the chair opposite his. "Ms. Burris, how can I help you today?" He observed her work boots, faded jeans cuffed at the bottom, and faded barn coat.

Sharp, brown eyes narrowed when they caught him assessing her appearance. He smiled, hoping to disguise any unprofessional looks leaking out of his face.

"I need your services for an important matter, but we'll get to that later." She wiggled out of her coat and settled back into the chair.

An important matter? A loan, for sure. But for what? What would she need to buy now? If her crow's feet told the tale, she might be close to eighty years old. Her laser-like eyes, however, chronicled everything in the room. Her body movements indicated a spryness not always shared by her contemporaries.

Not so fast, Ms. Burris. This is still my office, temporary or not. "Right, ma'am. First National Bank provides several kinds of services to our clients. Loans—"

"I know what banks do." Jutting her chin forward, she emphasized each word with a tap on the chair arms. "I want to know about you. You're not from around here, are you?" Her face revealed she already knew the answer. She delivered a challenge, not a question.

"No, ma'am." Take charge of this conversation. He leaned toward her. "Are you here to apply for a loan, Ms. Burris?"

She blinked away his attempt at leading the chat. "We'll get to my business. Don't worry. Where're you from?"

"Charlotte."

"A long way from here." She stroked her chin. "So, you're taking over for Thumb Nelson."

He trapped a chuckle just before it escaped. Who is this woman? "Terrence Nelson?" He planted his elbows on the arms of the wingback chair and clasped his hands.

"Indeed. Some people call him Thumb. Unfortunately, he has no neck. His head juts out of his shoulders like a thumb."

"Right, ma'am. Ahm."

Her mouth twitched. "I'm glad you've got his job."

"Temporarily. Till a permanent manager is hired."

"Neither here nor there." She flicked her hand to delete his words. "I'm just glad they got rid of Thumb. Finally."

"Terrance Nelson retired." Engaging in gossip is never a good look, Ben. Redirect the conversation. Put the kibosh on these rumors.

"So you say, but I know what the scuttlebutt is. His vices finally caught up with him, the Namby Pamby."

"Ms. Burris—"

"Call me Yancy if we're going to be working together." She narrowed her eyes. "My plain talk shocks your sensibilities, but I never cared for Thumb. Unfortunately, my money was already here when he got the job.

"Mr. Nelson—"

"Was a Namby Pamby."

"You've said. Now about your business—"

She cocked her head. "How do you find surfing?"

"I'm sorry. What?" This woman had clearly fallen off her rocker. Surely someone would be searching to return her to the rest home she must have escaped from this morning.

"Surfing. You know, waxed boards."

"Yes, ma'am. I've tried it a few times. Never got the hang of it. Not too many gnarly waves where I come from." He grinned over his clasped hands.

She captured his gaze with a severe, brown-eyed stare successful in melting his grin. "You think you know some of the language though, don't you, young man?" She raised an eyebrow. "I've never cared for silly new words myself. Silly old words like my favorite, pixilated? That's a different story."

Heat rolled inside his chest and crawled up his neck. He shifted in the leather chair, hoping to distract from his discomfort. This old woman had teacher eyes. "Are you talking computer graphics?" A relatively new word, for sure.

"No, sir. I am not talking about computer graphics. I believe you're confusing synonyms. Look it up." She folded her arms. "So, you're not a surfer. Disappointing, but not a deal breaker. Get that Stowe girl to take you some time."

Ben's mouth dropped open. He snapped it closed.

"Scuttlebutt. Plus, I've seen you together here and there with my own eyes. You couldn't do better than Virginia Rae. Her family goes back a ways here on the island. You'll find some Stowes buried up in the cemetery in Old Hatteras Village." She nodded. "Surfing. Try it before you go back inland." She stood, slipping on her coat before he could offer assistance.

He popped to his feet to keep up with her.

"Thank you for your time today." She halted, turning at the door and smiled, her first one of the meeting. "I'll be seeing you again, young man."

"Yes, ma'am." He sagged against his closed door.

Yancy Burris, a character, for sure. Glancing at his watch, he chuckled to himself. Another island character, Hazel, expected him bright and early in the morning for help with a Christmas project.

Taking down decorations from her attic? Putting up lights?

Whatever the job, it didn't matter. Ginny would be there too.

Hatteras, your women fascinate me. What other attractions do you have?

6

Following Hazel's instructions, Ben poured two cups each of Brazil nuts, English walnuts, and pecans into the stainless-steel bowl. "That's a lot of nuts."

"Now, take this chopper and start chopping, not to nut dust, but just break them up. Makes for easier slicing." Hazel checked on Ginny's pot with the condensed milk and bag of marshmallows. "Is the eye on low? Don't turn it up high. Melt them slow and easy so you don't burn the bottom."

"Yes ma'am. Will do." Ginny stirred and sent a quick smirk to Ben.

"I'm teaching you the right way to make these fruitcakes, Miss Priss. Cook it low and slow so you don't—"

"Burn it. Got it." Ginny dragged the oversized spoon through the milky, gooey mixture.

"With all these nuts, shouldn't we call them nut cakes instead of fruitcakes?" Ben raked the chopper through the bowl, redistributing the whole nuts with the chopped ones.

Hazel greased another mini loaf pan. "The fruit comes from the raisins, dried figs, and maraschino cherries."

"Are those cherries really fruit, though?"

"Quit giving me a hard time. Chop, Ben."

"I'm chopping. I'm chopping. Let's think about a name change. Fruitcakes have such a woeful reputation. Nut cakes, now, they sound—"

"Nut cakes sound better than fruitcakes? Really?" Hazel turned up the volume on her CD player. Bing Crosby silky voice filled the kitchen. "I love 'Christmas in Killarney.'"

"Maybe fruitcakes need new PR." Ginny arched her eyebrows, a teasing set to her mouth.

Ben caught Ginny's glance behind Hazel's back and held it. The blush creeping into her cheeks raised the hair on the back of his neck.

"Christmas music already?" He focused on Bing instead of Ginny.

"Sets the mood, and you people like to talk. We need to work. You know you didn't have to help."

Ginny dropped her gaze to the pot. "Right. You guilted me into helping. You held your health, or rather, the ruination of your health over my head. No whining from you next week."

"If I'd had to chop nuts for three batches and stir all this gooey stuff together by myself, my arm and back would've been out of commission for more than a week. You're getting a great end of the deal. Sparkling company on a Saturday morning and a fruitcake to boot. Plus, I don't have to call in sick."

"Sometimes I think I—"

"Hey, ladies. Are these nuts okay?"

Hazel peered into the silver bowl. "Looks good. Now add the raisins. Golden and regular. Both boxes."

"Gotcha." Ben opened the red box and shook the clump of dark raisins into the nuts.

"Add the golden ones and stir. Then you'll be ready for the graham cracker crumbs." Hazel inched toward Ginny.

"I'm still stirring."

"Don't let it burn." Hazel checked the control knob and lowered the flame a touch. "Low and slow."

"If you say that one more time—"

"Ladies, let's keep our eyes on the prize." Ben smiled to himself. These two bickered like siblings. A pang squeezed his heart for the three he left in Charlotte.

GINNY PRESSED HER LIPS TOGETHER. Hazel had a knack for grating all over her nerves. And in front of Ben too. He probably thought their squabbling childish. Note to self: *Focus on the pot and the sweetly scented steam rising from the concoction. Stir from the bottom so the milk wouldn't burn.* She'd never hear the end of it if the milk burned.

Hazel was trying her hardest to matchmake the two of them. Why did she like Ben so much? Granted, he was good-looking, smart, kind, interested in island history, folklore, and events. She smiled to herself. He sounded like the full package. Except for one enormous hurdle. His life existed seven hours away near his tight-knit family who clamored for him to come home.

Excursions to fish, to eat together, and to make fruitcakes were fine and good, but she'd keep her head on straight ... and forget about the look they just shared.

"Hey. Ginny. Look out." Hazel bumped her away from the stove with a hip and grabbed the spoon. "Were you asleep, girl?"

"I was stirring."

"You were daydreaming. Oh, the fruitcake woman never had as much trouble as this."

"The fruitcake woman? A neighbor?" Ben dutifully stirred

his bowl, pulling the nuts, raisins, and figs up from the bottom to the top of the pile and going back down for more.

"No. She's in a Truman Capote story." Hazel shook the box of graham cracker crumbs into the bowl of nuts and dried fruit.

"Yeah. I remember it. What's it called?"

"'A Christmas Memory.'" Ginny circled her spoon all the way around the pan and then down through the middle casting her mind to the sweet story of a little boy and his aunt.

"That's it. A professor read it in class one day during a freak snowstorm. Just a handful of us attended class. She got choked up reading it, and Christmas was past. Already January."

"People here celebrate Christmas in January too. Old Christmas. Ever heard of it? Nothing wrong with Christmas in January."

Ginny held her breath and began counting. One Mississippi. Two Mississippi. Three—

"In fact," Hazel paused, checking the stove knob again.

Here it comes.

"If you're still here in January, you can celebrate Old Christmas. Right, Ginny? Ride up to Rodanthe for the party. Maybe Big Buck will show up."

Stop coming up with outings, Hazel.

"January is a long way away. I'm sure the bank will have a new manager by then." Remember, Ginny. He's leaving.

"Trying to get rid of me?" Ben grinned. "We've had some résumés come in, but I'm not involved in the process. Big Buck, huh?"

"Two men dressed up like a shipwrecked cow that wound up here years ago." Ginny pointed to her pot. "This looks ready, Hazel. All the marshmallows are melted."

Hazel nodded. She dumped chopped cherries into the bowl

of nuts. "Now pour the bottle of cherry juice into your pot, Ginny, and keep stirring."

The juice tinted the milky mixture with a faint pink.

"Okay. Be careful now and pour your pot over Ben's bowl. Easy. Don't splash it. You'll burn your hands but good." Hazel kept careful attention on the process. "Yes, now stir it all together. Ben, you got strong arms. Put 'em to good use."

Ben chuckled. Ginny turned to the sink to rinse out her pan and keep her eyes off Ben's strong arms.

"Once all that's mixed up, we fill these little tin loaf pans and start all over again."

THREE HOURS LATER, Ben's strong arms ached as he navigated Highway 12 for the beach access. A run on the beach would get the kinks out.

Those cakes better be delicious. They were a bear to make. All that chopping and stirring, but Ginny was a trooper. She followed every one of Hazel's directions with just a couple of quirked eyebrows.

Turning off the highway, he coasted to a stop in the sandy lot. He jogged over the path leading to the beach and kicked off his New Balances. Digging his toes into the wet sand, he dipped his fingertips into the surf, a new take on his warm-up stretches. He checked his watch and aimed for the lighthouse.

Forty minutes later, he splashed through the surf to cool down and headed for his car.

He grabbed a towel from the back seat, wiped his face and hands, and picked up his phone. Ten messages from his siblings and one from Ginny. He read hers first.

Thanks for helping with the fruit cakes. You made Hazel's day.

She sent it an hour earlier. He checked his watch again. Almost four o'clock.

Make mine. Have dinner with me.

He sent the text and checked the ones from his family. Lots of chatter about Thanksgiving. No holiday at home for him. As the newest person in the office, and a temporary hire at that, he'd missed the time to request off the Friday after Thanksgiving. Only one person, Felicia Combs, would be off that day to enjoy her home-from-college children. His phone signaled a new message.

Sounds good. Did you fish this afternoon?

No. You're my fishing buddy. Ran instead. Let's go out.

~~~~~ ❄ ~~~~~

GINNY READ THE TEXT. Her heart fluttered. Fishing buddy. Calm down, heart. Fishing buddy equals buddy. Which is fine. Nothing's wrong with being a buddy. Helping Ben out. Having dinner with him to keep him from eating alone. She texted back before she could rain all over the fun prospect of being with Ben a second time in one day.

Sure. Where? What time?

Calmside? We can watch the sunset, right? 6:00? Text me your address.

Her heart flipped again. He'd pick her up? Was this a date or a don't-let-me-be-lonely dinner? What would she wear?

Sounds good.

She also texted her address and camped out in front of her closet going back and forth between casually chic and island dressy.

An hour later she slipped into the casually chic outfit she hadn't worn since Raleigh. It had languished in the back of her closet waiting for the perfect outing.

Please, Lord. Let this be a perfect night.

7

B en held the chair for Ginny. "Will your jacket be enough out here? I've got a sweatshirt in the car. Or we can get a table inside."

"I'm good. November evenings haven't turned too cold here yet. We want to see the sunset, right?" She nodded out over the calm water.

"Yeah. The view's great. So's the food."

"Some say the best on the island."

"You don't? The chowder was excellent."

"The food's delicious, but you'll find the best cooks at the church's potlucks."

"Gotcha. When's the next potluck?" He smiled at her.

And she wished for one on the calendar. "I'll let you know."

Their conversation, easy and fun and interesting, moved from one topic to another without falling into rough places or rocky patches, chasing one rabbit trail after another until dessert time. Ben scanned the menu. "Are you up for something sweet?"

"Always."

"Ah, a sweet tooth, eh?"

"Order the fig cake. It's an island thing."

"Figs? Again? Hazel promised us our own fruitcake, and you want to order one?"

"It isn't a fruitcake. It's a fig cake, and it's delicious. You have to try it before you leave." Yes, keep thinking about when he leaves. As fun as it is to chat over dinner, he will leave and go home. All the way to Charlotte.

"Is that okay?" Ben and the waitress waited for her to answer.

At her blank look, the waitress rescued her. "The slice is pretty big. You probably want to share."

She nodded. Sharing dessert. Hoo, boy.

* * *

"I ADMIT. This fig cake is pretty good." Ben stuffed another forkful into his mouth.

"Pretty good? Tell you what. You need to try one of Yancy Buriss's. She's the best."

"I've met her. She wants me to learn to surf."

"Oh, yeah?" Ginny laughed. "Is she going to teach you?"

"She said *you* should take me."

"She's the expert."

He sipped his coffee. "She surfed?"

"As far as I know, still does. I saw her on the waves twice last summer. She swims in the ocean almost every day. If the current's too strong, she'll swim in the sound. If you mention swimming pools in front of her, she'll call you a Namby Pamby."

"Right. She used that term in my office."

Ginny chuckled. "Probably about Terrence Nelson."

Ben glanced at her.

"Yep. I'm right. No love lost there. Not since he bowed out of a charity surfing tournament."

"Didn't donate money to the cause?" This isn't gossip, right? It's getting to know my clients, right?

"He didn't surf. She wanted to beat him."

Ben chuckled. "Sounds about right from the little I know about her. She thinks a lot of you." He drained his coffee cup, jolted by an impulse to smooth a wisp of hair behind her ear.

Shoving that reaction out of his mind, he broached a safer topic. "Hey, where's a good place for local gifts? I thought I'd treat my family to beach Christmas presents this year."

$$\cdot\!\!\rightsquigarrow\!\!\cdot\;\overset{\wedge}{\mathbb{M}}\;\cdot\!\!\leftsquigarrow\!\!\cdot$$

DARKNESS COCOONED them on the drive down Highway 12. Ben adjusted the radio to a local station playing piano music. He glanced at Ginny. "Are you warm enough?"

She nodded. "I enjoyed hearing about your siblings. And Josie's getting married next summer?"

"Yeah. To a great guy. We weren't exactly sure at first, but he's a keeper. He holds his own with all our smack talk."

"Sounds like a fun time when you're together."

"For sure. I'll miss them at Thanksgiving." Having planted the seed, Ben focused on maneuvering her driveway, waiting.

"You'll be here for Thanksgiving?"

"Uh-huh. I work Wednesday and Friday. One day off isn't really enough time to go home." He switched off the ignition and set the parking brake. Was that enough information to get her mind going? Would he have to straight up ask for an invitation? "I'll walk you up."

He met her at the front of his crossover, chanced a quick

glance in her direction. Her eyes scoured the ground. Was she considering asking him?

"Ahm. Hazel's having people over, including me. For Thanksgiving, I mean."

Bingo.

"I'm sure she'd love to have you too. I'll mention it to her."

"Well, I don't want to intrude." But he really did. A turkey sandwich in his room at the bed and breakfast verses a real meal? With Ginny? No contest.

"If she found out you spent Thanksgiving alone, I'd never get back on her good side." She continued toward her front porch. "You'll have the invite ASAP."

"I look forward—"

"Hey, Ginny." A disembodied voice carried from somewhere on the porch.

She gasped and made a hard stop. Ben knocked into her back.

"Tad?" Ginny's voice held surprise and some other emotion.

"The one and only." A smile colored the statement. A friendly smile or a menacing one?

She turned to Ben. "I'm sorry. Thank you for dinner. Ahm." She glanced to the porch.

A movement and the rocking chair, freed from a weight, rocked back and forth. "Don't let me break up your evening. I was just enjoying the night air."

"I'll tell Hazel, and ... and see you, okay?" She held up a flattened hand as if to ward him off.

Why didn't she want him to meet this person?

"Is everything good?" He lowered his voice to a whisper. "Are you okay? Do you want me—"

"Yes, I'm fine. Thank you for dinner." She nodded and headed for the porch steps. "Tad, why are you here?"

Ben hesitated. Ginny sounded more like herself after the momentary shock of finding someone rocking on her front porch. He watched as she unlocked the front door and let the man inside.

God, what to do here?

⋙ ❦ ⋘

WRUNG OUT FROM THE NIGHT, Ginny leaned against her bedroom door. The evening had begun so nicely with Ben picking her up, chatting over the delicious meal, watching the sunset, and sharing the fig cake. Perfect really until ...

Tad.

Why did he have to show up now?

Tad.

Her phone buzzed. She looked at the notifications. A text from Tad and two from Ben.

The first from Ben, a half hour ago.

Just checking in. Everything good?

The new text read,

Calmside was great. So was the company. Even the fig cake.

She tapped the message bar.

Thanks for checking in. I'm fine. Told you the fig cake was good.

Then opened Tad's.

Didn't mean to surprise you. Don't be mad.

A new text came through. From Ben.

Sorry. My older brother status is shining through.

You're a good brother. Good night.

Sighing, she headed toward her bathroom to pluck out her contacts. Tad had told her the beginning, but there'd be more. She swapped her tunic and tights for a hoodie and sweatpants. Might as well be comfy. Knowing Tad, the story would take a while to tell. A long night stretched in front of her.

She opened her door to the smell of coffee. A long night indeed.

8

B en grabbed the back of the pew in front of him to keep his fingers from drumming during the benediction. Why hadn't Ginny shown at church? He hadn't texted since the good night text last night, but his fingers itched to send How are you? or at least Good morning. Would he be overstepping, hovering like Josie always accused him of doing?

Dial back the concerned older brother routine. You already played that card last night.

He waited for Hazel near the cornucopia in the vestibule. "Good music this morning."

"Thanks. I try. Where's our girl?"

"I was hoping you'd know."

"Haven't heard from her since the fruitcakes yesterday."

"When I dropped her off last night, someone was on her front porch."

Hazel's eyes lighted. "Dropped off as in after a date? Where'd you go?"

"Not important right now, but we ate at Calmside. Do you know Tad?"

"Tad's back?" Hazel's eyes narrowed, extinguishing the light of a second ago.

"Who's Tad?"

Hazel made a face. "Oh, boy. And I'm on the church steps."

"You don't have to say anything you'll regret. Is it the guy who broke her heart in Raleigh?"

She sighed and shook her head. "He's her ... wayward brother."

Brother, huh? His shoulders released a bit of tension. "Wayward?"

She pulled him away from the diminishing crowd. "Tad's had a rough go of it for the past few years. Since he was a teenager really. Most of his own making."

"Gotcha."

"Didn't know he was back in town."

"He surprised Ginny too."

"Last night. Dang it. I want to hear all about your supper, but I need to get over to Ginny's. Check things out."

He tensed again. "Is she in danger?"

"Oh, no. Tad loves his little sister. It's himself he has a problem with. I'll drop by, ask her why she didn't come to church. You know. Be my nosy self." She gazed over the glistening sound and shook her head again. "Did you have the fig cake? Tell me that at least."

"Yep, and it was delicious."

❧❧❧ ❁ ❦❦❦

GINNY TIPPED her coffee cup to her mouth. Empty. The time on her phone screen nudged her to lunch, but she made no move to leave her chair on the back porch. She woke up an hour ago, too late for church. She switched on a favorite praise channel, hoping the music would lift her out of the funk stoked by her brother's appearance last night.

Tad. Why did you choose last night to come home? She released an extended sigh.

Thank You, God, for getting Ben away before Tad could ... be Tad in front of him.

How to explain Tad to Ben? Maybe she wouldn't have to. The checking in texts were comforting, but they'd made no mention of a next time. Would they have a next time?

"You hoo. You back here?" Hazel rounded the corner.

Ginny leaned her head on the back of her chair. "He's still asleep."

"Sleeping it off, huh?"

"No. Not this time."

"How much does he need?" Hazel dropped into the rocking chair beside her.

"He's got a job."

Hazel raised her eyebrows and rocked in silence.

"At a tackle shop up near Nags Head. For six months. In fact, he just got promoted to manager in September." She quashed the feather-light hope that wanted to settle in her heart. It was too early to contemplate her return to Raleigh.

"The college kids went back to school, eh?"

"Hazel."

"That boy." She tut-tutted and searched the horizon. "So much potential."

"Says he's been sober since Dad's funeral. He had a job in Hillsborough but wanted to get to the coast. He has a couple of days off."

"So, he just shows up out of the blue. Blindsides you instead of calling, not even texting you a heads-up first."

"Wasn't sure I'd talk to him. He came to apologize." Ginny swiped her thumb over the shell imprint in her mug.

"You've never not talked to him."

"The last time we talked I yelled at him. I ... it was bad."
She shuddered at the words in her mind she couldn't erase.

"You're expecting me to fail."

"I don't expect the people around me to fail. You just keep doing it. I expect the people around me to succeed. You've never stuck with anything long enough to succeed."

She'd show him more grace this time. *Please help me show him more grace this time.*

"Don't beat yourself up. He made his own bed. And now I guess he needs a ride back up the coast, or has he already lost his job?"

"Hazel, listen to me. We stayed up till 4:30. We yelled. We cried. We laughed some too. I've never seen him like this. He seems for real."

"Well, I hope to heaven it is, but he's gone sober before and fallen off the wagon more times than a shark's got teeth."

"He didn't ask for anything. I didn't promise anything. I just listened." But if he did stay sober ... Raleigh is a lot closer to Charlotte—stop. She pressed the back of her head into the wooden slats of the rocking chair. Don't count your pearls before you open the oysters.

"I hope you're right. For his sake and ours."

They rocked in silence and listened to the seagulls. Ginny counted three wind surfers on the sound.

"So, I heard you turned someone else on to fig cake."

"Hazel." She shook her head. "Leave it alone. He didn't want to eat another meal by himself."

"You could have ordered pizza at Gidgette's. You went to Calmside.

"He wanted to eat and watch the sunset."

"He's a romantic."

"He's leaving when the bank hires a new manager."

"Quit raining on my parade." Hazel rocked harder. "Let an old girl have some fun."

"You could have a lot of fun if you'd pay Red Basnight any attention."

Hazel fluttered her hand. "Pshaw. You don't know what you're talking about."

"Neither do you." Ginny grabbed her coffee mug. "Did you ask Red to Thanksgiving? Ben needs an invitation too."

"Wonderful. I'll see to it."

9

"Correct me if I'm wrong, but I think we just hiked through the Sahara Desert." Ben's baby brother, Sam, had a point.

The Jockey's Ridge State Park sand dunes, famous as the largest natural living sand dune system, dwarfed those nearer the seashore. Ginny had forgotten their stark, desert-like beauty in the fifteen years since she'd last been here for a youth group picnic.

Other groups had begun ascending the largest dune, heading toward the hang-gliding kites perched on top. She tamped down rising panic as she envisioned herself hanging from one of those kites and barreling toward the earth, screaming for help.

"And that looks like a mighty high hill we gotta climb." Sam's yellow helmet swung from his arm as he trudged over the sandy path. "You know, Ben, this jaunt sounded like fun before we had to get up at half past the crack of dawn just to get here."

"Sand dune, bro. If you're going to complain all day, go take a nap in the car. I'll take your flights." Ben bopped Sam on the head with his water bottle.

"Cut it out. I'm here and staying. Gotta show you how it's done."

The whole group laughed at Sam's bravado. Ginny hoped she'd be laughing at the end of this outing. Why didn't she bow out, opt for a morning on the water instead? She wanted to experience Ben's siblings again, that's why. Exactly the same, except twenty years older, they jostled each other, teasing back and forth in a choreography practiced for decades.

Right. A fun day except for the part about jumping off the side of a cliff strapped to a kite. Okay. Not a cliff. A really tall sand dune. With solid ground to hit after a fall.

"I'm still so full of turkey, I don't know how the kite will lift me off the ground." Ches tugged on his vest.

"Yeah, I noticed how shy you were digging into the turkey sandwiches yesterday. Not. Did you eat three or five?" Heath, the middle brother, chimed in.

"What can I say? Your sister's a great cook." He cupped Josie's elbow as they started the climb to the top.

"Thank you." Josie smiled and blew him a kiss.

Ginny mentally reviewed the steps from the mandatory lesson after all the consent forms were signed. So many steps to follow. How could she remember them all, not look stupid, and have fun all at the same time?

"Are you okay?" Ben's concern chipped away at her apprehension.

Pretending could lead to reality. Maybe. "Sure. It's all good." She wiped a trembling hand over a sweat-dotted upper lip.

"I can hear you breathing, and you're not out of shape." He grabbed her fingers. "Your hand is freezing."

"Kinda chilly today, don't you think?"

"Ginny, it's at least sixty-five degrees. Windy, yes, but the sun's warm." He dropped his voice lower. "You're okay with this, aren't you? It'll be fun."

"Heights aren't really my thing." She kept her eyes on the ground, ignoring her peripheral vision where waves broke on the ocean side of the island.

They crested the dune and took their places near Josie and Ches.

"We're not going up too high. We're just flying off the dune and landing in the sand down there." He pointed to the path they'd just traversed.

"Did you hear what you just said? 'Flying off the dune.'"

"Sailing then. Is that better?"

"If we were talking water, yes."

He chuckled. "It'll be fun. I promise."

"Don't promise—"

"Huddle up, folks." Brody, one of the instructors, directed everyone to group together according to the name on the yellow slip of paper he'd given them back at the rental shop. Groups formed based on weight.

Josie and Ginny were grouped with a dad and two teen-aged daughters. Ches and the brothers comprised another group. Three more groups made up the whole class.

"Remember each of you gets five flights. Everyone flies once, and we then start over. Okay, where's Brody's group?" The instructor called Eli moved over to a group of twenty-somethings sporting college sweatshirts and Vans.

He stepped toward Ginny's group. "All right. Who wants to fly first?"

Ginny's stomach clenched, and she stepped back.

"Me." One of the sisters hopped forward.

"Cool. Remember you're going to rest your hands on the crossbar like this." He held out his arms, curving his hands over a pretend bar. "Then bend your chest over a little bit. Remember the pterodactyl pose, right?"

He held up the kite as the youngest sister disappeared under it. The group to the left of them already had a person in the air, sailing down to the valley below. A peaceful sight, floating in the air, the kite landing gracefully like an autumn leaf.

Ginny glanced over at Ben's group. Ches, clipped to his kite, walked, then jogged, then ran, and then he floated in the air to the encouraging shouts from his future brothers-in-law. Holding a leader rope, his instructor ran beside him down the dune. Ches soared all the way into the sea oats on the other side of the path.

"Woo-hoo. He's a natural." Sam cheered the loudest.

"He's my guy." Josie chuckled and gave him a thumb's up.

Everyone was laughing and clapping and having an all-around great time. Ginny secured the last spot for a turn. While both waited their turn, Ben stepped over beside her.

"How's it going over here?" He smiled, his face full of hope.

"You must be excited. I can't believe you got openings this weekend."

"I kept calling for cancellations. The guy took pity on me and pulled in another instructor. Pays to be persistent." He trapped her gaze. "And I am." He pulled on the straps of his vest. "Hey, sorry they still didn't have room for Tad."

"No worries. He had to go back up to Nags Head."

"I enjoyed talking with him on Thanksgiving."

She nodded. "It was a good day." She smiled. "Thanks again for the flowers. Hazel got a kick out of them. I liked mine too."

"Glad to hear it." He motioned to the other groups. "So, you've had a chance to study all these beginners. Got a game plan?"

"Giving my turn to that eight-year-old in the next group who could be the star of his own hang-gliding show sounds like a plan. Josie's pretty much a pro already too."

"Generous gesture but no fun for you. It'll be great. Just relax."

"All right. Ready for the last one in our first round. Come on up." Eli motioned to Ginny. "Step over that bar and lie on your stomach. I'll clip you to the kite. Loosen up your shoulders. Relax and have fun." He stepped to the side of the kite. "Okay. Stand up. Remember hunch over a bit. Pull in your elbows. No chicken wings." He laughed. "Chickens don't fly. We're aiming for the house with the three gables straight ahead. See it?"

Her stomach bottomed out. "All the way to the beach?"

"No. We're aiming for it. Now, rest your fingers on the bar and relax. Remember walk. Jog. Run when I tell you. Then push your arms straight forward. Got it?"

Ginny sucked in a breath. So much to remember. Relax the shoulders and keep the elbows in. Hold the bar lightly.

"Okay." Eli moved with her. "Walk. Walk. Jog. Jog. Run. Run. Run! Push out. Push out!"

Her feet bicycled in the air one moment, and the next she slid on her stomach in the sand. She wiggled her ankles. Nothing broken. Good.

"All right we won't count that one. Let's get back and try it again." He released her from the kite.

She'd floated all of four feet down an eighty-foot dune before belly flopping. And it didn't even count. She brushed the sand from her vest. Oh, joy.

BEN WINCED as Ginny's kite nosedived into the side of the dune. Again. He'd feel slightly better if she'd let him pay for today's lesson, but she'd refused. She refused to give up also. When the family of five bagged their last flights in search of a fast-food experience, their instructor had taken on Ginny as a pet project, pulling her out of Josie's group and giving her one-on-one instruction.

A good sport, she'd taken it in stride joking about remedial lessons with a private tutor.

Heath stepped beside him as they watched another attempt at flight. "Man, these instructors are ripped like Olympic athletes, running down the dunes then back up with the kites who knows how many times a day. No wonder their water bottles are gallon jugs." He shook his head. "She's determined, eh?"

"Stop staring at her. You're making her nervous." Josie took a swig of water. "Say a prayer instead, you goons. She's trying so hard."

"Maybe she needs to just relax and go with the flow." Sam stretched his arms over his head in a good morning yoga pose. Heath jabbed him in his side. "Oof. Cut it out, man."

"Eli told her to relax every time he hooked her to the kite. She's doing better with Hannah. Hey, look. There goes Ches." Josie grinned at her fiancé.

Ches sailed just as before but some difficulty wobbled the kite, bringing him down well short of his impressive first flight's mark. He managed to salvage it with a landing on his feet, however. Doing a happy dance, Josie cheered and waved.

If nosediving farther down the dune counted as improvement, then yes, Ginny was getting better. Incrementally, at least.

God, give her some success before the end, please.

Listening to her instructor, Ginny nodded and laughed. Ben's heart lightened.

Hannah stepped to the side and called out the commands. Catching air, Ginny's kite rose and floated down the dune.

"Yeah, baby," Brody watched from his kite.

But as quickly as she went up, she came down again before the bottom of the dune.

Oh, man. Her last try. Hannah disappeared underneath, and then Ginny crawled out from under the kite. She jumped up and down and gave a thumbs up sign.

The crowd at the top of the dune went wild with Josie leading the charge. "Good job. Way to go."

"That's it, folks. The last flight of the morning. Another group's coming in at one o'clock."

Ben retrieved Ginny's water bottle and met her at the bottom.

"Great job. You got the kite going. How'd it feel?"

She laughed. "For the ten seconds I floated, fantastic. I think I'll stick to watersports, though."

"There's still some sand on your Henley." Josie brushed it off. "At least you improved. My best flight was my first one. I belly flopped on my last one." Josie gave her a side hug. "I like your positive attitude."

The walk back to the rental office consisted of tallying up belly landings and feet landings and voting on who looked the goofiest in the helmets. More teasing occurred at the equipment return window.

Hannah approached Ginny with a folded slip of paper. "Sorry we couldn't let you try again. You were really getting the hang of it. Gotta get ready for the next crowd." She waved goodbye.

Ginny opened the note and laughed. "A twenty percent off coupon for my next adventure." She offered it to Ben. "Here you go."

"Not a chance. It's yours. Don't lose it. We'll try again."

That's a promise, Ginny.

10

"It's not far to the sound from here." Ginny shut the crossover's door and headed from the shop's back parking lot. They'd enjoyed quick, mid-week fish tacos at Pete's, and now the second part of the evening consisted of watching for shooting stars from the shop's dock. It extended farther out into the sound than hers and offered an unencumbered view. Hazel had insisted Ben couldn't miss the light show.

"There it is." Ben caught up with her.

"What?" She scanned the horizon.

"Your accent. Finally. It's back."

Her stomach tightened. She'd been so careful, talking like she still lived in Raleigh, but her comfort level rose every time they were together. One little *Ow* sound in one short sentence betrayed her. "Ugh. My dad paid a lot of money to universities for me to learn to talk without the Outer Banks brogue."

"Why would you want to? It's so cool."

She slid him an are-you-kidding glance.

"Ginny." His eyebrows bunched together. "What's up?"

"Come on. Let's get to the dock so we can see the stars better."

"Hey." He tugged the hood of her jacket as she glided past him, her posture rigid. "Something's going on. Why did you want to lose the brogue?"

Turning back to him, she stopped. He let go of the hood.

"It's not about losing it exactly. I know when and when not to use my Hatteras voice."

"I like the Hatteras speech."

She tsked. "You didn't used to."

"Huh? I don't remember you using it before tonight."

She pinned her eyes on him. "I'm not talking about now." Continuing onto the dock, she kept well in front of him. "Hazel'll be disappointed if we don't see any shooting stars."

"I'm not worried about the stars or Hazel's disappointment either. Let's talk. You're not telling me everything."

❧❧❧❧ 🎋 ❦❦❦❦

BEN STARED after Ginny's unyielding back as she left him for the end of the dock. What had just happened? His gut wrenched at her transformation from a light-hearted dinner companion to someone wounded and closed-off. What was going on in her mind? How could he get her to share her story? He wanted to know more about her, her hurts, and her dreams.

The rising anger at her pain surprised him. He wanted to protect her, help her. He caught up with her and clasped her hand. *Trust me, Ginny. I'll keep your story safe.*

At the end of the dock, she motioned to the beach towel he held with his other hand. "Spread it out to lie on or roll it up like a pillow."

He followed her lead to roll his towel.

She positioned her towel several inches from his. "We'll see some stars, but they'll be few and far between now. You'll have to be patient. The best time is supposed to be two in the morning. I plan to be asleep then."

"One of my strong suits is patience, Ginny. I'll be ready to listen when you're ready to talk."

Ben heard a flopping noise against the water near the right-hand corner of the dock.

"What was that?" He turned his head toward the blackness over the sound.

"Just a fish dancing on the water. You're fine. I won't let anything happen to you out here." She injected a light tone in her voice, probably hoping he'd forget about his questions.

"I remember all your skills—crabbing, shelling, driving a boat ..."

"Steering a boat, please."

"I can hear you laughing at me."

She quietened. "I don't laugh at people's differences."

"A loaded statement, for sure, Ginny."

No response.

"Talk to me." Ben broke the silence. "Please."

HER HEART POUNDED against her chest like waves during a nor'easter. Was she really going to have this conversation with him? After all this time, did it matter?

Why not tell him, Ginny? He's not the same as twenty years ago.

She'd redeemed the ten minutes that changed her life. Okay, God redeemed it. Used it for her good. Made her into the knowledgeable person of today. She had experiences and skills beyond the ones of her childhood.

The dark, a protective blanket, let her travel back to the defining scene without him watching her relive it. "The first time I saw all of you, you fascinated me. You laughed and scrambled together like a winning team after a playoff game. Even with the shoving and thumping heads and teasing, I could tell you loved each other. You enjoyed being around each other."

"We were crazy happy to be out of the car. We'd just spent all day in our minivan. Our parents let us walk up to the store so we wouldn't kill each other."

"I tried not to be jealous of Josie's pink shorts and sparkly top. I can still see the front of her shirt with a sequined strawberry in the middle. I wanted to be part of your group so bad." She blew out a long stream of air. "You talked about crabbing, and I offered to take you. The words were out of my mouth before I could think them.

"Your parents were gracious and invited me to dinner and to the lighthouse." She chuckled. "What a time I had with my fancy family from Charlotte."

"Fancy? You got us confused with another vacation family."

"Nope." She sighed. Why not spill all the beans? Isn't confession good for the soul or something like that? "And then, of course, I developed a little crush on the big brother."

"What?"

"Yep. My ten-year-old self thought you were all that and a bag of chips."

"And dip?"

She chuckled again. "Dip too."

Another fish slapped the water.

"Okay. That one was a lot closer and may be related to Moby Dick."

"We're fine." She reached over to pat his arm.

He captured her hand. "That week sounds like I remember it. Except for the crush part. So, what happened?"

"Look! There's one." Her free hand jerked toward the sky.

"Yes! I saw it. Cool." He jiggled her hand still in his.

"On your last day, I rode my bike to the path to your cottage. All of you were joking around, packing up the van. You said, 'Put it in the boot, Heath.' And Sam howled. He kept repeating, 'in the boot, in the boot.' Then all of you started saying words with our accent." He tightened his hold when she tried to wiggle free. "Vans don't even have trunks, but you made fun of the language."

Taking in a breath, she held it, willing her heart rate to slow. *I am not that little girl.* Ben is kind. It wasn't a big deal. *I just built it up to be.* Let. It. Go. She cleared her throat.

"I ... I heard all of you laughing. I realized the week was just a week to you, nothing special like for me. You'd let me tag along to listen to me talk and then you were trying to sound like it. And laughing."

"In the middle of the laughing, I hightailed it for home." She pushed out another breath. "I didn't want to stay and give you more words to mock."

He sat up and drew her with him to sit knee to knee, then clasped her hands. "Ginny, please believe me. We weren't laughing at you. Yes, we were being stupid, trying out different sounding words, but listen to me." He leaned closer. "We were not laughing at *you*."

She buckled under the intensity of his gaze, transferring hers to the moon beam shining on the water. Nudging her chin with one finger, he guided her face back to him, caressed her cheek with the back of his hand.

"We weren't. I promise you. All of us thought you were special. We were jealous of your girl-boss skills. We went to the store to say 'bye, but your dad said you'd gone to the beach."

"I know."

"He told you."

She shook her head. "I hid behind the counter, then went to the beach just to keep his honesty in tack."

"Do you believe me?" Ben's face inched closer to hers.

Strands of her hair swirled in the breeze reaching out to Ben, lighting on his jacket. "I want to."

He slid his hand beneath her braid, tugging her toward him and brushed his lips to hers. "I want you to too." He kissed her a second time with a firmness that proved his words. Conveyed he cared about her as an adult and as the hurt little girl. Breaking away, he held her gaze for a moment before claiming her again.

She forgot about the hurt, about the stars shooting overhead, focusing, instead, on the heat rising inside her and the man who was becoming more than a schoolgirl crush.

11

The sunlight winked off the sound. Ben's office window served a tantalizing view of two sailboats enjoying a Monday morning water adventure. He swiveled in his chair, allowing his mind to skitter over the events of the long weekend, beginning with the surprised joy on Ginny's face at the bouquets of flowers he'd brought to Thanksgiving, one for her and one for Hazel, then the hang-gliding experience, the family's early send off yesterday, Ginny's revelations from last night. And, finally, the kiss.

He lingered on the kiss and smiled.

She seemed different after the kiss, not as reserved. Playful even. She'd explained how her hurt led to her interest in language and subsequent studies in communications and French. He chuckled, remembering his ridiculous attempt at a French accent. *"Parlez-vous français?"*

"That's all you know, right?"

"Merci, rendezvous, fondue, canoe—"

"Canoe?"

"Sounds French to me."

Her full-on laugh rewarded his whimsy, emboldening him to kiss her again.

Revealing conversations, shooting stars, and tantalizing kisses. Maybe the special night would signal a change in their relationship. A knock on his office door brought him back to the present. Right. Yancy Burris's meeting today. Felicia opened the door and ushered the older woman in.

Closing his door on the Christmas carol playing in the lobby, Ben offered one of the chairs in front of his desk to Miss Yancy, taking the opposite one for himself. Dressed again in the brogans and brick red barn coat, she looked more ready to milk cows or muck out horse stalls than discuss wealth management.

"It's good to see you again, Miss Yancy." Ben focused on the woman before him, pondering words to explain steps to establishing a scholarship. He'd checked her account after she booked this meeting. True, she had healthy holdings, but how strong would her account be if she encountered a long illness? Or if she lived for ten, fifteen more years?

"I'm happy to see you too." She considered him. "What's the difference between pixilated and pixelated?"

A grin broke across his face. "Pixilated with an *I* means crazy, confused, or wacky. Pixelated with an *e* means the individual pixels are visible in a computer graphic."

"Thank you for following through." She cleared her throat. "Now, as I told Felicia when I made this appointment, I need your help setting up scholarships and other things." She opened a satchel and extracted a manila envelope. "I've got my portfolio here for you to peruse."

At Ben's raised eyebrow, she continued. "You're familiar with my account here, right?"

"Yes, ma'am."

"Well, I have that much each in seven other banks in Dare,

Pasquotank, Chowan, and Currituck counties, plus stocks and bonds."

Ben quickly multiplied seven times the amount he'd seen on her account balance this morning. He blanked his face as he'd perfected during board games with his siblings. Could what she said be true? Could she have liquid assets upward of half a million dollars. He swallowed.

She handed him the folder, eyes focused on him, and smiled. "Precisely. You're the perfect person for me. I don't like locals knowing about my business. You won't gossip because you don't know but two people, Hazel and Ginny. They're not gossipers either."

"How did you—" He slammed his mouth shut on his off-limits question. He wasn't used to a sum of money shocking words out of his mouth.

"Well. You are human after all." She laughed. "It's a valid question. I'm quite good at reading the stock market. And knowing when to buy and when to sell, of course."

Question almost asked and graciously answered. "But you don't know me from Adam. You're trusting me with your life savings?"

"I'm not as dumb as you think I look."

Ben opened his mouth.

"Stop. I know the impression I give. I also know the kind of person you are. I've done some digging. Your expertise is wealth management. I need my wealth managed."

"I'm the temporary manager for this branch."

"Yes, so we have to get the ball rolling, don't we? I've got the list of charities and how I want everything divvied up."

Ben read over the list. "Two scholarships at the high school?"

"Yes, one for the college-bound student. One for the skilled student. To encourage both. I've got the prompts for entry essays and requirements too."

She was thorough, he'd give her that. The high school, the public library, the turtle-saving group, the Keenekeet Church, the Hatteras lighthouse.

"You've got quite a list here."

"I've got quite a lot of money. I want to see it put to good use."

"Miss Yancy, you have all this worked out. You need a lawyer to make it official."

"Right. I have one."

"Then—"

"I'm consolidating my money. My lawyer tells me to choose one bank. Tells me it'd be best. I doubt that's true. I'm sure the bigwigs on Madison Avenue have money in more than one bank. I'm sure it'll be easier for him when he goes to drafting the letters and what not. But it's easier for me too, keeping up with all those bank statements."

She shrugged. "It's inevitable word will get out about my money now, but I've got it allocated along with the amounts. Nobody should come singing their sad songs to me. I don't want any hullabaloo either. We just have to finalize this and that."

"Yes, ma'am." He pinched the bridge of his nose.

"Got a headache, son?"

"No, ma'am." He shook his head. "Just didn't see this coming."

"How could you have?" She laughed again. "I want this tied up with a bow by my birthday, Old Christmas."

"Old Christmas."

"January sixth. You're too much of a gentleman to ask, so I'll satisfy your curiosity. I'll be eighty. You got about a month."

12

"Well, it looks like my first fish will be my best entry. No luck out there for me this morning." Ben had caught several in the waning hours of Hatteras's first Christmas Classic Fishing Tournament, but all were smaller than the one he caught on the first day of the contest. Ginny had continued to encourage him, but the fish weren't obliging.

"Your catch is respectable. Don't count yourself out." Hazel reached for the ringing phone behind the counter. "Stowe's Tackle." She listened, frowning. "Say that again." She harrumphed. "She's here now." She handed the phone to Ginny. "Tad."

"Hey." Ginny frowned. "I'm coming. Sit tight." She handed the phone back and glanced at Ben. "I need to go, but I'll see you at the gala, okay?"

"What's up, Ginny?"

"Tad needs help over on Shackleford Banks." Hazel pursed her lips. "Didn't exactly sound sharp, if you know what I mean."

Ginny made a face. "He needs me. I'm going."

"Need some help?" If the anxiety in her eyes rang true, she did—in a big way.

"Thanks. I'm good."

"Yes, she does." Hazel folded her arms together.

Ginny set her jaw. "No."

"Yes, girl." Hazel reached under the counter. "The sound's choppy today. You don't know what shape he's in. Thank you, Ben. She's stubborn."

The sound's choppy? Ben swallowed. Had he just volunteered to ride in a boat? *God, this won't be good.*

"I can be stubborn too." But could he ride in a boat with his dignity intact?

Hazel handed a key to Ginny. "Take the ski boat out back. It's got two life jackets. Take another one just in case." She pointed to one hanging by the back door. "Ben, we appreciate your help. Leave your wallet and anything you don't want to get wet here. I'll keep it safe."

Should he ask for Dramamine? He pushed his wallet and phone toward Hazel.

"Okay. Let's roll." Ginny's countenance matched the clouds swirling in from the ocean. No time for medicine, just a quick, *Help me out, please, Lord.*

A boat. On that choppy sound.

Shrugging on the extra life vest, Ginny stalked down the path toward the boathouse. She hopped onto the boat with ease. Ben hesitated on the dock watching the bobbing boat. Don't watch the boat. Look at her back.

His last boat ride, a humiliating fiasco with college buddies, was supposed to have been his last. He'd promised himself, but Ginny needed him. Tad's call shut her down, changed her from the encouraging fishing buddy to a silent, all-business woman bent on a mission. Her brother.

She pulled a vest from the dry well and tossed it to him.

"Come on aboard." She grabbed the wheel and brought the engine to life.

Clutching the vest, he planted a foot on the boat's deck, the bobbing deck. His head swirled in time with his lurching stomach. He forced his other foot into place beside the first.

"Hang on." Ginny maneuvered the boat out of the slip.

The G-force pushed him against the seat. He closed his eyes. Bad idea. A warning seized his gut. He searched for a fixed point on the horizon. The horizon swayed. The clouds undulated. His brain see-sawed.

Breathe, Ben. You will help Ginny. You will not vomit in front of her.

God, help here, please.

Concentrate, man. He rested his clammy head on his forearm along the side of the boat. Think. Kissing Ginny the other night. Fishing this morning. Eating lunch.

Lunch. He lost it over the side.

Help her, Lord.

✥✥✥ ❦ ✥✥✥

A BREEZE BUFFETING her face over the windshield, Ginny urged the engine faster.

The phone call had changed Ben. He'd gone silent, watching the exchange with Hazel. What was he wondering? What would they find when they reached Tad? Had Ben ever dealt with someone who was high or drunk or not perfect like his siblings?

Tad had been fine on Thanksgiving for the hour he ate with them, but now ... Would Ben get to see him in all his sullied glory? Would he thank God his siblings were fun and fully engaged as contributing-to-society adults?

It didn't matter what he thought anyway. He'd be back in Charlotte with his family soon.

Tad's slurred speech warned her what to expect when they found him. Hazel, why'd you have to drag Ben into the middle of Tad's mess? Tad, you promised you were for real this time. You said you weren't going back to your old life. You promised.

Ridiculous hopes of his taking the shop in her place evaporated like cotton-ball clouds before the rain. She growled, confident the motor's roar would smother it before reaching Ben's ears. She pointed the bow north and gave the engine full throttle.

The boat road a swell and slapped the water on the other side. She squeezed the wheel, planting her docksiders for balance. Cool, salty spray splashed over the bow of the boat, snatching her from the negative thoughts. She glanced back to check on Ben. Good. Still in his seat. The hard landing didn't bother him. Her attention back to the sound, she scanned the horizon and spotted the small island.

She glimpsed the Jon boat up near Craggy Point. Good, but where was Tad? Thank goodness he had enough sense not to drive himself back. Tad, why'd you have to come all the way out here to ... She spied him, leaning against the port side of the boat. Passed out?

Gliding the boat to shore, she dropped anchor. "Hey, Ben, could you—" Her request flew from her mind.

With hands clutching the side of the boat in a death grip, Ben's face was tinted green. He shifted then heaved over the side.

"Ben, you get seasick?" A coldness in her stomach matched the wind on her arms. "Why'd you come?"

He wiped his mouth on his shirt sleeve and groaned. "I wanted to help."

"Oh, man." She shook her head. *I'm in a fix here, God.*

"Okay. Sit tight. I'll get Tad, and we'll be back to dry land before you know it." She jumped off the boat and splashed through the waves to shore. For the first time, she got a good look at Tad. He was white as the foam on the surf.

"Tad!" She plopped down in the sand beside him. The rag tied to his foot seeped with blood. She sucked in a lung full of air and held it with her eyes closed. Blood. Not good. She nudged his chin. "Tad, can you hear me?"

His eyes fluttered open and focused on her. "Hey. A shell ... Sorry."

"I thought ..."

Pain marred his face. "Sober."

Tears burned in the corners of her eyes. "Can you stand? You've got to get on the boat."

He mumbled.

She tugged on his arm, and another hand slipped under his other arm. "Ben, I told you to—"

Ben bent over and heaved again.

❧❧❧❧ ✂ ❧❧❧❧

THE LAST OF Ben's dignity spilled onto the little island. He wiped his mouth on shirt sleeve again and avoided eye contact. "Ready to lift him?"

"Ben, you don't have to."

"On three. One. Two. Three." They lifted Tad to standing. He swayed, but Ben caught his shoulder. Leaning together, they waded into the surf. The boat rocked on the waves. Ben groaned at the sight and tasted bile.

Man, oh, man. *Please, God, need some strength here.* His head beat out a sick island rhythm.

By God's grace, they sloshed Tad to the boat. Ginny hopped over the side and lifted him as Ben pushed from underneath. Tad rolled over the side and slid onto the deck. Ben forced his fingers around the ladder and climbed onto the bobbing boat. Gritting his teeth at rising nausea, he focused on fresh drips of blood dotting the wood.

He ripped off his vest and long-sleeved T-shirt and unwound the saturated shirt on Tad's foot. He sucked air through clenched teeth at the freshly bleeding gash. A bright red spot quickly spread on his shirt he wrapped it over the wound.

The wind whipped up a massive crop of goose bumps. Ben slipped on his life vest.

Ginny blew on her fists, then worked to get a vest on her brother. She tried to latch the hooks but missed the closures three times in a row.

"Let me." Ben grabbed the hooks, determined to connect them even if his head exploded in the process. The closure fit together on the second try, but success offered little pleasure against the war in his body.

"Thanks. He's lost so much blood." She met his eyes for the first time. "If I go back to the shop ..."

"Go wherever he needs." He waved her on and dropped to the deck beside Tad.

She raised the anchor, fired up the motor, and turned the boat in the opposite direction, covering new territory on the choppier surf.

From his vantage point flat on his back, the gray sky threatened rough weather. *God. Help.*

❧❧❧ ❁ ❧❧❧

An eternity later, Ben pushed to sitting as Ginny slipped the boat alongside the Avon Medical Office dock. She threw a rope toward the dock and cut the motor.

A male nurse waited with a wheelchair. Arms akimbo, Hazel shook her head, grim-faced. She bent to secure the rope.

"Well, you made it before the storm hit. Good girl."

Praise God for huge blessings like slowed storms, radios for calling reinforcements, and for Hazel's coming to the rescue.

Ben pulled on Tad's arm to help him sit up as the nurse hopped on board. Holding his breath as the boat rocked again, Ben prayed. Don't let me throw up in front of this man.

"Looks like you lost a ton of blood, buddy. Let's get you inside." Bracing one leg against the dry storage, the nurse gripped Tad and stood him in one move. "Hold him like this, ma'am, and I'll hop up. We'll get him on the dock and in the chair. No problem."

Clutching her brother, Ginny glanced at Ben. "Thank you. I couldn't have done it without you."

Her thanks, though well-meaning, missed the comforting mark. Retching scenes splayed prominently in his mind.

With the rope tied around a galvanized cleat on the dock, Hazel reached toward Ben to help him out of the boat. "Not a boat person, eh? No wonder you stick to pier fishing so much."

Ben grunted and let her steady him on the dock.

Satisfied with the safety of his patient, the nurse trekked to the building.

"I'll take it from here, Hazel. Thanks again, Ben. Go home and feel better." Ginny kept her hand on Tad's shoulder and skipped-walked to keep up with the wheelchair.

Gritting his teeth, Ben warned Hazel, "I'm not leaving yet." He set out after the group with the wheelchair. Hazel followed him, unusually silent.

Saving the last of his energy reserves, he rested his aching head against the wall in the Avon medical office. A miniature Christmas tree winked at him from the reception desk. With the pain hosting a party between his temples, he squinted at the swinging door to the examination rooms.

The male nurse emerged and offered him a scrub shirt with tiny Santa hats decorating it. "You might be more comfortable in this."

Comfortable had left the station a couple of hours ago, but a wet life vest or a dry scrub shirt? Even covered with Santa hats? No contest.

"Thanks, man." Ben popped the buckles and changed out of the vest. The soft cotton soothed his skin, cloaking him in a soapy smell.

The door swung open again. Ginny.

"I thought you two were leaving." She narrowed her eyes at Hazel. "He needs to go home."

"He wanted to check on you."

Her gaze flickered toward Ben. "I'm fine. Tad's getting stitched up right now. You need to get ready for the gala."

"I'm not worried about the gala." Ben shifted in his plastic seat, thought better about standing.

"You need to celebrate."

"Celebrating an honorable mention isn't important right now. Being here with you is important now."

Tears sparkled in her eyes. She lifted her chin. "Thank you, Ben, but it's all good. You need to go."

"No—"

Hazel rose from her chair. "Do you see that set of her jaw, Ben? She's decided, and there'll be no changing. Figure out the gala later, but you need to get home." She sniffed. "And cleaned up."

Despite the Muzak version of Jingle Bells playing in the background, defeat settled onto his shoulders. Ocean salt, vomit, sweat. He probably smelled worse than a dead fish.

"Come on, son. You're still looking a bit green too."

With the final blow to his confidence, he acquiesced and plodded out of the waiting room with Hazel.

Okay, Ginny. You've won this round, but I'm not giving up. I'll be back on my game with a settled stomach and a shirt without Santa hats. Get ready.

꿈꿈꿈 ❦ 꿈꿈꿈

TAD RESTED PEACEFULLY on Ginny's couch, and another thank-you prayer formed in her mind. Although he'd lost almost a pint of blood and needed twelve stitches in his foot, he'd recover with a scar and a new tale to tell. She tried to pray away the anger she felt every time she remembered the race across the sound and poor Ben throwing up the whole time. She picked up her phone to text him, but Tad opened his eyes,

"Hey, sis." He shifted on the couch. "Thanks for coming to the rescue. Again."

She sipped her decaf coffee, dismissing his thanks. "The doc says you'll need to hang out a couple of days. Get your strength back."

"Yeah. How's Ben?"

She glanced at her phone. "Enjoying the gala probably."

"The gala? You're supposed to be there."

"I'm not going."

"You don't need to babysit me. I'm fine. Go."

"I'm not going."

"Yes, you are."

"It's too late."

"The mingle time's just started. Go get ready."

"I'm not going." Ginny clamped her jaw shut.

"Yes, you are 'cause you're not laying this on me. I'm sorry about the rescue, but you're back now. Get dressed and go. Celebrate with Ben. You taught him all he knows."

13

The throbbing in Ben's head banged like a timpani when the buffet of seafood and salads came into view at the gala. Would he ever feel like eating again? He asked for a ginger ale from the bartender and sipped on the bubbly liquid. The Christmas lights decorating the archway in the community center twinkled in time to the pattern pounding between his temples. He relieved his eyes of the dancing lights and surveyed the room. No Ginny. Would she show?

What a day. She barely spoke for the entire boat trip except to bark orders. Her brother was out of his head most of the time.

He'd expected to stay with her and be a friend, be a comfort, be a shoulder for her, but no. Instead, she pushed him into Hazel's care, dismissing him with a wave and a thank you.

Appreciating the string band's jazzy rendition of "We Three Kings," he took another sip before releasing the glass to a waiter's tray. His bed and a dark room beckoned him more than the anticipation of a thirty-dollar check. Turning toward the door, he stepped in front of a familiar face.

"Pastor Maron, Good to see you." It was good to see anything with the violent headache demanding all his attention.

"Good evening, son. I saw your name among the winners on the town's website. Congratulations for placing in the money."

"Yes, sir. Thank you. Honorable mention feels kind of good for my first competition. I can afford a few more Apple Uglies with my prize money."

"Ooh, they're just this side of sinful. I'm abstaining during December so I can enjoy my wife's Christmas cookies. Maybe the purse for next year's tournament can be a little healthier. Speaking of next year, how does the field look for our permanent bank manager? Any good prospects?"

"Felicia Combs mentioned two new résumés."

"Nice. Yours wouldn't be one of them, now, would it?"

Ben laughed. "Well—"

The crowd nudged him to his left.

Pastor Maron shifted with him. "I've heard good things about you, Ben. We'd be honored to count you as a neighbor. Hazel says she's asked you to play backup keyboard for us."

Commandeered better described Hazel's invitation to play when she'd discovered his piano skills. She didn't shy away from what she wanted, for sure.

Ginny spotted Ben talking with Pastor Maron the instant she entered the room. Wearing a dark suit and paisley tie, his hair gelled in place, he proclaimed Mr. Big City. A cold sensation bloomed in her stomach, freezing tingly paths to her fingertips. She shivered.

He didn't belong in Hatteras any more than he belonged on her boat.

But Pastor Maron asked him to stay. She inched closer to the two as they shifted with the push of the crowd. A three-hundred-pound fisherman stepped between her and Ben's back, blocking her efforts to join their conversation as she strained to hear Ben's response about playing backup keyboard.

"The island's a beautiful place, no doubt. She's mentioned it, yes."

She braced herself. *When he says, no, just keep smiling. There'll be plenty of time for other feelings later.*

The linebacker fisherman wedged into an opening in the crowd, and Pastor Maron faced her. "Hello, Ginny. We were chatting about new prospects for the bank manager. I hope he'll apply for it."

Ben turned toward her, a tentative smile on his face.

Don't worry, Ben, I understand, and I'll help you out. "As much as we have to offer, I'm sure the sparkling city life is calling him back home, not to mention his family." She flashed a quick smile to Ben's jacket and switched her gaze to the pastor before Ben could confirm leaving. "The Christmas Classic Fishing Tournament is off to a great start, don't you think, Pastor?"

"Indeed. Next year we should be big enough for a sit-down dinner rather than a heavy appetizer party." He eyed the buffet table.

"From your mouth to God's ears," Ginny hoped her voice sounded normal. "Oh, there's Miss Edna. I need to speak to her, please excuse me." She touched Ben's sleeve and stepped away.

"Want a cup of spiced cider? I'll get you one."

"I'm good thanks," floated over her shoulder along with another pasted-on smile. Excellent. She'd made her appearance, let Ben know she understood about his leaving, kept her emotions under wraps. She'd inform Miss Edna the rod and reel she'd ordered for her granddaughter had arrived and then go home.

Telling Miss Edna wasn't imperative tonight—she called every day since she placed her order—but leaving the party was. Mentally and physically exhausted from the day's drama, she didn't have energy to keep smiling at Ben with his leaving foremost in her mind.

She'd regroup before seeing him again, get her brain fully accepting a future without him.

14

"So how was the big night? Do you like your trophy?" Josie teased over the phone.

"I got a check for thirty bucks. No trophy for honorable mention." By the time Ben had received Ginny's goodbye text, he'd searched the crowd for that clingy, swingy black dress for several minutes. Man, she always looked great, but tonight, even after the hours spent on the sound rescuing her brother, she could have lit up a red carpet anywhere. He'd have made sure she knew, if she hadn't left.

"So, when can we expect you? Please say Christmas Eve Eve."

"No can do. I'm working then so that I can have the whole long weekend. My co-workers are being more than generous with days off."

"It's not like you don't have days to take off. You're not a first-year hire, you know."

"Yeah. It's never a good look to come in and take days just because you can."

"So, sometime Christmas Eve?"

"I'll be there with bells on."

"Silver bells?"

"Funny, Josie. See you soon."

He checked the text box again. Nothing. He'd send one more and then call this day done.

> Hey. Got my check. Need some help spending it.
> Any ideas?

While waiting for a response, he took out his contacts, and heard one come through.

> I'm sure you have great ideas. Congratulations again.

Hmm. Very non-committal.

> How's Tad?

Fine. Thanks. He'll be good as new before too long.

> How's your week look?

Swamped with last-minute shoppers.

> Gotcha. See you before I go home on Christmas Eve.

Okay. Good night.

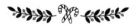

GINNY SET aside her phone and fingered the black crepe of her fancy dress. She'd been home for hours, kicking off her heels but lingering in the dress that made her feel special, like

Cinderella at the ball. The light in Ben's eyes when he saw her at the gala more than compensated for the money she'd spent on the full-price splurge.

She'd begun this friendship accepting its short-term status, but the fishing, the meals, the kissing—all those memory-making times had lolled her into a fantasy with Ben starring as lead. The daydream floundered a bit during the hang-gliding outing with the siblings' love sparkling all day and then again when Tad had arrived back in town.

Rescuing Tad, even though he was sober, gave Ben a glimpse of her not-so-sparkling sibling relationship while showcasing his kindness and strength despite a raging bout of seasickness. In case she still wondered if the friendship would grow into anything more, his magazine-cover look at the gala foghorned her foolishness.

Like Cinderella, she sighed, reality blanketing her own little corner on the island. Her brother slept in his old room down the hall. *Thank You, God, that he's on the mend. That he's still sober. Please keep him strong.*

Her life in Raleigh seemed as brief as the beam flickering every seven seconds from the lighthouse standing guard over the island.

Pastor Maron always exhorted his congregation to pray big to their big God. Fine. She took a breath. Okay, *Lord. I want him to stay but help me accept Your will.*

❧❧❧ ❀ ❧❧❧

No yellow Jeep at the tackle shop. So much for surprising Ginny with a lunch invitation. He parked his car in the only available space and headed inside. She was right about last-minute shoppers. He caught Hazel's eye and waited while she rang up a shopper holding a list and a credit card.

"She's not here." Hazel said without looking at him.

"Yeah. I didn't see her Jeep. She's not at her house either. Do you know where she is?"

"Nope, but she's with Tad."

"Gotcha."

The shopper gathered the two bags of equipment and opened up the spot in front of Hazel.

"She hasn't texted me since Sunday night." And those weren't too forthcoming. He leaned in. "I'm driving home first thing tomorrow morning. I'd love to see her. Help a guy out, Hazel?"

"I'd love to, buddy, but she didn't tell me much. Just that she'd be out and sent that teenager over by the bait cooler to help me during this crunch time." She made a face at the lanky teen. "She left these two presents for you." She reached under the counter and pulled out two small packages. "One's for you. The other's for your sister."

That's how it's going to be? Exchanging presents by proxy? The seasickness must have really disappointed her.

He sighed. "Hers is in the car. I'll go get it. And yours too."

After a quick hug from Hazel for the Ringo Starr biography he'd found in the island's bookstore, Ben drove north on Highway 12, scanning for a yellow Jeep. Not seeing one didn't deter him from continuing the search as he traveled onto the mainland into Columbia, his Christmas spirit absent from the westbound car.

15

H ome for Christmas. Josie had dressed the house to a *T*. She'd unboxed the elementary school ornaments, the fancy ones Mom gave them every year, the ones handed down from his grandparents. All of them hung on the shining tree.

The food ... delicious as usual ... the turnip greens with hot sauce alongside the beef tenderloin. Always an extravagance. Always worth every penny. Then the cookies. Dozens of cookies dressing up his great aunt's silver tray, and, of course, the apple and orange cake center stage on the dessert table with a side bowl of glazed pecans.

He grabbed a few pecans and tossed them in his mouth. The cinnamon and sugar tasted like home.

Every sight and smell proved Josie learned well from their mom. Perfect. But this year all the goodies, all the trimmings and smells and flickering lights did nothing to evoke the Christmas spirit in Ben's heart. His mind kept traveling back down Highway 12 to Hatteras.

What was Ginny doing? Did she think of him at all?

Josie's present.

He'd placed it under the Christmas tree with the others when he arrived home three hours ago, but it had shifted to the far side. He retrieved it, knocking off a shiny ball, and set it on a side table. He rehung the red ball and lost himself to more thoughts of Ginny.

"Hey, earth to Scrooge. Where've you been?" Josie entered the family room after saying good night to Ches. Heath and Sam had left too.

"Scrooge. A little harsh, don't you think? I came home bearing lots of gifts for all of you yahoos, and I get called Scrooge?"

"All right. You're not Scrooge, but where's your Christmas spirit? You've been in a mood all night. What gives?"

"Just tired after the drive, Jo."

"That may be part of it, but there's something else. Or rather someone else." She studied him.

He focused on the Christmas tree, ignoring her comment and her scrutiny. Thoughts about his job in Charlotte, his three months on the Outer Banks with Ginny pushed everything else aside.

"I saw the way you watched her Thanksgiving weekend. You're smitten with her."

"Smitten?" He turned toward her with an arched brow.

"It's a good word."

"For a history professor."

She chewed on the inside of her cheek. "You're taking the job, aren't you?"

His mouth dropped open. "I haven't made any commitments—"

"Out loud maybe, but you're thinking about staying. I can see it in your eyes."

"Okay, Miss Dog-With-a-Bone." He looked over her head

at the wooden Advent calendar they'd had since childhood and sighed. "I've considered offering to stay longer. The incoming résumés aren't exactly lighting up the search committee."

Josie's chin trembled, prompting a hug from her brother. "What about the promotion?"

"Yeah, I've a lot to sort out. The promotion would be great, but I like what I'm doing on the island." The gift on the side table caught his attention. "Hey. You've got another present." He handed it to her. "It's from Ginny."

"Sweet." Josie ripped the ribbon and the wrapping off in one tear. Opening the box, she gasped. "A conch shell. She gave me a conch shell. Like she promised." She flattened her lips. "You've got to go back, Ben."

"What?"

"You have to go back."

"I am. Monday."

"No. You have to go back tomorrow." She caught her bottom lip with her teeth, then sighed. "Spend at least part of Christmas with her. Wait." She turned and ran away from him, stomping all the way up the steps. Five minutes later, she carried a small, square box, dropped it into a tossed-aside gift bag and stuffed tissue paper from the used pile she'd refold sometime after Christmas. She handed him the package. "Here. Take this to her."

"You got a present for her in five minutes?"

"It helps that I'm back in my parents' house. No problem finding my treasure box." She pushed it toward him. "Give it to her on Christmas, please."

"Josie."

"I'll move breakfast to eight. Sam can grouse all he wants. You'll eat fast and be on the road by eight thirty. You'll be back on Hatteras by early afternoon."

His heart rate ticked up. Emotion mushroomed in his chest. "Well, if you want her to have this present on Christmas Day."

"She absolutely has to have it tomorrow." Josie grinned at him.

He grinned back. "I can FaceTime with Mom and Dad from there, right?"

"Maybe have her join you."

"You think?" He laughed.

"There he is. You finally made it home for Christmas, Ben."

<hr/>

"WANT some hot chocolate before we start the movie?" Ginny stretched and rose from the couch. "Or are you still stuffed?"

Her brother clicked the remote and pulled up a streaming service. "Sounds good. Hey, thanks for including me with your Christmas lunch. It's good to be home, sis. Hazel seems to be warming up to me too."

"She loves you. Give her time to come around." Her new slippers from Tad cushioned her feet like pillows as she padded into the kitchen. She poured milk into her Santa mug and, just to tease him, poured some into the Grinch one.

Crossing to the pantry, she glanced out the window. Sunlight glinted off a car pulling into the driveway. Did Hazel forget something? She surveyed the counter tops. Nothing. She glanced out the window again, her stomach dropping to her feet.

Ben.

He left yesterday, and he's back today. What? Sucking in a long breath, she held it as he walked up the path to the house. She released the breath with a prayer for help and strength and for her mouth to stop smiling so big.

Calm down, girl. You don't know why he's here.

But does it matter? He's back and here for Christmas even though he'd already left her present. She twisted the bracelet on her wrist, a silver braided chain with an Ichthys symbol clasp and one dangling aquamarine piece of sea glass. Hazel had made googly eyes when she saw it this morning.

He rapped on the front door. She breathed a steadying prayer.

"I'll get it." She jogged to the foyer, finger brushing her hair. Opening the door, she mirrored the tentative smile on his face.

"Hey."

"Hey back."

"I hope you don't mind me crashing Christmas."

"But you went home."

"Christmas Eve was great. Then Josie made me leave this morning."

"What?"

He peered behind her. "Could I come in, please?"

"Of course." Shaking her head, she stepped back. "You caught me off guard. Want some hot chocolate?"

Ben glanced at the two mugs. "Hazel?"

"Left a little while ago. Tad's queuing up a movie."

"Feel like a walk? I need to move around after the drive."

Tad appeared in the hall. "What's up, Ben? Merry Christmas."

"Merry Christmas. It's been a good one so far." They shook hands.

"Hey, man." Tad dipped his head and rubbed the side of his nose. "I never thanked you for helping my sister. I really appreciate it."

"Well, if you mean throwing up the whole time—"

"Naw, man. She said you helped get me in the boat. I was out of it."

"It's all good."

She set the Grinch mug in the microwave. "Your hot chocolate will be ready in a bit. We're going for a walk, okay?"

"Right. I can manage the microwave. Take your jacket. I see white caps out there. The sun's out, but the wind's up."

Ben lifted her jacket from the hall tree and held it for her. As she slipped her arm through the sleeve, he touched her wrist. "Hey. You're wearing it."

"Uh-huh. Thank you, by the way." She draped the sea glass charm on her index finger, let it go and shrugged her jacket on both shoulders. "Hazel oohed and aahed over it."

"What did you do?"

"I put it on." She smiled and lost herself in his green eyes with the gold flecks.

Without planning, they headed for the dock behind her house.

"That reminds me. Josie sent you something." He pulled a gift bag from an inside pocket and handed it to her.

"Oh, that's so sweet." She stopped and turned to him. "She didn't have to."

"She loved the conch shell. I think it tipped things in favor of my early return. Did you really save it all these years? Or was it a different one?"

"I almost threw it back in the ocean, but I changed my mind and kept it. Who knows why? I never expected to see you again." She peeked inside the bag and drew out a square box. Opening it, she chuckled. "It's a friendship bracelet." One end whipped in the breeze when she held it for him to see.

"Safe guess it's twenty years old too." He laughed. "Hot pink, purple, lime—her favorite colors back in the day."

She extended her arm toward him. "Could you tie it for me?"

"Are you sure you want it on the same wrist? It'll have to compete with that bracelet Hazel loves."

"I love it too. I love both of them. They mean ... a lot. Trust me."

Silence accompanied them to the end of the dock. During their last dock visit, he'd kissed her for the first time. Her heart raced at the thought.

Ben pulled up the collar of her jacket. "Tad was right. The wind's strong out here today."

Hair swirled around her face. Catching a lock, he smoothed it behind her ear. His thumb found her earlobe. Her insides melted, warmth rippling through her body despite the relentless December wind.

"Why'd you pull away last week?" He scanned her face. "I thought we were—"

Unlocking her gaze from his, she focused on the seagulls soaring on the current.

Gently, he guided her chin back to center with his index finger. "Tell me. What went wrong? It's my lack of seaworthiness, right?"

She laughed at the crazy thought, but his face showed concern and a curious bit of hurt, not levity. He stepped back.

"Ben, no." She grabbed the edges of his jacket. "Tad's right. You helped me so much. I couldn't have gotten him on the boat. Your presence meant a lot. I was scared, and your prayer settled me. Got me going again."

He frowned. "Did I pray out loud?"

"Short and to the point, but it worked."

"Then what? You didn't deny pulling away. What made you?"

The last time she explained her feelings, darkness gave her courage. This time ... *God, help me out here, please.* "Your life is back in Charlotte with your family. Mine is here, at the shop, helping Tad. He's on his way to fine, but ..." She shrugged.

"Seeing you all spiffed up in your suit helped me remember

our places. Helped me get ready for when you go back to Charlotte for good."

His fingers slid along her jaw, down the side of her neck. "What if I could stay here longer?"

She shivered and quelled the immediate urge to latch on to the lapels of his jacket. "What does that mean exactly?"

LIGHT-HEARTED FEELINGS WHIRLING in his heart, Ben cleared his throat. "It means I'm considering accepting a long-term position here."

Her eyes widened. "Long term as in how long?"

"Six months or more."

A tiny smile perked up the corners of her mouth.

"I have to get some things settled back home, but it could allow me to rent something more than one room at Teachy's. He drew her toward him. "I think we have something interesting happening between us, and maybe we should explore it some more. What do you think? Should I accept the position?"

Her smile grew. "I think, yes. Please accept it."

"Good." Heat thumped in his chest. "Because you still have to show me Ocracoke."

"Right. Will do. And we haven't been surfing yet either."

"Speaking of surfing, Yancy Buress's eightieth birthday is Old Christmas. Would she hate us if we threw her a party?"

"You can tell her."

He laughed and kissed her temple. "I hear the turtle season is pretty spectacular." He whispered near her ear. "And you have that hang-gliding coupon."

"Mmm. I love a coupon." She wrapped her arms around his waist. "You really need more practice fishing too."

"You want me to do better than honorable mention?" He trailed kisses along her cheek. "See, I have to stay longer."

"This is turning out to be a great Christmas."

"Maybe I can make it even better." And he lowered his lips to hers.

ABOUT THE AUTHOR

Hope Toler Dougherty holds a Master's degree in English and taught at East Carolina University and York Technical College. Her publications include four novels, *Irish Encounter* and *Mars...With Venus Rising, Rescued Hearts,* and *Forever Music* as well as nonfiction articles. A member of ACFW and RWA, she lives in North Carolina. She and her husband enjoy visits with their two daughters and twin sons. Visit her at hopetolerdougherty.com.

A Pennie for Your Thoughts

A Novella by

Linda Fulkerson

To my daughter, Elena, who has been my constant encourager since the day I decided to write fiction.

1

Never pack more than you can carry, unassisted, through a busy airport. Because statistically, those self-serve luggage cart rental racks are located an average of 17,002 steps in the opposite direction of where you need to go.

~ Pennie's travel tip No. 14

Rain plinked against the lakefront cabin's windows as Pennie Vaughn slid the adding machine tape through her fingers and scrolled to the end. She stared at the final figure. That number couldn't be right. She shuffled the stack of bids and, once again, punched in estimate amounts. Before she finished re-tallying the total, her phone's ringtone blared Smash Mouth's "Road Man," interrupting the soft *clackety-clack* of the 10-key device.

She tapped the answer icon. "Hey, Cal. What's up?"

"You're in!" Her best friend Callie Jorgensen's voice squealed with excitement.

"I'm *in* a lot of things. In debt. In over my head." *In love.*

Not that *that* mattered anymore. Pennie's gaze trickled toward the black velvet box, undisturbed in a cubby of the antique secretary's desk, taunting her to lift the lid. "You'll need to be more specific."

"The contest. *Wanderblog* posted the semi-finalist list today, and you're on it!"

Pennie tucked the phone between her ear and shoulder and flipped open her laptop. A few keystrokes and clicks brought her to a site topped with the headline:

Wanderblog Award Semi-Finalists

She scanned the page until she saw it. "A Pennie for Your Thoughts." Despite the hokey title, her Dear-Abby-style travel-advice blog had grown in popularity. Not bad for someone who never went anywhere. Pennie read the tasks required by semi-finalists in order to advance.

"You there, Pen?" Callie's voice tugged Pennie back to reality.

"Oh, yeah. Sorry."

"Did you see the Grand Prize cash amount? Hefty sum!"

Hefty enough to put a major dent in the amount needed to repair Dottie's—now Pennie's—cabin. "I saw that. But the rules say I'd have to publish a travel post by mid-January. With photos."

"So?"

"So, I'd have to actually *go* somewhere—not just tell Aunt Suzie how to cope with three toddlers on a long flight."

"That was one of your most-shared posts."

Pennie smiled but her face quickly contort into a frown. "If it weren't the dead of winter, I'd just do a piece about somewhere in Arkansas—like this lake." She peeked through a window and caught a glimpse of the usually serene surface white-capping in the wind. Lightning flashed, illuminating the sprawling waters.

"Pen-nie," Cal scolded.

"You got a better idea?"

"Duh! Use the ticket. He told you to keep it."

"I don't know, Cal." Her gaze returned to the desk, locking in on a thick envelope tucked beneath the ring box.

"If anyone deserves a trip to Hawaii, you do! Especially after what he—"

"Please. Don't go there." Pennie sucked in a deep breath. A water droplet plopped on her head. "Just a sec. Gotta get another bucket."

She grabbed a blue mop bucket from under the sink. After positioning the container beneath the newest drip, Pennie plopped in her chair and retrieved the phone. "I'm back."

"What did the roofer say?"

"You don't want to know. A bunch of blah, blah, blah about the skyrocketing cost of materials, attempting to justify his ginormous bid."

"You should go. Greg and I can watch the cabin."

"I don't feel right spending Jared's money now that ... now that we're no longer a couple." There. She'd said it. If only those were magic words and could make three months of pain disappear.

"The money's already spent. That package is nonrefundable, remember?"

"It was supposed to be our honeymoon trip." The puddle of tears welling within Pennie's eyes threatened to compete against the rainwater droplets seeping through the roof. She brushed them aside with the sleeve of her flannel shirt. "Besides, it's almost Christmas." The word hovered in the air like a hawk.

"Think about it." The phone amplified Callie's sigh. "What

advice would Pennie give if someone asked her whether or not to use an all-expenses-paid gift package to Hawaii?"

Pennie knew the answer. "She'd say go for it." Her voice's tone slid downward like a sad trombone.

"Exactly. You need to get out and enjoy the holidays instead of moping around the house." Callie had graciously left off the word *alone.*

"If I can't figure out how to get these repairs done, I won't *have* a house. And I can't do that to Dottie. Not after everything she did for me."

"Oh, Pennie." Compassion filled Callie's voice.

The rain had died down to a drizzle, but a howling wind continued, whistling through the crumbling chinking and slapping branches against the back wall. *Add tree-trimming to my list of things I can't afford.*

An insistent knock rattled the front door. "Someone's here. I'll call you back."

Pennie zigzagged around a trio of buckets like a car swerving between racing cones, wondering what urgent matter compelled the knocker to brave this weather. She paused to catch her breath after maneuvering across the room, then grasped the cast iron door pull and yanked.

"Mrs. Gul—Mrs. Gulliver." She sputtered the words, stopping herself short of calling the Lakeshore Homeowners Society president Mrs. Gulch, even though the woman resembled, in both appearance and attitude, the neighbor who had tormented Dorothy and Toto in *The Wizard of Oz.* "What can I do for you?"

Without an invitation to enter, Mrs. Gulliver pushed past Pennie and crossed the threshold. "For starters," she waved her hand toward the collection of containers, "you can get your roof repaired." She cleared her throat. "In fact, I have a list of repairs you'll need to have done on this ... shack."

Pennie pointed to her desk. "I know. I've received a number of bids."

"*Bids* won't save this dilapidated structure. It's an eyesore in our community, young lady."

The tone of her words, "young lady," sounded eerily close to the Wicked Witch of the West's pet phrase, "My Little Pretty."

Before Pennie could respond, Mrs. Gulliver thrust a piece of paper toward her. "Here it is. Signed by all the officers."

"Here *what* is?"

"A 30-day notice. If the repairs listed in this letter aren't in progress within 30 days, the Society will be forced to take measures toward having your ..." She paused and formed a menacing expression, apparently searching for the right term, "... *home* condemned."

"C-condemned?" Pennie choked out the word.

"Condemned." She emphasized the word with a smug nod. "Good day, Miss Vaughn."

Pennie closed the door behind Mrs. Gulliver-Gulch's retreating figure, punched Callie's number into her phone, and beelined to Dottie's old rocker for refuge. She sat with a huff and yelped when an alarming *crack* from beneath her sounded just as Callie answered.

"Hey, Pen—you okay?"

"I broke Dottie's chair."

The rocker now listed drunkenly on a shattered leg. That was it. There was no chance of halting the free-flowing tears at this point. "I want you to list the cabin," Pennie sobbed. "I'd rather sell it than watch it collapse around me." Through tear-blurred vision, she read the Society's notice to Callie.

"You want Greg to have some of his subcontractors take a look? He might be able to work out something cheaper than the bids you got."

Pennie sucked in a deep breath. "You know I don't like calling in favors."

"Stop being so hard-headed! This isn't the end of the world. The letter said the work must be 'in progress,' right?"

"Uh-huh."

"I'll talk to Greg. You go enjoy your trip, write your blog post, and win the contest. We'll take care of your place while you're gone."

"I'll think about it."

"And I'll pray about it."

"You pray. I'll think."

Pennie pushed the disconnect icon and reached for the velvet-covered case. She opened the lid slowly, as if its contents held more horror than that of Pandora's Box.

And for her, it did.

❧❧❧❧ ✦🎋✦ ❧❧❧❧

THREE DAYS LATER, Pennie followed her fellow passengers through Daniel K. Inouye International Airport's open-air walkway leading from the gate to the baggage claim area. A floral scent wafted through the air. Plumeria, she remembered from her impromptu crash course of what first-time visitors to Oahu should expect.

She stood, mesmerized by the sea of baggage floating across the conveyor belt, when a series of unexpected and unwelcomed thoughts flooded her mind. Jared should be standing next to her. She should be giddy with delight, a bride on her honeymoon. Tears fuzzed her vision, transforming the stream of colorful suitcases into a blurry blob.

Pennie dabbed her eyes. After a few blinks, she recognized her bag and yanked it toward the edge of the conveyor. One of the wheels caught on the carousel's side, and she tugged hard to free it. A loud pop echoed. She flew one way and the wheel flew the other.

"Woah there, little lady," a voice boomed behind her as a pair of arms balanced her. "You okay?"

She steadied herself and nodded, realizing her rescuer was a soldier. "Th-thanks." Pennie pointed to his uniform. "And thanks for your service."

"My pleasure." He gave a slight bow. "You here on vacation?"

"A sort of working vacation, yes."

"If it's your first time in Hawaii, I can give you a tour." The young man winked.

Pennie wondered if crashing her rear on the floor would have been a better option than being rescued. "Um. Thanks, but I'm good."

He chuckled. "I bet you are."

Heat rose up Pennie's neck. "I have to go." She spun away from him and jerked her hobbled luggage to an upright position, wishing she'd trimmed her packing list.

Pennie drug the suitcase behind her. Each *whump-whump* of the lopsided bag grated against her already frazzled nerves. After scanning the area for one of those luggage cart rental racks and finding none, she hoisted the crippled case in her arms, balancing it along with her purse, laptop case, and backpack, and waddled toward the rental car counter.

By the time she neared the area, she was huffing from hauling her bulging bag. Pennie set the suitcase down to catch her breath and noticed a man at the counter accepting a set of keys from the clerk. He brushed his hand through a head full of short-cropped curls dark enough to contrast with his well-tanned skin and rushed through the exit.

Jared?

2

When turning onto a one-way street in a city unfamiliar to you, take a moment to note which direction is the correct way.

~ Pennie's travel tip No. 59

Jared Ellison stepped into the elevator and punched the highest number. Music seeped into the small space from an overhead speaker. He recognized the tune. "What's it all about, Alfie?" One his mother often sang. Before ...

He pushed the thought away. Focusing on things he couldn't change wasn't productive. But the lyrics flowing from Dionne Warwick's smooth-as-honey voice haunted him. Did life truly belong to the strong, or was there something much more? The elevator's ding startled him. The doors opened, and he stepped onto the corridor's plush carpet, leaving the lyrics and his nagging memories behind.

A local woman wearing a bright floral *muumuu* stood from behind the reception counter, her tanned face etched with concern. "Mr. Jared. We weren't expecting you."

"I didn't expect to be here, Leilani, but I was summoned." He winked and gave a slight nod toward a set of double doors. "Is she in?"

"Yes. And she's ..."

The two leaned their heads close together and completed the sentence in whispered unison, "In. A. Mood."

Leilani laughed. "It's good to have you here."

"It's good to be here." He offered a warm smile. "I'll let myself in."

As Jared entered the office, he was immediately shushed by a woman pressing a phone receiver against her ear. She wore her blond hair pulled into a bun as severe as her scowl. He sighed. *It's good to see you again too, Kathleen.*

Thick draperies covered floor-to-ceiling windows of the corner executive suite, and Christmas music drifted through the speakers of the sprawling office. He moved across the room and opened the curtains, which drew an irritated glare from the woman. Jared marveled at the Pacific Ocean waves breaking gently along Waikiki Beach.

Turning from the ocean view, he hummed while he waited, noting the recent upgrades to the office, which included a massive koa wood desk.

"How much did that set us back?" He tapped a finger on the edge of the desk as Kathleen ended the call.

Exasperation flooded her face. "I didn't send for you to discuss trivial matters." She sucked in a breath and blew it out. "We're about to lose the Tanaka account."

"We?" He seated himself in a large leather armchair.

"Okay, *I'm* about to lose the Tanaka account. There. Does that make you happy?"

"No, Kathleen. It does not make me happy. If it did, I wouldn't have flown across multiple time zones when you said you needed my help."

Her features relaxed but stopped short of softening. "Thanks for coming."

He gave a half-nod. "Tanaka. Isn't your condo in that building?"

"Yes."

"Hmm. So, if you lose the account—"

"I'd have to move. I'd be ... *homeless.*" She spat the word, her voice tinged with disgust.

Jared opted to spare her a lecture on what constituted actual homelessness. For Kathleen Rutherford, the move would be a minor inconvenience until she could relocate to a perhaps even more luxurious location.

"He owns the Windward Coast Resort too."

"The place where I'm staying?"

"Yes. And three more properties. So, you see how vital it is that we save this account."

Again with the *we.* "And by *we,* this time you mean me."

Pride muddled the plea in her eyes. "Have you seen Father lately?"

"Changing the subject?" He reached for a gold-wrapped chocolate from a crystal dish on the desk's corner. "We still have dinner every month. I'm sure he would have sent his love had I told him I was coming."

"I'm meeting Mr. Tanaka at the resort restaurant at 6:30 p.m. I was hoping you could join us." She reached for her hair as if to brush away an errant lock but touched nothing. Every strand of perfectly styled platinum remained in place. "Look, Jared ..."

He peeled the foil from the candy and popped it in his mouth. "It's okay. I'll schmooze with your client. Besides, I'd blocked off this week for travel anyway."

Relief washed over her face, then changed to realization. "Your wedding. This was to be your honeymoon week."

The breakup had seemed logical at the time, with Pennie's sentimental hold on a lake house one leak away from demolition and him climbing the proverbial ladder of success. But now, the elevator song replayed in his mind, piercing his conscious.

He met his stepsister's probing eyes. "Yeah."

>>>>> ❀ <<<<<

PENNIE PILED her assortment of bags against the rental car counter and met the clerk's gaze. "I'm here to pick up a car." She retrieved the envelope from her purse and shuffled through some papers. "Ah, here it is."

The man barely glanced at the page. "Too late, lady. That vehicle's gone."

"Gone? How could that—"

"The customer who just left got it." He jerked a thumb toward the door.

So that *was* Jared. A flash of worry flooded her mind. If he'd picked up their rental, would he use the lodging voucher too? Pennie forced herself to remain calm. "Could I rent something else, please?"

"How many days?"

"I'll be here a week."

"So, seven days." His fingers moved quickly across the keyboard. "I have one left that's available for the full week." He quoted the rate.

Pennie gasped. "I-I can't afford that. Isn't there something cheaper?"

"Sure." He grinned and pointed to a row of cabs lined up outside.

His phone buzzed, and the young man gave a just-a-sec gesture. "One moment." He disappeared through a door behind him and returned within a few minutes, his attitude humbler. "My apologies, Miss." He handed her a fob embedded with the Lexus logo. "If you'll exit through the glass doors, Kaholo, our shuttle driver, will take you to your car."

A Lexus? She could probably roof the entire cabin for that price. "But I—"

"No worries. It's been taken care of—charged to Mr. Ellison's corporate account."

She thanked the clerk, took the key, and left in search of Kaholo, wondering how she'd ever pay Jared back.

A middle-aged local man wearing an aloha shirt, khaki shorts, and flip-flops rushed to help her with her bags. As he loaded her luggage into the back of a golf cart, his wide grin accentuated the sun-browned creases in his face. "Aloha! Welcome to Hawai'i."

She noted he pronounced the *W* as a *V*. "Thank you."

"*Mahalo.*"

"I beg your pardon?"

"It's how da locals say, 'thank you.'"

Good to know. Pennie remembered seeing the word on a garbage receptacle in the airport and thought it meant trash. "Mahalo!"

He pointed to the front passenger seat, "You sit here."

After climbing in the cart, he flashed another smile. "Got put tahp on truck. Gwan rain, ya."

"Could you repeat that, please?"

"Gwan rain." He pointed to the thick low-lying clouds and retrieved a tarp from behind the seat.

Ah, tarp. Rain. "Th-thank you," she stuttered, realizing her speech likely sounded as strange to him as his did to her. Being from Arkansas, she'd endured more than a few remarks about her Southern drawl.

After Kaholo covered her bags, he hoisted himself into the driver's seat. "How you like Hawai'i?"

Pennie breathed in a lungful of Plumeria-tinted air. "It smells good here."

"Wat da mainland smell like?"

She shrugged and laughed. "I never really thought about it."

"You need directions to hotel?"

"I'm not sure." She read him the resort's address.

"On da Windward side, ya?" He gave a low whistle. "Dat place too rich for my blood."

"Mine too. This trip was a ... a gift."

Kaholo nodded and rattled off a string of directions that made little sense to her. "Where else you go when here?"

Pennie browsed the itinerary. "A luau. Pearl Harbor. Diamond Head."

"Tourist." He gave a good-natured laugh. "You need see more den dat. Go Pali Lookout. High cliff. Big wind. Great view. Jes' don't jump."

"Don't jump?" Her life might be in a bit of a slump, but she'd never consider jumping off a cliff. She shuddered.

"Every so often some lolo throw some da kine into da wind tunnel to check for luck," Kaholo laughed. "Like the old saying, 'If you let something go and it comes back, it was meant to be.' But some say you jump, and wind bring you back, dat good luck. But wind won't bring you back." He shook his head. "Don't jump."

Pennie smiled. "Got it. I promise I won't jump. Thanks, er, mahalo, for the tip."

After he loaded her luggage, large droplets let loose from the sky. Pennie gave Kaholo a modest tip and drove in the direction he'd pointed just before she ducked into the car. Dozens of tall buildings breezed by as she maneuvered through the traffic. As soon as she passed by an exit marked Likelike Highway, Pennie realized that was the road Kaholo had told her to take. She'd been looking for a sign that said, "Leaky Leaky."

A short while later, she found herself in a maze of traffic, compounded by the myriad of one-way streets, bicyclists, and a steady stream of pedestrians, scurrying to get out of the rain. Panic edged up Pennie's throat when she realized she was driving into oncoming traffic. She'd gone the wrong way. Three cars stopped, allowing her to make an illegal U-turn, retrace her path, and search for her exit. Again.

When she emerged from the Likelike tunnel, the transformation was as dramatic as when Dorothy fell asleep in Kansas and awoke in the Land of Oz. Lush green mountains rose to her left, and the Pacific Ocean sprawled before her. Wispy clouds hung low on the ridged mountainside, and water trickled between their crevices. She sucked in a deep breath and suddenly understood the meaning of "breathtaking."

After locating the resort and checking in, she discovered she'd been booked in a three-room suite with a lanai overlooking Kaneohe Bay. A twinge of guilt moved through her at the realization this trip's cost could have covered Dottie's cabin's repairs. *Dottie.* She sighed. The woman had been her rock after her parents were killed during her early teens.

Dottie's days with cancer invaded Pennie's thoughts as she unpacked. She hoped she'd done right for her foster mom—caring for the cabin, reading her favorite books during the long hours at the infusion center. She'd even attended church with Dottie until she was too weak to go. But now, her final promise was on the verge of breaking.

Focus, Pennie. She'd force herself to take it all in while she was here. The sites. The climate. The culture. The food. All of it. Then she'd write the best blog post of her career and win. She'd do it for Dottie.

A yawn stretched her mouth, followed quickly by a loud growl from her stomach. The bedside clock read 5:45 p.m., but her body clock screamed, "go to bed!" Hating to waste her first full evening in paradise, Pennie selected a bright-colored sundress with in-seam pockets and headed toward the shower. After freshening up, she'd go downstairs and see what the resort's restaurant served for dinner.

3

When ordering from a five-star restaurant, make sure you don't judge the chef's offerings with a two-star palate.

~ Pennie's travel tip No. 42

Jared angled his chair to watch the gentle surf ripple onto the beach. The large reef-protected bay offered a stark contrast to the three-story pipeline waves crashing against the North Shore. Red and green lights twinkled in the palm trees lining the property, a gentle reminder that it was still Christmastime even in this tropical climate.

He felt a hand on his shoulder as Kathleen leaned in for him to kiss her cheek. Jared stood to perform the expected task.

She glanced over her shoulder. A smile breached her perpetual scowl.

"What?"

"I'll tell you later. I'm famished. Have you ordered yet?"

"I thought it best to wait on you. And our guest." He questioned her by raising an eyebrow.

"Ah, that. I'm not sure he's coming."

"He called you?"

"Actually, he never returned my call to confirm." She expelled a sigh.

Jared bit back his thoughts. Room service and reading a book in bed would have been an ideal way to spend an evening after a long day of travel. But instead, he sat with an unpleasant companion waiting on a no-show client.

The soft strains of "O Come All Ye Faithful" sounded through the speakers. Before the last note's resonation ended, Frank De Lima's voice broke into his trademark holiday song, "A Filipino Christmas." Jared's laugh temporarily drowned out the tune. "I know the local radio stations play this song a gazillion times during the holidays, but I haven't heard it in years."

"*That* can hardly be classified as a song," Kathleen muttered as she perused the menu.

Refusing to allow her mood to infringe upon his, Jared "*arf arf arfed*" along during the dog barking portion. "Come on, bawk with him," he urged as De Lima mimicked a flock of chickens.

Kathleen lowered her menu and glared over it. "I'm more concerned with Frank *Tanaka* than Frank *De Lima*."

"Ah, yes. Tanaka-san. Tell me the situation."

In between interruptions from the server, she explained the strained relationship with their most lucrative client. "Things were going fine until he handed over the account for his grandson to manage."

"Have you met him? The grandson?"

She paused to sip her water. "I would have, had he shown up for our dinner appointment."

Jared leaned back in his chair and stifled a yawn. "If he never confirmed, then you never had an appointment." He cut into his *mahi-mahi* fillet and savored a bite. "You can't get this in Arkansas."

"Then move back to Hawaii. I need you."

"No. What you *need* is to start treating clients like people instead of accounts." He could tell by her slight gasp that his words stung, but the truth often did.

"Fine, then." She twirled a spoonful of pasta and paused. "While we're playing the honesty game, I want to let you know how pleased I am that you finally came to your senses and dumped that peasant you were dating."

Jared set his fork down harder than necessary and bore his gaze into hers. "I'll not have you talk about Pennie that way. She's better than either of us will ever be."

"And yet you broke up with her?"

Despite the long day of travel with little food and the succulent entrée before him, Jared's appetite vanished. "For her sake. All this go-go, do-do lifestyle leaves me little time to work on our relationship." He emptied his water glass. "And relationships take *work*, Kathleen. They don't just magically sail smoothly along without any effort."

"Point taken." She stabbed a grape tomato with her fork.

"In fact, I'm wondering if this is even the life for me. If it's worth it."

"What do you mean?"

He sighed. "It's almost as though one has to choose between money and happiness."

"Money doesn't make you happy?"

"Does it make *you* happy?" He could see the answer in her eyes. "You know what makes—made—me happy? Pennie." His throat clenched, and he cleared it. "I should have never let her go."

Kathleen dabbed the corner of her mouth. "Well, whatever you said to break it off with her didn't work very well."

Jared held his water glass for the server to refill before turning his attention back to his stepsister. "What do you mean?"

"Do you remember that ridiculous song Father used to sing to us, 'The Cat Came Back' or some such thing?"

"Yes." He felt his patience growing thin.

She paused to squeeze some lemon into her water. "Well, you're having as much luck getting rid of that woman as the farmer had with that cat, because she's here."

"What? She's here?" Realization flooded him. The package. Had Pennie used their honeymoon trip package?

"You remember when I first arrived at the table, and you asked me why I was smiling? You had your back to me, but I saw her enter the restaurant as I came in. When you greeted me with a kiss, she ran out of here as if the fire alarm had sounded."

Jared scooted his chair back and stood. "And you let me stay here this entire time? Why, you—" He left his thoughts unspoken and rushed toward the exit.

"No worries. I'll get the check!" Kathleen followed the words with a sarcastic laugh.

❧❧❧❧ 🍬 ❧❧❧❧

PENNIE LET the waves wash over her feet, ignoring the sloshy sand between her toes as the chilly water covered her sandals. She clutched the box she'd tucked in her dress pocket and ran her fingers over the smooth velvet covering. Tears streamed down her cheeks. How could he? Jared had broken off their engagement, snuck off to Hawaii with another woman, and told her to use the vacation he'd paid for. Why? To taunt her?

Sobs came so heavy she could barely breathe. Without thinking, she jerked the box from her pocket, thrust it into the ocean, and then collapsed onto the beach. A moment later, she felt a soft thud against her foot. The ring box. Returned to her by the sea. Kaholo's voice echoed in her thoughts as she recalled him quoting the old saying about something you'd let go coming back to you.

But this was different. Pennie hadn't let the box go. She'd purposefully heaved it into the bay. She flipped open the box. The setting sun glinted off a diamond large enough to bring a pretty price if she were to sell it. Probably not enough to get her out of trouble with Mrs. Gulliver-Gulch, but it would be a start. She wiped the sand from the cover and tucked it back into her pocket.

She stood and spun around without looking, bumping against something solid. Taking a step back, she looked up at the handsome features of a Japanese man. He gripped her shoulders to steady her.

"Are you okay, Miss? I noticed you looked distraught, so I jogged over here to see if you needed assistance."

"I-I'm okay. I didn't hear you approaching."

"You need to be careful out here alone. It's getting dark."

Hopefully this man was truly a Good Samaritan and not the type of person he was cautioning her about. "Thank you. I think I'm fine now."

"You staying here?" He gave a slight head nod toward the resort.

She nodded.

"Can I buy you a drink? Or dinner? Have you eaten yet?"

Her hunger abandoned her when she saw Jared kiss the platinum blond in the restaurant. Were they still there? Perhaps room service was a better option.

The man didn't wait for her to decide. "Come on. Let's get you something to eat." He placed his arm gently around her waist and led her toward the hotel. "Have you ever tried *Unagi*?"

Pennie shook her head. "What's that?"

"Freshwater eel. I've heard the resort's chef makes the best on the island."

Pennie shuddered.

"Cold?"

"Um, no, but—" *I wonder if the chef makes the best burger?*

"Ah. Not a fan of eel? Hmm. How you Americans call fish with potatoes? Fish and chips?"

She gave a slight giggle. "That's what the British call it, but I do like fish." A memory of Dottie's golden fried catfish with a side of spicy fries poked at her appetite. Pennie could almost taste the crisp cornbread batter. She really should eat something.

Motion to her right caught her attention. A figure was running toward them. Taller than the man walking beside her. Tall. Dark. Handsome. As she blinked away the last remnants of her tears, his face came into focus. Jared.

When Jared reached them, he pulled Pennie away from her escort's grasp. He spun her to face him. "Are you okay? Why didn't you tell me you were coming to Hawaii? Who is this man?" His pointing finger punctuated the last four words.

Jared shot out the trio of questions in rapid succession. Pennie had a few questions of her own, but she'd not spout them in public.

The man stepped between them and returned his hand to the small of Pennie's back in a possessive manner. "I don't know the answer to your first two questions, but I can respond to the last one. My name is Frank Tanaka the Third, and I own this resort." He gave a slight bow and ushered Pennie toward the restaurant.

4

If you're planning an island tour in an open-air vehicle, braid your hair. Movies often portray windblown hair as romantic. In reality, wind transforms hair into an impossibly matted mess that can abrade your corneas, or worse, stick to your lip gloss.

~ Pennie's travel tip No. 36

"You what?" Kathleen's voice was pitched somewhere between a sob and a scream. She paced back and forth in her high-rise office. "I may as well schedule a moving service."

"It's not like I assaulted him or anything. I simply removed Pennie from his grasp." But he'd love to have a 'gentleman's discussion' with the billionaire. "I didn't know who he was, and I didn't know she was here until you told me."

"I thought you were over her." Kathleen paced along the bank of windows lining the wall. Twenty-five stories below, the morning sunbeams skittered atop the waves.

Jared reached for her arm to halt the incessant strides. "Have you never been in love?"

Her face blanched, and her bottom lip quivered.

A wave of compassion surged through him. He released her arm. "So, you get it. You understand."

Kathleen gave a slow nod.

Jared gazed at his stepsister. "Is that it? Is that why you've thrown yourself body and soul into your career?"

"Enough about me." She sucked in a deep breath, blew it out, and returned to her desk. "You obviously still have feelings for this woman. I never pegged you as one to let emotions lead your actions."

"I guess we both have a lot to learn about each other," Jared said softly.

Kathleen dismissed the thought with a wave of her hand. "The point is, now Frank Tanaka is offended. We must devise a plan to return to his good graces."

"Were we ever *in* his good graces?" He chuckled.

"It's a figure of speech." She tapped her pen against the desk for a moment, and her eyes took on a playful gleam. "We give him what he wants."

"What? If you're talking about Pennie—"

She held up a hand. "Hear me out, brother."

The something-close-to-a-smile that crossed her lips reminded Jared of the Grinch plotting to steal Christmas.

"Tanaka's never been to Oahu. I checked," Kathleen continued. "He asked your ex to dinner, also a first-time visitor."

"Pennie," Jared corrected.

"Whatever." She waved another dismissive gesture. "Why don't you take my Jeep and give them both an island tour?"

"You want me to chauffeur Tanaka and Pennie on ... on a *date*?" He was on his feet in an instant. "Forget it."

"You promised to schmooze the client."

"Yeah, but—"

"And you're the one who, well, who further complicated the matter." Kathleen punched the intercom button. "Leilani, contact Mr. Frank Tanaka at the Windward Coast Resort and let him know if it's convenient with his schedule, Jared will be escorting him and Miss Vaughn on a Jeep tour today." She paused for a moment. "He can pick them up in one hour."

"Better hurry." She tossed her keys toward Jared. "Rush-hour traffic will hit soon."

❧❧❧ ✿ ❧❧❧

PENNIE PADDED across the thick carpet. She could almost hear Dottie's voice echoing in her head about the horrors of walking barefoot in a hotel. Of course, she doubted Dottie ever stayed in such a swanky place as this. She pushed back the curtain, moved onto the lanai, and punched Callie's number into her phone.

After summarizing yesterday's activities, Pennie paused to catch her breath.

"And he owns the resort where you're staying?" Callie asked.

"He said he did. The staff treated him like royalty when we walked in, so yeah, probably."

"Wow. But you don't need to move from one too-busy-for-you boyfriend to another." She used her I'm-only-looking-out-for-you voice. "Especially one who lives halfway across the planet."

"He's not my boyfriend. I may not even see him again. In fact, when I told him I was exhausted and didn't want to go to the restaurant, he had food sent to my room. He was just being nice and taking care of one of his guests."

Callie said, "Uh-huh," but her tone said, *Yeah, right.*

"Anyway, I couldn't eat the food he sent."

"What was it?"

"Some sort of baked fish on a bed of sliced potatoes and onions. Red snapper, I think the server said."

"Sounds delish. You didn't eat it? Were you feeling sick?"

"Uh-uh. The fish was ... it was *looking* at me!"

Pennie waited for her friend to stop choking on a cackle and catch her breath. Then she turned serious. "So, Cal, what do you think about the ocean returning the ring to me? Does that mean anything?"

"It means the ring box didn't weigh enough to sink, and the tide was coming in. Don't take stock in superstitions, Pen. But if you're worried about it, pray."

Pray. Callie's answer to everything. Pennie reached into her tote and closed her hand around the ring box. "Okay. Maybe I will."

"Good. It helps." Callie's voice sounded reassuring. "So, what's on your agenda today? Going to play tourist and work on that article?"

Before Pennie could answer, someone knocked on her door. "That's weird. Someone's here. Just a sec."

She peeped through the hole and saw Jared. "I'll talk to you later, Cal." Pennie abruptly ended the call. Her heart fluttered as she turned the knob and held the door open a few inches. "Yes?"

"Sleep well?"

Pennie could feel the nervousness oozing out of him. "Yes. Did you?" She wanted to question him about the blond but reminded herself that his personal life was no longer her business nor her concern.

Jared gave a quick nod. "About last night. At the restaurant."

Apparently, her facial expression betrayed her thoughts.

She'd never make it as a poker player. "You don't have to explain. We're not engaged anymore. You're a free man."

"It's not like that—"

"Then what *is* it like, Jared?" She spat his name. "You break up with me because supposedly you love me too much to tie me down to someone who's too busy without even asking how I felt about it. Then, you insist that I take this pre-paid trip, knowing I'd do it because I'd feel guilty about wasting money you spent if the vacation package wasn't used. And when I finally do decide to go, I discover you've already snuck over here with another woman *and* brought her to the same place you knew I'd be staying?" She was babbling. She hated when she babbled.

"Pennie—"

"Don't 'Pennie' me."

She tried to slam the door, but he caught it and moved inside a few steps, closing the door behind him.

"Kathleen is my sister. My business partner. You've heard me speak of her."

Pennie cocked her head to the side and studied him. "Your sister?"

"Well, technically step. My mom married her dad after my father ... after my father died."

Her heart sank. Greg had told her Jared's father committed suicide when they were teens. Jared had never spoken of his father to her. And now, her little tantrum brought up bad memories. "I'm so sorry," she whispered and plopped onto the couch.

"Don't be." He eased down to sit next to her. "You'd never met Kathleen and had no idea what she looked like."

"She's perfect."

"Um, that's not the word I'd use to describe her." He

laughed. "But, she actually sent me on a mission, and that's why I'm here so early."

He hadn't come to see her because he missed her, to kiss and make up, but because his stepsister sent him. Her heart flutter died down. "What's the mission?"

"Frank Tanaka, the guy you went to dinner with last night—"

"We didn't go to dinner. I went to my room."

He raised an eyebrow.

"Alone." She folded her arms across her chest. "He had food sent up for me, and I went to bed early. I was exhausted and ... upset."

"I'm sorry."

"It's okay. What about him?"

"He's one of our company's biggest clients, and Kathleen has somehow irritated him. She wants me to schmooze with him. Make him like me, so he'll like the company."

"That shouldn't be too hard. Everyone who meets you likes you."

He cleared his throat. "Thanks. But, if you'll recall, I had a little run-in with him on the beach."

Pennie giggled. "There was a bit of a testosterone surge."

"Ri-ight. So, now I have to fix things."

"How do you propose to do that?" She'd forgotten how much she missed Jared. His easy-going attitude. His fun spirit. His gorgeous eyes. And his smile, like the one he displayed now.

A nervous teenage boy look crossed his face, and he sucked in a deep breath. "You wanna go on a Jeep tour?"

"What?" Was Jared asking her on a date? She felt her insides go all tingly.

"A tour. Of the island." He fidgeted as if unsure what to say next. "Look, Pen. Kathleen needs this account. She messed things up when Mr. Tanaka turned things over to Frank, his grandson. And I haven't helped matters, even though smoothing the business relationship with him was the purpose of my trip here." He paused.

"And?"

"And, well, we need your help. Frank likes you. We, er, I was wondering—"

"Stop." Pennie held up a hand, hoping it blocked his view of the tears pooling in her eyes. She turned away from him. "You want me to smooth things over with your client so you can keep his big account for your business? The same business you dumped me for?"

"Oh, Pen ..." He put his hand on her shoulder.

"Don't you 'oh, Pen' me." She shrugged out of his grasp, jumped up, and stomped across the room. Flinging open the lanai doors, she leaned against the rail and stared at the waves slapping the sand. The surf in the bay below broke gently, but the break in her heart erupted with the force of a volcano.

Pennie considered marching back into the sitting area and giving Jared the what-for when a text popped up on her phone. Frank.

Can't wait for the Jeep tour. Ready to go?

～～～ ❄ ～～～

OTHER THAN SPENDING over an hour detangling her unbrushable web of what Dottie would have called a "rat's nest," the morning went better than Pennie expected. Frank was a little flirty. Jared was more than a little protective. And she, for the most part, tolerated the outing well, despite the awkward tension. She managed to get a little shopping done and shot over 200 photos. Choosing which ones to include in her article would be a tough task.

Now, she looked at the bright pink floral *muumuu* spread across the bed. It would contrast well with her hair, which she had coaxed in a chic loose braid. Of all the items on her itinerary, this evening's luau was the event she most looked forward to. She slipped the new dress over her head, fastened her Bohemian beaded sandals, checked her hair one more time, and headed to the lobby to meet her "dates."

5

Be aware that your bathroom-finder app requires cell service to function. If your phone is searching for a signal while you're searching for relief, it is perfectly acceptable to ask for help.

~ Pennie's travel tip No. 1

Jared pulled the Jeep into the event center parking lot, and their group eased toward the luau's entrance. He was glad he'd convinced Kathleen to join them, preventing an awkward three's-a-crowd evening with Frank and Pennie.

Pennie. She looked radiant this evening. He'd blown it this morning. Made her feel used. Yet, she was a trooper during their island tour outing. And today wasn't the first time he'd blown it. What was he thinking, breaking up with her? His mind raced, searching for a way to make it up to her. To show her how he really felt.

A pair of young Hawaiian women in traditional hula attire approached them and draped a lei around each of their necks. Jared noticed Kathleen looked annoyed at the gesture, while

Pennie immediately lifted hers to breathe in its fragrance. Her face lit up.

The greeters led them along a path overshadowed by a variety of thick tropical vegetation. After a few minutes, the trail opened into a large grassy meadow. Palm trees wrapped with Christmas lights edged the area. A massive tent stood across the field, and a bamboo-framed stage sat to the right with dozens of chairs aimed toward it. Using graceful hand gestures, the Hawaiian women motioned them toward the tent.

A row of men in white chef uniforms stood at attention behind a table filled with silver warming dishes. Jared and company followed their escorts to a table, and within minutes a similarly dressed woman approached carrying a tray of punch-filled coconut cups. A young man wearing a grass skirt and whale-bone anklets arrived bearing an assortment of appetizers.

Jared observed as Pennie made a few choices, her face like that of a curious child. She'd been reserved since they arrived. His mind warned him to give her some space, but his heart fought against that advice, longing to engage her in conversation and hoping to hear her laugh.

When several other groups had arrived, a middle-aged man stepped onto a small platform within the tent and picked up a handheld mic. "Aloha, and welcome to our luau!"

Applause broke out, mingled with several guests shouting, "Aloha."

He bowed, then explained the evening's agenda. After the appetizers, the group would play a series of lawn games, followed by a sing-along session, a traditional feast, and, at dusk, the show would begin, which included hula lessons.

Jared noticed Frank attempting to make small talk with Pennie, but she looked a thousand miles away. The businessman apparently gave up and turned his attention toward another young woman, who sat nearby with a table full of friends. It looked like a girls' night out, but Frank seemed oblivious. Within a few minutes, he'd scooted his chair up to their table, leaving Pennie alone with Kathleen. Both looked miserable. As Jared pondered what could be wrong with Pennie, one of the luau attendants stopped next to him and put a hand on his shoulder.

"You, sir, have been selected to lead a team in our first game. Please stand."

Jared glanced toward Pennie. She gave him a shy smile, and he responded with a grin.

The young man held a mic toward Jared. "Please tell everyone your name."

"Jared Ellison."

"Good to meet you, Jared. I'm Makani." He gave a slight bow, and the crowd responded with applause. "*Mahalo*," he said, before returning to Jared. "And Jared, are you from Hawai'i, or are you visiting?"

Jared cleared his throat. "I lived here many years ago, but I'm here visiting for a few days." Pennie's full attention was on him, and although he'd never struggled much with stage fright, a sudden surge of butterflies invaded his gut.

"Very good. Then you may have heard of our traditional game, the hula skirt relay." Makani motioned to the young women who had greeted the guests. One pulled an elasticized hula skirt over Jared's head, and the other strung a pair of coconut cups around his neck. Both giggled as they stepped away.

Jared felt a blush creep up his neck. Pennie squelched a giggle behind the hand covering her mouth. Perfect. Maybe at least he'd have something to talk with her about when his period of public humiliation was over.

"And now, Alani and Malia," Makani gestured toward the

two women, "will dress the other team captain. You, sir." He pointed to Frank. "Please stand and introduce yourself."

Frank addressed the crowd with some blah-blah about visiting from Japan and mentioned his family's extensive holdings on the islands, but Jared noticed Pennie's attention remained on him. He pointed to the make-shift coconut bra and mouthed, "I can't believe this is happening."

She grinned and shrugged.

After Frank was "dressed," Makani instructed the entire group to move onto the lawn. As the guests scooted away from their tables and eased toward the grassy area, Alani and Malia worked the crowd, picking teammates for the two captains.

Jared noticed Malia approaching Pennie. A smile spread across the young woman's face as she led Pennie by the hand, placing her next to him.

"I think you two belong together." Malia winked at Jared and about-faced toward the other guests.

"Hey." He grinned at Pennie, wishing he could think of something more intelligent sounding, but that's all he could muster under the circumstances.

"Hey, yourself." She eyed the skirt and coconuts. "Nice outfit."

"Have you ever played this game?"

She shook her head.

"Watch and learn." He winked.

"And now, ladies and gentlemen," Makani began, "when the whistle blows, the team leaders will strip their grass skirt and coconut top and hand it to the next player. Each person must be completely 'dressed' before stripping off the outfit and passing it along. Our staff will monitor to make sure no team members are disqualified. Those of you who weren't selected to participate can choose a team to cheer for. Ready?" He pointed to a nearby man holding a whistle. "Go!"

As soon as the whistle blared, Jared slung the coconuts off his head and tossed them to Pennie. Then he shimmied out of the skirt and handed it to her. He was impressed with how quickly she donned and removed the hula garb. Both fell into a fit of giggles as they watched their teammates struggle.

One of the men on their team passed the coconuts to the next player without putting them on. Alani tapped him on the shoulder, shook her head, and made an ejection signal with her thumb. The man gave a shocked look and a who-me shrug, laughing as he seated himself among the rest of the crowd. Although the disqualification jeopardized their team's chances of winning, it produced more laughter from Pennie.

"It's good to hear you laugh," he spoke against her ear.

She smiled briefly and turned back to the game.

Frank's team won, and he gloated in the victory for a moment before walking over and high-fiving Jared. He turned to Pennie. "If all your team members were as skilled as you, your team would have fared much better." He bowed.

She returned his bow and smiled. "Thank you."

Next, the group gathered around a small bonfire and learned a few traditional Hawaiian songs, including the Christmas favorite, *"Mele Kalikimaka,"* made popular by Bing Crosby. Jared noticed Kathleen sitting apart from the group. She seemed content.

After stuffing themselves with generous portions of Kalua Pig and all the trimmings, the guests were led to the chairs aimed at the stage. Jared could feel the excitement among the group as anticipation grew for the evening's main event.

"I overheard one of the staff say we'd be paired off when the hula lessons start. May I be so bold as to ask you to be my dance partner?"

"Have you ever danced the hula?

Jared nodded. "It's been too long ago to count. But trust me, I'm no expert."

"That's disappointing. I was hoping you'd give me some tips." She offered him a fake pouty frown, which quickly converted into light laughter.

He followed close behind her as they headed toward the open-air theater and noted that Frank took a seat by Kathleen. Was he conceding? Even so, Jared hardly felt as though he'd "won." A twinge of guilt ran through him over thinking of Pennie as a prize to compete for.

But he felt no guilt observing her out here, enjoying God's creation and witnessing her childlike joy as she experienced new adventures. He noticed her face contort into a frown as she tapped her phone screen.

"Everything okay?"

"Ugh. No service." She leaned close to him and whispered, "Did you notice where the restrooms are located?"

Jared nodded. "They were to the left near the edge of the pathway we came through." He saw her cringe.

"The creepy one, with all the branches hanging over it?"

"Yeah. Come on. I'll walk with you."

"Thanks."

Placing his hand at the small of her back, he led her to a building near the clearing's edge. "I'll wait here."

A few minutes later, she returned. "Thanks for not making me walk over here by myself." She looked up at him and smiled.

He put his arm protectively around her shoulder, but instead of leading her back to the outdoor theater, he drew her a few feet off the path and pulled her close against his chest. Easing his hand from her shoulder to her face, he cupped her chin and brought his mouth down to hers. When their lips met, three months of missing her sprang forth from within him.

Although he'd kissed her before, this time was different. There was a rawness of emotions. A newness of purpose. Before, he'd held a barrier between them. In this moment, he bared his soul and offered his heart. Vulnerability mingled with hope as he deepened the kiss.

Pennie leaned into him and slipped her hand upward, behind his neck. His skin prickled at the touch of her fingers, and he curled his hand through her hair, bringing her as close as possible. Just when he thought he would burst from the emotions raging within him, she pushed away.

"No!" She slammed her palms against his chest and ran back to the audience.

Jared stood motionless, a wretched mess of guilt mingled with longing, as he watched her take a chair far from where they had been sitting. Instead of returning to the group, he slumped to the ground against a tree and watched as a pair of male hula dancers twirled fiery batons.

Like the dancers, he'd played with fire. But his thoughtlessness got him burned.

6

When traveling long distances, be aware that your body clock requires roughly 24-hours per time zone to adapt. It's normal to experience mood swings during the adjustment process. In fact, your temperament will likely range through that of all seven dwarves. At once.

~ Pennie's travel tip No. 27

Pennie scribbled over her last sentence. After re-reading what she'd written above the blacked-out scrawling, she shook her head, ripped the page off the notepad, wadded it, and tossed it on top of the trashcan now overflowing with crumpled papers. Her article was going nowhere.

She stared at the flimsy piece of cardboard in her hand that just an hour ago had backed a full pad of pages branded with the Windward Coast Resort logo. Now, it was empty. Wasted. Like the rest of her life.

Focus, Pennie! She stood and paced around the room. The aroma of plumeria permeated the sitting area. Glancing toward the source of the scent, she sighed. The bouquet had been delivered early that morning, with two simple words on the unsigned card. "I'm sorry."

Jared.

Had she overreacted? During their kiss, she'd whirled through a whole gamut of emotions—bashful, happy, dopey— all within a matter of seconds before settling on grumpy when she pushed him away.

The five-hour time difference between Hawaii and Arkansas was killing her. She needed to know what Greg learned about the cabin. Needed to get some inspiration for her unwritten article. Needed to process what happened with Jared. Needed her best friend. But by the time they returned to the resort last night, it was nearly 11 o'clock. Despite the late hour, she'd sent Callie a short text:

He kissed me.

No response. Not surprising, considering Callie was likely asleep at that hour. This morning, Callie was probably calculating when would be a good time to answer. Even though it was barely 8 a.m. here now, she could have called hours ago. Pennie hadn't slept. As if her thoughts had floated across the ocean and reached her friend, the phone rang.

"Callie! I'm so glad you called." The panic welled inside Pennie flowed through her voice.

"*Who* kissed you? The guy from Japan?"

The idea of Frank kissing her had never crossed Pennie's mind. "Um, no." She briefly relived the kiss, then gathered her thoughts. "Jared. Jared kissed me."

A low whistle came through the phone. "Girl, you've got some explaining to do. Spill."

"I will. But before I do, I want to know if Greg had a chance to walk through the cabin?"

Callie's silent pause wasn't a good sign. "Um, yeah. He did."

"And?"

Her sigh was worse than the silence. "It's bad, Pen. Worse than we thought."

"Worse than the estimates I already got?"

Another sigh. "Yeah. If you want it done right, we're talking serious money." She spouted a figure that made Pennie gasp.

Now it was Pennie's turn to alternate between silence and sighs. Finally, she spoke. "Sell it. The lot is worth something, right? Lakefront property and all." She could visualize the glee on Mrs. Gulliver-Gulch's face when the bulldozers arrived to level the place.

"Are you sure?"

Pennie brushed a tear aside. "List it now, please. There's no way I can pay for those repairs. Work your magic on the description like you always do. You have such a way with words, I should have you write my article."

"How's that going? Or should I ask?"

"You shouldn't." Pennie only half laughed. She tossed the cardboard backing on top of the other trash.

"It'll come to you. And it'll be great." Callie's voice, full of encouragement, was a welcome sound after the emotional rollercoaster Pennie had ridden the past few days.

"I'm serious about the cabin, though. I doubt it will sell before I come home next week, but I want you to list it. I'll give you power of attorney to handle the transaction if something crazy happens before I get back. Email me the documents, whatever I need to sign. If you need it notarized, I'm sure someone at the resort can help." She thought for a moment. "Or perhaps Jared's stepsister. I'm sure her office has a notary. I can have it scanned and emailed back to you ASAP." She paused. "Before I change my mind."

"You sure you don't want to wait until you get home?"

"No. I need this behind me. And be sure to give yourself full commission when you prepare the contract." She looked upward. *Forgive me, Dottie.* Pennie paused for a moment, then added *and God.*

Callie sighed. "Fine. I'll have one of my clerks get the property's legal description, and we'll get the paperwork drawn up before we leave today. Check your email after lunch your time. The documents should be there by then."

"Thanks, Callie." Pennie basked in the moment of relief that follows a major decision, knowing that the respite from her stress would soon be replaced by guilt and grief.

"No problem. Now," curiosity laced her voice, "tell me what's going on with you and Jared."

***

JARED PULLED his phone from its clip on the first ring. He sighed when he read the Caller ID. "Hey, Kathleen. What's up?"

"I was about to ask you the same thing." Her words carried her trademark smirk through the mobile device.

"Huh?"

"Don't play dumb, little brother. I'm talking about what happened with your little not-a-fiancée."

Had Kathleen *seen* him kiss Pennie? Had anyone?

"Jared? Are you there?"

"Uh, yeah." He paused to formulate his words. "About that—"

"Have you talked to her today?" she interrupted.

"Um, no. She said she had work to do today. I was trying to give her some space."

"As in *space* in your loft apartment?"

"What are you talking about? We didn't even live together when we were engaged." He wished she would get to the point.

"Ah, that's right. I forgot you're *old-fashioned*."

"You mean *Christian*."

"Whatever." She likely followed the word with a dismissive hand gesture, even though he couldn't see it.

"Cut to the chase. Why are you asking me about Pennie?" He sucked in a deep breath, hoping to quell the panic rising in his gut.

"You really don't know, do you?" Her smugness wafted through the phone.

"Apparently not."

"Well, she's listed her cabin, shack, whatever you want to call it, with a realtor. I guess the lot is worth something."

"She what?" As soon as the reaction left his mouth, he regretted letting his stepsister gloat that she'd obtained information he had no clue about. "Are you sure?" Kathleen didn't seem the type to become involved with petty gossip. But he knew what that cabin meant to Pennie.

"I'm sure, all right. That *work* she mentioned to you included an errand to my, er, *our* offices. She had Leilani notarize some paperwork for her. From Jorgensen's Realty in podunk Arkansas." She paused for a moment. "Jorgensen. That name seems familiar."

"That's her friend Callie's agency. Greg, Callie's husband, is one of my best friends. Since junior high."

"So, is that how the two of you met? Through this Jorgensen couple?"

Impatience swelled inside Jared. "Yes." He wondered at Kathleen's sudden interest in his and Pennie's history. "They set us up on a blind date. We doubled with them." And the attraction was instant.

"Ah. I think I remember something about that now."

He hated to give Kathleen more fodder for gloating, but he had to know. "Did she say why she was selling the property?" That cabin was more than a home to Pennie. It was Dottie personified.

"Well, I didn't intend to snoop, but she seemed distraught while she was speaking with Leilani, so I attempted to comfort her."

Jared couldn't imagine Kathleen *comforting* anyone. "And?"

"And in between sobs and sniffles, I gathered that the cost of repairs outweighed the structure's value. It will need to be demolished. It seems she cares nothing for the worth of the lot itself, just the cabin. Lakefront property can be a valuable investment." She paused for a moment. "I never understood sentimentality. It's not practical, and often, it's expensive."

The cabin represented more than a sentiment to Pennie. It represented someone who'd shown Pennie unconditional love. "Thanks for letting me know. I'd better get off here. I have another call to make. Have a pleasant afternoon."

"Thanks. I already have."

He shook his head as he ended the call and immediately punched in a number.

7

*Surfers range in expertise from novice to professional competitors.
It's advisable to have a clear understanding of where your
proficiency lies on this scale because many factors can injure or kill
ocean-sport participants, not the least of which is the ocean itself.*

~ Pennie's travel tip No. 92

The next morning, Pennie woke refreshed. Spending a day away from Jared hadn't eased her ache for him, but by the end of the evening, she'd made good progress on her article. Perhaps she'd given up too quickly, and there was still hope of winning the contest and saving the cabin. She'd discuss it with Callie later.

As she stood on the lanai, soaking in the beauty of the bay and surrounding mountains, her phone rang. She didn't recognize the number, but the device identified the number as being from Honolulu.

"Hello?"

"Good morning, Pennie," Kathleen's voice came across as bright, almost friendly.

"Good morning. Thanks for your help yesterday."

"That was no problem at all. However, I am hoping you can do a small favor for me today."

Jared had mentioned once how he scarcely asked anything of Kathleen because she had a penchant for keeping the favor score even.

Pennie hesitated to agree without knowing what she would be getting herself into. "What's the favor?"

"Before we get to that, I should ask if all went well? Your property is listed? And your article, is that progressing?"

So now they were besties. "Yes, on the property. I received a confirmation email this morning, and it's already displaying on the realtor's website." Guilt at giving up prematurely thumped her conscience, but she reminded herself she could always remove the listing. "And I had a breakthrough last night with the article's lead. It's so important to grab the reader in the first sentence. I'd struggled with that to the point of frustration. After getting the opening lined out, the rest of the words flowed quickly."

"Good. Good. I'm glad to hear things are going your way." The tone of her voice held a "but" behind it. "Unfortunately, I can't say the same about my business."

Here it comes. "I'm sorry." What else could she say?

"I'm sure it will work out as well as your problems have. But, I need your help."

There it was. The *but.* "How can I help you?"

Pennie had intended the question as more of a what-could-I-possibly-do-to-help-you inquiry, but Kathleen took the words literally.

"It concerns Frank Tanaka. He spent yesterday at the

resort's office complex, working on several projects. But today, he's ripe for another adventure."

Pennie didn't respond immediately, and Kathleen took the pause as an invitation to continue. "He'd mentioned a desire to give boogie boarding a try. I'd like you to take him."

"Boogie boarding." Pennie processed the words. Nothing about them appealed to her. In fact, an impending dread settled in as she considered what all boogie boarding would involve. Special clothing. Expensive equipment. Crashing waves. And, quite possibly, pain. "I've never done that sort of thing."

"Then it'll be a new experience for you as well." Her sentence ended with an uptick in her voice, as if she were pleased with herself at the concept of thrusting two beginning boogie boarders into the grip of the planet's most powerful waves.

"What is the safest place for beginners?"

Kathleen gave a half-laugh. "My apologies. I forget not everyone is familiar with the island. I'll have Jared drive you. He'll know where to go. Say, in an hour?"

One-hour warnings seemed to be Kathleen's mode of operation. Although the Pacific Ocean was certainly a force to be feared, and many careless lives had been lost in its depths, the warning signal blaring in her mind ignored the risk to life or limb—it warned of losing her heart. Again.

❧❧❧ ❀ ❧❧❧

If awkwardness were a steak, Jared would be slicing into one of those Texas-sized challenge cuts right now. Frank arrived at the Jeep, practically shouting into his phone in Japanese. Pennie showed up shortly afterward, looking cute in an aqua-colored wetsuit, with an expression that clearly stated, "I'd rather be anywhere else."

"Housekeeping brought this suit to my room. It is what I'm supposed to wear, right?" She looked back and forth between the two men, who were both wearing shorts, flip-flops, and aloha shirts.

Jared's voice caught in his throat. She looked amazing, the neoprene suit hugging her soft curves. "Yes. Yes, that's what you're supposed to wear. It looks ... you look ..."

"You look fabulous," Frank finished, covering his phone with one hand.

Perfect. He'd started the day with his foot in his mouth.

"But you two aren't wearing wetsuits."

Jared pointed to a pair of boxes in the back seat. "I had to grab these this morning from the surf shop a few miles away. We haven't had time to change yet. Yours was ... well, I had one in your size." *A present for our honeymoon.*

Pennie's expression told him she knew exactly why he already had a suit for her.

"I have tethered swim fins and socks for all of us too." Jared pointed to the rest of the gear.

Needing a distraction, he strapped two boogie boards to the rack and snugged the rope. Frank ended his call and pointed to the Jeep's hardtop. "Just two boards?"

Jared shrugged. "We can take turns."

"I volunteer to take pics and videos."Pennie offered a shy smile and dug a travel camera from her Hibiscus-themed tote.

Frank helped her into the back seat and reached across her to fasten her seatbelt.

"Thanks," she murmured.

Jared felt the heat rise within him but reminded himself that he was the one who'd broken up with her, leaving him no right to be jealous. And since he now needed to smooth things over with Frank for Kathleen's sake, he'd likely be biting his tongue all day.

When he was seated behind the wheel, he turned to Frank. "Since both of you are beginners, I think it would be best to head over to Waikiki. The waves are typically calm there."

Frank looked offended. "Where are the big waves? The Banzai?"

"On the North Shore. We can stop by there and watch if you want, but those are best left to the pros. Surfers, not boogie boarders."

"You're driving. Just go where you want, but I didn't come all the way from Japan to catch boring waves." His face contorted into a pout. A moment later, his expression brightened. "Oh, I know where to go."

"Where?" Jared was almost afraid to ask.

"Sandy Beach. That's a boogie boarding place, correct?"

"Yes, but again, that beach can be dangerous. The beginners—"

"Take us there. You said you would teach us the techniques."

Jared sucked in a sigh and headed toward *Kalaniana'ole* Highway, petitioning the Lord's protection with a silent prayer. He'd heard once you mastered riding a bicycle, it would always come back to you. He hoped the same held true for riding potentially deadly waves. Over a decade had passed since he'd been on a board.

An hour later, with the three of them decked in their gear, Jared helped Frank strap the bodyboard leash to his upper arm. At the water's edge, both men donned their fin socks and fins, attaching the tethers to their ankles. Jared performed a dry land demonstration on how to mount and hold the board.

Frank gave an eye-roll. "Can we get in the water already? People are staring at us."

"First, we'll walk out until the water is about knee-deep, then we'll paddle until we reach the breaking waves," Jared explained, looking back and forth between Pennie and Frank to make sure both understood.

"The next step is tricky and can be a bit scary for first-timers."

Pennie looked worried.

"It's called a duck dive maneuver."

Frank, who had been fidgeting with the leash's armband, looked up. "Duck dive?"

"It's how you'll get behind the wave. Basically, you grab the nose of the board and push downward until it's under the water while simultaneously pressing your knee on the board's tail. Next, take a deep breath and keep the board pointed down, then dive as deep as possible. Kick until the wave has passed over you and it's safe to surface." Jared pointed to a few boogie boarders nearing the waves. "Watch them."

The experienced wave catchers made the technique look simple.

"You know what," Pennie started, pulling her camera out, "I think I'm good right here on the beach."

Frank elbowed her playfully. "Aw, come on. I bet once you've tried it, you'll love it."

"You two go first. I'll watch."

Jared eyed Frank, who nodded.

"Once you're on the ocean side of the break, it's time to catch a wave. Start with a small one until you get the hang of it. When you spot a wave, turn your board toward the beach and kick hard. Keep your feet below the surface for better propulsion."

"And then?"

"When you crest the wave, ride it to the beach," Jared said. "If you need a bit more speed, you can push the board's nose down slightly, but be careful, or you could flip while you're on top of the wave."

"Sounds simple enough. Let's do this." Frank moved into the water.

Jared turned toward Pennie. "You'll be okay here?"

"Better than out there." She pointed toward the incoming surf.

"You don't have to go out there if you don't want to."

"I know." She nodded. "But I think I'd like to try it at least once. I mean, when in Rome ..."

The smile she gave melted his heart. "You know, Pennie ..."

She held up a hand. "It's okay, Jared." The tears welling in her eyes said otherwise, but she sucked in a breath and said, "Go on. Frank's waiting."

He nodded and hurried toward his client.

Frank caught on surprisingly fast. A few splashes and sputters, but for the most part, a casual observer wouldn't know it was his first attempt at the sport.

After the guys rode several waves in, Frank stepped out of the water and removed his swim fins. He ran over to Pennie. "You've got to try it. What a rush."

Jared lifted an eyebrow her way. She nodded.

"Great," he said. "Let's do this."

On her first try, she surfaced too quickly, and a small wave doused her harmlessly.

"Let's try again," Jared shouted over the surf.

Pennie nodded and paddled toward the waves. Just before she launched into her dive, Jared noticed the increased size of the breakers. He yelled for her to wait, but she'd already submerged.

"Dude, it's barreling! Gnarly!" A nearby voice yelled.

Jared watched the young surfer move into the whitecaps with experienced ease while he floated in place, waiting for Pennie. She surfaced in the midst of a swell, larger than most. He saw her arms flail helplessly as the board flung from under her. Then the grinder plummeted her to the ocean floor about twenty yards from him. He scanned the area where she went under. An eternity passed before he caught a glimpse of her neon wetsuit.

He struggled against the breaking tide, watching Pennie's body bob helplessly. With every stroke, the ocean fought against him. As Jared inched forward against the wall of water, the surf hurled him backward. Every breath burned his lungs. Salt water stung his eyes. His muscles ached. Still he swam, focusing on the elusive patch of turquoise.

Seconds transformed into hours. News reports he'd watched about boogie boarding mishaps flashed through his mind. Traumatic head injuries. Broken necks. Or worse.

Please, God. Keep her safe. Give me strength.

Adrenaline surged through his body as the distance between them shrank. Jared hooked his left arm around Pennie's shoulders and swam with his right. When his feet touched the ground, he hoisted her into his arms and fought against the swift undertow until he reached the shore.

A crowd had gathered. Jared could hear Frank screaming at the people to get back, but his voice sounded like a slow-motion echo. The movements of those nearby jerked forward like freeze-frames. He heard another voice yelling, "Call 9-1-1," and realized it was his own. Jared lay Pennie's motionless form on the soft sand. She wasn't breathing.

Jared rolled her onto her side and checked her mouth for any obstructions before taking in a lungful of air and pushing two breaths into her mouth. He followed up with a series of compressions and repeated the process. "Please, God. I can't lose her again." Time stood still. Far too much time had passed when he finally heard an ambulance's wail. Still, he continued breathing, pumping, praying.

8

The average Emergency Room wait time is 17,280 minutes, or roughly 12 days, so you may wish to bring along an ER waiting room activity bag to occupy your time.

~ Pennie's travel tip No. 74

Jared paced the length of the ER waiting room. He should have insisted they go to a safer beach. How could he have been so stupid to put Frank's wishes above his better judgment? He'd put his hope of saving the Tanaka account ahead of safety. Once again, he let Kathleen and the company influence his decisions. And now, Pennie's life hung in the balance.

He paused his pacing and sat, head in hands, praying. A Christmas song played in the background. He recognized the tune, "Fah Who Doraze," from *How the Grinch Stole Christmas.* Welcome, Christmas.

The scene played in his head as if he were watching it now. All the Whos in Whoville, circled, hand-in-hand, singing. His mind ping-ponged from the Grinch's question, "What if Christmas, perhaps, means a little bit more?" to a lyric that answered the "What's it all about, Alfie?" question he'd heard just days ago. Perhaps there *was* something much more. And suddenly, he *knew* what it was all about. The true meaning of Christmas. The meaning of life. They were one.

Love. Love was the answer.

"For God so loved the world that he gave his only begotten Son ..." God's Christmas gift to the world stemmed from love. And he'd found that love he missed, just like in the Alfie song. But he'd let her go. Tossed her away.

Now, if only she'd come back to him.

The waiting room doors opened, jerking Jared from his thoughts. Kathleen rushed to his side, followed closely by Frank Tanaka.

"Oh, Jared. I'm so sorry." Kathleen's voice held a sincerity he'd never heard from her before. "Frank called and told me what happened."

Frank. Jared had left him on the beach. "Frank. I'm—"

"No worries. You had far more important things on your mind than me." He looked at Kathleen. "Besides. Waiting for Kathleen to pick me up gave me time to think. And call my lawyer."

"Your lawyer?" Jared was confused.

"I asked him to draw up papers extending the property management with your company for another three years."

Kathleen's eyes widened. "I don't know what to say. Thank you, Frank."

Frank put a hand on Jared's shoulders. "Any family with a man as brave and loyal as you deserves my business."

"I appreciate that. And I know Kathleen does as well. But I must let you both know—I don't intend to remain with the family business. I want out."

"What?" Kathleen's voice squawked in a high-pitched squeal. She recovered quickly and lowered her voice. "I don't understand. Do you have plans for another position?"

Jared shook his head. "No plans. I just realized I've practically sold my soul to this company. If Pennie recovers …" He paused, the words choking in his throat. "*When* she recovers," he corrected, "I want to be with her. And if she needs … special assistance …" The possibility of brain damage was real with a near-drowning victim. He'd prayed about that too during his time of reflection. He cleared his throat. "No matter what, I want to be there for her."

"You really do love her," Kathleen said softly.

"I really do."

"Enough to relegate yourself to a mundane life?"

He looked intently at his stepsister. "I'm already living a mundane life. I want to be free from that."

"What will you do?" Frank asked.

Jared shrugged. "First and foremost, I'll take care of Pennie, regardless of her condition. Next, I'll see if my buddy Greg needs help. He's a contractor, and I can be pretty handy with building and fixing." He looked at Kathleen. "Will you buy me out?"

She nodded, wiping a tear. "Could you stay on as a consultant if needed?"

"Of course. But remember, I don't want to live on the go 24/7 anymore."

"I'm not sure I fully understand, but I'll have our attorney sort out the legalities."

"Thanks, sis." Jared pulled Kathleen into a hug.

"You are an honorable man, Jared Ellison." Tanaka bowed. "Now I know I want to trust my properties to your family's business. Even if you aren't directly involved."

The door leading to the treatment area opened, and a

young woman wearing scrubs motioned to them. "Miss Vaughn is awake, and she's asking for Jared."

He stepped toward her. "I'm Jared."

"Please follow me, sir."

❧❧❧❧ ❦ ❦❦❦❦

PENNIE'S EYES FLUTTERED OPEN. Above her, a bright light blurred her vision, and she blinked until she could better focus.

A nurse pulled the curtain back. Someone was with her. A man. Had the doctor returned? Pennie blinked her eyes again. "Jared?" She forced a smile.

"Hey, there." Worry etched his face. "They treating you okay here?" He gestured toward her temporary accommodations.

"Yeah. Well, I mean, I don't think I've been awake very long, but they've been great since I woke up."

Jared chuckled.

She lifted the edge of her hospital gown sleeve. "They cut off my wetsuit. I'm sorry. I think it's ruined."

"Don't worry about it. I'll get you another one. That is, if you want."

"I'll have to think about that." Pennie's half-giggle abruptly changed into a gasp. She wrapped her arms around a heart-shaped pillow and held it tightly against her chest.

"Are you okay?" He sat on the edge of the bed and brushed an errant curl from her face.

"Um-hmm. But I'm really sore, so the nurse gave me this pillow to hug. The doctor said I'd be fine. That I was lucky ... that if someone hadn't—"

Jared placed his finger against her lips. "Let's not think about that. The main thing is, you're okay." He kissed her hand and looked upward.

"Are you praying?"

He nodded. "I've been praying since you went under that wave."

"I prayed too." And she had. "When the water pulled me under, I didn't know which way was up or down. I was terrified, but after I asked God for help, I felt peace."

"Praying helps all the time. When you're scared. When you're happy. When you have a big decision to make."

"After everything went dark, I had a dream."

"What did you dream?"

"That you were kissing me. On the beach." She smiled. Then she scooted up in the bed with a groan and looked directly into his eyes. "And there were a lot of people watching."

He rubbed his thumb along her hand, sending tingles up her arm. "Are you sure it was a dream?" He winked.

Her eyes widened. "Did you kiss me? In front of everyone? While I was helpless and unconscious?"

Jared laughed out loud. "I would have loved to have kissed you on the beach, but I had to do CPR instead."

"So ... it wasn't a dream?" She settled back on the pillow, then sat up quickly, wincing at the pain. "*You* were the one. The one the doctor said acted fast and saved my life?"

He nodded. "I'm sorry if I hurt you."

"I'll be fine. Thanks for rescuing me."

"I'm just so grateful you're okay." A thoughtful expression filled his face. "I found something when you were unconscious."

"What?"

"I'm sorry to have snooped, but they needed your insurance card, so I looked in your bag." He reached inside his pocket and pulled out the black velvet box. "And I found this. Can I ask why you've been carrying it around?"

She looked away, suddenly feeling shy and embarrassed. "You can ask, but I'm not sure I'll answer."

His thumb made slow circles on the back of her left hand, then he moved to her ring finger. "Did you keep it with you because you want to wear it again?"

Tears pooled in her eyes, and she nodded.

"I want you to wear it again too." He opened the box and pulled out the ring. "That is, if you can forgive me for the way I treated you."

She looked at the large solitaire, glistening in the fluorescent light. "But what about what you said when you broke up with me?"

"I have put that business ahead of everything else in my life. God. You. Even my health. While I was in the waiting room, I had a talk with God about what life is all about, and I realized that love is the most important thing. Love for him. Love for you."

Pennie could feel the change in his attitude, his heart.

"I promised him I'd take care of you, no matter what." He choked back his emotions. "That is, if you'll have me. I can get down on one knee again if you want. That first time was for show, for the videographer to capture. This time, I'm asking you to be my wife from my heart."

He grabbed a tissue and wiped the tears from her eyes. "But you need to know this before you answer. I've asked Kathleen to buy my share of the company. I'll have to get a regular job. A job that will allow me to come home to you every evening instead of traveling all over the globe, wheeling and dealing. I plan to see if Greg needs some help."

"Oh, Jared. That is what I want. I don't need fancy stuff. I need you." She held up her hand, and he slipped the ring onto her finger.

Bending over the bed rail, he kissed her softly on the lips

and whispered, "This will have to do for now. I'm afraid if I kiss you the way I want to, that monitor will go nuts, and every nurse in the hospital will come running."

She blushed. "Okay, but you owe me. Don't forget!"

"Oh, I won't forget. Trust me." He gave her one more light kiss and stood. "Speaking of owing. You still owe me a hula dance. Remember?"

"Oh, yeah. That." She blushed again, remembering the way he kissed her at the luau.

"I have an idea. Why don't you rest for a bit and work on your article? Then, day after tomorrow, I'll take you on a sunset catamaran dinner cruise, complete with hula lessons if you're not too sore. Sound good?"

"Sounds perfect."

9

When selecting souvenirs, avoid those cheap, mass-produced dust-gatherers that the recipient has no idea what to do with. Instead, search for something meaningful. Yes, the thought does count, but it helps if the gift itself counts too.

~ Pennie's travel tip No. 49

Pennie fidgeted when the phone rang a third time. *Pick up, Callie.* She couldn't wait to tell her friend the news. Not only had she finished her article—and it sounded awesome if she did say so herself—she was engaged. For keeps this time. She gazed at the ring twinkling in the morning sun streaming across her suite's sitting area.

Right before Pennie was about to end the call, Callie's harried voice came through. "Hello?" She sounded out of breath.

"Hey, there. You okay?"

"I should ask the same about you. Jared called Greg last night. Wow, Pen. You could have *died*."

"I know. But God was good to me."

There was an expected silence. Callie had prayed for years that Pennie would come back to God. She never nagged, just gently encouraged. Now that she'd heard Pennie give Him credit for protecting her, Pennie knew Callie would need a moment to process.

"It's great to hear you say that." Callie's voice filled with emotion.

"It feels good. I've been thanking Him over and over ... for a lot of things. I have some news to share with you."

"Great. I have some news to share with you too, but you go first."

Pennie paused, considering which good news to share first. "Did Jared say anything else to Greg, other than the boogie boarding incident?"

Callie laughed. "Maybe ..."

"It's different this time, Cal. *He's* different. In a good way."

"And it sounds like you are too."

"I'm so excited. We haven't set a date or anything yet. I mean, it all just happened. I didn't get back from the hospital until late. The doctor wanted me to stay awhile for observation."

"I'm sure you'll get that all worked out soon."

"Yeah. And then we'll have to do the whole plan the honeymoon trip again." She laughed. "One of my teenage dreams was to have a beach honeymoon in Hawaii. Dottie and I talked about it. Her father was stationed here when she was a girl, and she shared a lot of memories with me."

"That's sweet. She was a special woman for sure."

"Yeah. But I guess getting re-engaged here will have to do." Pennie sighed. "Oh, speaking of Dottie, I have some more exciting news."

"What?"

"I finished the article. I wrote it as a dedication to Dottie. Her memories of Hawaii. My memories of her. I've read it about five times, and I hate to brag, but I think it turned out pretty good. Maybe even good enough to win, but if not, it's a nice tribute to her."

"That sounds sweet, Pen."

"I'm going to submit it today. I'll email a copy to you."

"Great. I can't wait to read it."

Pennie walked onto the lanai and breathed in the sweet floral scent. "I did a lot of thinking while I was in the hospital, and I realized I made a big mistake." She whispered a short prayer that Callie could quickly and easily take the cabin off the market. Jared was talented with handyman tasks. If he taught her and they worked together, maybe they could afford to repair the cabin.

"Really? What'd you do?"

"I'll tell you in a minute. I won't forget. But I just remembered you said you had some news to tell me, and I've been babbling on. What did you have to share?"

"Well, it's one of those good news-bad news things. Kind of bittersweet, but I think, in the long run, it'll be for the best."

Callie had a habit of hedging when she was nervous, but Pennie's patience had been stretched enough during the past few days. She paced back into the sitting area.

"You're stalling. Just spit it out already."

"Fine." Callie paused for just a second longer and blurted, "The cabin sold."

Pennie held her breath for a few seconds. "Sold? You mean someone made an offer, right?"

"No, I mean sold. A cash sale. It happened so fast. We signed the papers this morning."

Pennie felt her knees buckling, and she scooted against the loveseat and plopped onto the deep cushion. "Who? Who bought it?" She could hear the panic in her voice, but she didn't care. If Mrs. Gulliver-Gulch and her cronies collected enough cash to buy the cabin and tear it down, Pennie didn't think she could live with herself.

"We don't know. It was a sealed anonymous transaction handled by an attorney." Callie blew out a heavy sigh. "I'm sorry you seem upset about it. I thought you were firm in your decision."

"Is that even legal?"

"Yes, but it's rare. The buyer's lawyer had a cashier's check made out for the asking price. Whoever it was didn't even try to counter-offer."

Pennie wiped away a tear. "It's almost like someone was waiting for it to go on the market."

Like a vulture hovering over a dying animal.

❦ ❦ ❦

THE NEXT EVENING, Jared parked the Lexus near the marina and opened the door for Pennie. "Have I told you how lovely you look this evening?"

"Only about twenty times, but I'll let you say it again." She grinned.

He loved her smile. As they walked toward the catamaran, he stopped and looked into her eyes. "I have a surprise for you."

"Really?"

"A Christmas present."

"But Christmas isn't until tomorrow, and I haven't bought you anything yet."

He dismissed her concern with a wave of his hand. "You've been busy recuperating as instructed by the doctor *and* your fiancé." He pulled her hand to his mouth and planted a kiss. Then, he handed her a gift bag.

She reached inside and pulled out a red stocking covered with a white hibiscus pattern.

"A souvenir of Hawaii. You can hang it by the fireplace." He smiled.

A sudden onslaught of tears welled in her eyes.

"What's wrong?" Jared tipped her chin up with one finger.

"The fireplace. I don't have a fireplace anymore. I had planned to tell you later, but someone ..." An image of Mrs. Gulch riding her bicycle past Dorothy's house invaded Pennie's thoughts. "Someone bought the cabin." A tear trickled down her cheek.

He brushed the tear aside. "It'll be okay."

"How can you say that? I lost Dottie's cabin, and I don't even know who bought it!"

Pulling her in for a close hug, he whispered in her ear. "Do you trust me?"

Pennie nodded.

"Then look inside the stocking."

"A Christmas card?" She felt the envelope. "It's lumpy."

He gave a loud chuckle. "That lump is your Christmas present."

The front of the card had a drawing of Santa lounging on the beach wearing a pair of bright red swim trunks topped with an aloha shirt. When she opened the card, a keychain fell to the ground. Her fingers trembled as she bent to retrieve it—a hibiscus flower intricately carved in koa wood. "It's beautiful. Thank you."

"You're welcome." He kissed the top of her head. "But I have something to go with it." He dug in his pocket and handed her a well-worn key. Every scratch and groove was familiar.

"Is-is that the key to Dottie's cabin?"

Jared tipped her chin up to gaze into her eyes. "Yes. Only

it's *our* cabin now. And I've already made arrangements for a crew to repair it."

"Y-you? You bought the cabin? Really?" She wrapped her arms around his waist and clung to him.

"Really." Her reaction to his surprise made all the effort worth it.

"I thought I'd lost it forever." Pennie sniffled into his chest. "Callie told me the buyer was a secret. I thought Mrs. Gulch got it."

"Mrs. Gulch?"

"Her real name is Mrs. Gulliver. She's the president of the Lakeshore Homeowners Association. They threatened to condemn the cabin." She pulled away from him and gazed into his eyes, tears still glistening in her own. "H-how did you get the key here so fast? I gave it to Greg and Callie before I left. Did your lawyer overnight it to you?"

Jared gave her a wink. "I'll tell you all the details soon enough. But now it's time for our dinner cruise and that hula lesson." He slung his arm through hers and guided her across the gangplank.

10

Avoid cultural faux pas when traveling by observing and becoming aware of local customs. For example, in Hawaii, the shaka *sign is not an obscene gesture and should therefore not be responded to with a hand signal that is.*

~ Pennie's travel tip No. 64

The catamaran was nothing like Pennie had imagined. The sleek vessel was at least 60 feet long with a double deck mounted on two gigantic pontoons. It appeared more like a yacht than a catamaran.

As soon as she stepped onto the deck, Pennie realized Jared must have chartered the vessel for a private party. No other guests were onboard. She heard a squeal and braced herself for a hug as Callie rushed across the deck. Before she could throw her arms around Pennie, Jared stepped in the way.

"Be careful. She's still sore from the CPR."

"Ah, thanks for letting me know." Callie eased her best friend into a gentle hug.

Greg took a few long strides and joined the hug. He slapped Jared on the back. "*Ho brah!* Congratulations."

Thumbing toward Greg, Callie shook her head. "He's been on the island a half a day and is already trying to act like a local."

"Maybe *loco* is the better word." Jared gave a deep laugh.

"You two quit talking about me in front of my back," Greg teased. "Well, my friend, it's about time you came to your senses."

Jared laughed and nodded. "I'm almost as hard-headed as you."

Steps sounded behind Pennie. She turned to see Kathleen walking across the gangplank escorted by Frank Tanaka. What happened with them while she was in the hospital? She'd force her curiosity to wait for a private conversation with Jared.

"Are we late?" Frank asked, reaching to shake Jared's hand.

"You're right on time." Jared leaned in to kiss Kathleen on the cheek.

Pennie had opted to wear a simple white sundress but noted Kathleen looked radiant in a coral-print kimono.

Servers seated the group, then busied about, carrying dishes and platters. As Pennie marveled at the amount of food for such a small number of guests, voices carried across the deck. A troupe wearing traditional hula costumes boarded followed by an official-looking man. He walked over to Jared and shook his hand.

"I'd like you to meet my fiancée, Pennie Vaughn."

Pennie moved closer to greet the older gentleman.

"Pennie, this is a dear friend of our family, Ikaia. He was my mother's pastor before she passed away."

Ikaia bowed deeply. "It is my pleasure to meet the woman who has stolen Jared's heart." He took both her hands and kissed them.

Pennie felt a blush rising. "Pleased to meet you. Ikaia—I've not heard that name before."

Jared beamed. "It's the Hawaiian equivalent of Isaiah, so it means 'God will deliver.' Please, join us." He gestured to an open seat at the large table.

The menu was similar to that of the luau. After dinner, the group Pennie had suspected was the evening's entertainment pulled out their ukuleles and sang a few traditional Hawaiian songs. A trio of women flowed gracefully into a hula, and the small audience applauded.

One of the women walked behind a serving counter, and the other two moved toward Jared and Pennie, taking each of them by the hand. The third woman returned, bearing two boxes. She opened the first and removed a *ti-leaf* lei.

Jared lowered his head slightly as the woman reached to place the open-ended lei around his neck. She followed with a yellow-colored plumeria lei for Pennie. After draping the lei around her neck, the woman placed a matching floral headpiece on Pennie's head. The woman bowed and returned to her companions, wearing a satisfied smile.

Pennie wondered what was going on when the musicians and dancers returned to the small stage, motioning Jared and Pennie to join them. Pastor Ikaia followed. She saw Jared give a slight nod toward Greg, who stood and gave a hang-loose hand sign.

Callie poked her husband in the ribs. "It's funny that he waves the *shaka* now because this morning at the airport—"

Greg shook his head. "Let's not spoil the occasion by recounting my, um, miscommunication." He winked and turned to Pennie. "You know I love you like a sister, right?"

"Um, right. What's going on, Greg? Is this a surprise engagement party?"

"Not exactly." Greg laughed and motioned for Callie to stand beside him. "I think I'm going to need backup here, hon."

"Pennie, remember that dream of a Hawaiian honeymoon? Well, that's why we're all here." Callie nearly cackled.

Confused, Pennie glanced back and forth between Callie and Greg. "You're here for a second honeymoon?"

"I'm all for that." Greg winked at Callie. "But, actually, we," he pointed to Callie and himself, "had an idea, and we convinced Jared to go along with it."

Pennie looked to Jared for clarification. He gulped.

Before Jared could say anything, Pastor Ikaia spoke up. "Pennie, what your friends are trying to say is, we've gathered here this evening to unite you and Jared in holy matrimony. Then you can spend the remainder of your Hawaiian vacation as the originally planned honeymoon. In fact, if I understood correctly, Jared has arranged to extend the length of your stay."

"Yes." Jared nodded. "The roof and floor of the cabin should be finished within a few weeks. I thought we could enjoy some time here while the cabin is being renovated."

She'd heard of surprise birthday parties, but a surprise wedding? Shouldn't the bride be included in such decisions? A tiny part of her was upset, but she gazed into Jared's eyes, saw his unspoken plea for forgiveness, and her heart melted. She couldn't imagine how challenging it was for him and their friends to pull this off so quickly.

Pennie sucked in a deep breath and blew it out. "All right, y'all." She looked to Callie, then Greg, and locked her gaze onto Jared.

He gave her a sheepish look. "You know how you carried that ring box around with you?"

"Uh-huh."

"Well, I've been carrying this around." Jared reached into his breast pocket and pulled out an embossed envelope.

Their marriage license.

"Can we use that here?"

"No. It's expired. Plus, it's not valid outside Arkansas." Jared gazed into her eyes. "But I completed an online application, and Ikaia brought a licensing agent with him, so if you want, we can be married here. Today."

"Really?"

"Really." Jared pulled her close against him and kissed the top of her head.

After a moment of basking in the strength of his embrace, Pennie stepped back and spoke in a mock-scolding tone. "First the cabin. Now a wedding and honeymoon? I'm okay with surprises, but no more for now. Got it?" She broke into a giggle-laugh, and the entire group joined her.

After finalizing the paperwork, the wedding party gathered on the small stage. Callie stood to Pennie's left, and Greg to Jared's right, with the minister in the center.

Pastor Ikaia nodded to the entertainers, and the men played their ukuleles softly while the women danced the wedding hula. One of the men came to the mic and sang, "*Ke Kali Nei Au*," the traditional Hawaiian wedding song Elvis performed in *Blue Hawaii*.

When the song ended, one of the women stepped forward holding a *maile* lei. She took Pennie and Jared's right hands and tied them together with the lei. Ikaia explained this symbolized the binding together of the couple. The dancers then recited the traditional wedding chant in unison.

Onaona ka hala me ka lehua,
He hale lehua no ia na ka noe,
'O ka'u no ia e 'ano'i nei,
E li'a nei ho'i o ka hiki mai,
A hiki mai no ka kou,

A hiki pu no me ke aloha ...
Aloha e! Aloha e! Aloha e!

Pastor Ikaia then translated the words into English, "This is the sight for which I have longed. Now that you have come, love has come with you." He added some scriptures and sayings commonly used in Mainland wedding ceremonies, and finally, he concluded by asking Jared and Pennie to exchange vows.

Pennie felt as out-of-body during the ceremony as she had while Jared performed mouth-to-mouth on the beach. Was this really happening? Was she really marrying Jared?

When the time came to exchange rings, she realized she had nothing to offer, but Callie handed her an engraved gold band. The one she and Jared had chosen before the breakup. She smiled and placed the ring on his left hand, repeating the words prompted by the pastor. Jared placed a matching band on her left hand.

"And now," Pastor Ikaia bellowed, "by the power vested in me by Almighty God and the state of Hawai'i, I pronounce you husband and wife. You may kiss your bride."

As Jared bent over Pennie to kiss her, the man from the troupe who had sung lifted a *pū*, a conch shell horn, and blew it loudly. Jared startled, but then lowered his mouth to kiss his wife.

EPILOGUE

Six weeks later

J ared led Pennie up the path leading to the cabin. "You sure you can't see through the blindfold?"

"I'm sure. And this little idea of yours is stretching the honor and obey part of the vows pretty thin." She let out one of those giggles that melted his heart.

"Don't forget, I cherish you. I won't let you fall." He hugged her close against him. "We're almost there. Atta girl." Jared placed her hand on the rail. "Now we're at the steps."

Pennie grabbed the handrail with her right hand and clung to Jared with her left. "Can I take it off now?"

"Sure." He laughed and lifted the dark mask from her eyes.

She gasped. The cabin had looked like her when she left, defeated and more than a little drippy, and it looked like she felt now—strengthened and shining. The porch didn't sag under their feet, and even the trimming had been sanded and touched up. She could smell fresh paint mingling with the scent of the Ozark pines, yet the old wood was still there. He had saved the heart and soul of Dottie's cabin for her.

"Oh, Jared. It's amazing!" Tears welled in her eyes. "It's ... it's more than I could have ever hoped for."

"Wait until you see the inside." He winked and lifted her into his arms. Balancing his bride against him with one hand, he inserted the key and turned the knob with the other.

"What are you doing?"

"Carrying you over the threshold. Kathleen told you I'm old-fashioned, right?"

Pennie laughed, but as soon as they eased past the doorway, she slid out of his arms onto the solid floor.

Light streamed through new windows and lovingly touched the familiar shapes of home. Familiar, but not quite the same. Pennie truly understood the care Jared had taken when she saw Dottie's rocker, on four solid legs above polished runners, with a plush new cushion in cornflower blue.

She heard a noise behind them and turned. Mrs. Gulliver tapped lightly on the door, which still stood ajar. Jared raised an eyebrow at Pennie.

"May I help you?"

Pennie stepped forward. "Jared, this is Mrs. Gulliver, the president of the Lakeshore Homeowners Association. Mrs. Gulliver, this is my husband, Jared Ellison."

The older woman's perpetual smirky frown eased into a smile. "It's good to meet you." She looked around the cabin. "And I'm pleased with the work you've had done while you were gone."

Pennie opened her mouth, but Mrs. Gulliver shushed her with a hand wave.

"I talked to the man in charge of the crew. Greg something-or-other. He told me when you'd be back."

"Greg Jorgensen," Jared said. "A talented contractor and my best friend."

She gave a slight harumph and almost smiled again. "Owning a cabin this old, it's good to have a contractor as a best friend."

"I'm glad he was able to fit this project in. And with this view, it'll be worth every dime."

Mrs. Gulliver reached into a large tote she was carrying and pulled out an envelope. "It's not much, but the Association asked me to present this as a way of congratulating you on your new marriage as well as your newly renovated home."

"Thank you." He took the envelope.

She nodded toward it. "You can open it."

The greeting card had a home-sweet-home poem on the front, and inside was a gift card to a favorite local restaurant.

"Take your wife out to dinner on us."

"Thank you, Mrs. Gulliver." Pennie smiled, feeling all sorts of guilt for the past thoughts she'd had about the woman.

Mrs. Gulliver gave a slight nod and made her way down the path.

Before the older woman reached the edge of their property, Pennie's phone buzzed. She shook her head and grinned. Callie. Pennie punched the answer button and held the phone to her ear. "Hey, girl. What's up?"

"You won!"

"What?"

"The Wanderblog contest. Didn't they call you?"

Pennie glanced at her phone's screen. Two missed calls and a voicemail. "Someone called. I'm not sure who."

"Well, you need to call them back because you won."

"Seriously?"

"I might be in cahoots to plan a surprise wedding, but you

know I wouldn't kid about something like this. Check your voicemail."

She hung up the phone. Jared leaned in close and whispered in her ear. "A penny for your thoughts." He winked.

Pennie laughed. "Apparently, I won the blog contest. I'll need to call them to verify it, but I want to talk to you about the prize money. It's a significant amount."

"What did you have planned for it?"

Pennie shrugged, then looked up at him and spoke in a serious tone. "First, I need to reimburse you for these repairs." She gestured around the room with her hand.

"No need." Jared shook his head. "The buyout from Kathleen funded this project, and there's still plenty left in that account. Besides, the renovations were your Christmas present, remember?" He planted a kiss on her forehead.

"Well, there is one thing I would like to do." She felt a shy grin sneak across her face.

"What's that?"

"I'd love to make a donation to the children's home where I went after my parents got killed. The place I met Dottie. I want to donate some money in her memory."

He settled into the sturdy old rocker and drew her into his arms. "You wrote the article as a tribute to Dottie, so I think it's fitting to donate the winnings to honor her legacy."

"Thanks. I love you, Jared Ellison. I'm so grateful you came back to me."

"I love you too. And I'm grateful you welcomed me back."

"Really? Then show it by giving me one of those luau kisses."

ABOUT THE AUTHOR

Linda Fulkerson began her writing career as a copyeditor and typesetter at a small-town weekly newspaper. She has since been published in several magazines and newspapers, including a two-year stint as a sports writer, and is the author of two novels and several non-fiction books. In 2020, she purchased Mantle Rock Publishing's backlist and founded Scrivenings Press LLC.

She and her husband, Don, live on a ten-acre plot in central Arkansas. They have four adult children and eight grandchildren. Linda enjoys photography, RV travel, and spoiling her two dachshunds.

(Someday she hopes to slow down long enough to get a professional headshot made.)

Mr. Sandman

A Novella by

Regina Rudd Merrick

To all those who think snow makes life better—especially when you live in the South! Have a blessed Christmas!

1

Insanity: doing the same thing over and over again and expecting different results.

— Albert Einstein

Taylor Fordham stared at her computer screen, eyes glazed over as she scanned facts and figures. Those numbers equaled business for Pilot Oaks, the beautiful South Carolina antebellum mansion-turned-bed-and-breakfast and event center owned by the Crawford family.

Once again, she'd stayed up too late last night, watching her Sci-fi show, *StarPort: SP-1*, imagining how her favorite characters could end up together.

What was wrong with her? She loved her job. After Mike *—gotta get my mind off that—*she chose to stay in the Pawleys Island area, for Pilot Oaks. Nearby friends helped, but finding her niche in the hospitality industry and working for the Crawfords at their B&B made it worth staying.

"Excuse me ..."

Her head whipped up when a masculine voice filtered

through her brain fog. Taylor looked around the bank of miniature decorative snowmen on her desk, her nod to holiday décor. The heat on her cheeks felt anything but professional.

Way to go, Taylor.

"I'm so sorry." She rose, smiling, her insides doing something weird when the brown-eyed, dark-haired young man smiled back.

He's cute.

"Not a problem." He gave her a half-smile. "I'm Ian Rutledge, here for the chef interview?"

Okay, he's more than cute ...

Her mind went blank for a second, then it all came back to her. She closed her eyes for a second to re-group. "Oh, I'm so sorry."

"There you go, apologizing again." He raised his eyebrow in amusement.

"I'm ..." She grimaced. "I'll let the Crawfords know you're here." She walked away before she could embarrass herself completely.

It's the lack of sleep. I'm never this scattered.

She followed her nose to the scent of gingerbread baking.

One thing you could say about the Crawfords, they believed in doing Christmas BIG. For some reason, Taylor could handle it with them. Robert and Linda Crawford, their daughter, Susan Harris, and the cook, Prudie Matthews, all looked up when Taylor entered the kitchen.

"Is he here?" Prudie asked.

"Mr. Rutledge is in the reception area. Shall I show him to your office or here?" It was a chef's position, after all. Wouldn't they want to quiz him about his specialty? Um, cooking?

Robert narrowed his eyes at the spry woman. "Now Prudie, are you sure you want to share your kitchen with a young whipper-snapper?"

The older woman laughed. "I think I can manage. The breakfast crowd is my favorite anyway. Large groups are getting to be too much for this old woman."

"You are not old." Linda shook her head, salt-and-pepper bob swinging. With one look, she put Prudie in her place. "You're less than twenty years older than me, and I plan to be a vibrant seventy-something when I get there."

"Sweetie." Prudie patted Linda's hand. "I'm old enough to be your mama and Susan's grandmamma, so don't argue. Besides, I might just have plans of my own." She twisted her lips in a smile and squeezed each woman's hand.

Prudie? Blushing? She had been such a comfort to Taylor, possibly because many years ago, she'd also lost the love of her life.

"Let's have him come back here." Robert sought approval from the ladies.

"Sounds good." Prudie smiled. "Bring him on back."

"Yes, ma'am."

Taylor retraced her steps, then detoured through the servant's back entrance to the study. She wondered what Mr. Rutledge would think when she appeared behind him, seemingly from the solid-oak paneling. She touched the hidden door, and the spring-loaded apparatus opening silently.

No need to worry about the man being shocked or surprised.

He was asleep.

STARPORT: SP-1

Linc knew he shouldn't expect things to work out. When had they? But Alex was here, in his arms, where, he surmised, she belonged. Now to figure out how to keep her there.

2

Ian floated on a raft along the Waccamaw River. No alligators or snakes to be found, not even a single mosquito. Everything was perfect, including the temperature and humidity. The overhanging trees draped with Spanish moss wafted overhead in the breeze, and nothing could drag him away.

Except for that voice. That beautiful voice ...

"Mr. Rutledge, are you all right?"

He opened his eyes from the dream only to stare into the concerned blue eyes of the young woman from before. She bent over, her hand gingerly touching his arm. Was it weird that after the eyes, her lips drew his concentration?

I don't even know her name.

"Sorry, I ..." He cleared his throat.

"There *you* go, apologizing." She put her hands on her hips and shook her head, laughter on her face. "By the way, I'm Taylor Fordham, the Event Manager."

He held his hand out as he stood. "Nice to meet you, Ms.

Fordham." He'd already noticed the sparkling rock on her left hand. Married? Engaged?

Of course, she is.

His hand tingled as he held hers for a moment. A blush? Surprised, he let go, refusing to think about it any further.

"I think you know Prudie?"

"Yes." He grinned. "She's my grandfather's neighbor."

Ms. Fordham nodded. "She and the Crawfords would like you to join them in the kitchen. It's the slow time of day."

"Which way?" He pointed to the door.

"I'll take you back." She waved a hand, then led him into the main foyer. "Bad night?"

Small-talk. How do you tell people you might be working with that you hadn't slept since your last job ended on a sour note? Chalk it up to having one of the top ten most stressful jobs?

He shrugged. "Still not used to my bed at my grandfather's house."

"I understand." She seemed to have a difficult time meeting his eyes. "Here we are."

The door swung open to reveal a long worktable with Prudie, and he assumed the Crawfords. And another woman.

"Thank you, Ms.—"

"It's 'Miss.' You can call me Taylor."

Engaged.

"I'll leave you to it." She smiled.

"Thanks, Ms. ... Taylor."

She raised her eyebrows. "You're welcome. And good luck." She left in a different direction from where they'd come.

Curiouser and curiouser. He reminded himself he wasn't here for a woman, especially one who wasn't available. Proving he deserved to be an executive chef was foremost on his mind. He turned to the table and smiled.

Get it in gear, Rutledge. His father's militant voice broke through the sleep-depravation fog, encouraging him to stand at attention. So he did.

"Mr. Crawford, ladies. I'm Ian Rutledge." Ian stepped forward and held out his hand, which Mr. Crawford shook firmly.

"Nice to meet you, Ian." He introduced the ladies. "This is my wife, Linda, and my daughter, Susan Harris, the catering manager. And you know Prudie."

Ian smiled, relaxing a bit when Prudie spoke up. "I've known Ian since he was a little boy. His grandfather and I go way back." She glanced back at Ian. "Your grandma was one of my best friends."

"I remember." Back when his grandparents held annual Independence Day celebrations in their backyard, Prudie was always there, helping Grandma carry out platters of food. She was adept at swatting away little hands—mostly his—wanting to snitch a cookie before supper. He loved spending time there.

"Prudie tells us your last position was as executive chef at Montagu, in Charleston?" Susan asked the first question.

He gritted his teeth. That would have to be the first question. "Yes."

"I hated that it closed. My husband and I ate there a year ago. Excellent cuisine." Susan shook her head. "That's the restaurant business for you."

What else could he say? He nodded.

<hr>

When Ian came back through the office, Taylor looked up from her desk. "How'd it go?"

"All right, I guess." He gave her a nervous smile. "We'll see." *Would it be unprofessional to loosen my tie?*

"I'm sure they'll let you know soon. Prudie wants to have a chef in place before the New Year's Eve Gala."

"I heard. Pretty big deal, huh?"

"Big for here." She chuckled. "Probably not for you, used to Charleston-big."

"Maybe." He glanced at the clock. "Again, thanks for your help."

She shrugged, eying him with concern. "No problem. Have a nice day."

He lifted a hand and made his way out the door.

When he got to his car in front of the antebellum mansion, he looked back at the tall columns on the porch and the comfortable rockers scattered along the front. The place was beautiful and inviting.

The Crawfords said Prudie would still take care of breakfast except for large groups. His position would allow Pilot Oaks to offer lunch and dinner options for overnight guests and private parties. He'd worked enough events to feel secure in his training. All he needed was confidence.

The sleepless year was another issue. What if he blanked out at a crucial time? It had never happened, but until lately, he'd never experienced long periods without sleep either.

Ian's unexpected unemployment came at a great time since Grandpa needed someone to stay with him after his hospitalization. He'd given up his Charleston apartment since his lease was up, and without work, he couldn't afford the rent. Besides that, the responsibility he felt for his perceived part in the failure of his friend's restaurant made him want to disappear. It wasn't a hard decision.

So, Ian moved to Murrells Inlet and searched for a job close enough to his family and far enough from Charleston. At first, he thought about trying a new career, but cooking was what he knew. A job at Pilot Oaks would put him smack dab in the middle of the food industry again.

Pulling the car onto Highway 17, he remembered errands, including groceries and Grandpa's pharmacy. He took a deep breath while heading north toward the commercial center of Pawleys Island.

His chest felt tight, so he loosened his tie. Just nerves, right?

The pounding headache wouldn't go away. Somehow, he'd passed Food Lion and Bi-Lo, both supermarkets closer to Grandpa's house, but he made it to Lowe's Foods, the last grocery establishment before crossing the rivers into Georgetown.

Where's my brain?

As he parked the car, he felt off.

Deep breath, Rutledge.

Nope. He couldn't do it. *What is going on?* He closed his eyes and tried to relax.

The vice on his chest would not stop tightening. His heart pounded. Why was he here? Food. No. Medicine. Oh, medicine AND food.

He glimpsed his reflection in the rearview mirror. Very pale. More than pale, he looked dead. A blinding, crushing feeling allowed only one conclusion. He was having a heart attack. Should he call 911? No. No health insurance. Could EMTs get here in time?

While I can still think, I need to get to the hospital. Now.

STARPORT: SP-1

Dr. Elizabeth Garrity met the alien-but-all-too-human Bartok in the hallway, stopping him. "Bartok, are you okay? You look pale."

"That is a distinct impossibility, as my skin is darker than the night sky."

The doctor blushed and looked away for a moment, trying to gather her thoughts.

"Yes, but something is wrong ..."

3

The breathing exercises Ian learned at the gym helped.
He put the car in gear and headed south to the nearest
hospital, Georgetown General. He hadn't been there since he
sprained his ankle jumping into a shallow part of the river
about twenty years ago.

It's only ten miles to Georgetown from here. You can do this.

Part of his brain argued the rationale of driving himself to
the hospital, but the part of him in full-on survival mode took
over. It wasn't so much that he couldn't see that worried him,
but the dizziness. He made it over two bridges crossing the
Great Pee Dee and the Waccamaw rivers, then he followed the
signs to the hospital, and headed straight to the Emergency
Room. When the car came to a stop, he put it in park and sat
there.

If I get out of the car, I'll pass out.

A knock sounded on the car window. He tried to look up.
Reality became more and more blurred with the dream from
earlier. Wasn't he floating on the river?

Wait. Someone is here. Pain. Can't breathe.

"Sir, can you hear me?" A man in hospital scrubs tried to open the car door. "Unlock your door!"

What did the man want? Oh, unlock the door. That, he could do. Where was the button? Oh, he could just open the door.

As he pulled at the door latch, the man in scrubs caught him, or he would have fallen out of the car.

***

"GET ME A STRETCHER." The order shouted at close range sounded far away.

An oxygen mask slipped over his nose and mouth. Finally, he could breathe.

In.

Out.

"Sir, are you in pain?" A different nurse leaned over him, slid a cuff on his arm and grabbed his wrist.

He nodded.

"Where are you hurting?"

He put his hand on his chest and looked up at her.

"Get the doctor on call," she shouted. "Does it hurt anywhere else?"

"All over." He stared at her. Was he dying?

His attention drifted in and out as someone attached pads and wires to his chest and drew some blood.

The nurse fired more questions at him. He closed his eyes for a second. A lower voice joined hers. The doctor? When Ian opened his eyes, he met the concerned, yet familiar gaze of Rance Butler.

"Did you get demoted or something?" Ian's voice sounded raspy, even to him.

"Naw, I heard some Bozo having a potential heart attack

drove himself to the Georgetown hospital from Pawleys." Dr. Butler arched a brow. "How are you feeling?"

"Not good." Ian tried to take a deep breath. Still couldn't. "You said potential. Am I having a heart attack?"

"Waiting for the blood work and EKG results." The doctor leaned on the rail close to Ian's head. He looked worried. "When did this start?"

"On my way home from a job interview." Ian looked up. The oxygen helped, but he still felt short of breath. "What's happening to me?"

"I'm not sure. I have an idea, but I'll let the test results advise me before I advise you. Sound like a plan?" Dr. Butler spoke the words, but Rance, the friend, put a hand on Ian's arm and squeezed.

The nurse arrived and handed a clipboard to the doctor, who thanked her.

Am I dying? Tell me. The words kept running through Ian's brain.

"I'll have the nurse give you something to relax you." Rance gestured to the woman beside him. "Jackie will give you the shot—I'm terrible at it. I'll be back in a bit." The doctor turned back to Ian. "You know, if you'd wanted to get together and talk about old times, we could have gone out for a milkshake."

"I'll remember that next time."

"If I have anything to do with it, there won't BE a next time." Giving his arm another squeeze, Dr. Butler nodded at the nurse.

"This will stick a little." The nurse spoke softly.

The shot was nothing compared to the crushing pain he'd been feeling. Before long, the pressure eased. Relaxation was bliss.

In all the gin joints, in all the towns, in all the world, Rance Butler walks into mine.

And he was out.

STARPORT: SP-1

Dr. Elizabeth Garrity, Beth to her friends, placed her hand on Bartok's strong, sinewy appendage. "Are you sure about going through the drug trial? It's completely experimental."

"I am. If my people are to benefit from your research, then I must be willing to offer myself as a test subject." He stared into her eyes. "I am in good hands."

Blinking back tears, she nodded. When she picked up the needle to place the solution in the intravenous port, she paused and looked him in the eye. "If anything happens to you ..."

4

"**N**o." Taylor shouted at the television screen, angry tears poised on her lashes. "Oh, no they didn't."

Every. Single. Time.

She sighed as the credits rolled, the clock reading 2 a.m. Taylor finished fifteen seasons of *StarPort: SP-1* for the umpteenth time, and, once again, was highly dissatisfied with the ending.

Only her closest friends knew of her obsession with the '90s sci-fi series. Why? Because ... well ... because she was a little embarrassed at the utter nerd within her.

She could organize everyone except herself, and all the know-how in the world was useless in the face of sleepless nights.

Too much.

Wide awake, Taylor channel surfed, pausing briefly on the Hallmark Channel. Ugh, Christmas movies. Small towns, snow, happy endings.

Where was *her* happy ending? Two Christmases ago, her happily-ever-after was just around the corner.

Until last summer when her life fell apart.

No sweet romance for her. She gave up on love, and put the SYFY channel in her list of favorites, removing Hallmark and Lifetime. Neither her life nor *StarPort: SP-1* went in the direction she wanted. Life you couldn't predict. Her show? She'd watched it in its entirety more times than she would admit, and still unreasonably and unashamedly hoped for a happy ending.

Taylor snagged her laptop from the coffee table laden with candy wrappers, a half-eaten bag of chips, and a glass of what used to be iced tea. The computer lay on a stack of magazines, safe from the former tea's condensation puddle. The only casualties were a few pieces of mail that she hoped weren't vital.

She scooched down on her comfy couch, a hand-me-down from her parents —and her favorite sofa ever—toes hooked on the edge of the coffee table. Maybe if she did a little Internet surfing, she'd get sleepy and get a few hours of sleep. But her brain couldn't stop running scenarios that would have given her the ending she wanted.

Why couldn't she get hooked on soap operas like people used to? They were on constantly during the day, and you didn't have to worry about endings. The shows just kept going. A baby born one year was four years old the next year, and the next year? Eighteen with a love interest.

She pulled up Google and stopped, her fingers resting idly on the computer. What to search for? She took a sip of her watered-down tea and tried to relax. Strumming her fingers, thinking, she gave in, typed *StarPort: SP-1*, and hit Enter.

Maybe there were more episodes that her streaming service didn't offer—as if she didn't know each episode inside and out. Cast interviews? Outtakes? Blooper reels? Maybe the creators had made a video or written a blog about what they had planned to happen, but didn't, because of the heartless studio execs.

Okay. In 1.5 seconds, nine million results came up from her *StarPort: SP-1* search. Nine. Million.

She scrolled down, yawning into the back of her hand as she read past the Wiki page, the IMDB page, ads for buying the DVDs, and conspiracies as to why the show was canceled after a mere fifteen seasons. She delved into a rabbit hole.

After reading a few posts, she looked up, her lips tightening, and shook her head. These people didn't know what they were talking about. The characters of Linc, Alex, David, and Bartok should live forever. Who cares if the main actors were aging out of leading man and lady status?

Farther down the line, she paused.

Whoa.

There it was. On page two.

Fanficwow.net.

Stories. Hundreds of them.

About any television series you could think of. All by fans who felt the show had ended too soon. Just like her. The shows were listed in order of how many stories were published about that series. To her delight, *StarPort: SP-1* was third from the top, behind "Dr. What" and "Bunny the Werewolf Hunter."

She laughed, thinking how useless an actual bunny would be against a werewolf. That's Hollywood for you. Space and time, along with wormhole technology? Now *that* was reasonable.

She shook her head.

I NEED SLEEP.

Clicking on her choice, she saw over thirty thousand stories were devoted to *StarPort: SP-1*. Her heartbeat quickened in an excitement she hadn't felt since—and she hated to admit it—since Mike had proposed to her two years ago.

Out of the blue, he was gone. Taylor was devastated. Sure, she'd seemed to move on, but deep down? She was on a never-ending treadmill of home–work, work–home, weekday–weekend, Saturday–Sunday. The same thing, over and over again. The part-time job she'd taken monitoring sleep studies at the hospital—Thanks, Rance—bored her out of her mind, but it kept her from having so much time on her hands, alone.

She still wore the engagement ring. A few months ago, her mother asked when she planned to start dating again.

Date? It felt too much like cheating.

She had to get her mind off her personal drama. Maybe someone, somehow, had written a scenario in which Linc and Alexandra—Alex—finally got together after their fifteen-year slow-burn romance. That was enough drama for her, now.

STARPORT: SP-1

Alex stood on her tiptoes to kiss McNeil and he pulled her to him to help her reach him more easily.

"When did you first know?" Alex ran her fingers through his short, military cut, loving the feel of his bristly, yet unbelievably soft, hair.

"When you told me off in the first staff meeting. I didn't want a woman on my team until I met you. Alex, you were the toughest woman I'd ever come across …

5

Taylor's stomach grumbled again. Thankfully, Pilot Oaks offered a soup-and-sandwich buffet, and today's special was potato soup. In addition to the gingerbread, she detected notes of oranges and cloves. Spiced cider?

Boycotting Christmas had crossed her mind several times this year, but the food? No way would she skip that.

"What did you think about Mr. Rutledge?" Susan caught up with her in the buffet line.

Taylor hesitated. "He seemed nice." Should she tell Susan about finding him asleep?

"I thought so too. His references are excellent."

Placing a half BLT on her plate, Taylor moved on to the steaming soup pot. "Shouldn't a chef cook something for an interview?"

Susan tilted her head. "I didn't think about that. Probably ..." She filled her plate. "Although, I ate at Montagu, where he cooked, and the food was excellent."

"I guess he couldn't be that bad, or he wouldn't have good

references." Taylor picked up a glass of sweet tea. "Want to sit over there?"

Since Taylor began working for the Crawfords, she found herself gravitating to Susan. As the catering manager, they worked together a lot. The ten-year age gap didn't faze their relationship. Susan became the big sister Taylor never had. She played aunt to Susan's ten-year-old twin girls. Watching them and all the other kids in and out of Pilot Oaks made her long for her own.

At one time, she would have thought, *Someday.* But now?

Now I just want to get from one day to another.

❧❧❧ ❀ ❧❧❧

"LIKE I TOLD you yesterday before we released you, you had a panic attack."

"That's your diagnosis? You've got to be kidding me." Ian's heart thudded, and he resented its traitorous action. "Just shoot me. At least a heart attack is something you can't help."

"You can't help a panic attack, either." Rance narrowed his eyes. "Has this ever happened before?"

"No. I've never felt like that, and I hope I never do again." His mouth went dry thinking about it. "Can I expect this to happen every time I stress?"

Rance chuckled. "I don't think so. How have you been sleeping?"

Ian paused and took a deep breath. That felt good. "I haven't had a good night's sleep in six months."

Rance scribbled on a piece of paper.

Somebody's going to have to translate that chicken-scratch.

"I'm scheduling a sleep study." Rance looked at him more seriously than Ian had ever seen him. "I'm pretty sure your heart is fine, but this will help determine if the problem is physical—" Rance grinned. "—or mental."

"Believe me, it could go either way." Ian shook his head in disgust, then considered his friend. "You've found your niche here, haven't you?"

"Yep. Sometimes I wonder why I've been blessed the way I have."

"And I wasn't even around to play wingman. You found Charly and the job on your own." Wasn't this the guy who was supposed to do big things? Shoot for the stars? Instead, he'd settled for a position in small-town Georgetown, South Carolina, and a home-town girl.

The smile that had won Rance more dates and gotten him out of more scrapes than Ian could count played across his lips. This was the guy who always landed on his feet. "I'm glad I was here, for you."

"Me too." Ian settled his gaze on Rance. "Is it necessary?"

"It is if you don't want this to happen again. It's either the sleep study or pills. Your choice. I'm assuming warm milk and counting sheep haven't helped?"

"I've tried every old-wives-tale remedy the Internet holds." Ian shook his head. *Face it, Rutledge, you're a wimp who can't sleep.* "What's involved with this study?"

"You come in around nine in the evening, and we hook you up to all kinds of monitors. No screens of any kind—computers, phone, television—during the test."

Once Ian agreed, he left Rance's office. The cold December air coming in the car window was invigorating, and it felt good to be alive. Ian knew he had insomnia but hadn't realized it could be serious.

As the sun lowered, Ian pulled into Huntington Beach State Park. He changed from his good shoes to the boat shoes he kept in the backseat. In a beach town, you never knew when you'd end up on the beach. He grabbed his jacket and climbed the dune to get to the beach, empty except for a few dog-walkers and a runner. Even better.

Walking to the edge of the cool Atlantic surf, he turned toward Pawleys Island. Only the anti-social, the serious exercise nuts, or, like him, people in crisis mode, frequented this part of the beach. He stopped and stared into the horizon. He had the beach all to himself.

At least, he thought he did.

STARPORT: SP-1

Alex walked around her kitchen island and sniffed this morning's bouquet from McNeil. So far, he'd sent flowers, candy, or ammunition weekly since they'd declared their love for one another.

Such a romantic ...

So why did she have this uneasy feeling?

6

Taylor left her Litchfield Beach condo complex, Sandpiper Run, and walked toward Huntington Beach State Park. She was exhausted and had no energy. Not far beyond the beach house community lay a great stretch of coast too far for most beach-goers, making it a beacon of solitude for her.

The overcast sky was breaking up. Hopefully, before dark, she'd see blue sky. The brisk breeze heightened her senses. Her usual route took her north from her condo to Huntington Beach. That was the goal.

Taylor made it to the edge of the park property and stopped.

Am I getting so soft that I can't walk without stopping?

She stood there a minute, bent over with her hands on her knees. When she stood, she zipped her fleece jacket as an unwelcome chill went through her.

Move or freeze.

Straightening, she resolved to get at least halfway from where she stood to the public beach entrance.

I can do this. I do this all the time.

Legs heavy as lead, she slowed down as she reached her goal. She'd kept her head down, watching. One. Step. At. A. Time.

"Hey."

Her head whipped up, and a smile tugged at her lips. Ian.

"What are you doing here?" She stopped, gasping for breath.

"Probably the same as you." He grinned, a pleasant sight. One little dimple, ever so slight, threatened to appear.

I wonder if he has two dimples if he all-out smiles?

She tried to catch her breath. "Hyperventilating?"

"No." Ian laughed. "But I've been standing here a few minutes."

Why couldn't she catch her breath? Her lungs and legs were conspiring against her. Talking was a chore. "I think I can make it back if I rest a minute." She stood next to him, staring out at the winter waves. "You found my favorite spot."

He looked down at her and nodded. "I found this place a long time ago."

"That's right, you have family here."

"My grandfather. As a kid, I spent summers at my grandparents' house. My cousins and I explored every nook and cranny out here on our bikes. It was a good way to spend the summer."

"Sounds like it." She looked up at him, smiling when his dark brown eyes met hers. "Where did you grow up?"

"Charleston. You?"

Unexpected, but not unheard-of. Not everybody in a big city knows everybody else. "Seriously? Me, too. What part?"

"Goose Creek. My dad taught at the Naval Nuclear Power Training Command." He looked at her and shrugged. "Before that, we were all over."

"Wow. I grew up in Mount Pleasant, the child of two high school English teachers." She snorted. "Nothing exciting there."

"But you didn't have to move every two years, did you?" When she shook her head, he twisted his lips. A smile? A grimace? Hard to tell. "What brought you to this area?"

"My fiancé lived and worked here. So I came, and I stayed."

⋙ ❧ ⋘

LIVED? WORKED? Ian wondered as Taylor referred to her engagement in the past tense. She must have a broken heart, yet hoped to reconcile with the guy. Wow. She didn't look like the total denial type, but you never knew.

"I have friends in Georgetown. If it weren't for that and my job with the Crawfords, I would have gone back to Charleston. Oh, and Rance." She unconsciously pushed a tendril of brown hair behind her ear, then took a deep breath and exhaled slowly.

"Rance?" Now he was really confused.

"Rance Butler. We've been close since grade school." She smiled sadly. "He's how I met Mike."

"Talk about a small world."

The slight crease between her brows intrigued him, and he wanted to see it go away. She intrigued him. They'd met in a professional setting, but out here? Here, they were just two souls trying to work things out.

Wait. Who is Mike?

"Rance and I met in college." He laughed. "I was his wingman."

She laughed out loud. "Do guys really DO that?"

With a straight face, he nodded. "Of course. A good

wingman can mean the difference between a viable date and one you'd be better off avoiding."

"Seriously?"

"Seriously."

"And what are the perks of being the wingman?"

"Leftovers."

She laughed, and it did his heart good to see color in her cheeks.

Maybe she needed a distraction. "Rance has changed a lot in the last few years."

"In a lot of ways. Have you met his biological father?"

Ian nodded. "Some story, huh?"

"Can you imagine finding out the man you thought was your dad was actually your step-dad? Oh, and that you have a brother you've never met? Talk about messing a person up." She shook her head and stared out at the waves again. "How do you get past something like that?"

"Rance would say it's all about *grace.*"

Taylor looked down at her feet, then back at the lowering sun. "I should head back. I just needed a rest."

"I don't mean to pry, but are you okay?"

"I'm fine. I haven't been sleeping well." She smiled and glanced over her shoulder again. "Better go. Hope to see you soon."

"Do you know something I don't know?" *Like if I got the job?*

She turned and walked backward a few steps in the sand, her smile relaxed. "No, but it's a small community."

He nodded, staring at her a minute, wanting to know her better.

Much better. But she was still hung up on Mike. The last thing Ian needed was a romance on the rebound. Better to keep her in the friend zone. No matter how much she intrigued him.

‌❦

By the time Taylor returned, dark had overtaken her. She was, to put it mildly, exhausted. She stuck a small frozen pizza in the toaster oven and put a few dishes in the dishwasher. Then she went trolling through the apartment to see if there were any stray glasses or plates around. If she could at least do these dishes, she'd have one part of the apartment clean.

It was all she could do, these days, to get up and go to work. After work? She had nothing left.

Who needs clean dishes anyway? Pizza in hand, iced tea on a coaster, she opened her laptop. She'd check FanficWow and read more stories about *StarPort: SP-1*.

Some of the stuff was surprisingly good. *I've read books written like this.*

One particular writer, *SPfan89*, was a romantic. She tried to comment but was blocked. She would need to create a profile. Great. Another login and password to remember. She hesitated, and then gave in to the desire to comment. Who knows? Maybe this online community would fill a void she'd had since Mike died. How she missed him. He *got* her.

He'd loved her obsession with science fiction because it was so unexpected. It also made her very patient with his addiction to superheroes. He was a doctor but was fascinated with physics, so he loved the story of the Incredible Hulk. The quirk made her love him even more.

She picked *Lincsgirl* for her fangirl crush, General Lincoln McNeil. That would be a good username. Nope. Taken. She tapped her fingers against the keys. *Lincsgirl91*. What were the odds that it was available? She waited a few seconds and BAM. Accepted.

Awesome!

What to say ... She started typing, giving *SPfan89* all the reasons why his wonderful story wouldn't be realistic in real life, as much as she loved the story and wished it could happen.

She typed a few paragraphs and bulleted points, and then, before she could chicken out, bit her lip and clicked on *submit a comment.*

It was out there, in the ether, *awaiting moderation,* whatever that meant.

STARPORT: SP-1

Dr. David Carter, an archaeologist, came around the corner, stopping short when he noticed his superior officers in a clinch. "Uh, guys."

Bartok, his alien strength always a surprise, put his heavy hand on David's shoulder. "Do not interrupt them."

"But they'll get in major trouble. I mean, if the General sees them..."

Bartok's brow arched almost menacingly. "Is not McNeil also a General?"

7

I an kicked up the footrest on the recliner after cleaning the kitchen. Grandpa snoozed in his bed after Prudie's supper of white bean soup and cornbread. After the day Ian had, he was more than happy to accept the gift of nourishment. He couldn't tell them about his episode yesterday. He'd need to work something out for tomorrow night so he could do the sleep study.

For now, Ian wanted to relax. Relax and not think.

He pulled out his laptop. After reading a couple of emails, he moseyed over to his favorite website. Maybe a newbie had posted a story on Fanficwow.net.

While Ian enjoyed binge-watching television and reading, he also liked to write. Nothing serious, just an online forum he'd found a few years ago where people posted stories, got feedback, and kept writing. He made a few cyber friends. They'd chat and email back and forth. It was much easier than facing his friends in real life with his failed career.

A notification. That was a surprise. He hadn't posted

anything in a year, so he pulled it up, curious. When the long message came up, he almost laughed.

Here was someone—female from the looks of the username, *Lincsgirl91*—prepared to argue her case. While she would love to see Linc and Alex together, there were real-life obstacles they'd have to cross to make the relationship work.

This is too good.

❄❄❄ 🍬 ❄❄❄

TAYLOR WAS MISERABLE. This unfamiliar and all-consuming fatigue was getting to her. She'd almost fallen asleep at her desk. Almost.

"Good morning, Taylor."

"Morning, Susan." She smiled, trying to hide the fatigue. "Anything exciting happening today?"

"Just hiring a chef." Susan raised her eyebrows. "We're hiring Ian if he accepts the offer."

"Why wouldn't he?" What would it be like to see him every day? She admitted to herself, she was curious about that dimple.

"He'll be great. I'm going to call him, now." Susan paused waggling her eyebrows at her. "Want me to tell him you said 'hi!'?"

Taylor shook her head and gave her friend a disgusted look. "I think not. Thank you, anyway."

Susan plucked up a stuffed snowman from the collection on Taylor's desk. "Hey, you can't date a snowman, you know."

"If only." Taylor grinned. "One wrong move and into the greenhouse he goes."

"Ouch."

Taylor laughed at Susan, waving her off.

STARPORT: SP-1

Dr. Carter, David, read through military rules and regs until he was cross-eyed. He'd always heard officers couldn't "fraternize," whatever that meant.

The last thing he wanted was for his comrades to miss the chance of a lifetime. Linc and Alex were together, a General and a Colonel, with or without the permission of the powers that be ...

8

I an arrived at the sleep clinic yawning. Just watch. *Tonight I'll sleep like a baby.*

If only.

Walking up, Ian smiled, seeing two familiar faces. Jackie, the nurse who had been in the ER with him the day before, and Taylor.

Wait. Taylor?

"You work here?"

"As needed. It gets me out of the house." Taylor shrugged. "Rance didn't mention you were the patient. He said to tell 'the patient' he'd be here as soon as Lamaze class is over." She leaned forward and spoke quietly. "I think tonight is when they watch 'the video'."

"What's 'the video'?"

"Childbirth." She chuckled. "Of course, since Rance is a doctor, it shouldn't bother him as much as it will Charly."

"Probably not. I understand they met when he was an intern here."

"He was on his OB/GYN rotation and delivered her

brother's twins." She laughed. "Apparently her obstetrician was in his garden and got to the hospital just in time to see Rance catch twin number one."

"I got into the wrong profession." He grinned at her heightened color.

Picking up the clipboard, Taylor read the orders Rance left with her. "Jackie will hook you up to the monitors, so I suggest you get comfortable."

Ian looked down at his sweats and T-shirt and grinned. "I think this is about as comfortable as it gets." He held up his notebook and another book. "I brought entertainment without screens, per doctor's orders."

She held out her hand, and his first instinct was to take it, but he didn't ...

"Phone."

Oh, yeah.

He read a while, then wrote a while, and, settling in, Ian knew he should at least try to sleep. What if he'd forgotten how?

Pray.

That, he could do.

God, let me sleep. Please. Whatever is keeping me awake, let me think about it tomorrow. After praying, he started reciting several Bible verses he'd memorized. Starting with John 3:16, then random verses. He even hit the highlights of the Christmas story, finally landing on the twenty-third Psalm.

He makes me lie down in green pastures beside still water

...

If that wasn't peaceful, he didn't know what was.

TAYLOR SETTLED in with her laptop at the monitoring desk of the sleep lab, hoping to go over table arrangements for the Hurricane Rescue New Year's Eve Gala and catch up on reading her new favorite website.

The beeps and blips were above her pay-grade, but she knew the basics. Heart rate was good. Blood pressure, good. He seemed pretty chill.

He'd pulled out a notebook and started scribbling in it. She noticed when his heart rate and BP went up, he had a look of intense concentration on his face. What was he writing? Maybe a letter to his girlfriend?

There. That would stop her from thinking about the good-looking chef.

Several times, she'd checked FanficWow, hoping for a message back from *SPfan89*, but alas, nothing. Maybe she'd made him angry and he'd never write again?

Taylor had done all she could with the Gala plans without input from Susan and was unable to settle on a new story to read. An idea popped into her mind. She began to type. Sure, she'd given *SPfan89* her reasons why Alec and Linc couldn't be together, but what was fanfiction for, anyway? She couldn't resist the chance to *right the wrongs* of the television writers.

Decision made, she highlighted her words, copied them to the forum, and hit submit.

She'd published the first chapter of her first story.

Let's see what SPfan89 thinks of MY writing.

STARPORT: SP-1

"How is he?" Linc walked up to the doctor.

"His vitals are amazing, as usual." Dr. Garrity arched a brow.

"That's our Bartok." Shaking his head, Linc struggled with what he had to ask. "Will it work?"

"Only time will tell." She glanced up at him, a sheen of tears in her eyes. "The hardest part will be getting him to rest as he recovers ..."

9

Taylor paid for letting Rance take Charly out after Lamaze class. With little to no sleep last night, exhaustion overtook her. It usually hit after lunch. This felt different, somehow. The spreadsheet on the screen in front of her blurred, and she wanted nothing more than to lay her head on her crossed arms and snooze. Instead, she closed her eyes and propped her head up with her hands.

I'll just relax for a few minutes. That'll get me back on track.

"Taylor?"

Her head jerked up. She checked the time on the computer screen. Ten minutes had passed.

What have I done?

"Taylor, are you okay?"

She looked up to see the concerned eyes, not of her employer, thank goodness, but Ian Rutledge. Her face heated and then cooled, nausea in her stomach growing. This was the most unprofessional thing she'd ever done.

"I can't believe I did that." She cringed.

"I feel your pain. Now we're even." His brows went down. "Is everything all right?"

No, it isn't. She couldn't say it.

When she stood, trying to cover her embarrassment, her knees buckled, sending her back down to her chair.

Thank goodness I hadn't pushed it back.

"Whoa." He was by her side in an instant. "Let me get you some water." He looked around at the exits.

"Through there."

"Right. Don't move."

Instead of the snarky remark that came to her lips, she nodded her head and watched as he rushed in the direction of the kitchen. He came back with a bottle of cold water, Prudie right behind him.

"What happened?" Prudie leaned in toward her.

"I fell asleep." *This is humiliating.*

"Are you sure that's all? Ian told me you were pale, and I have to agree." The older woman looked up at the hovering chef.

Tears smarted.

Linda chose that moment to come into the office. "What's wrong?"

"Taylor's not well." Prudie tilted her head at Taylor.

She opened her mouth to protest.

"Now don't you argue." Prudie's gaze cut to Linda. "Doesn't she look pale to you?"

Ever the mom, Linda touched the back of her hand to Taylor's forehead. "She's not feverish. If anything, you feel cold and clammy."

"I'll be fine."

"You need to take care of yourself and see the doctor. It's time you used that health insurance policy."

The boss had spoken.

Taylor glanced from Linda to Prudie, and then to Ian. They obviously agreed. At this point, she didn't have the energy to argue.

❧❧❧❧❧ ✻ ❦❦❦❦❦

"ANEMIC?" Taylor knew the term meant her body was low in iron, but she hadn't been iron-deficient since ... ever.

Rance looked at the paper with the results of the blood work he'd ordered, then back at her. "Extremely, so we have a few choices." He was serious. His brilliant blue eyes had never been magical for her but were famous among all her female friends.

"And?" Her muscles tensed. Here it was the midst of the holidays, the fundraising gala coming up at work, and she still hadn't figured a way to get out of going home for Christmas.

"We can give you a blood transfusion ..."

"Yikes. No!"

"More common than you'd think. We can also do iron injections or iron tablets. Transfusion is fastest, injections a little slower, and pills the slowest, yet maybe the most reliable." He raised his eyebrows in question. "What'll it be?"

Quick decisions were not her forté. "How about we try the injections?" She didn't prefer shots, but if it would get her better faster, it might be worth it—without the horror of exchanging all her blood. Her skin crawled a little at the thought.

"Sounds good. Maybe we'll get you better in time to get home for Christmas." He chuckled, and then sobered when she looked away. "What's wrong?"

"Busy time at work. That's all." She wrinkled her nose. "And going home isn't the incentive you think it is."

He quirked a brow. "Is the Charleston crew still trying to fix you up with anybody and everybody?"

"You might say that." She cringed. Family holidays meant pitfalls and intrusive questions such as, 'Are you seeing anyone yet?' and 'Did you hear about so-and-so? They'll be grandparents next year.' "I suppose I'm being ungrateful."

"No, just human." He paused a moment. "Although, I know this guy ..."

"Don't even start with me." She struck him down with narrowed eyes.

"Just kidding." He winked at her. "You need to take some time off."

"But ..."

"No buts. I'd like to see you take at least a week off and do nothing but rest and maybe walk on the beach." Rance wasn't kidding this time. "I mean it, Taylor. If you don't take care of yourself, this can cause long-term health issues."

STARPORT: SP-1

"I feel well." Bartok's frown remained. Was that a slight pout on his lips?

Beth wanted to laugh yet she smiled as his brows came down even further. "You're more than well, but I don't want you to be off-world and find yourself in a pickle."

"A ... pickle?" The pout turned to confusion.

10

Grandpa's appointment with the orthopedic surgeon went well. He'd been upgraded to a walker or cane. No more wheelchairs.

"Now I can think about being Grand Marshall in the parade."

Ian's pulse picked up. "Are you sure?"

"Of course I am." Grandpa winked at him. "I've got plans, my boy. Big plans."

Big plans, huh? But he'd learned not to ask questions. When Grandpa was ready to share, he would.

Today had been a full day. He paused, thinking about Taylor's episode that morning, wincing as he remembered falling asleep in the office the day of his interview.

After the excitement of Taylor leaving, Susan Crawford offered him the job, which he accepted. The pay was good, the benefits amazing, and he'd be able to work alongside people he already liked and respected. How had Taylor fared after the incident this morning?

His sleep study had come back about the way he thought. Stress, burnout, etc. Rance had prescribed sleeping pills, low-dosage, for immediate relief, and a few sleeping tips. Basically, don't lay awake in bed. If you're not sleepy, get up and read until you are.

So, he tried that by catching up on his fanfiction. Was it contrary of him to try proving a point to *Lincsgirl91* by using all her reasons for Linc and Alex to NOT be together? He planned to make it as real-life as possible.

Logging in, he was surprised to see not only a message but the first part of a story—by *Lincsgirl91*.

The message:

Hi. I'm sorry if I overstepped! Are you mad?

He grinned. Yep, it was a girl, all right. Guys would ignore it and move on.

He rattled out an answer:

Not mad, just busy last night. You make some good points. More later.

Was it enough? Ian closed out the messaging window, then opened it back again. Strike while the iron is hot.

Ian, AKA *SPfan89*, began typing his rebuttal. He'd been thinking about it since her message yesterday and decided she deserved a thorough answer. Plus, if he overwhelmed her with words, maybe she'd keep her opinions to herself from now on.

StarPort: SP-1

Alex waited, hoping Linc wouldn't be late again. She knew the demands of command were great, and she sympathized. But as a woman? She longed to be more important to him. Chin in hand, she gazed out the window overlooking the San Francisco Bay and the Golden Gate Bridge. Beautiful.

His lips brushed her neck just below her ear, and she shivered.

He was right on time ...

>>>>>> 🦯 <<<<<<

TAYLOR WALKED ON THE BEACH, read a novel, and took naps. At least she was sleeping.

Since she'd always wanted to try crochet, Prudie gave her a lesson.

It. Was. Horrendous.

What some considered a relaxing creative endeavor became, for Taylor, a stress-inducing pathway to irritation and increased blood pressure.

So, she stopped, reminding herself that needlework wasn't for everybody any more than Sci-Fi was.

She'd pulled up FanficWow to see if *SPfan89* had been around. His last message had made her laugh. Definitely male. Brief, to the point, no exclamation points. Her heart rate increased when she saw comments on her story. Already? She clicked on the icon, thrilled to see three comments, all positive, and two from other writers whose stories she'd read.

How cool is this? They like me! They really like me!

After the high of reading praise and encouragement from perfect strangers, she moved on to the messaging feature to see if the lengthy response could be from whom she hoped. It was.

As she read, she wondered if this guy was for real or not. Should she be angry? Reading more, she smiled. Finally, she began laughing and couldn't stop.

He ended his rant with this: *I planned to write a story using all of your reasons to keep them apart, but I couldn't. Maybe I'm an incurable optimist. Maybe I'm crazy, and maybe I'm trying too hard, but I intend to convince the world that it would be possible for Linc and Alex to be together. My next story will convince you.*

STARPORT: SP-1

Linc gazed into her eyes. "I'll do anything ..."

"Don't say it, Linc." Alex's whispered voice pleaded with him. "We've been down this road before."

His hand caressed her cheek. "A road filled with potholes ..." His voice turned into a frustrated growl.

11

I an realized he was writing his story for an audience of one —namely *Lincsgirl91*. She left a comment on each post, and while she didn't always agree with him, she admitted when he made a good point. He returned the favor by one-upping the romance in his story for every twist she put in hers.

It had become a dance, of sorts. He couldn't help wondering about her. She'd mentioned a few personal things, but nothing concrete. Even so, he found himself looking for her in the message area as well as the story comments.

"Hey, Ian, mind if I join you?" Taylor broke into his thoughts.

He'd opted to eat in the kitchen rather than the dining room so he could catch up on his fanfiction reading. He gave his situation another minuscule thought but had no trouble pushing down the lid of the laptop and turning his attention to the hazel-eyed beauty in front of him, pouring herself a glass of water.

Am I so easily swayed between two women? Maybe

Lincsgirl91 wasn't hung up on another guy. But *Lincsgirl* wasn't here in the flesh, looking amazing.

"Hey. Are you back?"

"Ish." She wrinkled her nose adorably and shook her head. "Don't tell Rance, he wants me to take another week off." Shrugging, she sat down at the table with her bowl of soup. "Prudie makes the best potato soup."

"She is a wonder, isn't she?"

"She is." Taylor's mouth hung open. "I'm so sorry. I mean, you're a great cook too."

He held his hands up to ward off the apology. "There you go, apologizing again." He grinned broadly when her lighthearted laugh came forth. She was more relaxed than he'd ever seen her. Well, except for when she was asleep. That didn't count, did it?

"I'll try to stop." She pursed her lips and looked away for a moment. "Linda and Robert wanted me to take off until after Christmas, but I can't with the gala coming up soon after, so we compromised—part-time with breaks."

"It's a big deal, isn't it?"

"It is. Remember the hurricane that came through here six or seven years ago?"

He nodded as he blew on his soup. "I do. I came up here with a group to help flood victims clean out their houses. It was rough."

Taylor took a bite. "When I started working here, I learned Jared Benton ..."

"Isn't he the Crawford's son-in-law?"

"Yes, he's married to Sarah, Susan's younger sister. Anyway, he almost died in the storm."

Ian tried to imagine how it would feel to be so close to death. "Hurricanes are nothing to fool around with."

Taylor shook her head. "They're not. That year they lost

their hurricane relief fund when it was embezzled by a police officer. Since then, the community has rallied around the sheriff and police stations to raise money so it never gets low again."

"Susan and I have been working on the menu for the event. She says it will be the best one yet." Scooting his chair back, Ian stood and looked past Taylor at the clock. How had the time passed so quickly? "Speaking of the best one yet, some of us have to work for a living."

There it was again. Her laugh. It was infectious. No, not infectious. Habit-forming.

Taylor picked up her dishes and carried them to the sink. "Then I will leave you to it. Never let it be said I kept a chef from his appointed rounds." When she fluttered her fingers in a friendly wave, he had to smile.

"See you soon."

When her eyes met his, her smile grew slowly as she tilted her head. "Count on it."

WHO KNEW you could get a suntan in December? During her off time, Taylor walked up and down the beach daily. She'd also made a discovery that cut her to the core ... she liked sappy Christmas movies. Who knew?

Or maybe she was more comfortable thinking about romance these days.

On a particularly sunny day with weather in the upper sixties, she put up her Christmas tree. She covered it with seashells, starfish, and sand dollars, all found on the beach during her wanderings, then stepped back to survey her handiwork. It was progress. At one time she thought she'd never celebrate again.

Maybe there was something new on FanficWow.com. Her story was coming along nicely. She and *SPfan89* were corresponding regularly, and their stories were getting more and more convoluted and hilarious as the days went on. It was as if they were co-writing a story, and their *fans* were commenting to that effect. She shook her head. They had *fans*.

Taylor sat down and opened her laptop to find a message from *SPfan89*. It stopped her in her tracks. He'd sent her an email address.

She pulled her hands from the keyboard and stared at the screen. Did she want to go up a level of intimacy and start emailing? He'd put the ball in her court.

The image of a certain dark-eyed chef with one dimple— maybe two—made her hesitate. She'd sworn off romance because it hurt too much when she lost Mike. What if God had other plans for her? Had he put two men in her path?

To email or not to email. That is the question.

❧❧❧ ❀ ❧❧❧

TAYLOR WOKE up the next morning to a cold, cloudy day at the beach. More like December than the weather they'd been having. The wind blew, the surf roared, and it matched her mood.

Shivering in her fuzzy robe, she turned up the heat, then went to the coffee maker to brew her morning life-giving elixir. Sometimes the aroma of brewing coffee made her feel better. Today, it would take more than aromatherapy.

She put two pieces of bread in the toaster and pulled out her laptop. No email to speak of, unless she wanted to purchase an extended warranty on a piece of electronics she didn't own or borrow money at 25 percent interest.

As had become her habit, she clicked on FanficWow.net.

She saw a post on *SPfan's* story and a numeral on the messenger notifications indicating a new message since last night. A delicious shiver went through her.

Should I email him?

She moved the laptop to the coffee table and looked down at the ring on her left hand. Mike was gone. He wasn't coming back, and he'd want her to be happy. *Wouldn't he?*

Working the ring off over her knuckle, she held it in front of her eyes, turning it this way and that, watching as the clouds parted and morning sunshine reflected shards of light and color all over her living room. She hadn't done that in a long time.

A new day was dawning, and the thought filled her with awe.

Are you talking to me, God? Did you bring back the sunshine to let me know You're here?

She put the ring back on. A sense of despair clung to her as if she were being punished for something she had no control over. It had increased the bitterness and sadness in her heart to the point that she extended only an outward appearance of faith. Here at Pawleys Island, away from family and life-long acquaintances, she could skip church when she simply didn't want to face people. Easier to keep to herself instead of getting out and meeting new people.

The beep from the coffee maker caught her attention. Toast cold and coffee brewed, she pushed the lever down for a quick re-heat and poured her coffee, popping the toaster and slathering apple butter on the overcooked bread.

It's not burnt—it's perfect.

Settling in on the sofa, she pulled the computer into her lap to read *SPfan's* message:

Hey, Lincsgirl. Just checking on you. You mentioned not feeling well, and I hope you're better. I was being presumptuous and forward sending you that email address, and I apologize. Do you mind if I pray for you? See you on the forum.

He apologized. Somehow his old-fashioned manners, and his asking permission to pray, cheered her. She felt a little energy flowing through her.

Maybe it's time.

STARPORT: SP-1

Alex gazed up into McNeil's—no, Linc's—eyes.

Her feelings didn't change according to what she called this man. His hands rubbing up and down her back made her almost forget HER name, much less, his.

12

A frown formed between Ian's brows. He'd worked all day with Susan, creating the menu and making lists of ingredients and serving pieces to order, and his brain was mush. Also, he'd shared an email address with *Lincsgirl*, but she still hadn't acknowledged it, either in a message or with an email. Maybe she was skittish about meeting someone online.

Good grief. I created a new email address so I wouldn't be sharing my information with a stranger. And I'm questioning HER?

"Will you be all right by yourself tonight?" Grandpa's voice interrupted his thoughts.

Ian chuckled. Who cared for whom? "I suppose so. Got a hot date or something?"

"Something."

Did Ian see a tinge of red on his elderly grandfather's face? He stared. Grandpa had a date. "Do you need me to drive you somewhere?"

He hesitated, looking at the clock on the wall. "No. I have a ride."

"Uh-huh." Ian tilted his head curiously. "Something going on I should know about?"

Grandpa gathered himself up and put on his fiercest patriarchal glare. "I think I'm old enough to have a few secrets from the younger generation."

"You'll get no argument from me." He lifted his hands up to ward off the ire emanating from his usually easy-going grandfather.

"Besides, isn't it about time you made your own friends around here and started dating yourself?"

The image of a certain event manager floated through his mind, and he squelched it, remembering the sparkling ring on her hand. The elusive *Lincsgirl* crossed his mind ...

"Working on it, Grandpa. It's been pretty busy at work."

"Excuses, excuses." Grandpa chuckled, belying his earlier statement. "Life's short, son. You're not getting any younger, you know."

Ian twisted his lips in a reluctant grin. "You're doing better than me."

Although Grandpa was hard-of-hearing, he perked up at the crunch of the driveway's shell-and-gravel mixture. "That's my ride."

"Need any help getting to the car?"

"No. I'll be fine." He held up a highly polished walking cane and headed to the door, a spring in his step despite his limp. He opened the door and waved, then turned. "I won't be too late."

"See that you're not. Curfews aren't for nothing, you know, young man."

The old man winked and gave him a thumbs-up. "Yes, sir." And he was out the door.

Ian strolled to the window to see his ride and saw a familiar red SUV in the driveway. Prudie.

Grandpa and Prudie?

"Go for it, Grandpa."

Back to the comfort of the recliner, he pulled out the laptop. He checked email—both his old address and his new one—and saw nothing of note. Disappointing. Still no movement on the new email address.

The last message mentioned taking time off from work, which explained why her story seemed to be updated quicker than his. He posted his in the middle of the night. *Lincsgirl?* She posted in the middle of the day.

A fleeting thought came to him. Was it possible? Could it be? No. That would be crazy.

I'm crazy.

❧❧❧ ❄ ❦❦❦

TAYLOR FILLED out the online form and reviewed the information before she hit *submit* to create a new email address. She bit her lip, hesitating for a moment, but she hadn't revealed anything on there that would identify her if *SPfan* turned out to be a creep. There was always that possibility.

I've watched Dateline. It's always the quiet ones ...

A nervous giggle bubbled up from somewhere within as she clicked on the icon.

Working between the two tabs, she copied the email address *SPfan* sent into the *to* field. She took a deep breath. He'd given her an out if she didn't want to pursue a correspondence. But she did. As she thought about what to type, the light sparkled on the diamond in her engagement ring.

She held her hand in front of her, and a mist of tears impeded her vision.

It's time.

Taking her ring off, she stood and walked to her bedroom.

She placed her engagement ring in the velvet slot in her jewelry case. Realization hit her. She wasn't engaged anymore. She simply owned an amazing ring given to her by someone she loved and would always love.

Tears flowed. Memories crashed in on her. Rance introducing her to Mike. Snow falling in Charleston on their first date anniversary. Mike kneeling in the cold, wet slush to propose to her, and then treating her to a white Christmas in the mountains with his family. Then the heartbreak of watching as the life drained from him on the street during the half-marathon that he'd been so excited to run.

She closed the case and pulled a tissue from the box, wiping her face. Staring at herself in the mirror, she nodded, agreeing with the voice within that another chapter in her life was about to start. But that didn't make it any less scary. What if she got hurt again? Was she strong enough to handle another heartbreak?

Maybe she should stick with making new friends. She'd keep Ian and *SPfan* in the friend-zone.

13

After a busy morning of ordering food for the fundraiser, Ian was glad to sit alone in the kitchen with his sandwich.

He opened the laptop, surprised to see two new messages on his anonymous email account. The first "welcome to your new email account" message told him how to use email.

I think I can handle it, but thank you for caring.

But the second email? An unknown address flagged as potential spam. He smiled. *Lincsgirl91@hmail.com* was anything but.

Hi,

I waffled back and forth over whether to email you or not. Please tell me you're not a creepy ax murderer?

LOL

It took me a little time to get my courage up. It's not in

*my nature to be so brave as to email a perfect stranger,
but it's not quite as scary as calling you on the phone, or,
perish the thought, meeting in person.*

*Sorry, but I wanted to put that out there. And as a friend
would say, "there you go apologizing again."*

*Let's see if we can't wrap up this crazy story before
Christmas, please? Ha!!*

Lincsgirl.

Ian was stunned.

Stunned, exhilarated, and a little nervous. 'There you go apologizing again' wasn't exactly a coined phrase, but it had become a joke between Taylor and himself since their first meeting. He'd been suspicious, but this? This was getting closer to proof, and if he were honest, a relief. And scary. There was still the engagement ring and the specter of Mike, who'd obviously bailed on her, but still held her heart.

Should he tell her? Get his secret out in the open? Would she freak out?

❦❦❦❦ 🍬 ❦❦❦❦

IN THE DOCTOR'S OFFICE, a little thrill shot up Taylor's spine as she read the email from *SPfan* a second and then a third time.

Hi Lincsgirl,

Thanks for the email. I thought it might be easier to talk this way instead of in the message part of the forum. I'm

*never completely sure messaging there is private, not
that I plan to say anything untoward.*

*I agree. We need to finish up these stories. They're
starting to get a little over-the-top, aren't they? Although,
I think the ten people reading and commenting will
miss them when we're done. Maybe we should write one
together? I know of other members of the forum who've
done that.*

*Interesting that you wrote the Bartok and Dr. Garrity
characters pairing. I always wondered why they didn't
give the poor guy a girlfriend.*

*I have a lot going on at work, so if you email or message
me and I don't get back to you, it's not you, it's me.*

*Are you feeling better? I was concerned when you said
the dr wanted you to take some time off.*

Gotta go. Lunch is so over.

SPfan

If she were home, she'd answer him immediately. Would
that seem needy? Let him wait a little while. Like until after
her doctor's appointment.

"Ready to give me more blood?" The phlebotomist in the
lab used the usual Dracula accent and always laughed at his
own joke.

"Just don't take too much." She grinned at him. He was
cute, in an endearing, fresh-out-of-school way.

"I'll be gentle." He drew more than one vial, then pulled

out the needle and covered the wound with a cotton ball and tape. "I'll get the results to Dr. Butler before you make it to his office."

"Awesome." She pulled down her sleeve and reached for her jacket. "Thanks."

"Any time." He waved her away.

She walked out of the lab at Georgetown General and smack into Rance. "Whoa. What's the rush?"

He'd grabbed her upper arms to keep from knocking her over, a crazed look in his eyes. "It's time."

"Time for what? My appointment? I ..."

"No, Taylor. It's TIME." He looked over her shoulder to the exit. "I've got to go get Charly now."

"Go. I'll call your office and reschedule the appointment."

"Appointments. Office." He closed his eyes for a moment. "Forgot everything except water breaking and contractions starting and two bridges between her and me." He stared down at her. "Call my office and tell them what's going on. They know what to do."

She saluted. "Yes, sir."

He hugged her quickly and ran down the hallway to the exit. "You're a lifesaver."

"As long as I'm the tangerine-flavored one," she called out, knowing he hadn't heard a word.

STARPORT: SP-1

Bartok's face was a rather fearsome sight, "Are you saying that I will be unable to fulfill my duties with the SP-1 team for two weeks?"

"I'm afraid so." Beth was sympathetic. She knew he'd placed his confidence in her, and that his identity came from his work with the team.

14

"I 'll be right there."

Ian hung up and hurried to Susan's office. "I got a call from Prudie that Grandpa has fallen. I need to meet them at the hospital."

"Oh, I hope he's okay!" Concern etched her face. "Go. And let me know how he is."

He paused and looked at the clock. Two in the afternoon, and they had guests. "About supper ..."

She dismissed his concern. "Don't even think about it. Mom and I have cooked for guests before. We only have two couples. Family comes first."

"Thanks so much."

"Go. We'll be praying for Mr. Rutledge." She patted his arm. "And for you."

He nodded and took off his chef's coat, made his way to the kitchen, and hung the coat on a hook next to the door.

What have you done, now, Grandpa?

TAYLOR PEEKED into the maternity waiting room to see Charly's sister-in-law Lucy pacing back and forth, her short blond bob bouncing with each step. "Hey."

"Hi, Taylor." Lucy's attention darted back and forth between her, the door leading to labor and delivery, and the entrance to the waiting room.

"Is everything okay?" Taylor took a cue from Lucy and clenched her hands together.

Lucy waved a hand. "Don't mind me." She shook her head. "They'll be fine. The doctor is here, and the rest of the family is on their way. Three weeks isn't dangerously early. The twins were three weeks early and look at them, now." She laughed.

"Speaking of the twins, where are they?"

"Sarah's got them."

"Ouch. Plus one of her own. That makes three two-year-olds."

"Yeah. Sarah always wanted a houseful of kids. I guess this is a good test." Lucy sighed in relief when her husband, Tom, came through the door with his mother, the beautiful Mrs. Mary Ann Livingston. "Finally. I thought you'd never get here. Is this payback for Charly being here alone waiting for the twins to arrive?" Lucy melted into her husband's side as he drew her close, laughing.

"What's the latest on my baby?" Mary Ann looked concerned. It was hard enough being a mama, but she was blind. "And by my baby, I mean Charlotte." She always called Charly by her given name, as was proper.

"Rance came out here a few minutes ago. The doctor is here, and things are moving pretty fast. So much for first babies taking a long time, huh?" Lucy crossed her arms in front of her, mild annoyance written all over her face.

"Good. Charlotte came pretty fast, but Tom, here? Took him a day and a half to decide to come."

"Well, he is a pretty big boy, after all." Lucy hugged her mother-in-law. "The twins were no walk in the park, either, but they're here, and they're healthy. That's the main thing."

"Amen."

Taylor's attention was drawn to the door when a nurse escorted another group into the room, Rance's family.

"Any word?" Without preamble, Rance's mother, Anna, wanted an update.

Taylor hugged her and smiled, since she'd known Ms. Anna most of her life. "Things are going well."

"That's a relief. I was so afraid the baby would be born before we got here." She looked up at her husband, Ashton Butler. "I hounded this poor man all the way here to drive faster."

"I told her I wanted to get here to celebrate a grandchild, not to be taken to the ER." His bright, welcoming smile dimmed slightly when Clifton Watson came through the door. Ashton walked over to Rance's biological father and shook his hand. "You made it."

"No way I'd miss my first grandchild's birth." Clifton looked ill-at-ease, but the last two years had done much toward healing the hurts from so many years ago.

"I'm glad you're here, Cliff." Anna's smile was genuine. Clifton nodded, relaxing.

"It's getting pretty crowded in here, so I'll head out." Taylor began to feel claustrophobic. She took Anna's hand. "Text me when the baby gets here?"

"I will, sweetheart. I can't believe they didn't want to know if it was a boy or girl. This being 'surprised' is for the birds if you have the opportunity."

Taylor laughed. "I'd want to know, too, but to each his—or her—own, right?"

She left the hospital, wondering how the day had filled up from sunup on.

When she reached her car in the hospital parking lot, she saw a car whip into a parking place close to the ER. Ian Rutledge exited the car and jogged to the door. She hoped everything was okay. With his grandfather's age and his health issues, it might be serious.

15

I an arrived at the emergency room at the same time as the ambulance carrying Grandpa. He rushed in, noting that Prudie exited the front of the ambulance along with the EMTs. Ian's stress level rose with each moment.

He reached the gurney carrying the patient sporting a large white bandage on his head, Prudie by his side. "Grandpa, what happened?"

Hiding a smile, Grandpa refused to meet his eyes. Instead, he winked at the lady next to him. "Just took a little tumble. Got too big for my britches, I guess."

"What were you doing?" Did he need to secure help for daytime as well as him being there at night? Was Grandpa's mind getting worse? With each question, his worry grew.

Grandpa's hand reached for Prudie's, and they looked at one another and laughed. "I'll be fine. I didn't break anything. I hit my head, and Prudie panicked."

"Your grandpa was trying to show me how to dance the two-step." She blushed.

"The two-step?" What could Ian say? *Young man, you knew better?* "Are you in any pain?"

"The leg took the brunt, and then my hard head."

"You didn't mess up where they did the surgery, did you?"

"I don't think so." Grandpa looked at him sternly. "Don't you go blaming Prudie. She told me to settle down."

"Oh, I don't blame Prudie." Ian cocked a brow at the gray-haired woman standing beside his grandpa. He wanted to laugh, now that he knew it wasn't serious.

"Good." Grandpa seemed satisfied as he looked up at the nurse who'd come to wheel him in. "Let's get this show on the road. I've got a parade to *grand marshal* in exactly five days."

"Now, Grandpa ..." Was riding in a parade on the doctor's list of approved activities?

"Don't you 'now Grandpa,' me, boy." He pointed his finger and wore the most impressive *Grandpa* look Ian had seen in a long time.

"We'll see what the doctor says."

The nurse glanced from one to the other. "Can I take you back now?" She raised her brows.

"Sorry." Ian stepped back and watched as they took him through the ER doors, then turned to Prudie. "The two-step? Really?"

She shook her head. "I know. I told him an old man with a cane had no business dancing at all, but he wanted to prove he could. Unfortunately, the coffee table got in the way of his fall."

"I'm glad he's not hurt any worse."

"Me too." She sighed, shaking her head. "Your Grandpa. He's a doodle, isn't he?" Her lips twisted in a grin as she patted Ian's shoulder. "He'll be fine. His head is as hard as they come."

THAT EVENING, after settling Grandpa into a room and doing a little shopping, Ian stepped off the elevator on the maternity floor carrying a bouquet in one hand, and in the other, a gift bag holding a baseball mitt. Rance's son might be a little young for it yet, but you couldn't start too early, in his opinion. To be honest, if the baby had been a girl, he'd have brought her a pink one.

Ian stopped at the nurse's station, where a pretty blonde glanced up and smiled. "May I help you?"

"Charly Butler?"

"Dr. Butler's wife." She grinned when he nodded. "She's in 304, down the hall and to your left." She bit her lip. "Do you need me to show you?"

"I think I can find it. Thank you."

"You're welcome. Let me know if there's anything I can do for you." Her brows lifted and he raised a hand and walked away. At one time he would have flirted right back at an attractive woman who showed interest in him. He was either getting old or getting more particular.

He knocked gently and heard Rance's quiet "come in."

Ian pushed open the door to see Charly asleep on the bed and Rance in the recliner holding a wad of blankets. He carefully placed the flowers and gift bag on the rolling tray next to the bed.

"I'm assuming there's a baby in there somewhere?" Ian eased over to his friend, who maneuvered the baby so he could show him off.

"Ian Rutledge, meet Reed Livingston Butler, my son." In a voice lower than a whisper, Rance spoke with emotion.

"He's awesome." Ian caught a hint of tears in his buddy's voice, and when he looked up, Rance was smiling and teary at the same time.

"He is, isn't he?" The new father held his son close, shaking his head. "Sometimes I have to pinch myself that I'm a husband and a father." He chuckled low. "Who knew?"

"Right?" Ian smiled. He wanted to mention knowing Taylor. How could he work it into the conversation? "I'm surprised the room isn't full of visitors."

"You just missed them. They were going out to celebrate, and come back later when they can, once again, fight over who gets to hold him longest." Rance chuckled. "Hey, how's the new job going?" He looked up quizzically. "Any more panic attacks?"

"Are you my buddy, or my doctor?"

"Both."

Ian grinned. "Great, and no, thank goodness." He spied a side chair by the door and tiptoed over to bring it nearer Rance.

"How's your grandfather?"

"You're off-duty, remember?"

"I know, but I'd ask even if I weren't a doctor."

"He's good. They're keeping him overnight for observation. Just a knock on the head." Ian couldn't help staring at his friend, the father. Weird.

"What about the job?"

"Love it."

Rance nodded. "I had a feeling. The Crawfords are good people."

"I'm finding that out." An opening. "I understand you know their event manager, Taylor Fordham?"

"Yeah!" Rance looked surprised. "We've been friends since middle school, I think."

"That's a long time." Ian eyed his friend. "Did you two ever date?"

Rance's laugh burst out before he could slap his hand over his mouth. Charly shifted in the bed, and the baby stiffened in surprise.

"Gotta remember to keep my laughs to myself." He watched as little Reed relaxed and went back to sleep.

"Hi, Ian. How long have you been here?" Charly pushed up to a sitting position. "Ooo! You brought presents!"

She sniffed the bouquet and handed it to Rance to place on the windowsill with a few other arrangements. When she opened the gift bag, she laughed. "What every newborn needs. A baseball glove."

"If he's a lefty, we'll have to get a different one."

"Thank you, Ian. You're very sweet."

"You're more than welcome. You've got a fine boy there, Charly."

"I think so too." She sighed, her attention divided between her guest and her husband comfortably holding the newborn.

"Sorry I woke you, babe." Rance winced.

She smiled. "I was starting to wake up anyway. I had to hear the answer to Ian's question about whether or not you and Taylor ever dated."

"Very funny." Rance turned his attention to Ian. "No, we never dated—except in emergencies. We were buddies, like you and me, only she refused to be my wingman."

"I can imagine. She seems nice."

The speculative gleam in Rance's eyes matched his arched brow. "She is nice." He stood and handed little Reed to his mother, who'd held out her arms as if she couldn't wait for another second to hold him again. Successful transition without waking the baby, they all relaxed. "Anything you want to know about Taylor?"

The unexpected question threw him off. He hadn't thought that far ahead. "Is she engaged?" Where did that question come from?

You idiot, you've been wondering that ever since you saw her engagement ring.

"Was." A sad expression crossed Rance's face. "Do you remember Mike Sloan? A couple of years ahead of us at Clemson?"

"Sure. I didn't know him as well as you."

"He was pre-med, like me, and kind of took me under his wing when he tutored me in Organic Chemistry."

Charly spoke up. "That sounds horrible."

"You have no idea, sweetheart. Anyway, I introduced them when we were at a pizza joint in Charleston one weekend." He drew in a breath. "Great guy."

"What happened?"

"He died."

16

"Died?" Dumbfounded. He'd been ready for a called off broken engagement and shattered heart, but not this. His soul ached for her. It was unfathomable that she'd suffered so much loss and pain at such a young age.

"It was during a half-marathon last summer. He had a massive heart attack right there on the street. Taylor was there. Heck, me and half of the hospital staff were there, and there was nothing we could do. Later, I found out he had an undiagnosed valve issue that chose that moment to blow."

"All the training he'd done, and his number comes up then." Rance closed his eyes for a moment. "He was a good guy. Good friend. Engaged to be married, great job as a hospitalist here at Georgetown General. The sky was the limit."

"I had no idea. I noticed her ring ..."

"Oh." A statement, not a question. Rance's eyebrows rose.

Heat started at the back of his neck and traveled upward. Hopefully, it would stop before it reached his face. "Guys notice these things."

"I've heard that." Charly laughed, then gave Rance a saucy

grin. "That's why when I caught this guy, I didn't let go for anything."

"I'm glad you got me." Rance leaned down and kissed her lips softly. "And I got you."

"Okay, single guy here." Ian waved his hand.

Rance cleared his throat and gave him a pointed look. "Taylor is great. She's funny and a little nerdy."

"How's that?"

"She was always trying to get me to watch this one show." Rance laughed, and realization dawned in his eyes. "That same show you used to watch on repeat all the time ... I can't remember the name of it ..."

Ian had to look away. "*StarPort: SP-1*?"

Rance pointed at him. "That's the one. Wonder if she still watches it?"

Oh, she watches it, all right ...

❦

TAYLOR'S FEET moved forward as if walking through molasses. There was no spring in her step. Some of the feelings she thought she'd gotten past were rearing their ugly heads.

If Mike hadn't died ...

Stop it. Stop it right now, Taylor Fordham. Sure, if Mike hadn't died, I'd be married and maybe even having my own baby by now. But he did, and I may as well accept it.

One voice inside her head kept telling her to 'suck it up.'

Then there was another one. The one that let her wallow.

I'll never find happiness again. I'll be old and alone with no children and no more love in my life. Why even try?

That one had a name—no, several. Despair. Pain. Melancholy. Satan. Yeah, he tried to knock her off her feet every chance he got. She tried not to listen to him.

Exiting the elevator, she followed the signs and found Charly's hospital room without incident. She paused when she heard voices. Good, nobody is asleep.

She put on her public face and pushed the door open to see the new mom, baby, new dad, and a very discombobulated Ian. Curious.

"Hey, guys."

Charly held out the arm that wasn't holding Reed, and Taylor accepted the invitation for a hug. She needed hugs more often. Physical contact with a good friend lifted a little of the load off Taylor's heart.

"I had to come and see this little guy." She handed Charly the gift bag she carried and stole a peek at him. It was love at first sight. Tears filled her eyes, and she never knew she liked babies before. An only child, she had no nieces or nephews, but since she'd started working for the Crawfords, kids—toddlers to pre-teens—were all around her.

"What am I, chopped liver?" Rance put an arm around Taylor's shoulder, and she reached to hug him too.

"No, Rance." She looked down at the baby. "Y'all did good."

"We did, didn't we?" Charly beamed. "Do you want to hold him?"

Could she? "What if I drop him?" Her heart began beating a mile a minute, her desire to hold the baby escalating unexpectedly.

"You won't drop him." Rance took the baby from his wife and held him out to Taylor.

Unable to resist, she took him in her arms, holding up his little head and relaxing into a natural sway that seemed to come out of nowhere.

Charly pulled the gift from the bag Taylor brought. "Baby Yoda!" She laughed and hugged the stuffed animal, her eyes going wide when it made the sounds of a newborn. "This is so cool."

"Only you." Rance chuckled.

"I'm determined to share my love of Sci-fi with the younger generation." Taylor smiled.

"If anybody can, it will be you." Rance watched her for a minute. "You're a natural."

"I agree." A lower voice joined the conversation.

She'd forgotten about Ian, and heat crawled up her neck and cheeks. He looked at her as if he'd never seen her before.

Drat those tear ducts. "I wouldn't go that far."

Ian walked over closer to her, looking at the baby, touching his tiny hand. Little Reed grasped his finger, and Ian looked at her in wonder. "Does this mean he likes me?"

"I'm sure it has nothing to do with the natural grasping reflex in all infants." Rance chuckled.

"Don't ruin the moment with medical jargon." Ian frowned. "I'll take what I can get."

Reed started wriggling and scrunched up his face, still not making a sound, but clearly waking, working hard at an activity Taylor wanted no part in at this juncture.

"I'm thinking he will need a parental figure—and soon."

"It's Rance's turn." Charly sent her husband a cheesy grin.

17

W hen Charly's dinner tray arrived, Taylor took her leave. Ian following after her. The blonde at the nurses' station looked disappointed when he came down the hallway with Taylor.

He didn't know what to say. Taylor was *Lincsgirl91*.

To tell her now, or wait?

Wait. Definitely wait. She was still hung up on Mike. Even though the poor guy was dead. Despite his best—friendship only—intentions, Ian wanted more. But grief couldn't be rushed.

"How are the gala plans coming along?" Taylor broke the silence when they entered the elevator.

He stuffed his hands in his pockets and looked up at the ceiling of the moving cubical. "Good. We've got all the food ordered, and Susan is working on the layout."

Taylor covered her face with her hands, then looked up at him, her mouth in a thin line. "I'm supposed to be doing that."

"Hey." He touched her arm to get her attention. "It's not all on you."

"I know, but that's the fun part, and I'm missing out." She gave him a sidelong glance and a half-smile. "How about that baby?"

"Way to change the subject." He laughed. They walked off the elevator and stopped.

"I'm a master at it." She grinned.

"Little Reed gets my vote."

She sighed, with a faraway look in her eyes. "Mine too."

If she could change the subject, so could he. "I'm going to check on Grandpa before I leave."

"Is he okay?"

Ian snorted. "He'll be good. They're keeping him for observation since he whacked his head on the coffee table."

"What in the world ...?"

"According to Prudie, he was teaching her the two-step." Their eyes met. Ian raised a brow, and Taylor laughed out loud. He had to join in. "I know. Crazy, huh?"

She quieted. "I hope to be that crazy when I'm his and Prudie's age."

"Me too." He hesitated, and it seemed that Taylor did, too. "Have you had supper yet?"

"No"

He didn't want to leave just yet. "Would you join me for dinner?"

"Why Mr. Rutledge. On such short acquaintance?" She used an exaggerated Southern accent and put her hand to her chest as if shocked at his suggestion.

"There's not a non-fraternization policy among Pilot Oaks employees, is there?" He narrowed his eyes, wondering if she'd take the bait. After all, that's what had kept their favorite characters apart for fifteen seasons.

"I don't think so." She tapped her chin with her finger,

looking at him curiously. "I could be persuaded, as long as they serve sweet tea."

He smiled. "I think you're safe in this neighborhood." A thought came to him. "Do you want to wait for me here, or tag along and meet Grandpa?"

She bit her lip, then met his gaze. "I'd love to meet your grandpa. Prudie talks about him all the time."

"Oh, she does, does she?" Ian held an elbow out and she took it. "You'll have to fill me in. I have a feeling there's some fraternization going on between those two ..."

✾✾✾ ❀ ❦❦❦

"I'll have the crab cakes, please." Taylor handed her menu to the server and linked her fingers together, elbows on the table.

Ian perused the entree menu at Big Tuna, an eatery on the Harbor Walk in historic Georgetown. "Don't think less of me for not ordering seafood, but I think I'll have the ribeye." He looked the server in the eye. "Medium Rare." When the server nodded, Ian shook his head. "Write it down, because you can't uncook a steak, and I know your chef."

"Yes, sir." The young man grinned and wrote it down. "Can I get you an appetizer?"

"She-crab soup?" Ian looked across at Taylor, who smiled.

"That sounds good."

"She-crab Soup for both of us." Ian handed over his menu.

"And lots of sweet tea," Taylor interjected.

"Coming right up. Would you like me to send the chef out to see you?"

Ian laughed. "Let's wait until after the meal."

The server nodded, then hurried to the kitchen, leaving them alone.

Unsure what to talk about, Taylor looked around, then dove in. "This is nice. I haven't been here in a while."

"I like it. And I usually order seafood." Ian shrugged. "The chef is Greg Powers, a friend of mine. We went to culinary school together."

"Ah. It might be nice to eat with someone who has connections." Taylor grinned, more relaxed than she'd been in a long time. Though Ian didn't make her nervous, she kept fingering the spot where her ring had been. It felt so naked, it distracted her a little.

Which is probably a good thing.

The server brought the rich She-crab soup and bread, along with their drinks.

"This smells amazing." Taylor stirred her soup so it would cool. "So, your grandfather will be the grand marshal in the Murrells Inlet parade. How exciting for him."

A shadow crossed Ian's face. "Yeah ... I'm not sure it's a good idea, but he's determined."

"How did he hurt his leg?" Taylor blew on the spoonful of soup.

"He stepped off his fishing boat. A buoy shifted and knocked the boat crooked. Just one of those things when you're a fisherman. He was alone and lay there with a broken leg for three hours before anyone found him. Fortunately, he landed back in the boat instead of in the river."

"That's rough." There was something more in Ian's tone. She couldn't quite put her finger on it. "Does he usually have a partner?"

Ian shook his head. "No, but at his age, it would be better if he did." He dipped a piece of bread into the soup and took a bite. "Not much family left that's close by. I think we've all neglected him since Grandma passed away."

Taylor thought a minute. "He doesn't seem lonely." The

garrulous old man won her over upon first meeting, and from what Prudie had said, he didn't have much chance to be alone, much less lonely.

"How could he not be?" Ian shrugged.

"How long has your grandmother been gone?"

"Three years. I thought about coming up here to work when I got out of school, to be nearby for him, but then Greg and I had the opportunity to open the restaurant in Charleston."

"And now, here you are."

He scoffed. "Here I am." His half-smile came across as sad. "I'm here for Grandpa, but only because the restaurant folded, no thanks to me."

"I imagine there's more to it than that."

He quirked up one side of his mouth. "There is." He drew in a breath. "We started low on both experience and capital with expensive tastes in ingredients."

"It doesn't sound as though it was all on you."

Ian shrugged. "Maybe. I felt responsible, as the head chef. Greg's a good chef, but he tried to hold the business together while I kept ordering food. When I found out how much in the hole we were, it was too late to save it."

Tilting her head, she read sincerity and humility on his face. "Sounds like he should have kept you in the loop more."

"Maybe." He shook his head as if trying to throw off the serious topic. "Fortunately, he doesn't hold a grudge."

"I guess we'll find out when you get your steak." She smiled at him, hoping to lighten things up, and it worked.

For the first time since she met him, he laughed out loud, and her eyes widened.

He DOES have a second dimple ...

Just friends. Just friends.

Maybe if she kept repeating it to herself.

18

W hen Taylor didn't feel particularly sociable, she ate lunch in the kitchen's sunny breakfast nook. Prudie was gone for the day, and Ian was supervising the cleanup in the dining room.

Today, she needed time to think. She stood and gathered her plate and silverware, then stopped when a notification came up on her shiny—if a bit scratched—phone. An email. From *SPFan*. The time sent was last night, and she was just now getting it? Oh well. It wasn't the first time an important communique had gone rogue and appeared late. She felt a smile tug at her lips when she sat back down and opened the message.

Dear Lincsgirl,

Hope you're feeling better. I'm sorry I've been out of pocket for a few days. Things are heating up at work, and by the time I get home, I'm falling asleep at the computer. Thank goodness we finished our stories. I concede to your superior storytelling skills. You not only gave Linc and Alex a happily-ever-after but demolished each reason they had stayed apart so long. I'm impressed.

I've been thinking, and before you start complimenting me on using my brain, hear me out. I'd like us to meet. I think we've shared enough about ourselves that we are ready to connect. I can always use a new friend.

What do you think?
SPfan

Taylor's lip would be raw if she didn't stop chewing on it. *Meet?*

SPfan wanted to meet? It was scary and exciting at the same time.

I'm not a thirteen-year-old girl meeting a predator.

At least she hoped not.

Ian walked up to her, plate in hand. The cook always ate last.

"Hey, Ian."

"Hey." He had a nice smile. Dependable. Solid.

Dimples.

She couldn't help the chuckle that tumbled out.

"Are you okay?" He looked at her strangely but in a friendly way.

"I'm fine, thinking about something I read before you walked up." She took a sip of hot chocolate and gestured for him to join her across the table.

He settled in with his perfectly constructed sandwich, then looked across at her.

She had a fleeting thought. *Why do my sandwiches never look like that? Random.*

"Drinking your dessert today?"

Sighing with pleasure, she nodded. "I've got to get Prudie's hot chocolate recipe."

"Cinnamon and cayenne pepper."

"Come again?" Her mouth dropped open.

"Yep." He waited as she took another sip. "Notice the lingering heat after a few sips?"

"I'm going to experiment tonight." They'd become friends in the last weeks, solidified by their impromptu dinner a few nights ago. "May I ask your opinion on something?"

"Sure." He took a large bite of his turkey club.

Taylor hesitated. Was this too weird? *Too weird that I'm attracted to Ian and asking his opinion about meeting another guy that I may be attracted to as well?*

"... I met this guy online."

"Creeper?" He had an odd look on his face. Maybe it was her imagination.

"I don't think so?"

"You put a question mark on the end of your sentence. I heard it." Ian's expression gave nothing away.

"Anyway ..." She glared gently. "We've been emailing back and forth, and now he wants to meet." She scrunched up her face, hoping it wouldn't stick that way as her mother had always threatened.

He took another bit of sandwich and lowered his brows. "Do you want to meet this guy?" His deep brown eyes seemed to bore into her. At least he was showing interest now.

"Part of me wants to because we seem to have so much in common. Another part of me is anxious at the thought."

He nodded. "Sounds reasonable." Frowning, his gaze sank

to the floor for a moment, then bounced back up at her. "What kind of things do you have in common?"

Here we go.

She had a hard time meeting his eyes. "We both like this ... television show."

※→≫ ✿ ≪←※

IAN KNEW he'd made a mistake the moment he laughed out loud, so he got his act together quickly. The last thing he intended was to make fun. When he saw her reticence to admit her guilty pleasure, so much like his, it came out naturally— relief more than anything. He couldn't remember being this attracted to a woman. Her shy glow only intensified his feelings.

"You asked." Taylor set her cup down on the table and crossed her arms, leaning away from him.

"I'm sorry I laughed." He leaned forward. "So, you have this TV show in common."

"We met on a fanfiction forum."

"Fanfiction?"

She looked sheepish. "Fanfiction is where you take a TV show or book series, and write stories in that story world, with those characters. You can make them do anything you want."

"Like a little community of superfans?" He cocked an eyebrow.

"You make it sound like a bunch of forty-year-old guys living in their mom's basement playing video games."

"That wasn't the image I was getting." He grinned.

Laying her silverware on her plate, she gathered her things to leave the table. "Anyway, we exchanged emails and have had nice conversations. That's all."

He reached for her hand as she reached to pick up her mug

and leave. "Taylor, if you think you want to meet this guy, do it."

Twisting her lips, her expression was unsure. "I don't know ..."

"You only live once." He said nothing else until she looked up at him. "Who knows? He may be your soulmate?"

From my mouth to God's ears ...

STARPORT: SP-1

"Fly back to Denver with me?" Linc's boyish plea caused Alex to grin.

"Can't. I have a meeting with Major General Sherwood first thing in the morning. I thought while you were gone, I'd crash at your place if it's okay with you." She was able to sneak a quick kiss between sentences.

The military vehicle arrived all too soon to take McNeil to the airport.

"And here I was hoping to get you all to myself on a flight between here and Denver."

19

I t wasn't a glowing recommendation, but Ian's advice meant a lot to Taylor.

She put away the few groceries she'd bought, then checked both email accounts. On her personal one, her mom had emailed, asking for the fifth time what she wanted for Christmas.

Running it pretty close, eh, Mom?

And then the inevitable 'When are you coming home for Christmas?' and 'Will you be able to stay a week?' Like Mom thought she had school breaks.

She'd answer her mother later, after dinner. Now for the new, anonymous email. He hadn't emailed again, leaving his question hanging, and giving her plenty of time to consider it.

A tiny part of her wanted him to ask her again. Was that being selfish?

Do it.

Taylor hesitated, her fingers poised over the keys. Part of her wanted to close the laptop, forget this email address, and fade into the background. The other part? The other part wanted to move on. Wanted to see what would happen.

Take a chance.

Easier said than done. What if Ian was attracted to her, as she was to him? Shouldn't she allow him to ask her out, at least? After their dinner the other night, Taylor felt more comfortable with him, and he seemed to enjoy being with her as well. Was it wrong to be interested in two guys at the same time? How had she gotten past thinking of them as friends?

A long, desperate sigh whooshed its way out of her being. She made it much more difficult than necessary, and she knew it. Type already.

Hi SPfan,

I'd love to meet the person who is as obsessed with this show as me. You tell me when and where, and I'll let you know how to recognize me ...

❦

Taylor's email surprised Ian. He knew how conflicted she was at the thought of meeting someone she'd only met online. He hovered the cursor over the unopened email, ready to click it open when he heard a voice.

"Ian, could you come back here for a minute?"

"Sure, Grandpa." He set his laptop on the table next to his chair and made his way there. "What do you need?"

"Your opinion." Grandpa looked a little discombobulated, which was unusual.

Ian laughed. "Since when do you need my opinion?"

"I can't decide what to wear to ride in the parade. I want to look good, not like an invalid riding in the back of a convertible, wrapped up in blankets." The older man narrowed his eyes. "Any ideas?"

"You're serious." Ian crossed his arms, suspicious. "What are you up to?"

"None of your business. I just want options."

"Options that won't make you look like an old man." He knew his eyebrows were lifted to his hairline by now.

Grandpa pinned him with a glance and nodded. "Bingo."

Most of grandpa's shirts were in the blue family. "It's supposed to be in the 50s on Saturday, so you'll need a jacket."

"I thought so too." Grandpa rifled through the articles of clothing. "Nothing is speaking to me."

A laugh threatened to explode from within Ian, but he kept it together. "How about your red sweater over this shirt, then your leather jacket?" He quirked a brow at him. "That youthful enough for you?" Ian's lips wobbled, trying to hide a grin. "If you want to look young, leave your shirttail untucked and don't wear socks."

"Let's not get carried away." Grandpa rolled his eyes. "I think wearing jeans instead of polyester is about as much of a concession as I can make in that department."

"Good call." Ian tilted his head. "Two-step, huh?"

Grandpa's eyes cut him a side-glance as he grinned. "Two-step."

Ian nodded, studying the old man's face, knowing that things were about to change. "You're sure you don't want me to drive you in the parade?"

"Nope. I want you out there watching, taking pictures for posterity."

"I can do that."

"And who knows, maybe that young lady I met will be at the parade too."

"Maybe."

"Nice girl." Grandpa arched one brow. "And I think you've noticed that."

Ian pushed his hands into his pockets and nodded his head. "Should I ask her if she knows the two-step?"

"Couldn't hurt." Grandpa winked and patted him on the shoulder as he walked out of the bedroom, his limp barely visible.

TAYLOR READ his email again as she stood in front of her closet that evening, trying to select the perfect outfit.

Hi Lincsgirl,

How about we meet at the Murrells Inlet Christmas parade? There's an ice cream shop on the Marshwalk, and it's never too cold for ice cream, is it?

Looking forward to seeing you ...

Was she too easily swayed by a nice turn-of-phrase?

Hi SPfan!

I can't wait! I'll be wearing a red hat and will be in front of Twister's. Is that the place you were talking about? How will I know you?

In a matter of hours she'd meet *SPfan*. Her thoughts veered to Ian for a few minutes, making her wonder, but she'd already reasoned it out. She'd meet this guy and satisfy her curiosity with no expectations other than meeting a new friend with something cool in common.

She pulled out her favorite blue turtleneck sweater. The soft wool and deep color made her hazel eyes pop blue. At least that's what she'd been told. Blue sweater, jeans, and her favorite brown leather boots. Looking over the hats in her cold-weather-gear bin, she pulled out the second red hat she found. This one wasn't just red. It had snowflakes on it. She smiled. If she were to ask for a sign from God these days, it would include snow.

That's silly. Isn't it, God?

The hat she'd bought for the trip to the mountains with Mike. She fingered the soft knit. Before tears could form, she held it to her chest for a moment, thinking about the happy memories it brought to mind. She'd always love Mike. Always. And she knew recovery after losing someone so important to you is a process, and it doesn't have a timeframe.

She also knew that God loved her and wanted the best for her. Was she ready to learn what that *best* was?

❧❧❧❧ ❦ ❧❧❧❧

THE CALVARY CHURCH couples Christmas party was a good testing ground for the gala in a few weeks. He knew several of the attendees—Rance and Charly included—and Ian felt confident it would go well. The menu they'd settled on was one he could cook in his sleep—which he was doing on a more regular basis now. His mind was divided tonight. Part of him was keeping tabs on the kitchen, the other, thinking about meeting *Lincsgirl*, AKA Taylor on Saturday at the parade.

Soft Christmas music filtered into the kitchen every time the door swung open, and the extra staff they'd hired kept things running smoothly.

"Ian?"

A smile tugged at his lips when he heard Taylor's voice from the region of the door. Looking under the rack of pots between himself and where she stood, he crouched lower to see her face.

Sometimes just looking at her reduced his blood pressure. And sometimes, it increased it.

This time? The worried look on her face affected him all the way to the pit of his stomach.

"What's wrong?" Scanning the room, he was becoming more confused by the second. "Taylor?"

"There's smoke in the dining room."

Bile collected in his throat as he glanced at the wall holding four wall ovens and a bank of warming drawers. Looking around, he could see a haze up high, but the high-powered vent hoods near the ovens kept it clear in the kitchen. He rushed to the swinging kitchen doors leading to the dining room and his heart fell.

Sure enough, there was a thick haze of smoke hovering over the room. At that precise moment, the smoke alarms went off, alerting the diners who began looking around for exits and instructions.

Taylor took charge. She waved, then shouted to get their attention after the murmuring died down. "Folks, I don't think there's anything wrong, but we have an exit plan. Those of you on the last row of tables will exit through the French doors behind you, the next row to the door near the hostess station, and the ones nearest the kitchen to the hallway and out the front door."

Ian watched the evacuation like it was a dance in slow-motion. The hosts and hostesses had thought this through. Taylor was the emcee, and Robert, Jared Benton, and Mike Harris—Susan's husband—each took a door and made sure everyone exited in an orderly manner. He came to himself, realizing he had his own duties, but he couldn't get the girl with the microphone off his mind.

A crisis seemed to bring out the best in Taylor, which didn't surprise him. He evacuated the kitchen with the others, thankful they were dealing with smoke, which wouldn't set off the heat-triggered sprinkler system.

Once the kitchen and waitstaff were clear, he went through the stations working on various stages of meal prep. Cooktops, off, no evidence of scorching or burning. When he got to the ovens, however, his heart seized within him.

Smoke seeped out of one oven and then sucked out through the nearby ventilation system. He tried to pull open the oven door, but it was locked.

The Crawfords had two new ovens installed a week ago, not trusting the old ovens that had been in service for many years. It was top-of-the-line, but its day had come and gone, and now it was clear why new ovens were needed before the gala on New Year's.

At some point, when all the ovens were supposed to be turned off and the roasted pork loin left in a closed oven for another hour and a half, the door of this oven had inadvertently been locked and the self-cleaning feature activated. The temperature, instead of going down slowly from 450, had risen to well over 800 degrees.

He pulled at the door. Nothing. Tried the lock lever. Would not budge. There was still an hour left on the timer, and unless they wanted to ruin the oven, it would have to sit there and finish the cycle, incinerating one-fourth of the meat meant to serve the fifty people now shivering on the patio.

The pressure in his chest increased. In his head, he knew it was like the panic attack he'd had while driving a few weeks ago. In his current state of agitation, knowing what was riding on this one dinner, his head wasn't reliable.

The last thing he remembered was Taylor's hand on his shoulder, then nothing.

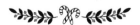

TAYLOR HAD SEEN a heart attack before. When Mike collapsed on the pavement, her world had turned upside down. He'd grasped at his chest, face sweating suddenly, and then, he was out. It had been so massive, she couldn't even get to him before he was dead.

Watching Ian grasp his chest and go down, it was *déjà vu*.

No. I can't go through this again. I won't.

"Help!"

Robert and Prudie came through the door. Robert to Ian's side, Prudie to the oven that was putting out more and more smoke. She pushed a few buttons, then turned to them. "Is he okay?"

"I called 911." Taylor's voice shook. She felt useless.

When Ian's eyes flickered, they met Taylor's, but she couldn't maintain his gaze. She turned, leaving the kitchen, but knew she would never forget the look of agony on her friend's face.

Was he more than a friend?

No. I've gone through this once. Never again.

She saw Susan in the hallway. "Taylor? Are you okay?"

"It's Ian ... he's ..." Tears came. "I have to leave."

Susan frowned. "Is he okay?"

"I don't know. He was unconscious." Raising teary eyes to her friend, she shook her head. "It was so much like Mike ..."

Ian's eyes closed again when he saw the look of abject fear on Taylor's face before she practically ran from the room. The pain had eased, but when the EMTs came in and checked his vitals, she was gone.

"What's going on?" Ian took in a deep breath when he heard Rance's voice.

"Taylor called 911. I think she thought I was having a heart attack." And it sure felt like it.

The EMT handed Rance his stethoscope. "I think you'll live to cook another roast." He pulled Ian to a sitting position. "Another panic attack?"

Ian nodded. "This time it was definitely stress-induced." He looked around, seeing Rance, Prudie, Robert, and Linda looking at him with concern.

Susan rushed in and expelled the breath she seemed to be holding. "Thank the Lord." She stopped, hands on her hips, shaking her head. "I think you scared poor Taylor to death."

Was it possible to feel the blood drain from your face? "She thought I was having a heart attack." Ian closed his eyes and bowed his head, repeating his statement from earlier, then looked up at his friend

"I'll talk to her." Rance nodded.

"I sent her home." Susan spoke up. "She was close to falling apart and just said she had to go."

"One of these days when I think I'm having a panic attack, I may actually be having a heart attack." *Maybe Taylor should guard her heart against me, after all.*

"I think you're putting way too much importance on a couple of episodes." Rance reached his hand down to help Ian to his feet. "If you want me to run more tests, I'd be glad to."

"Ian, I wish you would. I don't want you to take any chances." Linda's mouth twisted in concern.

"Couldn't hurt." Rance looked more serious than he'd seen him in a while. "Better safe than sorry."

Taylor got back to her condo and couldn't stop shaking. Part of her wanted to go to the beach and walk off some of the horror that continued to fill her mind with images of Mike, then Ian, lying on a highway, dead.

The other part of her wanted to go to bed and pull the covers over her head for the foreseeable future.

She changed from her holiday hostess attire and pulled on a pair of well-worn jeans and a hooded sweatshirt with *Pawleys Island* emblazoned on the front.

The muted ding on her phone alerted her to a text message. Susan.

You okay?

Not sure.

There was a pause while Taylor watched the little dots dance, indicating someone was typing a message.

Ian's okay.

What happened?

He's having some tests run to make sure there's nothing wrong. He's up and about now.

I'm glad.

Looking around at the muted Christmas decorations in her

living room, she felt angry. She'd almost given in to the holidays and to the idea of having someone in her life again.

"What's up with this, God? Am I being punished for something I did? If so, what IS it?"

She sat on her couch, head back, looking at the ceiling, hoping for some kind of divine guidance, or at least a little reassurance. What about the Holy Spirit, the Comforter? Where was He?

Nothing. Nothing but pain, heartache, and the pressing feeling of despair she'd almost forgotten. It wasn't as if she and Ian had a relationship beyond that of friendship. Not yet, anyway. She'd wondered ... but no. *It would be better to be alone forever than to put myself through this hurt again.*

Life would go on. She wiped the tears from her eyes and took a breath. Her laptop called to her. Maybe she could get her mind off this latest sorrow.

Opening her email program, she felt her heart leap a little when she saw an email from *SPfan. Tomorrow's the big day. I finally get to meet SPfan.*

She didn't want to get her hopes up. After today, she'd be even more wary than before. Maybe she should be thankful for the friends she had and not put herself out there to hope for more. What was the point?

Settling into her favorite position on the sofa, she clicked on the unread email.

Dear Lincsgirl,

Can I just say I'm more than a little excited that we get to meet day after tomorrow? I don't want to scare you off by being too anxious, but it's been a crazy week, and I'd like to think about something besides work.

I hope you're not disappointed.

> Soon,
> SPfan

Taylor shut the laptop and leaned back, closing her eyes. She knew she wouldn't be disappointed. But what about him? Was he prepared to meet a shell-shocked woman who was afraid of new relationships because of the hurt she *might* experience?

Fingers hovering over the keyboard, she thought a minute before answering.

Dear SPfan,

I'm looking forward to meeting you, too. It's been a strange day. We had a big event at work and a friend of mine collapsed. It was horrible. Oh, and then there was the smoke, but that's not the important thing. That sounded weird, didn't it? Let's just say there wasn't a fire. Like you, I hope you're not disappointed. Sometimes I wonder if it's worth it to have relationships if it's going to be so hard? Sorry. Way too serious.

See you at the parade. Or not. I'll be there, and if I've scared you off, I won't blame you!

> *Lincsgirl*

BLOOD DRAWN—AGAIN—AND stress test taken, Ian was exhausted by the time his lunch hour was over and he returned to Pilot Oaks. He'd refused to take off work because the kitchen needed a major cleaning after all the smoke from the night before.

"How was it?" Prudie's brows went up, and as usual, she spoke without preamble.

"Fine. Rance said he'd let me know how my tests were tomorrow.

"Good." She eyed him closely. "You sure you're okay today?"

He nodded. "Has anybody talked to Taylor?"

The serious look on Prudie's face almost crumbled when her lips quivered in a semi-smile. "Susan told her to take today off." She rinsed out the rag she held and placed it in the cleaning bucket. "She was feeling better."

"Good." Ian avoided the older woman's eyes. "I hated that I scared her like that."

Prudie patted him on the arm. "I know. She'll be okay."

"By the way, thanks for saving the evening." After Ian was forced to choose between going home and riding an ambulance to the hospital, Prudie had come through for him like nothing he could have asked for or expected.

"We cooks have to stick together. The meat wasn't all burned, so we managed to feed everyone after the smoke cleared."

"We?" Ian arched a brow at her. "I'm not sure anybody else could have pulled it off."

Maybe I'm out of my league.

"You stop that, ya hear?" Prudie glared at him. "That stove had been spoiling for a fight for a long time. It just chose that moment for the self-cleaning feature to work." She shook her head. "Lord knows it hasn't wanted to work for the last five years. Why would it choose last night to decide to lock up and prove it could do it?"

"Jealous of the new ovens?"

Prudie laughed out loud. "Exactly what I was thinking." She sobered. "Susan did say she wanted to see you when you came back after lunch."

Great. Time to look for another job?

STARPORT: SP-1

Alex roamed the empty SanFranciso apartment as she made herself a cup of tea in the sparse kitchen—at least Linc had tea bags—and settled into the sofa, wishing he were there with her.

This apartment was more modern than his cabin outside StarPort, but like the wilderness lodge, the apartment was relaxed, slightly messy, and, oddly enough, smelled faintly of wood smoke.

From where she had no idea.

20

I an delivered Grandpa to the parade lineup in plenty of time. His brows rose when he saw the Crawford's son-in-law, Jared Benton, and Prudie next to the Porsche convertible. Grandpa went straight to Prudie.

"So, you're the driver today?" Ian approached Jared, hand extended.

Jared chuckled. "Prudie said she wouldn't ride on the back of, as she put it, 'just any car with just anybody driving,' so I didn't have much choice."

"I hear you. Ian narrowed his eyes and cocked his head toward the older couple. "Is there something going on between those two?"

"I'm not saying." Jared shrugged. "My instructions were simply to drive and keep the heat going."

"Um-hmm. Keep an eye on them." Ian peered around at the crowd gathering, trying to keep his eyes open for a red hat. He hadn't answered *Lincsgirl's* question about how she'd know him, but he had an idea.

After her last email, he was a little concerned. She said she'd be there, but would she change her mind? He hadn't seen her since he'd been laid out on the floor of the kitchen the other night, and she had looked completely traumatized.

Ian turned to leave but with one last glance, he had to grin when he saw Prudie slathering sunscreen on Grandpa's bald head.

✦✦✦ ✦ ✦✦✦

HEART FLUTTERING, Taylor arrived at the ice cream establishment and glanced around. *Anyone here look like a superfan of a defunct sci-fi television show?*

She'd tried all morning to tamp down her anxiety about meeting *SPfan* and shook off the worry that had taken over since Ian's attack.

There were at least one hundred red hats in the vicinity. It reminded her of the Union Station scene in Hitchcock's movie, *North by Northwest*.

Poor *SPfan*. She laughed out loud, surprising herself. He'd have a tough time picking her out of a crowd. She spotted Ian in the distance. Should he be here? Was he well? She could ask him, but she couldn't bring herself to approach him.

His grandfather was the grand marshal of the parade. *That's why he's here.* She lost him in the crowd. Her eyes roamed, hoping to see someone zeroing in on her. What were the odds, considering how many red-hatted persons were in the immediate vicinity?

The parade started. Local high school bands, scout troops, churches, and civic groups of all kinds had entered floats pulled by tractors and trucks. There were the requisite beauty queens in their tiaras and finery. Local politicians pitched candy to the children, who scrambled to pick it up before the next group came through.

Maybe *SPfan* wouldn't show up. Disappointment niggled at her, but she tried not to take it personally. It was a shot in the dark, after all. She'd probably scared him off with her last email.

STARPORT: SP-1

When Alex flew back to Colorado after the morning meeting, Linc was at her house. She held him as close as humanly possible. Her meeting with General Sherwood proved to be life-changing. Linc had put his career on the line to be with her. The selfless act was more than she could fathom—although it had crossed her mind to do the same. He'd done it for her so they could be together without consequence.

21

I an was glad he knew the identity of his date because he couldn't believe how many red hats he saw in front of Twister's.

Stands to reason. It is a Christmas parade, after all.

He'd spotted her before finding a place to buy a rose, not wanting to arrive empty-handed. Keeping out of sight as much as possible, when he heard "White Christmas" playing, he knew he had to reveal himself.

Working his way through the crowd, he arrived behind her. She stood on her tip-toes trying to see the float from church and then sank back on her heels as she clapped. He watched her for a moment, taking in her natural beauty. There was a look of strain on her face, but then she smiled. When he heard a satisfied sigh come from her, he knew it was time. Fingering the ribbon on the de-thorned rose, he went for it.

Stepping closer, he slowly reached the hand holding the rose around her so she could see it.

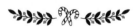

TAYLOR SIGHED as the band transitioned from "White Christmas" to a drum-line rhythm. She was surprised when a red rose came from behind her, a masculine hand holding it.

Could it be? How did he pick her out from a veritable sea of red hats? All these thoughts tumbled through her head before she had a chance to turn and see who held the rose.

Wondering at the way things around her seemed to stop, Taylor held her breath. It seemed longer, but likely no more than five seconds before she turned around to see a familiar face.

Was he ...? Could it be possible.

"Ian?"

He offered the rose. *"Lincsgirl?"*

Taking the flower, her smile grew, and then dimmed. "You're *SPfan.*" It wasn't a question.

Ian nodded, and they stood there, staring at one another, both of them forgetting there were other people around.

What could she say? When Ian collapsed, she'd determined that no matter how she felt, she wouldn't put herself through the pain she'd experienced when Mike died. She couldn't do that again.

But Ian ...

When a car horn honked, their attention returned to the parade route.

❧❧❧ ❀ ❧❧❧

THE ROSE BETWEEN THEM, Ian turned toward the street to see Jared's Porsche carrying Grandpa and Prudie. It halted, and both of them waved.

"What in the ..." He grabbed Taylor's hand and pulled her to the edge of the street.

"Somebody wants a picture taken." Jared shouted over the din and laughed as Prudie swatted at him.

"Grandpa?" Ian was still muddled. Between revealing himself as *SPfan* to Taylor and his Grandpa's arm around a blushing Prudie, he didn't know what to think.

Grandpa hugged Prudie to him and kissed her before calling out to Ian. "Get our picture, Son. We need it for posterity."

After snapping a few pictures, Ian laughed when Grandpa held his lady-love's hand up to reveal a sparkling diamond ring. "That old sea-dog," he muttered under his breath, even as he laughed.

"Are they ..."

"I'd say they're engaged." Ian shook his head. "You know, Prudie said she'd never marry. I guess she didn't count on the Rutledge men."

"Pretty special, huh?" Taylor laughed as Ian turned toward her, smiling, and her hand somehow ending up in his. Her eyes narrowed. "Are you okay?"

"I'm sorry I scared you. It was a panic attack. I had one a few weeks ago brought on by insomnia. This one was stress-related." He brought her hand up to his lips. "You're not upset?"

She shook her head, her eyes bright with unshed tears. "No. Surprised? Yes. Relieved that you're okay? No question. But upset?" She paused, gazing into his eyes. "Absolutely not. I'm sorry I ran out on you. I was just so scared. But you're really okay?"

"No apology needed. Rance ran tests." He placed her hand against his heart. "My ticker is fine. I promise."

STARPORT: SP-1

The sun was setting over the mountain holding the classified military installation they'd called their second home for nearly fifteen years. Across the valley, at Linc's cabin, Alex looked at her new husband and friends as they sat around a lake suspiciously absent of fish.

Bartok and Beth Garrity had discovered their feelings for one another, their shy happiness adorable.

Would they all get their happily-ever-after?

A shooting star assured her that, indeed, they already had.

22

Taylor and Ian made their way to the end of the parade route to see the happy couple, who still basked in the congratulations they'd received.

"When is the big day?" Taylor admired the ring on Prudie's hand.

Mr. Rutledge beamed down at his fiancée, and she nodded. "New Year's Day."

"Are you serious?" Ian looked from one to the other and laughed.

"We're not getting any younger, you know." His grandfather winked at him, and Prudie swatted at him.

"Can I give the happy couple a ride home?" Jared gestured to the car they'd emerged from minutes before.

Prudie nodded. "I think that would be nice, don't you, Ira?"

"You? Me? Back seat? I'm all yours, young lady." Mr. Rutledge kissed her on the cheek and winked, laughing when she blushed in front of everyone.

"Behave yourself, old man." Prudie shook her head but couldn't wipe the smile off her face.

Jared helped them both into the car and waved at Taylor and Ian, who stood there, watching as they drove off. The low rumble of the sports car belied the age of the passengers.

"If that don't beat all ..." Ian stared after them.

"I think it's sweet." Taylor looked up at Ian and narrowed her eyes. "So, how long have you known I was *Lincsgirl*?"

He twisted his lips in a smile. "Your first email to me."

"How ..."

"It was when you said, and I quote, 'there you go, apologizing again,' end quote." He lifted his eyebrows.

Her mouth dropped open in surprise, then she laughed. He looked down at his shoes, and then into her eyes. "I should have told you."

Tilting her head, she thought a moment. If he had, she wouldn't have had this time of anticipation. "No, I think it worked out perfectly."

His lips curved in a smile. "Walk on the beach?"

❧❧❧❧ 🎄 ❦❦❦❦

THEY WALKED in companionable silence for a little while when Taylor stopped. "Ian. Look."

She saw a snowflake on his shoulder, then another, and another. They looked around, mesmerized by the snowflakes falling all around them. It was a little private miracle especially for her.

"Are you okay?" Ian saw the tears she tried to hide.

"I'm fine." She smiled, trying to get the lump out of her throat. After being so worried about him, she was overwhelmed with both relief and anticipation. "Have you ever asked for a sign?"

His eyebrows went up. "You mean a sign from God?"

She nodded, hardly knowing where she was going with this. "When I see snow, I think of Noah and the rainbow." She shrugged. "A little nudge, telling me that God's here, and He loves me." She looked away, feeling her face warm. "Anyway, maybe I'll tell you about it sometime. It sounds a little crazy when I say it out loud."

"I don't think so." He turned her to face him, smiling as he brushed a fluffy flake from the tip of her nose.

When his brown eyes met hers, she couldn't look away. His smile faded into a look of wonder, which made her tremble with more than the cold wind off the Atlantic. She'd been so sure he wasn't the one. Couldn't be the one.

Ian took Taylor's hands and leaned in to kiss her gently. She smiled into his kiss, knowing, somehow, that she'd gotten her sign through the swirling snowflakes. Life would never be perfect on this side of Heaven. But at this moment? Pretty close.

When he stepped back, she pulled her hands free and rested them lightly on his chest, her heart in her throat. "I never did look into that non-fraternization policy, did you?" Taylor grinned as Ian laughed and pulled her closer.

"No, and I don't know if I can keep secret how I feel about you." His lips found hers once more. "I think I may love you, *Lincsgirl*."

Hugging him closely, she whispered in his ear. "Maybe you could call me 'Iansgirl,' instead ..."

ABOUT THE AUTHOR

Regina Rudd Merrick is a multi-published writer, church musician, wife, mother, former librarian, lover of all things beachy and chocolate, and grateful follower of Jesus Christ. Married to her husband of 35-plus years, she is the mother of two grown daughters and a son-in-law, and the keeper of a 100-year-old house where she lives in the small town of Marion, KY. Connect with Regina on Facebook, Twitter, Instagram, or on her website at www.reginaruddmerrick.com.

Coastal Christmas Charade

A Novella by

Shannon Taylor Vannatter

To my dear friends, Vicki Harris & Jeannine Wallace for always listening to my stories and getting me out of my office for fun days.

1

"This will never do." Lark scanned the massive great room. The week after Thanksgiving and no Christmas decorations, with a winter wonderland wedding scheduled for next week. How had Gran and Gramps had any guests with the Shell House Inn in such a state of indifference? They'd obviously lost interest long before they officially retired. Though they slept soundly in their private quarters, their hearts were already in Dallas.

"Yip." Peaches' ears perked as she paced at the front door.

"Shh, you'll wake up the old folks." Lark nabbed her leash.

Peaches went into Pomeranian orbit, bouncing around her feet.

"You have to be still if you want to walk. Sit."

The little orange powder puff sat.

"Good girl." Lark snapped the leash in place and scratched behind Peaches' ears. "I need somebody to cover this place in lights before the bride, who's more high-strung than you are, arrives. But a walk comes first." She opened the door, and

Peaches shot out at warp speed, pulling the slack tight. Straight toward the water.

"At least we think alike." Lark sighed, breathing in the ocean air as the gentle swish of the tide rolled in. Even though Christmas was right around the corner, here at Surfside Beach, Texas, the sunny, seventy-degree day tempted her to kick off her shoes and wade the coastline. A breeze off the water whipped her hair about her face, soothing her stress level.

But being here also reminded her of the last summer she'd spent here as a teen. The dark-haired boy with thick glasses. And their kiss. Surprisingly sweet and promising. Until he'd learned the truth about her. Her cheeks heated. If only she could find him and apologize, explain her shallow teen reasoning for going along with the dare.

A racket sounded behind her. Like the steady rumbling thud of horse hooves? Lark turned around. A pale golden horse with a lone rider thundered toward her. Her pulse spiked. Should she stand still or dodge?

"Yip, yip, yip." Peaches launched into incessant barking.

The horse reared up with a panicked neigh.

"Whoa, girl." A man's voice soothed. Just before he sprawled into the sand.

Free of her rider, the horse pawed the ground, stopped long enough to drop foul-smelling-fertilizer, then bolted on along the shore.

"Nice." The man sat up, spitting sand.

"What are you doing?" Lark stooped to pick up a still-agitated Peaches.

"Testing a horse."

"This is a public beach. You can't do that here." She pointed at the manure.

"No worries." He stood, dusted himself off. "I'll take care of it."

A younger man caught up with them, used a contraption with a blue bag on the end to scoop up the stench and tie it off.

"Thanks Wesley, if you'll catch her, I'll handle that."

"Sorry, ma'am." Wesley winced, handed over the gadget, and hurried after the horse.

Her jaw gaped and she forced it closed. "Isn't riding a horse on the beach against some law or something?"

"Not at all. In fact, I'm assessing a new mare for *Romantic Beach Rides*."

"You've got to be kidding." Peaches squirmed and Lark set her back down.

"I assure you, I'm not. Our services are quite popular."

"She could have run me down." A complaint would be launched first thing in the morning. The beach was no place for horses.

"Horses try not to step on people." He adjusted his Stetson. "But I apologize for startling you. She's feisty and got away from me. Normally, our horses don't run and are quite tame. We won't be buying her." He pointed at her feet. "What about you? Are you prepared for that?"

A pungent odor warned her before she ever glanced down, where Peaches hunched in a most unladylike position. Heat warmed Lark's face.

"No worries. I can take care of that." He held up his scooper as if it were a prized possession. "There is an ordinance against leaving waste, whether dog or horse."

"Thanks." She mumbled as she turned Peaches back toward the inn.

"You're welcome. And again, I'm sorry for startling you. I can assure you *Romantic Beach Rides* only purchases safe, tame horses if you ever feel the need for our services."

"No, thank you." She scurried away. Maybe she and

Peaches could walk down the street. Avoid horses. And cowboys.

Every house along the shore was lit up. Except the Shell House. A woman sat on a porch immersed in the newspaper.

"Ma'am," Lark cupped her hands around her mouth. "Could I ask who did your Christmas lights?"

The woman looked up, smiled. "A young man flipping a house, across the street, three doors down. I think he does most everyone's décor every year."

"Thank you." Lark tried to steer Peaches in the direction the woman pointed, but the stubborn Pomeranian stopped to sniff every bush, every clump of seagrass. "At this rate, Christmas will be over before we get there."

WITH A GRIMACE, Jace trudged after Wesley, his ranch foreman. The mare stopped, blew a burst of air out her nostrils. Wesley caught her reins and cut across between two houses.

She didn't remember him. Lark Pendleton in the flesh. The blond of his dreams with are-they-blue-or-green eyes. Every summer, she'd arrived in May to spend three months at her grandparents'. And every time, he'd fallen a little more in love, though he never summoned the courage to speak to her. She was summer folk, with family ties to Surfside Beach. Rich and snobby.

As the handyman's son, Jace Wilder was nowhere near her league. Or class. Not even on her radar screen. She'd never even acknowledged him. Not once. Except for that lone kiss. And she obviously didn't remember it or his existence.

Rather than take the chance of looping back and running into Lark again, he followed Wesley's trail and crossed the street.

At his flip project, Wesley waited by the horse trailer with his shoulders slumped. "Sorry 'bout that."

"It's okay. You didn't buy her."

"I should have known." Wesley blew out a sigh. "The seller wouldn't ever come clean on why he wanted rid of her."

"No worries. You'll get better at reading people. And horses. Comes with experience."

Jace set a soothing hand on the mare's shoulder. "There now. Nothing to get worked up about. Just a yappy little poof of a dog. Probably as snobby as her owner."

Wesley tugged the mare's bridle. "I'll get her back to her ranch and find you a more suitable horse."

"I appreciate it." Jace stood aside while Wesley loaded the mare, helped secure the door, waved them off, and then went inside.

Sunlight shone through the windows, spotlighting the mixture of drywall and sawdust floating through the air, puddled in the floor, coating everything in the front room. With the rest of the house walled off by plastic, the kitchen was almost done. Then he'd complete the living room and move upstairs.

He went back to his table saw and cut the two by four. As he carried the beam to the kitchen, the air compressor buzzed into action, and he secured the board in place. With his brace level, he lifted the upper cabinet until it sat on top of the two by four. He stuck his head and left shoulder inside the cabinet and reached for his nail gun as the compressor stopped.

"Do you need help?" Lark asked.

"What are you doing here?" His voice echoed surprise inside the wooden cage.

"I knocked, but you didn't hear me. Here, I've got the gun."

"Thanks." The tool slid into his right hand. The thwack of

the nail gun filled the silence as he attached the cabinet to the studs.

"I took my grandmother's dog for a walk and saw how great all the Christmas lights look. And since I need to get my grandparents' inn in shape for a wedding before I sell it, I asked who did them."

He bumped his head as he tried to extract himself from the tight space.

"Sorry." Her cringe sounded in her tone. "I guess this is a bad time. I'll leave my card and you can call me."

"Don't run off yet." He managed to free himself, hopefully with a bit of grace, and turned to face her. "Still want to hire me?"

Her color-defying eyes went wide. "It's you?"

"I guess you'll want to retract."

"No." Her face went crimson. "Maybe we should start over." She offered her hand. "Hi, I'm Lark Pendleton, and I'm in desperate need of a light guy."

He stared at her hand as if it might bite, then forced himself to clasp it. "Jace Wilder. I do a few lights on the side, flip houses, and own *Romantic Beach Rides*." Why did he tell her all that? Was he still trying to impress her?

"You own the business?"

"Does that surprise you?"

"Well." She bit her lip. "Actually. Yes. Since you were testing your horse, I assumed you were a guide or ranch hand."

"I like taking a hands-on approach. And she's officially not my horse. Sorry again about that."

"It's okay. I'm sorry I got so uptight. I'm a tiny bit afraid of horses." She giggled, as if admitting it was difficult for her. "And not-my-dog made as big a mess as not-your-horse did."

"Not nearly as big." He chuckled.

HER LAUGH CAME OUT STILTED, forced. Why was she suddenly so nervous? And why had his handshake sent a tingle up her arm? He checked all her *hard no* boxes. Despite sea glass green eyes that seemed to look right through her, strong jaw, hair the color of the night sky, he was a local. And a cowboy. A deadly combination.

"You're talking about the Shell House Inn, right?"

"The one and only." Mom's words echoed in her head, 'Stay away from locals unless you want to live here, and never fall for a cowboy unless you want to end up on a ranch.'

She was only here to whip the inn into shape, host Hillarie's wedding—establish the inn as *the venue* for events in the area—and sell the property. Then she could get back to her cowboy-free life in her Dallas condo.

"I've considered buying the property. The Pendletons said they had a realtor handling it. I guess that's you?"

"It is. And I've got an offer you can't refuse." While she spoke, Peaches circled her ankles. "What do you say, I pay you to help me decorate the inn, and after I host my Christmas wedding, you can buy it."

"It would be perfect if I hadn't already bought this place. I try not to get more than one flip going at a time. I usually hire out my lighting skills, but I'm not taking any more jobs so I can focus here."

An idea niggled, an opportunity to advertise her side career. "Have you ever worked with a professional stager?"

"A what?"

"I bring in furnishings and décor items to create mood, to make the home inviting and warm. Staged homes sell faster. So, you hang my lights and help me turn the Shell House into a winter wonderland, and once you complete your reno, I stage this house for you."

"Why would you want to do that?"

"My bride gets her Christmas wedding, you get a quicker sale, and I get a bit of advertisement for my services." She managed to sidestep out of the lasso Peaches had created. Since the little dog had relieved herself on the beach, his hardwood floors should be safe.

"How long will your lighting project take?"

"A few days. My bride and groom arrive Friday." Peaches circled again and Lark picked her up. "The wedding isn't until next weekend, but I want everything in place when they arrive."

"Friday, as in this Friday?"

"If you get behind on your flip, once the wedding is over, I'll get the inn on the market and help you with your house. I can hold stuff for you, paint, lay tile, whatever you need along with offering my excellent taste in decorating."

His gaze narrowed as he inspected her. "You lay tile?"

"My dad used to do some house flipping when I was a teen. When a project was on deadline, my mom and I helped wherever we could."

Obviously skeptical, as if trying to picture her doing anything hard, he shrugged. "If you can do all that, why not do the lights yourself?"

"I could, but not in two days. And besides that, I don't have a ladder or one of those." She pointed to his scissor lift.

"Why not call Daddy?" A hint of sarcasm coated his tone.

Of all the nerve. Her jaw clenched. "He hurt his back, so he's a contractor now. If I call him, he'll insist on doing the work himself. And get hurt again." She held her hand up, palm toward him. "Never mind. I'll find someone else."

"I'm sorry." He hung his head, then dusted off his hands

and offered his right one. "I'm afraid deadlines stress me. Two days won't make or break me, but the staging thing sounds like a good deal."

"Really?" Her voice came out too high. Why the turnaround?

"I'll hold you to your end."

"Not a problem. Thank you." She clasped his hand, and despite him being on the verge of rude, another tingle worked up her arm.

2

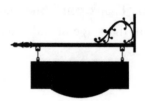

Jace parked in front of the Shell House Inn the next morning. Memories of rich kids snickering echoed around him, calling him Tool Face Jace. Heat crawled up his neck. Why had it bothered him so much? Because he'd been a kid. And he desperately wanted to fit in.

He grabbed his tools from the bed of his truck.

Even though Lark was rich and hung with the snobby, mean girl crowd, she'd always seemed like their barbs embarrassed her. He thought she was nicer. Until their kiss. The one he later learned only happened because of a dare.

If the staging thing could speed the sale of his flip house, maybe he could buy the inn before someone else did. Since it had gone on the market, he'd dreamed of buying it. As a kid, staying there seemed like the height of being ... someone. To own it would put him on a level playing field with the rich folks who'd always looked down on him.

Or he could sell the property to some developer, have the source of all his bad memories leveled, and watch condos take its place.

The door opened before he reached it.

"Thank you so much for coming." Lark stepped aside to let him pass. "Where should we start?"

Even in an oversized T-shirt and stained jeans with her hair in a ponytail, she looked model-worthy. Better than most models, since they were usually underfed.

He scanned the massive great room. Plaster walls, huge chandelier in the middle of the ridiculously high ceiling, hardwood flooring, seashell wallpaper border along the spiral staircase.

Just like he remembered. As if trapped in a time capsule. "I can't believe this old border is still here. I'd get rid of it."

"No!" The word ripped from her. "Hillarie loves this wallpaper. Gran said she based her bouquet and wedding colors on this border."

As in Hillarie Chambers, the mold for mean girls everywhere? The darer in the most embarrassing moment of his life.

"Relax. I meant if I bought the place. Your wallpaper is safe."

"Oh. Sorry." Aqua eyes collided with his and a hint of a grin tipped her lips up.

"Where will the wedding be?"

"Here in the great room." She spread her arms wide. "She'll come down the staircase. The preacher will stand in front of the fireplace, and chairs will line the area facing it."

"I'll put lights up in this room first, then the exterior, then the rooms where your guests will stay."

"I can handle the guest rooms, just a small tree and a bit of décor in each one." She gestured to double doors across from the staircase. "But I need you to do the ballroom. The reception will be there."

Though he'd never been in the ballroom, fancy dresses,

weird hor d'oeuvres, and uptight orchestra music filled his illusions of it.

"All right, then." He set down his toolbox near the winding staircase. Looked like something straight out of *Gone with the Wind*. "Just a caution. We don't have time to spend agonizing over the perfect décor. We've got two days."

Her cheeks sucked in, as if biting her tongue. "I'm not one of those women who can't make a decision."

And again, he'd insulted her. Did he have her pegged wrong? Had he misjudged her all these years?

"Time's wasting." She headed up the staircase. "I know exactly what I want." At the top landing, she peered down at him. "You coming? All the Christmas stuff is in the attic."

❦

AFTER THEY DETANGLED ALL the lights and weeded out the strings that didn't work, Jace unloaded the hydraulic lift and drove it inside.

Lark cowered while he climbed in the cage atop the contraption with five working strands looped around his left arm. A whirring sound started as the platform lifted him upward. He stopped when the ceiling was within reach, then slid the lights off his arm and set them in the middle of the work surface.

The thwack of his nail gun filled the silence as he secured clear twinkle lights along the ceiling perimeter while she made her way down the staircase, wrapping translucent garland.

"Where's your grandmother's dog?"

"Gran and Gramps left early this morning with their U-Haul packed and Peaches in tow, headed for their new condo."

"Good. I didn't want to squash her." A beep sounded as

Jace steered the lift a few feet over. "I guess your folks live near their new place."

Rolling around at least twenty feet from the floor as if it were nothing.

She did a little shiver and tried not to watch. "Yes. I'm close as well. They can relax and be near family."

"I'm falling!" His shout echoed.

She screamed, scurried closer and held her arms out, as if to catch him.

Laughter reverberated above her. "Sorry, I couldn't resist."

"Not funny." Hands on hips, she glared up at him.

"I promise I won't fall."

For the next thirty minutes, they worked in silence.

"Done. Now what?" He peered down at her.

"Gramps used to drape lights on the chandelier. The plug in the ceiling should work, but he had the wiring for the light unhooked after a bathtub leak caused a massive short."

"I'm on it." The beeping started up as he drove the lift to the center of the room.

He grabbed a string of lights, plugged them into the socket, looped them over each upturned arm of the fixture. "Like this?"

"Perfect."

"Uh-oh."

The chandelier did an odd tilt. A tearing sound echoed above.

"Watch out!"

The fixture lurched toward Lark near the bottom of the staircase, swung low as wiring snaked out of the ceiling, and then snapped. Crystals and brass crashed to the floor in a dusty, clattering heap. Like *Phantom of the Opera*. Only smaller and without dramatic organ music.

"You okay?" Jace lowered the lift.

"I'm fine." She brushed debris from her hair, obviously unaware of the drywall dust smeared on her face.

He climbed out of the basket, clenched his fist, resisting the urge to wipe it away for her. "Someone patched the plaster, which camouflaged the water damage to the support beam. I'm sorry about the chandelier."

"It's okay. It hasn't worked in years, and I never liked it anyway. I'd much rather get one similar to the updated model in the ballroom. I'm just thankful the wires weren't live."

"But the ceiling is another story." He blew out a big breath.

"Fixable by Friday?" She winced as she examined the long gash with the massive gaping hole.

"Definitely. I'll take out all the rotten studs and make sure the new fixture is stable and useable."

"Charge me whatever you need for this."

He frowned. "I don't charge according to what I need. I set my price by project and timeframe."

"I didn't mean to insult you."

"Trust me, I'm well aware you've got money." His tone turned mocking. "And I don't need it."

A muscle in her jaw twitched. "Do you have a problem with me?"

"Not at all."

"I'll have you know that my family worked hard for their money." She propped her hands on her hips. "Gramps was a plumber. Daddy hung sheetrock and did drywall before getting into contracting. And I make my living selling houses. So don't treat me like I'm some snobby, rich girl, born with a silver spoon. You don't know me."

"I'm sorry. Maybe I don't."

"You've had a chip on your shoulder since I met you. Can we just get the work done without all the snarky remarks?"

He let out a heavy sigh. "I guess I'm a bit bent out of shape because you don't remember me."

"We've met before?" She scrutinized his face. "Were you one of the summer kids?"

"I've lived here my entire life." His shoulders slumped. "I used to wear glasses. My dad was the handyman."

Her jaw dropped. "Tool Face Jace?" Her cheeks went crimson. "I mean that's what everyone called you. But not me, I never called you that." She closed her eyes. "I mean, until just now."

"It doesn't matter."

"It does. I'm sorry. I didn't recognize you without the glasses." She studied him. "Why didn't you tell me who you were on the beach? Or at the flip house?"

"I shouldn't have to. Contacts and a different hairstyle don't change who I am."

"You're right." Her gaze held his, as if still questioning how he could be the same awkward kid she used to know. "Is your dad still around?"

"No. He retired, remarried, moved to the Hill Country, near San Antonio."

"Funny how people work their entire lives to retire near the water. But coastal folks work their entire lives to escape it. Gran said she's looking forward to good hair days for a change."

"I better get to work on this mess." He grabbed a trash bag, picked up pieces of the ceiling and the chandelier. "So, is the bride Hillarie Chambers?"

"The one and only."

"Weren't y'all archenemies?"

"My nemesis of the worst kind. I signed up for choir, cheerleading, and the drama club. She did too." She smirked. "But I got the solo, the lead role in the play, and head cheerleader, while she ended up president of the debate club. She couldn't stand it."

Made sense. Hillarie's best event was whining. "No wonder she's envious of you." Enough to bust up Lark and her boyfriend which tangled Jace up in their rivalry. "But you're hosting her wedding?"

"A big fancy, high-society wedding is just what I need to put this place on the map as *the venue* to bring buyers flocking. That's my best chance of it staying an inn instead of some developer tearing it down to build condos." She knelt to help. "Aaaachoo."

Had she read his mind? "Bless you."

"Drywall dust always irritates my allergies."

"Step back. I'll get it."

"Aaaaaachoo."

"Bless you."

"Is it on my face?"

"Just a smidge on your right cheek."

"I'll only make it worse." She held up her dusty hands.

"May I?" He wiped his hand on the inside tail of his shirt.

She sniffled. "Please."

Ever so, gently, he dabbed his thumb over her cheek.

The front door opened, and a brunette stepped inside behind Lark. Hillarie Chambers. Her mouth dropped open, then closed, and opened again.

Lark spun around. "Hillarie, what are you doing here?" She went to work trying to brush herself off. "I didn't expect you until Friday."

"What happened?" Hillarie's high-pitched whine echoed through the massive space. "What about my wedding?"

"Don't worry. We had a little chandelier mishap, but it's a good thing we discovered the problem now. This could have

happened in the middle of the wedding. Death by chandelier."
Lark laughed.

But Hillarie didn't. "Look at this mess. And there aren't even any Christmas lights up outside." She wailed in full meltdown mode. "You always did try to sabotage me, and now you're after my wedding."

"Don't be ridiculous, Hillarie. I hired Jace to have the lights done by Friday. He's fixing this too. By Friday, right, Jace?"

"Jace?" Hillarie focused on him, then squinted. "Tool Face Jace?"

"At your service." Hillarie recognized him. But Lark hadn't.

"Why are you here two days early?" Lark leaned on the staircase.

Hillarie tore her gaze away from the destruction. "Your grandmother said we could come early. I said no. But I've been stressed, so my fiancé talked me into it."

"Technically, we're closed." Lark smiled. "To prepare for the wedding."

The brunette splayed her hands. "I left a message on the machine late last night."

"Is he with you?"

"Oh." Hillarie's eyes went wide. "I didn't know you'd be here." She grimaced. "Why are you here?"

Lark's eyes narrowed. "Gran and Gramps had their name on a waiting list for a condo in Dallas. One became available. If they hadn't jumped on it, they'd have had to wait at least six months, so I offered to handle the wedding."

"Great." Hillarie's fake smile looked more like a cringe. "Do you know who I'm marrying?"

The door opened again and a blond man with a suitcase in each hand entered. Familiar. One of the summer rich kids. Lark's ex-boyfriend. Thanks to Hillarie.

"Warren?" Lark frowned. "What are you doing here?" Her

voice went up an octave. "Oh, you must be in the wedding party."

"Right." He shot her a million-watt smile, but it faded as he scanned the room. "What happened?"

"Just a little sprucing up before Hillarie's big day." Lark's smile looked as fake as her nemesis's. "Jace promised we'd be in ship shape by Friday."

"Look, darling." Hillarie sidled up against Warren. "It's Tool Face Jace."

"Nobody calls him that anymore." Lark frowned. "They never should have."

Lark defending him?

Her gaze narrowed, pinged back and forth between Hillarie and Warren. "Darling?"

"Um." Hillarie's baby blues bounced to the floor. "That's what I wanted to tell you. Warren is my fiancé."

"Oh." Lark cleared her throat. "Congratulations."

"Thank you." Hillarie's gaze darted to Lark. "I mean, we all knew it was meant to be. Right?"

"I'm just here to make sure you two have your dream wedding." Lark smiled.

Hillarie's attention turned back to Warren. "I had no idea Lark would be here. I expected Gran and Gramps."

"I'm not sure about staying." Warren's eyes never left Lark. "Or getting married at the inn. I don't know what you were thinking, Hillarie."

Did he wish he were marrying Lark instead?

"I've dreamed of getting married here since I was a little girl."

"Which I never understood. What about the Apex or Platinum? Both have more room and are much more suitable." Warren's mouth twisted as he surveyed the rubble.

He had a point. Both hoity-toity venues would suit them better.

"They're both in Galveston. And you know why I want our wedding at the Shell House Inn. The first time I ever saw you, was here."

"While I was dating Lark. That's where you want our marriage to start?"

"Come on, guys." Lark huffed out a laugh. "That was a long time ago, and we're all adults. If you want to get married here, Jace and I will make it happen. The chandelier is a minor problem." Her voice was a bit too cheery. "We'll have this place whipped into a winter wonderland before you know it. The guest rooms are good to go."

"We can't change location this late." Hillarie looked up at Warren, all dreamy eyed. "I doubt we could get another venue on such short notice." A lack of self-esteem hid in the clingy, possessive way she latched on his arm. "And the invitations have gone out."

"Whatever makes you happy." Warren spewed out a sigh. "If you want to get married on my ex-girlfriend's stomping grounds, who am I to argue?"

Hillarie's face crumpled. And Jace almost felt sorry for her.

"We were kids." Lark scoffed. "And we've all moved on."

"Right." Hillarie's gaze bounced from Jace to Lark, and a smile bloomed. "Besides, Lark has a new man in her life. Isn't that funny, Darling? After all these years, Lark ended up with Tool—I mean—Jace Wilder."

His jaw dropped. "Whoa. I was only wiping dust off her cheek."

"Oh, come on, babe." Lark slipped her arm through the crook of his elbow. "There's no need to hide how we feel about each other among friends. Busted."

He froze as she moved in close. Her mouth touched his and

fireworks went off in his veins. As quickly as it happened, it was over. She stepped back, but kept her arm linked with his.

For the second time in his life, Lark Pendleton had kissed him. Just as fake as the first time, using him as a pawn. Her gaze met his, pleading for him to play along. This was his chance to embarrass her as badly as she'd humiliated him all those summers ago.

3

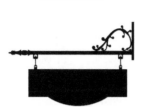

B ut it might be more fun to watch Lark squirm, forced into a pretend romance with Tool Face Jace for the next week and a half.

He slipped his arms around her waist and this time, he did the kissing. Rigid at first, her hands slid up his chest and around his neck. Lark went limp in his embrace as he made sure she was good and thoroughly kissed. When he finally drew away, her eyes stayed closed, lips searching for his.

"I'd like to continue, but we have company, sugar dumplin'."

Her eyes popped open, and she pulled away from him, but he kept her solidly against his side. Stiff as a statue, she plastered on a smile and faced her guests.

Warren huffed. "If you're finished making out with Tool—"

"Jace. Can we cut the childish taunts?" Lark defended him once more. "I'll show you upstairs along with the back exit."

"Lark is right." Warren managed a strained smile. "We're all adults. And those summers were a long time ago."

"Oh, thank you." Hillarie bounced up and down, like the

want-to-be-cheerleader she was. "We'll need two rooms. Warren and I moved in together years ago." Her proud gaze cut to Lark. "But we decided to do things the old-fashioned way leading up to our wedding."

Warren guffawed. "Hillarie's old-fashioned nonsense."

"Are you running the inn permanently?" Hillarie's tone went petulant child again.

"Just until it sells." Lark slipped away from him, stepped toward the couple. "Now, let's get you settled in your rooms, so Jace and I can get back to work."

"I can't wait to be Mrs. Warren Abernathy." Hillarie did a little bounce, shot Lark an I-got-him-and-you-didn't smile.

"How about the sea glass room for you, and Warren can have the driftwood room?"

Hillarie's mouth formed a small *o*. "They're still like they were?"

"Exactly. I'll show you."

"No need. I remember." Hillarie grabbed Warren's arm and practically dragged him up the stairs. "I'm so excited."

As the couple climbed the staircase, Lark kept her smile in place. Jace stood near, setting her nerve endings on high alert. She willed herself not to move away.

Finally, doors opened and closed upstairs, and she sidestepped him.

"I'm sorry for that little display." Her stomach clenched. Even though she'd never called him hateful nicknames, she hadn't treated him fairly. Then or now. "I panicked when I realized she's engaged to Warren."

"So, you're still hung up on boy wonder?"

"Of course not. I haven't seen him since graduation eight years ago."

"Then why the kiss this time? Another dare?"

She flinched. "Definitely not. I guess I wanted them to know I've moved on. Hillarie was probably hung up on Warren back then, and that's why she dared me to kiss you. It all sounds so childish now." She cringed. "I'm sorry you got caught up in the middle of it. Then and now."

"They're perfect for each other—two of the shallowest people I've ever known."

"True." Lark winced. "But Warren was raised that way. His parents are into high society, and he doesn't know any better."

Back in high school, it made sense for the head cheerleader to date Warren, the captain of the football team. They'd gotten along well enough, and it was easy and comfortable not to worry about who would ask her to prom. But once graduation neared, Lark wanted an out. She'd taken Hillarie up on the dare, hoping Warren would break up with her. Which he had.

If only she could explain it to Jace. But it sounded so —shallow.

"I don't know much about Hillarie, but I always wondered if her life wasn't as grand as she wanted everyone to think."

"At least Queen Hillarie recognized me."

"Like I said, you look different." All filled out and muscley. And how had thick glasses camouflaged those piercing, electric green eyes?

"You know after you kissed me—this time—and your eyes pleaded with me to go along, I thought about outing you. To embarrass you, to make you feel like I did that last summer."

"You should have." Her insides wilted. "I deserve it."

"But then I thought, hey, I can torment her with a pretend romance until the wedding is over and torture her even more."

Her gaze narrowed. "You're too kind. That kiss you initiated was a bit over the top."

"I try to make my kisses count."

She rolled her eyes. "I should come clean about us now and let you off the hook."

"However you want to play it, I'll go along."

"The truth will set us free." But did she want to be free? She'd dated a few guys over the years but had never been kissed like that.

Talk about shallow. There was more to a relationship than kisses. And she didn't have time for distractions. Her potential staging career was in Dallas. Ace this wedding, secure the inn's future, and get back to her life in the city. Period.

⁕⁕⁕⁕⁕ ✼ ⁕⁕⁕⁕⁕

EARLY MORNING SUN felt good as Lark swayed the white wicker porch swing back and forth with one foot. Quiet, peaceful, and with only the squeak of the chain to interrupt the stillness.

The backdoor opened, and she stiffened. It could only be Hillarie or Warren. The latter stepped outside. Which was worse? A tossup. She should come clean now about her Jace charade, swallow the embarrassment, and move on.

"Hey." He strolled toward her. "The great room looks better. No debris, new chandelier on the ceiling instead of the floor."

"We pulled a late night to get it cleaned up, then installed the new one early this morning." She didn't make room for him on the swing.

After an awkward silence, he claimed the rocker to her right. "I hate this tension between us. I don't want this week and a half to be uncomfortable."

"No tension here. And I'm happy for you and Hillarie. Y'all are perfect for each other." The swing had stopped. She set it back in motion and the chains resumed their squeaking.

"You must have questions."

"Just one." It didn't really matter. But had they made a fool of her? "It was Hillarie who dared me to kiss Jace that last summer. Was there something between y'all then?"

"Nothing. But not long afterward, Hillarie's father and mine worked together on a business deal. We started seeing each other. After we got serious, she admitted she'd had a crush on me for years."

"I wondered then." Probably why she always tried to best Lark. "So, you've been together all this time?"

"On and off. We fight and make up a lot."

A couple strolled along the shore, hand in hand, with seagulls swooping above their heads.

"I love her, but she's so jealous. She's convinced I can't truly love her and that I'll dump her for someone else like her mom did her dad." His shoulders sagged. "You being here only made it worse."

"Why? It was so long ago. We were kids. And were never serious." They'd basically used each other to get through high school.

"I know. But she's gotten it in her head you were my first love. And she broke us up with that dare. If it hadn't been for her, we'd still be together."

"That's ridiculous."

"I've told her that. But Hillarie's mom left when she was young, and her stepmom was emotionally abusive."

"That's terrible." Something hard sank to the pit of her stomach.

"Her mom's abandonment and Tilda's words took a toll over the years." His gaze latched on something in the distance. "Hillarie hides it well, but she has very low self-esteem."

"But you love her. And she loves you."

"Yes. I hoped proposing to her would prove my devotion." He leaned forward, propped his elbows on his knees. "Maybe it's good that you're here. Maybe she'll realize once and for all, she's my one and only. Especially since she's seen you happy with Jace."

Her stomach churned. So much for coming clean. "Does she know you're with me right now?"

"No. She's still sleeping. Doesn't do mornings. Especially since—"

"Since?"

"She's pregnant."

"Oh." Had she trapped him with a baby? Was she that desperate?

He scanned the coastline. "What about you and Jace? Was there something to that dare?"

"No. I never saw Jace again until I came back here for the wedding."

"And that was?"

"A month ago." True. She'd barely left the house and spent every waking moment getting Gramps and Gran packed. As a result, she hadn't run into Jace until two days ago, but Warren didn't need to know that.

"You hired him, and feelings developed?"

"Something like that. We're in the discovery stage. And crazy about each other." The lie tumbled from her lips.

A familiar green pickup pulled up. Jace killed the engine and stepped out. His glance bounced from Lark to Warren then back, and his dark brows formed a *V*. Certainly playing his jealous boyfriend part well.

WHAT HAD Lark ever seen in this guy? Warren had given Jace his nickname all those years ago and never missed an opportunity to make him feel lower than a snake's belly. Why was she out on the back porch with him?

"Morning Jace." Warren stood. "Just enjoying the peaceful view."

Of Lark. Jace's jaw throbbed.

"I better go check on my fiancée." Warren stopped at the door. "By the way, Hillarie wants us to all go to dinner tonight. Around six?"

"Why?" Lark frowned. "It's not like we were ever friends."

"She's not the same person she was in high school. I think she wants to make amends."

"Okay. I guess we can do that." Lark shrugged.

The screen door clapped shut behind Warren.

"The only view he seemed interested in was you."

"Stop. We were just talking."

"Scoot over." Jace strolled over to the porch swing, stood there until she looked up at him. "He might come back out. And I assume we're continuing our charade since you agreed to dinner with them."

With obvious reluctance, she made room for him.

"He's a complete jerk." He put his arm around her shoulders. "Making time with his ex-girlfriend while his fiancée is upstairs."

"It wasn't like that. He's completely in love with her." She moved his arm. "He's gone, and we don't have to be in a clinch every moment."

"Are we coming clean at dinner then?"

"I wish we could. But—" she squeezed her eyes shut "—there's more at stake."

"Such as?"

"Hillarie's pregnant and very jealous."

A chill crawled up the back of his neck. "Toward you?"

"Somewhat." She brushed hair away from her face and filled him in on her conversation with Warren. "I need them to stay together."

"Because?"

"This wedding. It's the biggest event of the season, and I've got the photographer from *Coastal Society Magazine* coming."

"You want your nemesis to marry the wrong man so you can sell the inn?"

"I want this inn to stay in existence." Her mouth set in a firm line. "Hillarie and Warren couldn't possibly be more perfect for each other. You said it yourself. And there's a child involved. We need to keep pretending we're a couple for her peace of mind and their baby's sake."

A teen jogged along the shore with a golden retriever, as if without a care in the world.

"It doesn't sound like they have a healthy relationship."

"I can't let her insecurities about me ruin their future. So, will you please keep pretending to be my boyfriend?" She closed her eyes. "I can't believe I just said that."

"Since it's such a hideous concept for you, I'm not sure."

"That's not what I meant. It's just that, I try to be honest. I'm a Christian."

"Really?"

She blew out a heavy sigh. "I know I haven't acted like it where you're concerned. But I got saved when I was twelve. After a disturbance at my school, some of the summer parents talked up their hoity-toity private school. My folks transferred me, but I didn't fit in. I made friends as best I could and tried not be shallow like them."

"You never called me Tool Face Jace."

"No. But I humiliated you."

"I survived." He waggled his eyebrows at her. "And now, I've got my chance to torment you with my attentions."

She chuckled. "That means you'll do it?"

"I'm a Christian too. Rescuing damsels in distress is right up my alley. But you, you need to work on your cuddling, young lady."

Her cheeks bloomed pink. "We don't have to cuddle."

"If we're gonna be a couple, you can't be all stiff." Jace twined his fingers with hers.

"But we're not gonna *be* a couple." Her gaze shot to their hands, and she tugged hers away. "They're not here, and we're only pretending."

"True. But when they're here, we have to pull it off. If you keep being so uncomfortable with me, they'll get suspicious."

"I guess you have a point." She took in a sharp breath. "Are you sure about this?"

If he truly harbored a grudge toward her, it would be a chore. But this closeness with her felt like an opportunity. Maybe that old crush never died. But this time, he'd guard his heart. Lark Pendleton wouldn't get the chance to break it twice.

"It'll be easy." He covered her hand with his again.

With a big sigh, she threaded her fingers through his, shot him a glare. "But absolutely no more kissing."

"Not on the agenda." Definitely off limits. He stood, pulled her into a loose hug. Stiff and unyielding. "Relax." He said it for himself as much as her while her heady perfume and shampoo did a number on him. This is only pretend.

"Okay, we can do this." A shudder moved through her, but she relaxed.

"We got this. Just enough truth to keep it real."

"You're good at this." She slugged him in the chest. "That worries me."

Of course, Warren picked the most expensive restaurant in town. Overly attentive, Jace pushed his plate away and covered her free hand with his. Lark's gaze dropped to the table. If only pretending with him would be an unpleasant task. But instead, every touch set her nerve-endings on fire.

She pushed a jumbo shrimp around her plate.

"This steak is excellent." Warren forked another bite. "Tender and cooked to perfection."

"The chef has won several grilling competitions." Her seafood was perfect too, but her appetite was off.

"How's yours?" Warren glanced at Hillarie, quiet beside him.

"It's good." Hillarie sipped her tea. "The inn looks great. I never should have doubted you."

"Jace did a great job." He'd spent the day scaling the ballroom and the outside of the inn hanging lights, while she'd put a small tree in each of the guestrooms. The result gave a twinkling, Christmas Cottage feel. "Tomorrow, we put up the tree in the great room."

"I'm sorry for the things I said yesterday, about you trying to derail my wedding." Hillarie folded her napkin. "I'm so stressed."

"It's okay." Lark pushed her plate away. "You've got pregnancy hormones firing too. It's a wonder you can function at all."

Hillarie's gaze jerked to Warren. "You told her?"

"I was afraid she might kick us out, so I wanted her to understand why you're so uptight."

"I'm sorry." Lark winced. "I didn't realize it was a secret."

"Well, obviously, we're not telling everyone. Until after the wedding." Hillarie glanced at Jace.

"My lips are sealed." He locked his mouth with an imaginary key and threw it over his shoulder.

His acting skills needed work.

"So, when did you two reconnect?" Hillarie leaned toward them, as if eager for details.

"Once Lark came back to the inn, things just developed." Jace locked eyes with her and she couldn't seem to look away.

"To Lark and Jace." Hillarie raised her tea glass—unaware of the torment she caused. "May y'all have a very long happily-ever-after. Like Warren and me."

They humored her, clinked their tea glasses.

"Do y'all live together at the inn?"

Lark choked on her tea, sputtered, and coughed into her napkin.

"Not unless Lark has changed." Warren grinned. "A lot."

Didn't anyone believe in waiting for marriage anymore? Her face heated. But here she was, a professing Christian, living a lie.

"She hasn't." Jace's words came through clenched teeth. "And I'm glad." He broke his mesmerizing eye contact and leveled a scathing glare at Warren. "I own a ranch in Rosharon, but at the moment, I live in my current flip project, the old Morris place."

"You? Own a ranch?" Warren's condescending tone grated on her nerves. "And you're flipping a house?"

"This is my tenth flip. It's a very lucrative business and how I bought my ranch." Jace's gaze latched on hers again.

Warren's face turned purple. Was he really so self-important that Jace's success made him uncomfortable?

"Are we ready for dessert?" Lark couldn't wait for dinner to end. Eager to escape her arrogant former *boyfriend*. Eager for Jace to stop looking at her like that.

Before she started believing their charade.

"Tell me about this flipping business of yours." Warren's voice dripped disdain, but the smell of money always interested him. "Dad and I have talked about investing in such matters if you need a financial backer."

"No thanks." Jace smiled. "My finances are quite healthy. Though I appreciate the offer, I prefer to work alone and keep my profit margin for myself."

"I see. Well, hit me up if you ever change your mind."

"I won't. With my flips, my ranch, and my beach horseback rides, I do quite well."

"Beach horseback rides?" Hillarie's eyes lit up. "Do tell."

"Jace owns *Romantic Beach Rides*." Lark set her napkin by her plate. "You can rent a horse from him to ride on the beach."

"In fact, that's how Lark and I ran into each other again. I was testing a mare and she spooked over Lark's grandmother's dog."

"The mare almost took me out, so I blasted him."

"And I managed to tame her." He slipped his arm around her shoulders.

Behind a plastic smile, Lark's teeth set on edge.

"Oh, how romantic. And you rode off into the sunset."

"Not really. I didn't buy the mare. And we haven't had time for a romantic beach ride."

"Oh, let's do it. The four of us." Hillarie clapped her hands.

"Whoa, wait up." Warren held both palms up as if to ward off the idea. "I've never ridden."

"I have, and we've got our very own horse pro here." Hillarie gestured toward Jace. "He can show you, can't you Jace?"

"Sure. I'll check the schedule."

"Y'all have to come with us." Hillarie reached across the table and grabbed Lark's free hand. "You can't date a guy who owns *Romantic Beach Rides* and never experience one. That would be like me or Warren never staying in any of the condos our dads build."

"You're on." Jace tucked her against his side, his chin resting on her head. "We should experience that, sugar dumplin'."

It took everything she had, not to bury her elbow deep in his ribs.

4

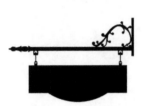

L ark scurried to the pile of boxes, and opened the one containing the tree.

"Just for the record, I'd have picked a real blue spruce." Jace pulled a piece from the box. "Who ever heard of a plastic tree?"

"A woman who doesn't want to vacuum pine needles." Lark put the stand together. "Feel free to get a live evergreen for your flip house." She set her hands on her hips. "And knock yourself out cleaning needles."

"It's already up."

"Really?" A bachelor putting a Christmas tree up in a house he planned to sell? Not many men like Jace.

"I love Christmas." He put the two lower parts together, then climbed a few steps on the ladder to set the top in place. "It forces the world to acknowledge Jesus's birth."

"If only they'd realize there's much more to Him than a cute little baby." Lark sighed.

"Yes, but acknowledging His existence is a start."

With Jace back on level ground, they busied themselves

fluffing out lower limbs, filling in holes. The plastic bristles were spiky against Lark's fingers.

Movement on the staircase and Jace automatically slipped his arms around her waist, buried his lips in her hair.

Thanks Warren. She squelched an eye roll. And a shiver.

"Break it up, y'all." Hillarie clapped her hands, with a giggle.

Gladly. Sort of.

"Where are the ornaments?"

"In that box by the door." Lark pulled away and pointed Hillarie in the right direction.

Warren dragged the box over.

"Oh, these are the cutest ornaments." Hillarie nabbed a glittery sand dollar. "Look honey, they're all beachy with sea life and shells."

"Gran collected them for years." Lark picked up an aqua frosted seahorse. She stepped back, risked a glance at Jace. "It's looking great."

"Mine, at my ranch, has cowboy boots, stars, and hats." He snagged a starfish and hung it on a branch.

"That's fitting." Hillarie giggled.

Bouts of chatter and silence accompanied the foursome as they placed ornaments. Her hand brushed Jace's several times as they went for the same branch, and she even bumped into him twice as they both turned to get more ornaments. She'd never known trimming a tree could be so nerve wracking.

"I think we're ready for the topper."

"But we still have ornaments." Jace held up another starfish.

"Gran always had a taller tree, but I don't want it to take away from the bride, so I got a smaller one this year. You don't want it too cluttered." Lark grinned at the young boy Christmas drew out of him.

"What a lovely star." Hillarie picked up the tree topper. "Can Warren do the honors?"

"Of course." She agreed with an inward cringe.

Warren cleared his throat. "It seems like Jace's place to do that."

"At your service." Jace took the tree topper, climbed the ladder, and set the lighted starfish in position.

Lark plugged it in, then they stepped back. Oohs and ahhs echoed. Warren put his arm around Hillarie, and she laid her head against him. Lark's gaze went to Jace as his fingers twined with hers. Her insides fluttered. Not a good sign.

"Now we're festive." While the tree usually stood in the center of the great room and tall enough to almost reach the chandelier, this year's smaller version was tucked against the back side of the staircase. The perfect backdrop for Hillarie's dramatic bridal entrance down the staircase with candid shots to end up in *Coastal Society Magazine*. "I think we can call Christmas at the Shell House Inn complete."

"Thanks for letting us help." Warren ushered Hillarie toward the door. "We're off to the beach."

Hillarie turned back. "Don't forget to set up our *Romantic Beach Ride*, Jace."

"Scheduled for next Tuesday."

"Yay." Hillarie squealed and the door shut behind them.

"I expect a bill for fixing the chandelier and ceiling."

"We'll wait and see what all you do with the staging thing. And probably call it even." He retrieved his light jacket from the hall tree, and slipped it on.

As the door closed behind him, Lark climbed the stairs, stashed the empty boxes and tubs in the attic. Decorating with the handsome cowboy was fun. She shook thoughts of him away. Wow, did she need to get back to Dallas.

JACE NEEDED HIS DRILL. How could he have left his most important tool at the inn? At the door, he was tempted to knock. But with the inn officially open and fully staffed now, it wasn't like it was a private residence. The knob turned. Unlocked. He stepped inside, scanned the room. No sign of his tool. He'd have to find Lark.

Voices on the landing above.

"I'm really sorry for daring you that last summer." Hillarie apologizing? It sure sounded like her. "I knew Warren was there and I wanted y'all to break up, so maybe I'd have my chance with him."

Jace leaned against the wall, hidden from their view.

"It's okay," Lark said. "It's ancient history. I knew Warren was there too. I wanted him to break up with me."

"Really?"

"That's the honest truth. I knew we were all wrong for each other, but I didn't know what to do about it."

If that was true, why had she been mooning over Warren on the porch the other day? No, it was a silly dare. And Lark was a control freak. She'd taken the dare to be in control.

And she'd gotten control. Of his heart. Face it, you oaf, she only has eyes for Warren. She'd never jeopardize his relationship with Hillarie, but she'd never give her heart to Jace.

"All the guys always fell for you." Hillarie whimpered. "I wish I could pull off your casual look. You have such a natural beauty, I always felt like I could never compare. Like I was overdone, and no one would ever look at me as long as you were around."

Lark cleared her throat, obviously uncomfortable with the compliment and probably with Hillarie in general. "Thanks. But there's no reason to feel vulnerable. Especially toward me.

Trust me, I'm no threat to you." The inadequacy in her tone tugged at him.

"I didn't intentionally get pregnant, but sometimes I wonder if Warren would have proposed if I hadn't." Hillarie's voice cracked. "I mean, if I hadn't broken you and Warren up that last summer here, maybe y'all would've ended up married."

"We never loved each other. He loves you, but you shouldn't have to depend on Warren for your happiness. Find your joy and let a loving husband be the icing on your cake."

"I used to find my joy in Daddy. Before he married Tilda."

"Do you ever get to spend time with your dad?"

"Only at work." Hillarie's voice quivered. "That's why I agreed to have an office. Tilda never shows up there."

Poor Hillarie, her mom had abandoned her and then she'd lost her doting father too. No wonder she seemed so lost.

"Do you spend time with Warren's parents?"

"They're traveling." Hillarie huffed out a sigh. "And I don't think they like me all that much."

Warren's mom kept her nose too far in the air to approve anyone. Though Jace would have thought Hillarie would suit her standards. His dad spent his time following his wife around repeating, 'Yes, dear.'

"If it makes you feel any better, they didn't approve of me at all."

"I can totally see that." Hillarie giggled. "I didn't mean that as an insult at all. You're way too real for them. But that's a good thing."

"Do you go to church?"

"Once Warren and I got together, he started making me go. He gets it, but I don't." Hillarie's tone dripped sadness.

"Come to church with me tomorrow. With an open mind."

"Maybe." Sniffling.

A door opened above.

"What's going on here?" Warren to the rescue. "Lark? Did you make her cry? What did you say to her?"

How dare he use such a scolding tone? Jace hurried up the stairs.

"Of course not. We were just talking." At least Lark stood up for herself.

"Lark has been very nice to me. Even when I didn't deserve it."

"What's going on?" Jace finally made it up the endless stairs and put his arm around Lark's waist, relished having her close.

"Hillarie and I were just talking." Lark pressed her cheek into his shoulder. Needing strength or glad he'd broken up the one on one with the fiancée of the man she still loved. Probably both.

Their eyes locked on Jace—holding Lark close.

"I think Hillarie had a bout of pre-wedding jitters along with pregnancy emotions." Lark patted the brunette's shoulder. "But you only have six more days to wait for the wedding of your dreams. And then all this bridal stress will be behind you, and happily-ever-after will be all yours."

"Why did you propose to me, when you did?" Hillarie's chin trembled.

"Because I love you." Warren pressed his hand to her back. "Let's discuss this in your room."

"No. I need to know. Would you have proposed to me if I hadn't gotten pregnant?"

"Of course, I would have."

Jace wanted to slink down the stairs and escape this drama. Would Warren and Hillarie disintegrate right here, allowing Lark to ride off into the sunset with the jilted groom?

"But you asked me to marry you only after I told you about the baby."

"Because I had the ring already and you surprised me with the good news. It just came out."

Hillarie laughed, clasped both hands over her mouth. "You had the ring already. How did I miss that?"

"What?" Warren frowned, confusion lining his brow.

"You proposed after I told you I was pregnant. But you had the ring already. Which means you bought it—" she giggled. "—before you knew about the baby."

"Yes." He pulled her into his arms.

"You really love me."

"I've been telling you that for years. Marriage is a big step, a life-time commitment. I wanted to make sure we were right before I bought a ring."

"We're right." Hillarie couldn't seem to stop laughing. And crying. "Oh, I'm a soggy mess."

"But you're beautiful. And I love you."

Lark took Jace's hand, motioned toward the stairs. He followed her down and onto the back porch.

"Wow, I'm emotionally exhausted." Lark slumped into the wicker swing.

Because she was still hung up on a man who was in love with his pregnant bride-to-be. He settled beside her. "Poor Warren. That much drama could suck a guy dry. Talk about high-maintenance."

"But he loves her. I think they'll be okay now."

"Does that mean we don't have to pretend anymore?" He held his breath.

"She's got wedding stress and pregnancy hormones firing. If thinking I'm crazy about you gives her peace, we should continue."

Jace started breathing again. "All right, then. I'll be your trusty pretend boyfriend for another week."

A week to live his fantasy.

"Why are you here?"

"Huh?"

"Why did you show up today?"

"Oh, I can't find my drill. Did you happen across it?"

"I did." She stood. "I stashed it in the closet. I'll get it for you."

The loss of her warmth so close sent a chill over him.

Back to reality. He needed to stay there. For good. In a week, Lark Pendleton wouldn't be his pretend girlfriend anymore. And in a few weeks, she'd be gone from his life. This time for good.

❧❧❧ ❀ ❦❦❦

In church with Lark sitting beside him, Jace could get used to this. But Warren?

Forgive me, Lord. But it's hard to sit through anything with him.

"For there is no respect of persons with God." The pastor read Romans 2:11, then scanned the crowd. "With God, we're all on equal footing. Rich, poor, black, white, college education, or not. None of us are any better than anyone else."

The words sank into Jace's soul. For so long, he'd let a blue-collar job define him as low class. But God didn't see him that way at all. With God, there was no social status.

"Anyone can come to him, with an open heart." The pastor continued. "Won't you come forward and receive Christ?"

The altar call began as the pianist played "Have Thine Own Way Lord." Voices blended as several went forward.

Whispering beside him, then Lark stood, and followed Hillarie and Warren to the altar.

She was a good person. Despite her lingering feelings for Warren, Lark truly wanted him to be happy with Hillarie.

Warren waved the pastor over. He knelt between Lark and Hillarie and prayed. A few seconds later, Lark stood, returned to her spot beside him, and bowed her head.

The couple stayed there for a long time with the pastor. The pianist ran out of verses and started the song over. If Hillarie was down there getting right with God, maybe her upcoming marriage could survive.

Selfish of him. But Hillarie's marriage was so intertwined with Jace's chance for happiness with Lark. And he was beginning to hope for a future with her.

"Be with Hillarie, Lord." He whispered. "She needs you. And help me to be more selfless."

Finally, Warren stood, and helped Hillarie up. As they returned to their seats, the brunette wiped away tears, and Lark gave her a hug.

He couldn't wait to see them off Friday. But in seeing them off, he'd lose Lark. And he'd miss her. If only he could have the real thing with her. No more pretending.

Even if Warren stuck with marrying Hillarie, if their union failed, he'd run right back to Lark. But the dark circles under her color-defying eyes spoke volumes. She wasn't over Warren. She'd be there to pick up his pieces.

But if Warren left for good, stayed with Hillarie, maybe Lark could eventually forget him. And if she did, Jace would be there to pick up her pieces. Even if he had to move to Dallas to do it.

5

Prep launched into high gear the next day, starting with wedding favor production in Hillarie's room.

"Thank you so much for helping me with this." Hillarie pressed a gold label embossed with her and Warren's names and the date on a tiny plastic tube of bubbles, then set it on the coffee table. "I hoped my maid of honor and bridesmaids could come early and help. But none of them can make it until the day before the wedding."

"I'm glad to help." Lark squeezed Hillarie's hand.

"Are you in love with Jace?"

"I think I might be falling." It slipped right out. And it had nothing to do with appeasing Hillarie.

But she did not, could not love Jace.

"How do you know?"

"Because my insides buzz just talking about him." The truth and nothing but. "And when he's not with me—I miss him." Also true. Oh, boy.

"That's exactly how I feel about Warren." Hillarie

squealed. "Even though you didn't love him, I'm sorry I stole him from you."

"It's okay." Lark chuckled. "I'm glad you got him. I think y'all will be fine now. Just base your relationship on God and honesty." Boy, was she one to talk. Falling for Jace during a fake relationship for Hillarie's peace of mind. Pretending her feelings were fake for her own peace of mind.

"Me too." Hillarie's blue eyes squeezed closed.

"The only true joy I've ever found is in God. He never lets me down. Ever." Warmth spread through her chest.

"Thank you for helping me see that. You've been way too nice to me."

"You're a good person." Deep down. Just spoiled. "I've enjoyed getting to know you." The real Hillarie.

"I'll miss talking to you after this week."

"We can keep in touch."

"We can?" Hillarie's eyes lit up.

"Of course. I'll give you my number."

"Thank you, Lark."

"No problem." Lark hugged her.

"You have no idea how much that means to me."

"I'll actually miss you." And she really would. But more than that—she'd miss Jace.

Her pretend relationship, that involved very real developing feelings for Jace, would end.

No more holding hands, no more cuddling, no more kissing. Her chest hurt.

A knock sounded on the door. "You awake, hon?" Warren called.

"Come in."

The door swung open, and Warren's eyes widened, then ping-ponged between the two women. "Everything okay?"

"Just fine." Hillarie stood and burrowed into his arms. "We're putting wedding favors together."

"Okay?" Uncertainty rang in Warren's tone.

"She's been telling me how crazy she is about you." Lark caught his gaze, then tied the final bow and scooped the bubble tubes into a white basket. "I'll take these." She slipped out of the room and hurried downstairs.

"Morning." Jace stood in the great room looking up at her.

She promptly dropped the basket. Bubble vials bounced and rolled in all directions. "What are you doing here?"

"Obviously scaring the daylights out of you." He stooped to pick up the tubes that made it all the way to the first floor.

"Did any of them break?"

"No. What are these things anyway?"

"Bubbles. Guests blow them as the bride and groom leave."

"What happened to birdseed?" He frowned.

"I think some people still do that."

In the middle of the staircase, he met her, and handed over the tubes he'd retrieved.

Her fingers tingled at the contact. "Hillarie and I put these together. And talked."

"How'd that go?"

"Quite well. I really like her."

"You do?"

"I do." She shot him a sheepish grin. "When I first met her in school, I hated her, then I felt sorry for her. Now I like her."

He retreated down the stairs, and she followed.

"I got a glimpse of the real Hillarie." She lowered her voice. "She's fragile and believing our relationship is real definitely reassures her."

"Not that I mind this reassurance thing, but she's a bombshell. What's she got to be insecure about?"

No one had ever called Lark that. Especially not Jace. "Bombshell or not, her sense of worth is a mess."

"No worries. I don't mind convincing her. Not at all." He whistled at her.

"Stop it." She whacked his shoulder and almost dropped the basket again.

With a deep chuckle, Jace scooped the basket from her, and pulled her into his arms. "I've missed you."

"Taking it a bit far, don't you think?"

"It seems like we've been running in two different directions all day long."

Weird, but he smelled too good, felt too good, to pull away from—all warm and firm muscles.

"Break it up, y'all." Hillarie giggled.

Ohhhh. That's why he hugged her. Pretending to miss her. But she really had missed him.

"I gotta get my Lark fix while I've got the chance." Jace's embrace was convincing.

Enough to kick her heartbeat up to double time. He didn't let go, and she didn't either.

"We're going out for lunch." Warren tugged his grinning fiancée toward the door.

"But I'll be back soon to help with ribbons on the chairs like we talked about. And we still have to decorate the dining room for the reception." Hillarie turned pouty eyes on Jace. "We're still on for our *Romantic Beach Ride* tomorrow night, right?"

"I'll have the horses saddled and ready."

"I actually had my own horse in Dallas. And won some dressage competitions and jumping shows."

A vision of old-fashioned puffy jodhpurs popped into Lark's head. It fit. Although Hillarie probably had the modern, sleek legging style riding pants.

"I'm not so sure this is a good idea." Warren pressed his hand against Hillarie's stomach.

"There won't be any jumping. I'll be fine." Hillarie's smile broadened. "I even packed my riding clothes since I hoped we might find a dude ranch close by." She did a little squeal and the door closed behind them.

And Jace still held her.

"You can let go now." She turned her face away from his way too tempting throat, but his muscled shoulder muffled her words.

"They might come back. Maybe I should kiss you, just in case." Jace's low chuckle heated more than her face.

It took all her faculties to keep from turning to accept that offer. She craved the freedom to explore her growing feelings for him. So tempting. Just for today, could she throw caution to the dry Texas wind? Her insides sweltered.

What would happen when Warren and Hillarie left? Her heart clunked to the pit of her stomach. She didn't even want to think about after. When life would go back to normal. A few days ago, she couldn't wait for Warren and Hillarie to leave. But now? She missed Jace already.

Warmth threaded through her. His embrace going right to her head—threatening to crowd out all rational thought. Take a step back, her brain commanded. But her heart refused.

"I think the coast is clear." Lark let out a sigh, pulled out of his grasp. "I forgot about the ride."

"Your enthusiasm crushes my soul, sugar dumplin'." He clasped a hand to his heart.

"If you call me that one more time ..." she glared at him, but then winced. "Did I mention, I'm kind of afraid of horses?"

"You did. But you'll ride with me."

That thought made her quiver.

"Fear not, fair maiden." He winked. "I shall choose my tamest steed."

She rolled her eyes and jabbed her finger in his chest. "Do not stick Warren with a stallion." Pure muscle. She couldn't even threaten him without her pulse racing. She took a step back, dropped her hand to her side. "Hillarie and their baby need him in one piece."

"I can't believe you'd think such evil of me?" A wicked grin spread over his mouth. "But that would be fun."

She could picture it. A smile teased her lips.

"You know you'd love watching him land on his backside."

"Promise." She used her sternest tone—shot him the stink eye.

"I promise." He raised his hands in surrender. "But only because I'd prefer not to get sued." His sigh spewed out from between gritted teeth. "Why do we have to ruin a perfectly good beach ride by dragging along the gruesome twosome?"

"Be nice." But she couldn't squelch her giggle. "I expect a bill for the ride."

"I'll bill the gruesome twosome. But not my sugar dumplin'." He blew her a kiss.

She rolled her eyes. "What are you doing here?"

"If we're continuing our charade, I figure I should stop by often."

"Oh. Right. Thanks."

"No problem, sugar dumplin'." He waved as he exited.

What had she gotten herself into? Her charade with Jace was more volatile than Hillarie's pregnancy hormones.

<hr>

OH, no. Jace closed his eyes.

Hillarie and Warren approached with Lark. The brunette

wore an obviously expensive red jacket, white tights, and funny boots that came up all the way to her knee. Holding a riding crop in her hand, she looked like she needed to put some pants on. Ready for some fancy jumping horse show? Or an English fox hunt? Not a romantic beach ride.

Warren stuck with his usual skinny pants, though they were khaki—proof he didn't own jeans—and a button-down shirt. His shiny boots probably zipped up the side and ended above his ankle.

"Luckily Hillarie brought along her uniform." Lark, somehow managed to keep a straight face.

"Um, you won't need the crop today." Jace pried the whip from Hillarie's fingers. "These horses don't jump, and if you want to go faster, you use the reins."

Hillarie's eyes lit up. "Which one's ours?"

"This is Alabaster." He stroked the buttery Palomino's shoulder. "She's gentle and easy to handle."

"I know my way around a horse." Hillarie huffed.

"Yes." Warren helped her mount. "But we don't want to take any chances with the baby."

"I won't." She patted Alabaster's neck.

"Saddle up." Jace envisioned Warren on his neighbor's stallion, then sailing through the air. It would help him sleep tonight.

Awkwardly, Warren followed his instructions and flailed his way into the saddle behind his bride-to-be, completely out of his comfort zone.

Jace hurried to help Lark, as she cringed near the porch.

"Come on. She won't hurt you. I promise."

Tentatively, she crept closer.

"Lark, this is Caramel."

"You've got her, right?"

"Yes." He waved her over with his free hand.

"What kind of horse is she?"

"A quarter horse with Buckskin coloring. They have gold or tan coats with black mane, tail, and markings. Pet her."

"Where?" She fisted both hands, drew them to her chest.

"Here." He took her fist in his, got her to open it, and smoothed it along the Buckskin's gold dust shoulder.

"Good girl." Her fingers shook, but she soon relaxed, following his lead.

"Now her face." He placed her palm between the mare's eyes and stroked down.

"Oh, her muzzle is so soft, like velvet."

"I think she likes you." He swung into the saddle, then offered her his hand. "Put your left foot in the stirrup, jump up behind me, and swing your right leg back and over like I did."

"Whoa." She wobbled a bit but made her way up. Her arms clamped around his middle, as if hanging on for dear life.

If only she'd never let go.

"Good job. That was smoother than Warren." He whispered.

"I heard that," Warren groused.

"I can't believe you own *Romantic Beach Rides* and you've never taken your honey for a ride." Hillarie whimpered. "I'd be insulted if I were you, Lark."

"We've both been pretty busy. But there's no time like the present." Jace reined Caramel into motion. "You good, Hillarie?"

"Fine. We'll follow you."

The sand silenced the horses' hooves as Warren and Hillarie's chatter muffled behind them.

"Alabaster is a Palomino, right?" Lark's grip on him didn't let up.

"Right." And he was fine with that. A little too fine.

"I've always thought they were the prettiest horse."

"You can relax. Caramel doesn't spook, bolt, or rear up."

"Oh, sorry." Her grip loosened slightly. "I just feel very out of control."

"I always knew you were a control freak."

She let go with one hand, long enough to swat him in the ribs.

As dusk set, a flame lit the beach ahead. Two couples sat around the fire.

"That looks like fun." Hillarie squealed.

Thankfully, the horses didn't even twitch.

"Maybe we could have a bonfire sometime."

"I don't know. I still have a lot of wedding décor to do and Jace has his hands full with his flip house."

"I'll always make time for my honey." Jace muttered.

She pinched his side.

"We don't work for our daddies, but no worries, darlin'. If my sugar dumplin' wants to have a bonfire with y'all, I'll be there."

Lark pinched his other side.

At the rate they were going, he'd be bruised before the evening was over. But having her warmth against his back was worth it. Here he was, tumbling for Lark all over again.

"I want us to go to Wednesday night Bible study," Warren said. "But maybe we can manage a bonfire tomorrow night afterward."

"Perfect." Hillarie cooed.

It did sound pretty perfect. But in three days, the wedding would be over. Their charade would end. Shortly after that, she'd be gone, and he'd probably never see her again. He had to build up an immunity to her. And fast.

6

The bonfire cast a glow on each face in the circle. Bible study had really sunk in for Lark tonight. The preacher had read Proverbs 3:5, "Trust in the Lord with all thine heart; and lean not unto thine own understanding." It hit her hard. She was a control freak, just as Jace had said, and she needed to rely on God.

Tenderness and love glowed out of Warren as he watched his soon-to-be wife. Hillarie seemed relaxed, like she was enjoying herself.

Her comfort came from God, not Lark's pretend relationship with Jace. If it wouldn't cause drama, she'd come clean. But tomorrow would be busy with wedding guests arriving, the rehearsal and dinner. Then the wedding the next day and their charade would end. Lark shivered.

"Maybe we should call it a night." Jace suggested.

"But this is so much fun." Hillarie snuggled close to Warren. "I don't want it to end. Y'all cuddle up, share your body heat."

"I've got a better idea." Jace jumped up and headed for the gear he'd brought.

What was he up to? Snuggling by the fire with him might be too much for her wayward heart to handle.

"The perfect solution." He came back with sleeping bags, dropped one in each lady's lap. "Bundle up."

Warren unzipped theirs, spread it around his and Hillarie's shoulders, while Lark stood and shimmied into hers. No way was she sharing with Jace. Besides, she'd been around him enough in the last week to know he was hot natured.

"Ooh, thank you." Hillarie looked from one to the other of them. "Y'all aren't fighting or anything are you?"

"Of course not. Who would fight with such a treasure?" Jace winked at her. "I'm not cold and Lark likes to wrap up like a mummy."

"He's right." She settled beside Jace, pulled the blanket over her head, and tucked it under her chin. How had he known that? She ended up a bit closer than she'd intended, their knees touching. And despite the thickness of her sleeping bag between them, her nerve endings stayed on high alert.

It felt way too good sitting in the warmth of the fire next to him. Especially since she wouldn't get to be so near him for much longer.

"What about once you sell the inn? What about you and Jace?" Hillarie's gaze pinged back and forth between them. "This isn't just a Christmas romance, is it?"

"Of course not." Lark wiggled closer to him until their shoulders touched. "I couldn't do without this guy. We'll travel back and forth, make it work. Dallas is only four and a half hours from here."

"Or I might talk her into becoming my missus and living on my ranch." Jace turned her way, the firelight capturing every contour of his handsome face.

Somehow living on a ranch didn't sound hideous anymore. "We'll see what the future holds for us. We don't want to rush it."

But they had no future. Not as long as he was here, and she was in Dallas where she'd carefully established her staging career. A few more jobs and she'd have a down payment stashed away to start her own business. She could not let her heart land her in Rosharon, population eleven hundred or here in Surfside with not quite five hundred.

No one sold houses here unless they were for rental properties. And despite how she'd advertised her services to Jace, staging didn't really help in the rental business. At least, not in Dallas anyway.

"I think it'll work out. Y'all have been destined to be together since those long-ago summers. Just like Warren and me." Hillarie yawned.

"We better get back to the inn." Warren tweaked Hillarie's nose, then stood and offered his hand to help her up. "It's getting late, and you need extra rest."

"I am tired. Sorry guys." Hillarie took Warren's offer. "But y'all can stay. Don't leave on our account."

"Sounds good to me." Jace slipped his arms around Lark's shoulders.

"Night guys." Warren clasped Hillarie's hand. Soon the couple disappeared in the darkness.

"At least hanging with the gruesome twosome is almost over. After the wedding, we won't have to pretend anymore. You stage my flip house, and we go our separate ways. If they ever come back here, I'll tell her about our Texas-sized breakup."

Why did the thought of that lodge a lump in her throat?

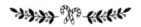

HILLARIE AND WARREN's families and the wedding party arrived throughout the next day. Later that afternoon, with everyone settled in their rooms, Lark did a final check of reservations. Only one couple hadn't arrived yet. The Hightowers—more snooty, former high school classmates.

The front door opened, and Jace entered. "Hey, are you finished with my ladder?"

"I am. It's behind the staircase. As usual, your timing is impeccable."

Jace scooped her up and swung her around.

"What are you doing? Stop."

But when he set her down, the room kept whirling. She wobbled into him.

"Oops. Didn't mean to make you dizzy." He steadied her.

After the world stopped spinning, she couldn't seem to make herself step away.

Before she could blink, his lips were on hers. What? She pushed against his chest, but he held fast, his arms a steel band around her. As his lips teased, her brain fogged. All resistance melted. Her hands snaked up his shoulders, around his neck, cupped the back of his head. And she kissed him right back. For all she was worth.

He pulled away and she chased after his lips, but Jace set her firmly away, a message in his gaze she couldn't quite read.

"Um, we seem to have an audience."

"Ahem." A feminine giggle. Footsteps descending the stairs. Hillarie.

Skin steaming—from the kiss and embarrassment—she looked up. Hillarie's red dress accentuated every curve as she clutched the stair railing. She even descended the stairs gracefully, with Warren trailing her.

Lark's gaze darted back to Jace. Their eyes locked and hers

dropped to his chest. He'd kissed her because he heard them coming. And she'd chased after him when he finished with her.

"Oh, my." A familiar female voice. "Looks like we're behind on developments." Katherine Hightower.

Inside the door, Katherine posed with her husband, Charles. Lark's eyes widened, met Jace's again. It took everything she had not to pull away from him. She blinked, tugged her gaze from his. The kiss had brushed all thoughts of their audience away. And they'd developed a bigger one.

"Welcome to the Shell House Inn." Lark managed to get her feet moving, shook Charles' hand and hugged Katherine.

"Hello." Katherine did a ta-da motion with her hands.

"It's so good to see you." Hillarie made it to floor level and hugged Katherine. "I saw you from my window and just had to come welcome you."

But Katherine's attention riveted on Jace. "Who's your guy, Lark?"

"Surely y'all remember Jace Wilder." Hillary squealed.

Charles's jaw dropped as he recognized Jace. "You and Tool—I mean Jace. Who knew?"

"Yeah." Jace pointed above them. "Mistletoe. We were just trying it out."

"You and Jace." Katherine pointed a finger at them. "I always thought y'all would make a perfect couple."

"Looks like some highly effective mistletoe." Charles grinned at his wife. "Maybe we should try it out."

Oh, yeah, that. Lark didn't want to talk about or think about mistletoe. "Feel free to make yourself at home. We still have a few hours before the rehearsal dinner."

"We need to pick up our wedding finery, but I wanted to make sure we could find the place. It's been a dozen years since we came here."

"See y'all in a bit then." Lark waved her fingers.

The door closed behind the couple.

"Isn't it great seeing all our old friends?" Hillarie clasped a hand to her heart.

"Just great." Lark pressed her fingertips to her temple where a dull ache throbbed to life.

"See y'all at the rehearsal soon." Hillarie went back upstairs with Warren on her heels. Doors closed above.

"I hate lying to everyone." Lark whispered.

"It's almost over, and we'll never see most of these people again." Jace surveyed the wedding decor.

"You're right. I'm just ready for this wedding to be over. The last time I checked, God doesn't approve of lying. And that's all I've done lately." At least he thought she'd kissed him back because she realized they'd had an audience.

"Don't fret, Lark. I think God understands you're only trying to help Hillarie. You're keeping her happy and off Warren's back." He glanced up the stairs. "She's kind of scary."

Did God approve of little white lies? No. Especially when she should have left Hillarie's happiness to Him.

She needed Warren and Hillarie to leave. To go on their merry way, so her life could get back to normal. In Dallas.

But at this point, could she ever return to ordinary life with things all wonky with Jace?

❄❄❄❄ 🍬 ❄❄❄❄

THE REHEARSAL and dinner had gone off like a well-oiled machine last night. Just the wedding to go.

Lark did a final check of her sea green dress in the full-length mirror. The ruffled hem swirled around her ankles with each step and made her feel feminine. The caterer and florist had taken over the kitchen, great room, and ballroom. The photographer got all the family pictures of the bride and groom separately, while joint pictures would take place after the nuptials.

As she descended the stairs, the front door opened, and Jace stepped in.

Typical jeans, western shirt, and boots with no hat and no drywall or paint splotches. She tripped over her own feet, grabbed the railing to keep her balance.

Green eyes met hers. "Hey."

"Hey." She made it to the bottom of the stairs without embarrassing herself.

"I thought I should be your plus one for the wedding." He whispered. "Isn't that what dating couples do."

"You're right. Good thinking." The last day to pretend with Jace. Her heart took a dive.

One of the floral assistants entered from the kitchen. "Ms. Pendleton, where should this arrangement go?"

"Let me check my chart." She hurried to the office.

The rest of the morning passed in a flurry of questions and last-minute details. Lark lost track of Jace. But when it came time for the ceremony, there he was, saving her a seat.

The vows were heartfelt, and Lark dabbed tears as the preacher pronounced Warren and Hillarie husband and wife. The pianist launched into a jubilant recessional. The bride and groom retraced the aisle to delighted applause and disappeared into the ballroom.

As the crowd followed the preacher's instructions, they dispersed to witness the couple's first dance as husband and wife.

With aching feet, Lark stayed seated and slipped off her heels. A sweet, melodious love song seeped into the room.

"Shall we?" Jace offered his hand.

"No one's watching. There's no need to pretend."

"But you dance, don't you? You worked so hard on this wedding, you ought to at least get to enjoy it."

"I can't bring myself to put my shoes back on. Not yet."

"Who needs shoes?" He tugged off his boots, bowed before her in sock feet.

She giggled. And couldn't seem to stop as she placed her hand in his. He drew her close and they fell into perfect rhythm, with her cheek against his chest, his chin on top of her head. At the moment, she could die right here and be happy as his spicy cologne filled her senses.

"You're a good dancer." His warm breath fluttered her hair. Gave her goosebumps. "Thanks. You too."

"When do you think you can stage the flip house?"

Stone cold reality hit. They weren't a couple. Only pretending to be. Within a few hours, Hillarie and Warren would leave in a cloud of bubbles and the charade would be over. But for now, she just wanted it to last a bit longer.

"Probably tomorrow. I'll leave Christmas décor up here for the Open House showing, so I'll just need to tuck the wedding paraphernalia away and I'm all yours." She wished.

"All mine, huh?"

She felt his voice rumbly in his chest. Couldn't pull away from him, even if she wanted to.

"Lark." A female voice called. "Oh, I'm terribly sorry to interrupt." Tilda, Hillarie's stepmom.

Jace did the pulling away.

"Hill wanted you to be there for the toast at the end of this song."

"Of course." She forced a smile and her feet to move, slipped her shoes back on.

Rebooted, Jace trailed her to the ballroom.

The next few hours filled with chatting, pictures, and food.

Though she didn't even have time to acknowledge him, Jace stayed by her side the entire time, like the dutiful pretend boyfriend that he was. Before she knew it, the reception wrapped up, and the happy couple, changed into their travel clothes, prepared to leave.

"One more hug." Hillarie sniffled as she wrapped Lark up again. "I never thought I'd enjoy our stay so much. I wish we could have visited more."

Lark gave her a squeeze. "Call me any time."

"You might regret saying that." Hillarie managed a soggy laugh.

"You'll be fine. Remember what I told you about not relying on Warren for your joy."

"I might object to that." Warren frowned.

"Silly man." Hillarie turned Lark loose, dabbed under her eyes with perfectly manicured thumbs. "She told me to rely on God for my joy."

"Oh." Warren grinned. "Good advice. Let's get out of here before the tears start again."

"Take care of her." Lark met his gaze. "And the baby." She helped Hillarie into her coat.

He gave her a stiff salute and ushered his wife toward the door. With one more tearful wave from Hillarie, they exited.

The guests followed the couple outside, leaving Lark and Jace alone.

"Isn't her family helping with clean up?"

"Nope. They paid extra for the staff and me to take care of it. Wedding Abernathy is officially over. I don't know about you —" Lark plopped in a chair "—but I'm glad that's a wrap."

"That poor girl wore me out." Jace straddled the chair back in front of her. "Almost makes you feel sorry for Warren. Almost."

"Be nice."

"It'll be weird. Not pretending, I mean." Jace cleared his

throat. "We were so convincing with our fake romance, I was beginning to wonder if it was real."

"You lied to me!" Hillarie wailed from the open front door.

Lark whirled around.

Warren did a facepalm behind his wife.

"I thought you were my friend, Lark. And all this time you were lying to me about Jace?"

"I was only trying to help." Lark bit her lip. "I thought if you didn't see me as a threat, you and Warren could be happy together."

"What else have you lied about? Are you still hung up on Warren? Is that the real reason for this little charade? So he'd think you were over him?" She turned to her husband. "Or were you in on it? Was the Jace and Lark show a cover to keep me from being suspicious? Are y'all carrying on behind my back?"

"Seriously Hill, when would I have time to carry on with anybody but you?" Warren shouted. "You're all consuming— like a fire that eats up anyone in range."

Hillarie wilted, her face crumpled, but she turned on Lark again. "You can't get a man of your own, so you have to steal mine and pretend you have a boyfriend to cover for it. You're such a loser."

"Shut it, Hillarie." Warren jabbed a finger at the door. "Go to the car."

"But—"

"Now!"

Spine straightened, head held high, Hillarie stomped out the exit.

"I'd like to speak to Lark." Warren's gaze caught hers. "Alone."

"I don't think that's a good idea." A tic started up in Jace's jaw.

"I do." Lark hugged herself. "I'll be fine."

"I'll be right in the other room—if you need me." Jace stared him down, did the I'm-watching-you-thing at Warren, then with obvious reluctance, left them alone.

An engine revved outside, and tires squalled. Lark winced. "We can talk later. You should go after her."

"I'm tired of going after her." Warren sank into a chair at the long breakfast bar. "I'm not sure I'm up to this farce of a marriage."

"But you have to. You said hurtful things to her, and she needs you. Your baby needs you."

"Maybe I'll just let her go, then once our child is born, I can fight for custody." Warren swallowed hard. "She's so exhausting."

"You love her enough to marry her." She hurried to the office, grabbed her keys. "Take my car."

He hesitated as if he didn't want to leave.

"You made a vow." She slammed her palm on the counter so hard it stung. "Not an if it gets hard, we'll bail vow. A lifetime commitment. She's just stressed. Over me. The baby. And battling morning sickness. Cut her some slack. Try to remember what drew you to her in the first place. Why you fell in love with her."

"I'll try." He straightened.

"Concentrate on her. Make it work."

He gave her a cocky salute. "I almost forgot. We came back for her bouquet." Warren retrieved it from a chair. "Wish me luck." He opened his arms, obviously expecting a hug.

"I'll pray for y'all." She accepted his embrace.

Just as the door opened and Jace stepped in the room.

His jaw dropped.

7

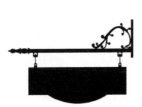

"Time's up." Jace managed to find his voice.

"Yeah. I was just leaving."

Unable to look at Lark, he followed Warren to the lobby, intent on seeing nothing but the back of him. Leaving. Even if Jace had to throw him out by his perfectly pressed shirt collar. And if he came back, Jace would deck him.

At the door, Warren turned to face him.

Jace's fist clenched.

"She's in love with you."

"What?" Totally not what he expected. Didn't Warren hear it was all a charade?

"Don't let her get away." Warren exited.

Jace sank to a chair in the great room. Lark would never jeopardize Warren's marriage. But she still had feelings for him. And as long as she did, Jace couldn't pursue her. Had she told Warren she loved Jace to throw him off balance, to get him to leave her alone?

Whatever had been said between them, Jace refused to be her cover. Or win her on the rebound.

"I've left Hillarie two messages." She paced the entryway. "She won't answer or call me back."

Lark always tried to smooth everything over and keep everyone happy. It was one of the things he loved about her. But sometimes she got so involved, other people's troubles threatened to consume her. And she certainly didn't need to be involved in Warren's marital woes.

"You can't fix everything." He gently gripped her shoulders. "Warren and Hillarie aren't your problem."

"But I'm part of their predicament. Hillarie thinks there's still something between Warren and me. She took off. Alone and upset. If she has an accident and gets hurt, I won't be able to live with myself."

"None of this is your fault."

Her cell phone rang. "It's her." Lark swiped her screen. "Hillarie? Are you all right?" She pressed a hand to her heart. "Oh, I'm so relieved. You had me so worried." She covered the mouthpiece with her hand and whispered, "Warren is with her."

Jace had to get away. "I need to get back to my flip house." He made his escape, bolted all the way home.

But even the sanctuary of sawdust and progress couldn't soothe him. After pretending to love Lark for the last ten days and falling for her during the sham, how would he pretend they were only friends? If only he could back out of their deal and avoid her.

Just get through her staging, send her back to Dallas, and sell the flip house. If he could buy the inn, and level it, she'd have no reason to ever return. Maybe then he could forget Lark Pendleton ever existed.

But why did he long to scurry back to the inn and spend as much time with her as he could?

"Are you sure you're okay, Hillarie?" Lark crossed the great room to her private quarters.

"I'm fine." Hillarie sniffled. "I'm sorry I worried you. And sorry for those horrible things I said."

"I didn't want to lie to you. And I promise my relationship with Jace is the only thing I lied about. Everything else was true." She winced. "I hope you can believe that coming from a liar."

Hillarie's watery laugh echoed through the phone. "I believe you. You were nothing but kind to me. A lot more than I deserved. I was just so jealous of you and worried about Warren's feelings for you."

"There's nothing between Warren and me. There never was. I wish I could convince you of that." She settled on the foot of her bed.

"It's just that you're so sweet and easy-going, and I drain him. You heard him say it—only much meaner than that. I'm a mess."

"You're not." *Please Lord, help me get through to her.* "But I think you should see a counselor."

"I'm not crazy!" Hillarie snapped.

"You're not. I agree." *Lord, give me the words.* "Mood swings can be part of pregnancy. But maybe a Christian counselor could help you see yourself in a different light."

"Maybe." Hillarie's voice went soft. "And I don't think it's just the pregnancy." A long pause. "Warren thinks you really are in love with Jace. That you weren't pretending."

The breath went out of Lark's lungs. She didn't want to open up like this. But maybe it would ease Hillarie's concerns if she knew the truth.

"Lark, are you still there?"

"He's right. I was pretending at first. But not toward the end."

"You should tell him how you feel."

"I can't. He doesn't feel the same. Even if he did, I'll go back to Dallas and he's here."

"Don't let geography end something that could be great." A wistfulness tinged Hillarie's tone. "Tell Jace the truth. Weren't you harping about honesty in relationships a week ago?"

"I may not be the best example on that." At the time, she'd been faking a romance. "But I'll think on it, if you'll promise to think on seeing a counselor."

"Deal. I wouldn't be surprised if Jace had feelings too. Y'all were awfully convincing." Hillarie giggled.

"You sound better."

"I feel better."

"Thanks for checking on us." Warren's voice in the background.

"Be happy, Hillarie. Pray, go to church, read the Bible, see a counselor, and love your husband. And child."

"I'll do my best."

"And call any time."

"I will."

Lark turned on her side, drew her knees up beside her. She felt better about Hillarie and Warren since he'd gone after her. They were together and married. She'd done all she could do to help them.

But inside, the place in her heart where Jace had taken up residence, felt empty.

WITH THE CLEANUP crew gone for the evening, Lark tackled the final task. One by one, she removed the swag from each white chair, folded them and hung them back on the storage cart.

The front door opened, and the best-looking cowboy she'd ever seen, stepped inside. "I guess you talked the newlyweds off the ledge."

"Hopefully. I got too involved, tried to fix everything, as usual." She forced a smile.

"I thought you might need help with cleanup."

Why did he have to be so thoughtful? She could resist him better if he was rude or impatient.

"What can I do?"

"There's not much left. I was stealthy with my décor. The bells fit weddings and Christmas, so they can stay. If you'll take the ribbon and flowers off these chairs and restack them, I'll sweep and tidy up."

"I'm on it." He plopped in a chair and worked at stripping the décor. "When do you plan to go back to Dallas?"

"The Open House for this place starts tomorrow, so I'll probably stay through next weekend."

"I won't be done with reno until Monday, so you can wait to start staging then." He stacked six more chairs on the cart. "I'm mainly down to the floors in the living room and bedrooms."

"Wow, I figured you were over here so much, you'd gotten behind."

"Sick of me, are you?"

"I didn't say that." She bit her lip. "I feel like I made a new friend."

"Agreed. It's been nice getting to know the real you. Maybe after—"

Her phone rang. Such bad timing. "McDonald & Associates," she read aloud. Her eyes widened. "I'm so sorry, but I need to take this." She swiped the screen. "Pendleton Staging Services. How may I help you?"

"Ms. Pendleton, this is Clarice Marcel, Mr. McDonald's assistant. We're hoping to secure your services for our new condos near the Galleria."

"I'm familiar with that area." She'd been salivating over those condos for months. "When will they be completed?"

"Now. I know it's short notice, but the staging service we usually use had a fire. Can you help us?"

"When would I need to begin?"

"Monday."

"Monday?" Her stomach sank as she turned toward Jace. "I see."

"Mr. McDonald wants the condos staged for our Christmas Open House on the fifteenth. I know that only gives you three days, but we're hoping you can work magic."

Take it. Jace mouthed. *Go. I'll be fine.*

"I'll rearrange my schedule and be there at nine o'clock Monday morning."

"Wonderful. I'll e-mail you the contract. We've heard good things about you, Ms. Pendleton. This could be the beginning of a valuable partnership."

"I look forward to getting started. Thank you." She hung up.

"McDonald's & Associates is one of the biggest names in Texas when it comes to condos." Jace shoved his hands in his pockets.

"I'm so sorry, Jace. But I can't let this opportunity slip through my fingers."

"No worries. I've sold nine flip houses without staging. I'll be fine." He looked everywhere, but at her. "But what about the inn's Open House?"

"I'll get one of my associates at Landmark Realty to cover

for me. But if I don't stage your flip, I need to pay for your services."

"I'm not a paid escort." Hurt coated his tone.

"That's not what I meant. For the lights, installing the chandelier, and you ended up helping with wedding décor too."

"Don't worry about it. Consider it an early Christmas gift. But I better get back to work." He headed for the door.

"Maybe I can still come back after the fifteenth and stage it for you."

"Don't bother. I hope to have it sold by then." He turned back to face her. "There's nothing for you here at Surfside Beach. There never has been." He rushed out the door.

And her heart crashed to the floor.

<hr />

"Oh wait, guys. Center the couch on that wall." Lark directed her crew provided by McDonald & Associates. "Perfect. Thanks so much."

"Where do you want the chairs?" The older man asked.

"That wall, at the edge of the rug." She set a large succulent on the coffee table, then unwrapped two teal vases from her packing box and centered them on the fireplace.

Her phone rang. *Landmark Realty.* Her other job. "Hey Lita. How's it going?"

"Great. Tabby just got an offer on your grandmother's inn and the buyer intends to keep it intact as an inn."

"Wonderful." But her stomach bottomed out. She sank to the couch.

"I've got the buyer's info for you."

Besides being in the middle of a time-sensitive job her boss didn't know about, she wasn't sure she could stomach the sale of the inn. "You know, since I needed to come home and Tabby handled the open house for me, let her have the sale."

"Are you sure? It's your family's business. You could give her a percentage."

"No. Let her have it. I've got a lot on my plate anyway." And too much on her mind. "By the way, what if I relocated to an area with rental properties instead of sales?"

"Like Surfside Beach?"

"Maybe."

"I'm not sure why you'd want to live there since your family inn is in the process of being sold." A pause. "Oh. Is there a guy?"

Her heart sped. She did not want to discuss Jace with her boss.

"Strike that. It's none of my business. I could definitely keep you busy. Commission on a rental is significantly less than a sale, but you'd get more of them."

"I'm in the thinking stage right now, but I'm glad you're open to the idea." Was there any reason to return to Surfside Beach? Was there anything to pursue with Jace?

"Of course, just let me know what you decide. I can use your skills wherever you decide to land."

"Thanks. I'll keep you posted."

The call ended and Lark dragged herself up from the couch. If the offer went through, the inn would be gone. This was what she'd wanted. She'd aced the wedding and the inn sold. It would remain an inn. But her family would never spend a holiday together there again. She'd never see Jace again.

Her mind replayed that last day. Before the call from McDonald & Associates, she'd mentioned them being friends. But he'd started to say something. Maybe after ...

He'd also said there was nothing in Surfside Beach for her.

Was she hanging her hopes on nothing?

JACE SHIFTED from one foot to the other and rang the bell. Why had he come? Spending Christmas with Lark's family at the inn would only make him miss her more. But Gran had insisted, and she'd always been hard to say no to.

The door swung open, and he was face to face with Lark. The two weeks since he'd seen her melted into nothingness.

"What are you doing here?" their voices blended together.

"You first." She leaned against the door frame.

"Gran invited me to dinner. Wouldn't take no for an answer. Aren't you supposed to be in Dallas?" If he'd known she was here, he wouldn't have come. She'd made her choice, picked Dallas over him. And he'd been doing just fine without her.

"The inn sold. Gran wanted us all to gather here one last time for Christmas." She stepped aside, gestured him inside.

"What about staging the condos?"

"I signed a long-term contract. But even McDonald & Associates takes off for Christmas, so here I am." She glanced around the great room and swallowed hard. With the wedding over, comfortable seating areas were back in place, making the room cozy and inviting. "I knew it was coming. Thought I was prepared. But I'll miss this place."

How would she feel about his news?

The kitchen door opened, and Lark's mom smiled. "Jace, come in." Nora greeted him with a hug. "I'm so glad you came."

"Thanks for the invite." He couldn't escape now.

"We couldn't let you have Christmas alone. It's a shame you couldn't join your family."

"I'm in the middle of selling my flip house, so I needed to stay here."

"You and Lark, like two peas in a pod, always working." She ushered them toward the kitchen.

Lark's dad, Will, met him with a firm handshake, while Gran and Gramps both gave him hugs. Everyone formed a line to fill their plates. Ham, stuffing, sweet potatoes, and all the fixings along with a smattering of pies and desserts lined the countertop. With his plate overloaded, he ended up across from Lark.

"Let's pray." Gramps said and everyone held hands around the table. "Thank you, Lord, for letting our family gather here one more time. We'll miss the inn, but we'll have good memories to sustain us. Thank you for our buyer and that the inn will remain a place for families. Bless this food and each person here today. Thank you for this day set aside to remember you came to earth to set us free. Amen."

Amens echoed and everyone dug in.

"I'm so glad the inn will still be an inn, but I never heard who bought it." Lark's gaze went to Gramps.

"You're sitting at the table with him." Gran grinned.

A frown marred her brow and then her color-defying eyes turned on him. "You?"

"Me."

"Are you planning to stay here and run it?"

"I am." Initially, he'd wanted to own it for status. Then to level it, to erase bad memories attached to it, including her. But in the end, he loved the old place. "The inn has been such an important part of the area for so many years. And there's been so much change here, I felt like something needed to stay the same."

"Will you still flip houses?"

"I'm not sure yet. I may hire a manager for the inn."

A genuine smile curved her lips. "If it's not in the family anymore, I'm glad you'll have it."

The rest of the meal passed in family chatter, with Lark contributing here and there while Jace was content to listen. But being near her again was hard.

Once the meal was over, he insisted on helping Gran wash dishes to escape Lark, while Peaches yipped from the mudroom. He said his goodnights and slipped out the back door.

❧➳➳➳ 🍬 ❦❦❦❦

LARK STAYED out of the kitchen for as long as she could stand it. But when she entered, Gran was alone. "Jace left?"

"Said he had a lot to do tomorrow, wanted to get to bed early."

"I'm glad you invited him. It was nice of you." Why had he left? It had been hard, seeing him, without getting close, without pretending. Especially when she didn't want to be away from him. Ever. She couldn't let him go.

"I think I'll go for a walk on the beach."

"Take your jacket."

If she had to beg, she would. She slipped into her coat, darted outside to get her thoughts in order before heading to his flip house.

Down the shore, a man walked alone. She slowed her pace to avoid crowding his space. But his movements were familiar. Jace.

"Hey." She hurried after him. "Wait up."

He stopped. Slowly, hesitant, he turned to face her.

"Before I got the call from McDonald & Associates, you started to say something, maybe after ... What were you about to say?"

"I don't remember." His mouth flatlined. "Nothing

important." But it was there in his eyes. Whatever he'd been about to say, he remembered.

She blew out a sigh. What if this was all one-sided, in her head? What if she'd been caught up in their charade and he didn't feel the same way? If she ended up a fool, she'd never come back here again. Never see him again. But she had to try.

"How are the newlyweds?"

"Doing well. Their pastor found them a counselor."

"That's good."

"It is, but I'm here to talk about us." She touched his hand.

"What?"

"When we were pretending, I didn't want it to end."

"Me either." His voice thick with emotion, he caught her hand in his. "Our little charade became all too real for me."

"Really?" Her gaze bounced up to meet his.

"I hoped maybe you'd fall for me." A sappy smile tugged at his handsome lips.

"I think I did."

His eyes tender, promised forever. "I think I did too."

Tears blurred her vision. "I don't want to be just friends with you." Heart swelling, she leaned into him. Soaked up his warmth.

"Are you truly over Warren?"

"There was nothing to get over. That was all a high school football captain, head cheerleader thing. We were basically friends and nothing more. And it's true, I used Hillarie's dare to get him to break it off." She gazed into his eyes. "But I've never forgotten our first kiss, even if it was a dare."

"Me neither." He let out a sigh. "But what about Dallas? And McDonald & Associates? And Landmark Real Estate?"

"It doesn't matter where I live for me to fulfill my staging contract. And my boss at Landmark said I can handle rental properties here. I figure I can stick around, see how things develop, maybe get into rental houses and staging, and travel to Dallas when I need to."

He pulled her into his arms. "It just so happens, I need a manager for the inn."

"Would this manager thing provide room and board?"

"For as long as you want to stay." He cupped her face in his hands.

"So, what were you about to say, before I got that call? Maybe after ..."

"Oh. I think it's coming back to me now. Maybe after I sell the flip house, we could go on a date."

Her breath caught. "I'd love to go out with you."

For once, there was no dare, no pretending. His lips met hers. She kissed him back with no charade, with her heart wide open. And in his kiss, she tasted their future.

ABOUT THE AUTHOR

Award winning author, Shannon Taylor Vannatter writes contemporary Christian cowboy romance and has over a dozen published titles. A romance reader since her teens, she hopes to entertain Christian women and plant seeds in the non-believer's heart as she demonstrates that love doesn't conquer all—Jesus does.

She gleans fodder for her fiction in rural Arkansas where she spent her teenage summers working the concession stand with her rodeo announcing dad and married a Texan who morphed into a pastor. In her spare time, she loves hanging out with her husband and son, flea marketing, and doing craft projects.

MORE CHRISTMAS ROMANCE FROM SCRIVENINGS PRESS

Christmas Tree Wars

Available October 5, 2021

Christmas is meant to be a time of goodwill, but there's no peace between two neighboring Christmas tree farmers involved in a longstanding feud. Can this year be different with a bit of holiday romance tossed into the season?

When the financial planner son and forestry major niece of feuding Christmas tree farmers come home to help their families in crisis, it takes Christmas tree wars to a whole new level. As the young people seek success by competing to provide a national Christmas tree, romance fills the air and connects them like mistle to toe.

Stay up-to-date on your favorite books and authors with our free e-newsletters.

ScriveningsPress.com